Also by Lucy Gilmore

FOREVER HOME
Puppy Love
Puppy Christmas

PUPPY Kisses

LUCY GILMORE

sourcebooks
casablanca

Published by Sourcebooks Casablanca, an imprint of Sourcebooks
P.O. Box 4410, Naperville, Illinois 60567-4410
(630) 961-3900
sourcebooks.com

Printed and bound in Canada.
MBP 10 9 8 7 6 5 4 3 2 1

chapter

1

Stealing a dog turned out to be much easier than Dawn had expected.

"Wait. So that's it?" She glanced down at the animal in her arms. The shaking, shivering golden retriever puppy whimpered and tucked her head into the crook of Dawn's elbow. "We walk out that gate, and the deed is done?"

"Well, we could climb over that section of fence with the razor wire if you really want to," her coconspirator said. He didn't even whisper, which went to show how anticlimactic this whole ordeal was. "But if it's all the same to you, I'd rather not. I like my fingernails where they are."

"It seems a little tame, is all I'm saying." Dawn ran a soothing hand over the back of the puppy's neck and contemplated their two exits out of the dusty backyard. Even if they *had* been forced to take the more perilous route, they could easily have tossed a piece of canvas over the top of the razor wire and come out unscathed. There was a whole stack of it sitting on the ground. "I always assumed that theft came with higher stakes. Geez. If I'd have known it was this easy, I'd have started a life of crime years ago. Here…grab the keys out of my front pocket, will you? You'll have to be our getaway driver. I don't want to let this poor honey go. I can feel every last one of her ribs."

Only a flicker of a frown for the dog's thin, scabbed body crossed Zeke's face before being replaced by a more pronounced expression of horror. "You want me to put my hands *where*?"

"Oh, don't look so worried," she said, laughing. She also jutted out her hip to give him better access. "I promise not to like it."

"You owe me for this," he grumbled, but he did as she asked. And was none too pleased about it, if the way he tentatively poked one finger in the tight fit of her jean-shorts pocket and fished around for the key ring was any indication. "I don't know why I let you talk me into these things."

Dawn did. "Because you love me and I'm the only reason you have a semblance of a social life. Now, come on. The sooner we get this girl to a veterinarian, the better. People who treat animals like this deserve to be in prison."

It was a subject on which Dawn would have gladly expounded—and at considerable length—had the situation allowed for it. She'd driven by this house at least half a dozen times in the past week. Each time, regardless of the hour of day or the fact that the summer temperatures were soaring well into the hundreds, the undersized puppy had been hooked onto a short, heavy chain in the backyard.

One time was unfortunate, but six was nothing short of animal cruelty—especially since it looked as though the chain weighed more than the animal did. The poor thing couldn't reach either shade or water and had done her feeble best to dig a hole in the dirt to cool herself off. But she clearly hadn't been fed in some time, and she barely had the strength to stand, let alone carve out a space where she could be comfortable. Just thinking about it started Dawn's blood running hot again. It always tended to be on the warm side, quick to boil over and liable to scald, but this went beyond anything.

Dawn drew a deep breath and adjusted the puppy until she was more comfortably encased in her arms. As much as she would have loved to get up on a soapbox and shout at the house until someone came out to face her, this was neither the time nor the place for such a tirade.

Especially since a light in the upper story of the A-frame house flickered on before she could take as much as a single step toward freedom.

"Oh crap!" Dawn clutched the quivering bundle tighter. She cast an anxious—and slightly accusatory— look at her friend. "I thought you said you rang the doorbell and no one answered."

"I did." Zeke finally managed to get hold of her keys and yank them out of her pocket. "Twice. Maybe the guy was taking a nap."

"Hey!" A window was thrown open and a head appeared. From her vantage point, Dawn could make out a gray, scruffy beard and the top of a filthy white T-shirt. "This is private property. What the hell do you think you're doing?"

"Running," Dawn said and did just that.

She didn't wait to see if Zeke followed. As a full-time

ranch worker and competitive triathlete, he was in far better shape than she could ever hope to be. In fact, he took a nimble leap over a pile of broken-down lawn furniture and passed her within the first ten seconds of their flight. Since he also paused to make sure she got through the gate and then opened the car door for her, she wasn't too insulted.

"Step on it," she urged as she swung the car door shut and slammed her palm on the lock. She caught sight of the man struggling into a pair of brown sweatpants at the front door of the house. He seemed to be having some trouble getting his second leg into the proper hole— most likely because of the shotgun clutched fervently in his right hand. "And step on it hard. I think he's going to start shooting at us."

It said a lot about her friendship with Zeke that he only sighed and muttered something about his inevitable death at her hands before following orders.

"It's moments like these that I wish you'd bought that Tesla," Zeke muttered as he shifted the car into drive and hit the gas. Her little Jetta was cute but not very powerful. A crunch of gravel kicked up behind them, followed by a slow, almost painful whip of the tail end of the car before they started moving forward. "I could use some zero-to-sixty action right now."

Dawn cast a look in the rearview mirror. "We both could. He's given up on the sweatpants and is going straight for the truck in his underwear. It's not an attractive sight. *Move*."

Zeke didn't have to be told twice. He hit the gas with a heavy foot and pulled them out of the drive.

It wasn't an ideal location for a getaway. The house

where the puppy had been tied up was in the middle of a semirural area north of Spokane, where pockets of houses were broken up by long, empty stretches of highway. It took them all of thirty seconds to pull out of the neighborhood and find themselves surrounded by the vast nothingness of eastern Washington. Unless they barreled the car into a field of corn or one of the many haystacks dotting the landscape, there weren't many hiding places.

Dawn suggested one of the latter, but Zeke just started to drive faster.

Since the pickup truck was already starting to smoke in the distance, and Zeke knew this area better than if Google and Apple Maps had a baby, Dawn settled back and turned her attention to the puppy in her lap. She'd never been one to worry about the things she couldn't control—mostly because her life had been one long series of things she couldn't control. If she took it into her head to get into a pucker every time someone tried to chase after her, she'd never leave the house.

"You poor honey," she murmured as she settled the animal more comfortably across her bare thighs. "Let me take a good look at you."

The golden retriever had stopped shaking by this time, opting instead to balance her head on Dawn's knee. As if sensing a kindred spirit, the animal showed no tendency to fight back against Dawn's gentle pokes and prods. This, in and of itself, was a good sign. Dawn wasn't the family expert when it came to dog behaviors—her older sister, Lila, was the one with the master's degree and an incredibly analytical mind—but she hadn't spent the last six years training service puppies for nothing. Abuse and neglect often caused animals to show their teeth and stop at nothing to protect themselves. And rightly so, if you asked her.

This puppy, however, only offered a feeble tongue and sighed contentedly, even when Dawn's hand moved over the silken fur on her stomach to find numerous neglected sores.

"I hope you run that bastard off the road," she said as she poked gently around the edges of the wounds, all of which must have been there for quite some time. One in particular seemed to have become infected sometime in the past few days. "I hope you aim for a cliff and propel him right off the end of it."

Zeke didn't look over. He was too busy gripping the wheel with both hands, the fields a blur around them. "There aren't any cliffs around here, but there's a good chance we'll end up turned over in a ditch before this is over. Are you wearing your seat belt?"

"Yep."

"Airbag is on?"

"Check."

"You've made peace with your maker?"

"Um." Dawn was forced into a laugh. "That depends on who you ask. I mean, *I'm* okay with most of my life choices. If you were to ask my mother, however…"

"Uh-oh. Hold that thought, D. We've got more company."

Since both her arms were wrapped around the puppy, there wasn't much for her to hold on to. Not that it would have been of any use to cling to the dashboard or those weird handles that people used to carry their dry cleaning. Just when the frenetic, wheezing pickup was becoming nothing more than a blip in the rearview mirror, their tail was replaced by a sleek green-and-white car with a whir of colorful lights up top. Unlike the truck, this new car managed to keep pace with them just fine.

"Oh dear. Is that—?" Dawn began.

Zeke finished for her. "Sheriff Jenkins? Yes. *Fuck*. I was going at least ninety. He's not going to like this. I hate to say it, but I think we'd have been better off with No-Pants Shotgun back there."

Dawn disagreed. She'd had enough encounters with the legal system to feel wary where they were concerned, but she'd take her chances with a backwoods officer of the law over an irate man without pants any day.

"Don't worry about the sheriff," Dawn said with a toss of her head. She bit down on her lips to bring the blood to them and gave her T-shirt a not-so-discreet tug. She'd dressed for the day's heist in functional jean shorts and a ratty shirt, but the top had been worn so many times that it was practically sheer. The deep plunge of the V-neck didn't hurt matters, either. Her boobs were far and away her best feature—too big for everyday comfort, but ideal when trying to bend people to her will. Whenever she got annoyed with the former, she tried very hard to focus on the latter. "I'm sure I can convince him to let us go with a warning."

Zeke snorted as he pulled the car over to the side of the road. "You obviously haven't met Harold Jenkins. The only thing he hates more than people who speed are *women* who speed."

"But I'm not the one driving," Dawn pointed out. She dropped a kiss on the golden retriever's dusty head.

"Besides, who would give a ticket to anyone holding such a sweet little love as this?"

The answer, as it turned out, was Sheriff Harold Jenkins.

"That makes the third time this month, Mr. Dearborn." The sheriff—a short, balding man with a swagger in his step and nothing but disdain for Dawn's cleavage—was every bit as disagreeable as Zeke had promised. He examined the driver's license in his hand as if inspecting the edges for lines of cocaine. "I told you last time that I'd suspend this if I caught you speeding again."

"Yes, sir."

"I clocked you at eighty-nine. That's an eight and a nine. Together. In one number."

"Yes, sir."

"Last I checked, we hadn't made any changes to the speed limit around here."

"No, sir."

It was almost more than Dawn could take. Meekly accepting one's fate was a thing she never could and never would understand—especially in a world as flawed as this one. They'd just saved this poor animal's life, for crying out loud, and her white knight was quaking more in fear over a traffic violation than over the man who'd been chasing them with a gun.

Since she appeared to be on her own in this fight, she leaned across the driver's seat and plastered on her brightest smile. "I'm so sorry about this, Officer. But it wasn't Zeke's fault—honest, it wasn't. This one was all me."

"Sheriff."

She blinked, somewhat taken aback by the gruff note in his voice. She also noted her error at once. "Yes, um.

Of course. That's what I meant, *Sheriff*." She batted her eyelashes for good measure. "Zeke was only going so fast because it's an emergency."

The sheriff's eyes narrowed as they ran over the car's interior. "Doesn't look like much of an emergency to me. Is there a reason you have the dog up front like that?"

"Yes." Dawn saw her chance and latched onto it. She was nothing if not opportunistic. "This puppy is in desperate need of medical attention. Look how frail and underweight she is—and at these sores on her stomach. She's in a lot of pain."

She thought both she and the puppy sold it pretty well. Not only did the animal give an appropriately pitiful blink of her sleepy brown eyes, but Dawn followed up with one of her own. No man would be able to stand up to the pair of them. She was sure of it.

At least, she was until the sheriff chuffed out a breath and handed Zeke a ticket. The ID he kept firmly in hand. "Then you're going in the wrong direction, young lady. Marcia Peterson is the best veterinarian in twelve counties—a thing Zeke Dearborn has known since his cradle. She's also located a good fifteen miles the other way."

Dawn's heart sank. That had been some of her best work.

"I'll have to see the lady's license, if you please," the sheriff added in a clipped tone. "Seeing as how she'll be the one driving you home. If she's unable to take the wheel, then I'll be happy to escort all three of you in the back of my car. This ID is no longer valid."

"But, Harold, you can't—" Zeke began with an agonized glance at Dawn. She knew what that look meant. He spent nine-tenths of his life working on his family's ranch and the other tenth at his triathlon training sessions. To lose his driver's license would be to lose his only means of transportation in and out of here—his only escape. He freaking loved those triathlons.

"We're not taking her to Marcia's," Dawn said, grasping at the only straw she could see. And she meant that literally. They were so far from civilization that not even a Google and Apple Maps baby could save them. "We're taking her to the ranch."

"The ranch?" Sheriff Jenkins echoed doubtfully. He paused, though, which was the most important thing, the driver's license hanging fatefully in the air. "What for?"

"Well…you see…the thing is…" Dawn heaved a deep breath to give herself strength. This next part was going to hurt, but she had to do it. "This is Adam's dog."

Despite the pang that filled her at such blasphemous words, she had the benefit of seeing a flicker of hesitation in Sheriff Jenkins's eyes. Of course, that flicker then moved to the puppy, taking in that hunched, traumatized form with a disbelieving chuff of air.

"Mr. Dearborn owns *this* dog?" he asked. "What for?"

"She's a service animal." Zeke was quick to pick up on the train of Dawn's thoughts. "To help Adam around the ranch and stuff when Phoebe and I can't be there."

The idea that this starving bundle of a puppy could be of service to anyone was ludicrous, but Zeke went on, driven by the silence greeting him on all sides. "Dawn here is a dog trainer," he said. "Didn't I mention that? She owns a company—a real business that trains and places puppies for the blind. You have some business cards on you, right, Dawn?"

Dawn saw nothing for it but to pull out her wallet and extract a business card. She was, in fact, exactly what Zeke was making her out to be. She worked with her sisters Lila and Sophie to take bright, eager puppies and train them to provide services to people of all kinds. Hearing service dogs, vision service dogs, emotional support animals—if a dog could do the work, they found a way to make it happen.

"Here you go," she said as she handed over the business card. It was a little ragged around the edges from being wedged in her wallet for so long, but the gist of it was there. "Our company is called Puppy Promise. We specialize in training young dogs so we can make sure they grow up to be a perfect fit. My sister Lila is the brains behind it."

Sheriff Jenkins took the card and eyed it carefully, almost as though he suspected her of carrying them around in case she someday got pulled over for speeding while caring for an emaciated golden retriever. "That so?"

Zeke held up three fingers in a Boy Scout salute. "On my honor."

For a long, suspended moment, Dawn thought it was going to work. The sheriff glanced back and forth between them, taking in the driver and the passenger, the puppy and the card. *Let us go*, Dawn willed him. *Send us on our way*.

Her hopes reached their zenith when Sheriff Jenkins gave a curt nod and returned her business card. He even handed Zeke back his ID. "Then of course you're free to go."

"Thank you, Sheriff," Zeke said, not wasting a

moment as he turned the keys in the ignition. "And it won't happen again, I promise. You won't regret—"

Sheriff Jenkins coughed, cutting Zeke short. "I'll go ahead and follow you two to the ranch. You'll want a police escort. An animal like that should be seen right away. We wouldn't want you to run into any more setbacks on the road."

Dawn could only open her mouth and close it again, watching as the sheriff turned on his heel and walked away. She continued following his progress in the rearview mirror. He lowered himself into the driver's seat of his patrol car, said something into his handset, and checked his mirrors.

And then waited—patiently and calmly—for Zeke to pull out onto the road.

"We're in for it now," Zeke accused. The engine gave an ineffective roar as he stepped on the accelerator before he remembered to remove the car from park. "Have you lost your ever-loving mind? We'd be better off going to jail than facing Adam. What in the hell made you introduce my brother into the conversation?"

Dawn gently massaged the puppy's silken fur, struggling to come up with a reasonable excuse. *Desperation. Stupidity. An overwhelming desire to see Adam again.*

"I'm sorry," she eventually said. "I panicked."

"Yeah, well, you might want to hold on to that panic a little bit longer." Zeke glanced over his shoulder before pulling out onto the highway. The sheriff was visible behind them, keeping an exact six car lengths back. "The second we walk in that door with your stolen puppy and a sheriff in tow, Adam is going to eat me alive. No—he's going to eat *you* alive while I'm forced to stand by and watch. Isn't that how torturers do it?"

"Don't be so dramatic. I'm not scared of your brother."

Zeke snorted on a laugh. Now that no one was pointing a shotgun at him and his ID was safe in his wallet, he was back to his usual carefree self. "Yes, you are. You're terrified of him. That and bees—the only two things in the world capable of bringing you down. And at least you have an EpiPen to fight the bees."

"I could probably use the EpiPen on Adam, too," she pointed out. "If it came down to hand-to-hand combat."

He snorted again. "My brother? Felled by one tiny needle? You've got some strange ideas, Dawn, but I draw the line at that one." He cast an obvious glance down at the puppy. "One of these days, those ideas are going to be the death of you. And me, probably."

"I'm not scared of your brother," she echoed, more firmly this time. "I can handle him."

"The same way you handled Sheriff Jenkins?"

She didn't bother answering. Okay, so the good officer had proven impervious to her charms. It happened sometimes. Not often, but sometimes. Zeke, for example, regularly told her that he'd rather sleep with a tiger on fire than get anywhere near the disaster that was her romantic life. Clearly, the honorable Sheriff Jenkins was formed from the same mold.

Adam Dearborn, however, wasn't impervious. Not to her *physical* charms, anyway.

"Now that I'm thinking about it, you weren't too adroit with No-Pants Shotgun back there, either," Zeke added. "For a woman who claims to be so good at manipulating men, you seem to have a pretty terrible track record."

"At least when an angry man runs after me with no pants on, I know what's on his mind," she retorted, nettled. "It's when they keep their clothes on that I start to worry."

chapter
2

There were two things Adam really didn't want to deal with today, and both of them showed up on his doorstep at the same time.

"Sheriff Jenkins," he said, tackling the lesser of two evils first. "Please, come in. It's always a pleasure."

"No, it's not," the sheriff replied. His voice carried its usual gruffness, a gravelly tonality caused by his life-long smoking habit. "The only time I see you is when there's a meeting at town hall or your brother is up to some mischief. And there's no meeting today."

Adam chose to ignore the implications of this statement. That Zeke was up to trouble—again—was no surprise. Especially considering the woman standing next to the sheriff. He'd have recognized that scent anywhere, though he'd have been damned if anyone asked him to point out how. Dawn Vasquez was the only woman he knew who wore no perfume, used no scented soaps or lotions, and even washed her clothes with an odorless laundry detergent. What he smelled were pheromones, plain and simple.

Those, unfortunately, she had in abundance.

"Dawn," he said, still in his blandest voice. "To what do I owe the honor? Or is it better if I don't ask?"

He didn't know why he bothered. As was usually her custom, Dawn pushed her way through the front door as though his opinion on the matter carried no weight whatsoever. She didn't make contact with him as she moved past, but that didn't seem to matter. Adam could always feel her coming. The air around her crackled with energy—most of it sexual.

"Did you forget I was coming by this afternoon with your new service puppy?" she asked in the light, breezy tone that almost always presaged mischief of some kind. "I thought about having Lila call to remind you, but you're always so organized. I thought for sure you'd remember our date."

Although he was already holding himself perfectly still, those words caused him to grow even more immobile. "Our date?" he echoed.

"She's in much worse condition than we feared," Dawn continued. "Do you mind if I set her on the couch?"

For the first time since he'd heard the crunch of two pairs of car tires in the drive, Adam wondered if he had, in fact, forgotten an appointment. Most of his days were so busy that he had to keep to a tight schedule or risk being out with the cows at all hours of the night. Phoebe did a decent job of keeping him apprised of his calendar, but she hadn't mentioned anything about Dawn stopping by today.

He definitely would have taken note of that.

"Zeke, be a love and make sure the vet is on her way, would you?" Dawn asked. Adam could tell, from the location of her voice, that she'd decided not to wait for permission and had moved straight toward the couch.

"Sheriff Jenkins, would you mind terribly getting a bowl of water? I'd like to get some fluids in this puppy sooner rather than later."

To Adam's complete and utter lack of surprise, both men went off to do her bidding. Zeke, because his brother never said no to Dawn, and Harold, because, well, he was male. It didn't seem to matter that the man was married and old enough to be Dawn's grandfather. When she issued a request in that sweetly lilting voice of hers, it was impossible not to want to move the sun and the earth to carry it out.

"I'll get the water," Adam said. Part of it was a perverse desire not to let this woman have the handling of his household, but most of it was his reluctance to be left alone with her. As he *wasn't* married and only had four years on her, he had none of Harold's protective armor in place. "Food, too, I presume?"

Dawn's approval was evident in the slight hum at the back of her throat. "Yes, actually. If it's not too much trouble. Some kind of canned beef or chicken, I think, and if you could mash it up to a soft consistency, that'd be great. I'm not sure what condition her teeth and gums are going to be in." She paused before adding, "Something to clean these wounds would also be a help."

Wounds? "What did you do to that poor animal?"

"Oh, she's been beaten, dehydrated, and starved," Dawn said in a voice that was strangely cheerful for such a macabre list. "But her spirit's strong. With the right training, she should make you an excellent service puppy."

That was the second time she'd said *service puppy*, and it didn't make any more sense this time around. Adam wasn't in the market for a service animal. He liked dogs just fine, but he had yet to meet a single one who could keep pace with him around the ranch. They always ended up being more of a hindrance than a help.

Kind of like a certain woman he knew.

"Anything else I can do for you while I'm at it?" he asked.

If Dawn noticed his note of sarcasm, she blithely ignored it. "I'd love a drink of water myself, actually. It's a hot one out there today. Sheriff? Can we offer you anything?"

There was no verbal response, so Adam assumed Harold must have shaken his head. At least, that was how he planned on interpreting the silence. He wasn't going to play the gallant host unless someone told him what was going on.

It was in a mood of budding annoyance that he moved to the kitchen and began assembling the items Dawn requested. The kitchen, like the rest of the single-story ranch house, was neat and organized, every item in the same location it had been for as long as Adam could remember. Keeping the saltshaker and water glasses in the exact same place didn't make for a very exciting life, but it did make for an independent one. At least where Adam was concerned. He might not have been able to see the kitchen in a literal sense, but the map was laid out in his mind's eye just fine. Bowls. Glasses. Water. Antiseptic wash. Paper towels.

Zeke was there, too, hovering in the hallway that led from the bedrooms to the living room. He was probably looking for a way to sneak past without Adam hearing him.

Taking pity on his younger brother, Adam began to

hum "Somewhere Over the Rainbow" under his breath. It wasn't much, but it gave Zeke the boost of courage he needed to slip past him and return to the safety of the living room.

Adam almost ruined it by laughing out loud. *Poor Zeke.* So many of the things his brother did around here were far less secretive than he thought. He and Phoebe both. From the way the pair of them skulked around, speaking in whispers and sneaking out when they thought Adam was asleep, you'd think he was running some kind of prison camp instead of the family ranch.

Unfortunately, that was what came with being the eldest—and with being the boss. Even though he was only four years older than the twins, it might as well have been forty.

"Oh yes. Golden retrievers make excellent service dogs. They're one of the smartest breeds out there, and they can concentrate on a task better than most humans. They're my favorite animal for this kind of work." Dawn was holding court when Adam returned to the living room, which was no surprise to anyone who knew her. She had a way of drawing all the attention in a room.

Determined not to fall into her inevitable orbit, he set the tray of supplies on the coffee table and wordlessly settled himself on the arm of the couch.

"And what kind of work is that?" Sheriff Jenkins asked.

"Ranch work. Manual labor. Traveling long distances to hunt down rogue cows." Dawn shot them off as if reading from a list. "You need a lot of strength and intelligence to keep up in a place like this. Wouldn't you agree?"

Although Zeke, who'd also been born and bred here,

could have easily answered that question, Adam had the feeling he was the one being put on the spot. What he didn't know was *why*.

"I'll have you know that my cows don't go rogue," he said by way of answer. "They're exceptionally well behaved."

"All two hundred of them? That isn't possible."

"Well, there is one that's been causing us a lot of problems near the west field lately. She keeps breaking down the neighbor's fence and forcing herself into places she's not wanted. We named her Dawn."

Although Zeke's laugh was unmistakable, Dawn hid hers behind an outraged gurgle.

"Because she usually escapes right before sunup," Adam explained. He held himself on the edge of the couch arm, his posture upright. "She's cost us a fortune in repairs already. I'm thinking about getting rid of her. Don't tell me *that's* what brings you all this way, Harold. I didn't know you were interested in animal husbandry."

"Actually, I was escorting the youngsters," Harold said. "Seeing as how this puppy is in such terrible condition and they were determined to bring her here rather than to Marcia's. What made you take on an animal like this one?"

"I told you already," Zeke interrupted. "Adam hired Dawn to help him find the perfect canine companion. He needs help around here."

On the contrary, he needed no such thing. The books were balanced, the expansion plans were shaping up, and Adam was in the best physical condition of his life. Considering that he ran one of the largest family-owned-and-operated cattle ranches in this part of the state with almost zero percent vision, this was no small feat.

But that clearly wasn't the story he was supposed to be selling here.

"That's right," he lied cheerfully. "I'm getting on in years. Unlike Dawn, I'm ready to start making myself less of a nuisance and settle down. Dawn the *cow*, that is."

He could hear Dawn the human struggling to keep her feelings to herself. More silence than sound, there was a definite sense of laughing indignation coming from the other side of the couch.

"So this really *is* your new seeing-eye dog?" Harold asked.

"Absolutely."

"And you ordered them to bring her to you?"

"With all possible speed," he said with a calm perjuring of his soul. Unless he was mistaken, things were finally starting to make sense. Zeke always drove with a lead foot, and Dawn always had a way of getting exactly what she wanted. If her goal had been to talk her way out of a speeding ticket, this was one way to do it.

A tortured, tangled, ridiculous way to do it, yes, but when had she ever done things any other way?

"I hope Zeke didn't take me too literally about the speed thing," he added, somewhat perversely. "We wouldn't want him putting his safety—not to mention the safety of his passengers—at risk. But what am I saying? I'm sure you would have told me straightaway if that were the case."

All three of them coughed at once. They also began talking at once. Harold murmured something about needing to go on his way. Zeke offered to walk him to the door. And Dawn was encouraging the puppy to eat something in a low, soothing tone.

From the sound of it, she wasn't having much luck. Casting aside all other considerations, Adam shifted from the arm of the couch to the floor, crouching near the warm, panting body laid out on the middle cushion. The first thing he noted was that the animal's temperature was high—*too high*—her breathing rapid, and her nose dry to the touch. The second thing he noted was that *beaten* and *starved* had been gross understatements. He was much more of an expert on cows than dogs, but the painfully bony rib cage and rough patches of balding skin were more than enough to convince him that his brother and Dawn had done right to bring the dog here—speed limits and Harold Jenkins be damned.

"Was Zeke able to get hold of Marcia?" he asked as his fingers prodded gently at the puppy's stomach. The animal gave a whimper of protest as he encountered several hard lumps. "I know, girl. I'm sorry. I'm being as gentle as I can. Where's the antiseptic?"

"I don't know," Dawn said. As she placed the bottle in his hand, she added, "About Marcia, that is. But if she's busy, I can always ask our vet to come out. Or even Lila. She'll know what to do about a dog in this state."

Adam had never met Dawn's older sister, Lila, but she had a good reputation when it came to animals. He could have easily—and guiltlessly—handed this problem over to her.

He didn't.

"No, thank you. I'd like one of my own people to tend to her." He began cleaning the worst of the puppy's wounds, a large abrasion on the downy fur on her belly. He worked gently but firmly, refusing to let the animal squirm her way out of the necessary care.

That was kind of his specialty. Adam Dearborn was the man who got things done—even if it hurt sometimes.

"What she needs is rest, not a bunch of strange people tramping in and out of here," he added. "It would only scare her. I don't treat my animals that way."

"She isn't your animal."

He ignored her. "Don't force any more food on her, please. I think she may have swallowed some rocks."

"She isn't your animal," Dawn repeated, more insistently this time. When he only continued working his hands over the puppy's body, gently testing her joints and bones for breaks, she asked, "How do you know she ate rocks?"

It had been his intention to tend to the puppy's wounds and leave Dawn to the full and solitary possession of the couch. He hadn't made any physical contact with her other than the light brushing of fingertips as she handed over the antiseptic, but he was still acutely aware of her presence. It was impossible not to be. Her body was warm and crackling with energy, her breath disturbing the air around him.

Her body was *always* warm and crackling, and her breath *always* disturbed the air around him. All she had to do was walk into a room, and Adam forgot about anything and anyone else in it.

Which was why he slid his grip up to hers, his rough, heavily callused palm easily capturing her softer one.

He needed to confirm that she was flesh and blood, that her hand, like everyone else's, was only a hand.

There was no magic to Dawn Vasquez. There was just attraction. It was important that he remember the distinction.

"Feel this?" he asked, pulling Dawn's hand down the puppy's bony rib cage to the swell of her stomach. He waited until her fingers ran over the hard protrusions. Like him, she was extraordinarily gentle, unwilling to push too hard for fear of hurting the animal more than she had to. "There are a few of those lumps shifting around in here. If she was hungry enough, she might have eaten them to try and fill her stomach. I'm assuming you found her abandoned on the side of the highway somewhere?"

Dawn's hand twitched but didn't pull away. "Yes. Abandoned."

"The rocks are probably blocking her digestive tract, which is why she's not eating. Marcia will be able to tell us whether or not they'll need to be surgically removed, but I prefer not to resort to such extreme measures on one of my animals unless I have to."

"You mean, you'd prefer not to resort to such extreme measures on one of *my* animals unless you have to."

"I think I'll call her Methuselah," he said with a bland disregard for Dawn's protest. "Because of how wrinkly all the fur around her neck is."

"You can't name a puppy that! She's only a few months old."

He rose to his feet and eased the hunch in his shoulders with a shrug. The gesture was largely for show—a way of proving to Dawn that he felt nothing for either of the soft, pliant creatures currently seated on his couch—but it also had the benefit of easing an ache in his upper back. He'd spent most of the morning reinstalling that damned fence by the west field. He hadn't been kidding about the rogue cow.

"I suppose I could name her Dawn, too, but that might be taking things too far, even for me. One woman and one cow is more than enough already." He turned toward the sound of the front door. "Oh, Zeke, are you back? I hope you didn't take up too much of Sheriff Jenkins's time. Dawn and I were just discussing what we should name my new service puppy. I don't think she approves of me calling her Methuselah."

His brother chuckled. "I don't know that I approve, either. We have enough Biblical names in this family already. You and Phoebe got off easy, but Ezekiel's a hard thing to live up to." Then Zeke hesitated and added, "Uh, Adam, about the puppy…"

"She couldn't have come at a better time." Adam nodded in Zeke's direction. "As soon as the expansion plans go through, it'll almost double the amount of land we need to cover in a day. A service dog will be a big help. Thank you for thinking of me—both of you. It means a lot."

This last part was said with the sole intention of getting a reaction out of Dawn. It was beneath him, he knew, but he couldn't resist. He'd obviously been used as a Get Out of Jail Free card—a way for Zeke and Dawn to avoid a speeding ticket—and nothing more. The least they could do was admit it.

"Well, the thing is…" Zeke began in a voice tinged

at the edge with sheepishness. "See, we were… Um, it was just…"

"Yes?" Adam prodded. "Were you afraid I'd balk at the puppy's condition? Is that it? Don't worry. I'm not *that* hard-hearted."

"Actually—"

"Actually, you can't have her," Dawn interrupted before Zeke could make another feeble attempt at explaining himself. "Even if I were willing to give her up, which I'm not, she's nowhere near qualified enough to become a service puppy."

"Well, well. *Now* who's being hard-hearted?"

"Adam!" Dawn released a sound halfway between a groan and a laugh. "That's not what I meant, and you know it."

"Besides, I thought you said you prefer golden retrievers for this kind of work," he said. When Dawn didn't answer right away, he added helpfully, "Because of her concentration and intelligence. That's what you told Sheriff Jenkins, wasn't it? I'm sure I could call him back to confirm."

The threat hung lightly in the air, flittering around them as Dawn weighed her options. As far as Adam could tell, there were only two. She could admit the truth—that she'd used him and his blindness to get out of a tight spot—or she could dig in her heels and brazen it out.

She chose the exact one he'd assumed she would.

With a dignity that could only belong to a woman as shameless as this one, she said, "Upon further consideration, I don't think she'll be a good fit for you. She's not trained for life on a ranch."

"Weird. You'd think a professional dog trainer would be able to work around that."

Dawn ignored him. "And it'll take months to get her up to her full health. It's not fair to ask you to shoulder the burden of her care."

"I'm happy to do it."

"Adam, this isn't what you think," Zeke said, once more trying to insert himself into the argument.

Adam stopped him with one raised finger. As much as he appreciated his brother's willingness to come clean, this wasn't his fight. It was Dawn's.

And mine. When it came to Dawn, the fight was his. It always had been.

"Well?" he prodded. "Is this or isn't this my new service puppy? I believe I was promised one. I'd hate for Sheriff Jenkins to come by another day and find me toiling in the fields all alone. What would he think?"

Dawn's struggle with herself was a silent one, but Adam could feel it just fine. Oh, how he felt it. It flooded the air around her, filled the corners of the living room, grew hot and heavy in his own blood.

"Of course she's yours," she finally said. Her voice was tight with suppressed emotion, but no less musical because of it. "But our service puppies don't come cheap. You'll be expected to pay the full price for her."

"Of course," he replied. "I'm delighted to welcome Methuselah into the fold."

"And you'll have to cover all her veterinary bills, too. Even if that means surgery to get those rocks out of her stomach."

He nodded, finding it incredibly easy to be

magnanimous now that he was winning. "I wouldn't have it any other way."

"Of course, all your fees will include the six-week training period, too," Dawn said. She appeared to be making a recovery, her voice gaining strength as well as that familiar tinge of mischief, as if she'd caught on to his game and was preparing to give him hell right back. "Possibly longer, given her current state. Lucky for you, I recently finished up a case with another client, so I'm wholly at your disposal."

A nervous qualm turned the hot, heavy blood in his veins to something more dangerous…something that felt an awful lot like lava. "You are?"

"Naturally. I wouldn't hand over a case as important as this to one of my sisters. It'll be great. Just you and me and the puppy, working together for eight hours every day."

"Eight hours?" Adam found himself echoing. The lava hardened. "Every day?"

"It's the Puppy Promise way. You know, I wonder if it wouldn't be better for me to live here for the duration of the training. Since I'm already such good friends with the family, I'm sure you guys wouldn't mind, and you have the extra space. It's an awfully long drive from Spokane."

Adam felt it was time to put his foot down on this little game. Both feet, in fact, with all the force he could carry in his steel-toed work boots.

"You wouldn't," he said.

Her laughter came out in a warm, liquid burst. "I would, actually, but you're in luck. It just so happens that both my sisters have moved out, and I can't leave the rest of our puppies alone in the kennel at night. But don't worry—I'll be here bright and early every morning. It'll be fun."

He should have put a stop to this charade at once. Dawn could keep both her victory and her dog. Nothing good would come of giving her free rein over his house. She'd already won over Zeke, and Phoebe practically ate out of the palm of her hand. There was no telling what would happen if she was given full access to Adam, too.

Actually, there was. That was the whole problem. It would be the same thing that always happened whenever he and Dawn shared a room for more than ten minutes at a time.

There would be fighting. There would be flirting.

There would be *fucking*.

Adam had no way of knowing if that last one pushed him over the edge, or if the decision had been made for him the moment Dawn stepped through the door. Either way, his voice was resigned as he accepted the challenge being offered.

"Perfect," he lied. "I can't think of anything I'd like more."

❧ ❧ ❧

"She's a sweet little thing, isn't she?" Marcia's soft, clipped voice was followed by the snap of her medical bag being closed. She'd come out to the ranch as soon as they'd called, her examination swift but sure. "Every time I press somewhere it hurts, she just licks me to try to get me to stop. It's breaking my heart."

"But she'll be okay, right?" Dawn asked anxiously. "She doesn't need surgery or anything? Just a little extra love and care, and she'll be as good as new?"

Adam was more grateful than he could say that Dawn put into words the exact thing he was feeling. He didn't want to speak for fear that it would dislodge the puppy. The entire exam had taken place on his lap because Methuselah wouldn't leave it. Five seconds away from any of the people currently in this living room, and she started shaking and whimpering as though it caused her physical pain.

Adam could relate. It was hard to give up a warm lap once it had finally been offered.

"Love, antibiotics, a strict feeding schedule, and a few weeks of good Dearborn Ranch air, and she'll be back on her feet." Adam could practically hear the smile in Marcia's voice. She *always* had a smile in her voice. He couldn't count the number of times he'd had to call her in the middle of the night to tend to a sick cow, but she rarely lost one. That was probably what made her so cheerful.

Well, either that or the fact that she was a happily married mother of three with the respect and admiration of just about everyone who knew her. It was a toss-up.

"She's lucky you found her when you did, though," Marcia said. "She wouldn't have lasted much more than a day or two like this. Where did you say you came across her?"

"I didn't" came Dawn's easy reply. "But it wasn't too far from here."

"Strange. It's not often you find a puppy like this one abandoned on the side of the road." There were a few more rustling sounds as Marcia packed up her gear and prepared to head out. It was growing late, and Adam was sure she had several more house calls to make before her day was through. Life out here wasn't easy on any of them. "If she's purebred—and from the looks of it, she is—that's over a thousand bucks someone left behind. She may have been lost. Do you want me to put out some feelers to find her owners?"

"No!" Both Adam and Dawn spoke at the same time and with the same passionate reaction. The volume caused Methuselah to give a nervous jump, but Adam put his hand on top of her head to calm her. She seemed to like that—burrowing somewhere warm, contentedly assuming that Adam was there to provide protection.

In a more moderate tone so as not to cause the puppy to jump again, he added, "You said yourself that these sores have been developing for quite some time. I'm not so sure that whoever lost her deserves her back."

"Suit yourself," Marcia said, still cheery. "If it were *my* puppy who'd gone missing, I'd be frantic to find some news of her. You would, too, Adam, even though you're much better than I am at maintaining emotional distance."

He couldn't disagree with that. Harboring sentimental feelings toward ranch animals was a hazardous approach to life in a place like this. You couldn't go around getting attached to every cow who lowed her way into your heart, or there wouldn't be anything left of it by the end of the first season. You could *respect* the animals. You could *appreciate* the animals. But there was no falling in love.

That was the first—and only—rule.

"I'll be by again in the morning to check on her progress, but don't hesitate to give me a call if you have any concerns," Marcia said. "Dawn, it was lovely to meet you."

"Likewise. I'll see you out."

Adam would have protested that—Dawn acting like the lady of the manor, escorting a veterinarian who'd been running around this place since she was a kid—but there was no way he could get up without moving Methuselah.

He realized his mistake the moment Dawn returned to the living room. The hot, heaving body on his lap had him pinned to the couch, unable to flee in any direction. Zeke had long since left to go for a run, and Phoebe never seemed to be around when he needed her.

In other words, he was trapped.

"Sheriff Jenkins wasn't kidding about Marcia, was he?" Dawn asked, perfectly casual. "I can tell why she's considered the best in twelve counties."

Adam ignored her. Maybe if he refused to rise to her bait, she'd take the hint and leave.

Nice try, Adam. When has that ever worked before?

As if to prove it, Dawn's weight sagged the arm of the couch next to him. Her hand brushed his as she reached down to scratch the puppy behind the ear.

"I can also tell that you'd like nothing more than for me to take myself off and leave you alone," she said. Coming from any other woman, those words might be intended to make him feel guilty. Coming from *this* woman, they were almost certainly a declaration of war. "But I'm feeling awfully exhausted from my long day of puppy rescue. Mind if I curl up next to you and take a nap?"

"Don't you have a house of your own?"

"Yes, but it's sad and empty and I don't want to go back to it alone."

"Then why are you laughing?"

"Because you two look so adorable, all snuggled up together and trying to get rid of me." Dawn paused, the laughter still in her voice. "She's the same color as your pants, by the way. A kind of warm, beigy tan with dark-golden ears. She'll eventually grow into those neck wrinkles, but right now she looks like she needs to be ironed."

Adam grunted a noncommittal reply. He'd never admit it to this woman, but the easy way she described the puppy to him was both helpful and thoughtful. A lot of people made a huge production out of painting the world around him, sounding more like art students let loose in a museum for the first time than actual human beings. *The play of the light over the leaves… The sun-dappled mountains rising in the distance…* Poetry was all well and good for some people, but all Adam needed were the basic facts, thanks.

There's a tree five feet to your right.

The dog is tan.

Dawn Vasquez is quite possibly the most gorgeous and dangerous woman to ever grace God's green earth.

Facts he could work with. Facts he understood. A bout with meningitis in early childhood had left him without much in the way of sight, but he had plenty of common sense. And common sense, that old bastard, was more than happy to make up for whatever else his life might be lacking.

"Oh, relax," she said. "I'm not going to force myself into your arms. I can see that they're full right now."

"I *am* relaxed," he protested.

"No, you're not. You're tense and all worked up and

look like you can't decide whether you want to throw
me out of your house or into your bed."

He had the answer to that ready to go. "It's definitely
the first one."

She knew it for the lie it was. With a light, musical laugh, she leaned down and dropped a kiss on
Methuselah's head. Adam held himself still, hoping
that by being immobile he could also somehow become
invisible, but it was no use. Dawn pressed another of
those soft, easy kisses on his cheek as she passed it by.

"You were my hero today, you know," she said. "Saving
me from that big, bad sheriff. Taking this poor, defenseless
puppy under your wing without a single question."

"Then why do I get the feeling you're about to make
me regret it?" he countered.

"Because I am." All the playfulness dropped from her
voice, her pretense at seduction gone in a flash. She was
exceptionally good at that—turning herself off and on,
and turning *him* off and on with it. "You can't keep her,
Adam. She's not a service dog. Even if she were in the
peak of health, which she's not, being a guide dog takes
a lot of work. Especially on a ranch this size."

It was no use asking him to explain why that simple
statement—offered in true Dawn Vasquez style without any bullshit—caused such a strong reaction inside
Adam's chest, but it did.

"You brought her here," he said, his hand curled possessively over the top of Methuselah's head. The puppy
seemed to sense that she was the topic of conversation,
but she was too exhausted to do anything more than
heave a small sigh. "You put her under my protection.
You made me lie to an officer of the law."

"Technically, I didn't *make* you do anything…"

His laugh ·was sharp and short. "You never do, Dawn. That's the thing I can't understand. No matter how determined I am not to fall for whatever it is you're trying to sell, I always end up holding the check."

"Fine. I'll go." He felt the weight of her rising from the couch arm. She took all the heat and comfort of her body with her. "I'll take the puppy home, where my sisters and I can look out for her. I won't answer the phone when you call. I'll tell Zeke that I'm allergic to cows or something, so he has to come to me in Spokane if he wants to hang out. Would that make you happy?"

Yes. No. Not even a little bit.

Adam found it impossible to express the roiling conflict of emotions he was feeling at that exact moment—or, if he was being honest, that he'd been feeling since the moment Dawn entered his life. More than six months had passed since he'd had the dubious honor of making her acquaintance, and he still wasn't sure how it had ended up like this.

Zeke often dated women like her—beautiful women, lively women, women who knew exactly how to appreciate a twentysomething ranch hand who spent most of his free time training for triathlons. From the outset, Dawn had been different. For starters, *she'd* been the one to pick up Zeke for a date, presenting him with a bundle of flowers and a giant, heart-shaped box of chocolates at the front door. She'd also sat herself down on the couch and chatted with Adam for a full half-hour while Zeke finished getting ready, sharing stories about a life that, if they came from anyone else, Adam would have found difficult to believe.

But not Dawn. When she'd told him about running away from home to join the circus instead of going to college, he'd thought, *Yeah. That makes sense.* When she'd admitted she'd once dated a cult leader, he'd chuckled and wished he'd been there to witness it. And when she'd taken his hand in hers and shook it, laughingly promising to have his brother home by eleven, he'd pretty much been lost. More than anything else, he'd felt a strong compulsion to clasp that hand, to beg her not to go out for a night on the town with Zeke, but to stay and keep him company instead.

He'd almost done it, too, which was the worst thing. He'd have trotted out the braille playing cards, challenged her to a game of poker with Zeke and Phoebe, pulled out a bottle of his favorite butterscotch schnapps, and lit a few cigars for ambiance. An evening spent that way was his idea of heaven, even if it seemed tame to everyone else.

Instead, Dawn had murmured something about how attractive the Dearborn brothers were and commented on her good luck in stumbling across such a hidden treasure. And then she and Zeke had gone dancing until three in the morning. Adam knew because he'd lain awake the entire time, counting the chimes on the grandfather clock as each hour went by.

It would have been fine if Zeke had taken the relationship no further than that, treating Dawn like the casual acquaintance she was at the outset. But although his brother had admitted that there was no spark between them, they continued to hang out as friends. A lot. So much, in fact, that Adam had been eventually forced to admit that he and Dawn didn't just have sparks.

They were on fire.

It was on the tip of his tongue to take Dawn up on the offer to bundle Methuselah home and to bundle herself home with her, never to return. There was no denying that his life would be so much easier if Dawn wasn't in it.

But it would be a hell of a lot less interesting, too.

That was the explanation he told himself, anyway, as he wrapped a protective arm around Methuselah and lifted his chin. "You heard Marcia. The puppy needs a few weeks of good Dearborn Ranch air."

"I'm sure the air in Spokane will do just as well. I've been breathing it for years and have yet to keel over."

"Yes, but you aren't a vulnerable animal who was left to fend for herself on the side of a highway. The last thing she needs is to be dragged around in the back seat of your car."

"Or to be forced into training before she's ready?" Dawn suggested.

"That too."

Dawn gave a frustrated grunt. "I swear, talking to you is like talking to a troll who lives under a bridge. Everything is a riddle. Do you or do you not want a service puppy?"

"I mean, I don't *not* want one…"

Adam did his best not to laugh as Dawn released another grunt of frustration, this one accompanied by an unladylike oath. "Let's try that again. Do you or do you not intend to let me take the puppy that *I* rescued home with me?"

"That one I can answer. No."

"Because Marcia said so?"

"Sure. That seems as reasonable an excuse as any."

He couldn't say for a certainty that Dawn threw up her hands, but it sure sounded like that. She sighed and leaned so close that her lips were only a few inches from his own. He could practically taste the waxy lipstick she always wore.

"You're a real pain in my ass. You know that, Adam Dearborn?"

He did. He also knew that being a pain in Dawn's ass was one of the only ways to keep her coming back. A woman who'd traveled with the circus and dated cult leaders wasn't likely to find much else to entertain her in a place where cows outnumbered humans fifty to one.

"The feeling is mutual, Dawn Vasquez," he replied. And because he couldn't help himself: "Are you going to kiss me now?"

She laughed and pulled away. "I was thinking about it, but you don't deserve to be rewarded for your behavior. That's how good puppies get ruined."

"What about good men?" he asked. "Is that also how you ruin them?"

For the longest moment, Adam was afraid he'd said something wrong, misjudged the situation. It wouldn't be the first time in his life that had happened, since he could only rely on verbal cues to read a room, but it would be the first time it had happened with Dawn. Most of the time, she was refreshingly honest about what she wanted and expected out of their not-relationship.

This time was no different.

With a laugh that he was more relieved to hear than he was willing to admit, she said, "If I ever find a good man, I'll let you know."

chapter

3

D awn, you can't go around stealing people's dogs—
even if they have been severely maltreated. There
are protocols for these things, *rules*. We could lose our
license if you got caught."

Dawn's older sister, Lila, stood shaking her head at
the top of the kennel stairs. Her hands were on her hips
and a look of concern furrowed her brow, but Dawn
didn't let either of those things bother her. She never
did. Lila was the best of big sisters, and there was no one
Dawn would rather turn to in a pinch, but there was no
denying that Lila loved rules more than was good for her.

"But I won't get caught," Dawn promised. The first
thing she'd done when she got home was head out to the
kennel to find Adam a more suitable puppy. She was still
deciding between the boxer to her right and the stately
Great Dane to her left. Her instinct said Great Dane, since
he'd already started the training to become a visual support dog, but the boxer had a weirdly oversized tongue
that lolled out at the least provocation. Surely even
impenetrable Adam Dearborn wouldn't be able to resist
that? "I mean, I had a police escort as I fled the scene of
the crime. It doesn't get much more official than that."

"Dawn…"

With a decisive nod, Dawn decided on the Great Dane. Every other human being on the planet might be resistless against a wet, sloppy puppy tongue, but not Adam. If he could have been won over with one of those, she'd have subdued him a long time ago. Alas, neither tongue nor lips nor any other body part had power over that man.

Not any *real* power, anyway.

"I think I'll take Uncle," she said and reached down to clip a leash on the Great Dane. Even though the puppy was only six months old, he was already shaping up to be a mammoth of a dog. She didn't trust her ability to lift him out of the half-walled pen he called home, opting instead to lead him out on his long, sturdy legs. "He's practically a cow anyway. He'll feel right at home on the ranch."

"Dawn."

She turned to her sister with a sunny smile, pushing back a wayward lock of dark-brown hair from her face. She'd pulled it into a short ponytail, but wisps kept springing free around her cheeks. "Lila," she said, her tone matching her sister's.

"Dog theft."

"Dog *rescue*."

"Criminal charges."

"Criminal *abuse*."

Lila sighed. Her own hair was pulled back in an intricate coil of braids that met at the nape of her neck, nary a strand out of place. It was as good of an indication of their differences as anything. Dawn could have made a list of all the ways her older sister was smarter, better, and more organized than her, but that would have defeated the whole purpose of the exercise. Lila was the list-maker in the family. She had hordes of them on her person at any given time. If Dawn were to snatch her sister's purse right now, she was sure she'd find at least half a dozen, all of them clipped together and stored in a manila envelope.

"I don't know why I bother," Lila said and dropped her hands from her hips. "The least you could have done after stealing the poor thing was take her to our own vet. It wasn't very nice of you to leave her to become someone else's problem."

Dawn paused long enough to praise Uncle for his obedience before heaving a sigh of her own. Although Lila had met Zeke several times before and knew Adam by reputation, she clearly underestimated the force of the latter.

"If I could have gotten her out the door without creating more trouble, I would have," Dawn said. "But Adam wouldn't hear of it. Believe me, when that man gets an idea into his head, it's impossible to move him from it."

Lila's slightly arched brow captured her disbelief, but Dawn didn't respond to it. Her sister had no idea just how far back her relationship with Adam Dearborn went, and she wasn't about to enlighten her. There would be questions. And concerns. And utter disbelief. When it came to Dawn and men, six months was a world record.

"To be fair, I'm kind of glad the puppy stayed there," Dawn added. "Marcia said that the less we move her around until those rocks pass, the better. Besides, Dearborn Ranch is the best place to store stolen goods. No one would think to confront Adam on his own turf. He's intimidating."

"Intimidating?" Lila echoed, blinking. "But you're not intimidated by anyone."

"Well, no," Dawn admitted. "*I'm* not, but I'll bet No-Pants Shotgun would take one look at him and reform his way of life. He'd probably even start paying his taxes."

"How do you know he doesn't pay his taxes?"

Dawn laughed as she pictured all those coils of razor wire and the speed with which the man had threatened to shoot. "Call it an educated guess," she said. "My highly developed intellect also tells me that Uncle will be a much better fit for Adam in the long run. Won't you, Uncle?"

The enormous gray puppy sitting at her feet gave an obliging wag of his tail.

"That's right," Dawn cooed and dropped to the animal's level. "We'll woo him with your admirable work ethic, since that's the only thing he cares about. Then Gigi can come with me where she belongs."

"Gigi?"

Dawn peeked up at her sister to find that she was being carefully watched. "Yes. That's what I'm naming the golden retriever."

"And you want to keep her? As…a pet?"

Dawn nodded and buried her face in the nape of Uncle's neck. His fur carried that distinct puppy smell—a mixture of the organic shampoo they used to bathe the animals every week and the grass that he loved to roll around in whenever the opportunity afforded itself. "I could use the company," she said, her voice muffled.

"Because the eight puppies out here in the kennel aren't company enough?" Lila asked.

Dawn knew what her sister was thinking. There was already more than enough to do around this place without adding recreational puppies into the mix, and Dawn was hardly the ideal candidate for long-term pet ownership. Of all the Vasquez sisters, she was the most unpredictable, the least reliable, and, yes, the one who would probably die at the barrel end of a shotgun.

But it wasn't as if she'd *asked* for any of this.

When she and Lila and Sophie had first purchased this house, it had been with the vision of the three of them enjoying a long spinsterhood together with the service puppies they trained and placed with those in need. Having the animals living in the kennel behind the house had been an ideal way to combine work and play, leaving them with plenty of time to see to the animals' needs without infringing on their social lives.

It had been a great plan, but Dawn's sisters had been a little more aggressive in the social life department than any of them had anticipated. Both Sophie, the baby of the family, and Lila had moved out to be with their One True Loves, leaving Dawn behind to do most of the work around the kennel. Dawn didn't begrudge them their happiness, of course, but there was no denying the underlying message.

Sisters fell in love. Service puppies found homes. All around her, people and animals were pairing off like they were boarding the Ark, leaving her alone to face the floodwaters.

Which would have been fine and all, except no one had thought to ask if she wanted to go for a swim.

"It might be nice to come home to a friendly face sometimes, is all I'm saying." Dawn kept her arms around Uncle, drawing comfort from his solid, massive form. "Someone who'll be here longer than a few months at a time."

"Yes, but—"

Dawn didn't wait to hear it. "I'm doing the best I can, Lil," she said, a hand up to stop her sister from saying something they'd both regret. "I know you think I can't handle this place on my own, but everyone is still alive and accounted for. I think I should get some credit for that."

"I'm here every afternoon," Lila said, somewhat defensively.

"I know."

"And Sophie takes the weekends."

"Which I appreciate."

Silence held for a moment before Lila sighed, her long limbs relaxing at her sides. "You're right, of course. It's not fair that you've had to take on the lion's share of work around here. Especially since…"

Dawn's smile held tight. There were countless ways to end that sentence, but all of them held to one common theme: *You're untrustworthy. You're chaotic. You'll run off with the first handsome face to offer something better.*

"I just think you adopting a pet isn't a good idea right now," Lila said in a neat side step of the actual issue. "Give me a few more weeks, okay? I'm working on a few things to take some of the pressure off you, but I can't make any promises yet."

"Of course," Dawn replied, the words rising automatically to her lips. Her sisters were so content—so *happy*—that it would only be cruel to get in their way.

"And you're right. I'm sure the mood will pass. You know how I get when I'm planted in one place for too long. I'm probably restless."

"Restless?" Lila echoed.

"I'm a free spirit, remember?" Dawn gave an airy wave of her hand. "I go where the wind takes me. I can't be tied to one place—or one person—for too long, or I start to get twitchy."

Dawn had no way of knowing if Lila bought her lie or not, since Uncle chose that moment to signal for a potty break. Latching on to the opportunity, Dawn promised to close up the kennel for the night so her sister could get home to her family.

As soon as Lila bore herself away, Dawn clipped a leash to the puppy's collar and led him outside, talking to him all the while. Since she didn't want to dwell on the unsatisfying conversation with her sister, most of what she said was a running dialogue of nonsense about what the dog could expect out of life on the Dearborn Ranch.

"Adam won't be cruel to you or anything," she said as Uncle circled his favorite spot to relieve himself. "In fact, he's inordinately kind to everyone and everything he considers to be under his care. But don't expect him to show you affection or, God forbid, a glimpse of what goes on inside his head. It's all business with him."

In reply, Uncle released a long stream from beneath his leg.

"You're all business, too, it seems. You two should be very happy together. You can spend long evenings discussing rural politics and steer poundage."

Uncle twitched his nose.

"It's better than it sounds," Dawn promised. "There's something very soothing about his voice. Now, come on back into the kennel. It's off to bed with you. We have to get an early start in the morning if we're going to rescue Gigi before she makes the mistake of growing attached to him."

She thought of the way she'd left the golden retriever—all curled up in the corner of Adam's couch, her head burrowed into the fold of his strong arms—and added, "Believe me when I say that there will be no saving her after that."

"No."

"His name is Uncle, and he has the longest eyelashes I've ever seen on a dog. I tried putting mascara on him once, but Lila yelled at me before I got the cap off the wand." Dawn paused. "You have awfully long eyelashes, too. Would you let me put some on you?"

Adam ignored the sultry, teasing note in Dawn's voice and shoved his pitchfork into the bale of hay at his feet. The satisfactory rustle of straw against metal was matched by the heavy weight that pulled at his arms as he lifted, heaved, and tossed the bale down from the truck. It might have seemed careless of him, to hoist seventy-five pounds onto the ground near where Dawn and her long-lashed companion stood, but Adam had long ago learned how to perfect his aim.

Granted, it had taken him about three years and a hell of a lot of missed landings, but Adam was nothing if not determined. He'd found that for most chores around the ranch, he was perfectly capable of doing things without assistance. It was like that with everything, really. For as long as he could remember, being blind had just been a way of life. He could go almost anywhere he wanted and perform almost any task he set his mind to. He needed a little more time to get the process down, that was all.

Fortunately, time was the one thing he had in abundance. Hours of it, in fact, long stretches of big, empty —

"The least you could do is come down and meet him face-to-face," Dawn said, interrupting him before he had a chance to grow morose. "Rejection is always easier to handle when it's personalized."

With a sigh, Adam stabbed his pitchfork into the last of the hay bales and hopped down from the loading bay. There was nothing else he *could* do. He'd brought this on himself when he agreed to this scheme in the first place. He'd hoped he'd have at least twenty-four hours before Dawn descended on him in full training glory, but she'd come all this way. He might as well make the best of it.

"What would you know about rejection?" he asked.

Dawn didn't hesitate. "Oh, you'd be surprised. For reasons I haven't been able to work out yet, some men seem to take one look at me — figuratively speaking, that is — and decide they'd rather spend their nights wrestling alligators."

"At least when you wrestle an alligator, you know what the risks are." He matched his tone to hers, all bland friendliness. "Dismemberment, disembowelment, death…"

A laugh caught in her throat. "All of which are preferable to me, I presume."

He hunched one shoulder in a shrug and drove a hand deep into his pocket. In the normal way of things, he wasn't a man given to fidgeting, but something about being around Dawn always made him acutely aware of his hands. They twitched and tingled and felt about three times their normal size.

"You're the one who introduced alligators into the conversation," he said somewhat gruffly. "I would have suggested bedding down with something safer. A grizzly bear, perhaps."

"I think I prefer the alligator, thanks. They make such lovely shoes." Her laughter sounded again. "Adam Dearborn, allow me to introduce you to Uncle. Uncle is a purebred Great Dane, and he comes from parents who have supplied half a dozen other service puppies to us over the years. He's gray all over—even his eyes, which, in addition to having long eyelashes, are droopy and beautiful."

"Beautiful, droopy eyes. How helpful on a ranch."

"He'll also grow to be the size of a pony and will be able to outrun every man, woman, and cow on this place. So don't turn your nose up at him yet."

"I told you—I'm happy with Methuselah." Despite his words, he crouched down and extended a hand, holding it there until he felt a tentative, wet puppy nose touch his fingers. "Hello, Uncle. I'm sure you're everything that's been promised, but I have a dog already."

Uncle responded by licking his palm. The animal's tongue was huge. As Adam ran a hand over the top of his head, he realized that Dawn hadn't been exaggerating about the rest of him, either. Already larger than a newborn calf, this puppy would grow to be an enormous creature.

And probably a helpful one. Now that the idea had

been planted in his head, Adam was starting to realize that he could use a companion like this one. Of all the things he did around the ranch, the most difficult was walking around outside. The orientation and mobility classes he'd taken as a kid and his cane made him confident in public places, but the great outdoors was the one thing he couldn't control. Rabbit holes, rocky paths, even one goddamn stick in the way could make a short walk into a hazard of the worst kind. Having someone the size of Uncle to keep him company would go a long way in making it possible for him to do things like routine perimeter checks on his own.

But "I'm sure that Methuselah will be more than capable of handling the workload as soon as she's feeling better" is what he said. "She's doing well, by the way. I left her in the office with Phoebe. She still doesn't like being alone for any period of time."

"She and I have that in common," Dawn said. "A lady likes to have an appreciative audience every now and then. Speaking of, what time is Marcia stopping by today?"

"She's not," Adam said, taking much more perverse joy in thwarting Dawn than a grown man should. It would have been so easy to accept a replacement puppy, this olive branch of Dawn's offering, but he wiped his hands on his jeans and rose instead. "She came by first thing this morning and pronounced herself pleased with the puppy's progress."

"Drat," Dawn said. At Adam's lifted brow, she hastily added, "About Marcia having come and gone already, I mean. I was hoping to see her again. I liked her."

The feeling had been mutual, but Adam wasn't about

to tell Dawn that. She already had an ego the size of a small planet.

"I'm afraid we keep early hours in these parts," he said, his voice taking on a marked drawl. He even hitched his thumb in the loop of his belt for good measure. The only thing he was missing was a piece of hay between his teeth. "None of your fancy city living out here. If you want to get anything done, you have to get up with the sun."

"Phoebe would sleep in until noon every day if she had the chance," Dawn retorted, unmoved. "Zeke too. In fact, he was getting up when I peeked in his room. He made me promise to tell you that he's been organizing the shed since eight."

Adam didn't point out the obvious—that Dawn's discretion left something to be desired. That woman had never been able to keep anything to herself. She said and did whatever the hell she felt like, consequences be damned.

Well, that wasn't strictly true. As far as he could tell, she'd never once told any member of his family—or hers—about the things they'd done under cover of night. And morning. And afternoon. And once, when both Zeke and Phoebe had visited friends on the other side of the state, an entire sordid weekend.

"They're terrified of you, you know." Dawn's voice came from closer than it had a moment ago, although he hadn't heard her take a step. "The big, bad giant, stomping around his castle. Or ranch, as the case may be."

"They are not."

"They don't dare contradict you or tell you what they're really thinking."

She was closer now, not just her voice but her presence

growing stronger. Adam wanted to put a hand out toward the Great Dane, to reassure himself that the animal was providing a necessary barrier between them, but he tucked his hands firmly behind his back. Otherwise, there was a good chance he'd reach out and touch Dawn, and that was definitely not what he wanted right now.

And not just because he'd been hefting hay bales for over an hour, smelling of sweat and straw. In one of her more determined moods, she wouldn't let a pesky thing like that stop her.

"They contradict me all the time," he protested.

"They warned me that you were in a mood this morning. 'Don't do it,' Phoebe said. 'You and that puppy are too nice to die like this,' Zeke said."

"Please. I would never hurt a puppy."

Dawn's laughter sprang up in the air between them, as warm as the sun on his back. Today would turn out to be another scorcher, he was sure. That was part of the reason he was up so early, why he was working so hard before most people had poured their first cup of coffee. *Life on a ranch is hard. Life on a ranch isn't for the reluctant.*

Life on a ranch also wasn't for a sweet, emaciated puppy or for a woman whose idea of physical labor was to walk the two blocks from her house to her favorite latte stand. Clearly, he wasn't doing so great at boundaries.

"Give Uncle a chance," Dawn said. "A two-day trial, that's all I'm asking. If you don't like him after forty-eight hours, I'll take him home and you'll never hear the words 'Great' and 'Dane' from my lips again."

Mentioning her lips had to have been some kind of tactic. Just the word—*lips*—had him remembering their shape and size, the way the bottom one was so much plumper than the top, how good they felt when pressed against his bare skin. She always warned him to scrub hard before he met up with any other women, since she left a trail of lipstick all over his body.

He wasn't seeing any other women, but there was no way he was telling her that. She already had him under her spell. He didn't need to be under her power as well.

"Thank you for the offer," he said tightly. "But I already like—"

"The one you can't have," Dawn finished for him. She was definitely closer now, the unmistakable nonscent of her mixing with the hay and dirt to whirl his senses. "That seems to be a sort of thing with you, doesn't it?"

He ran his hands through his hair, since it seemed suddenly important that he do something with them. It was also important to do something with this situation. If he let her continue like this, unchecked and uninhibited, there was good chance neither one of them was getting any work done today.

"As I recall, I've had you plenty of times already," he said, a challenge in his voice. "In fact, I bet I could have you right here and now."

Adam didn't know if he was the one who'd drawn closer to her or if she'd stepped up to him, but there was no longer anything between them. Not a puppy, not air, definitely not common sense. The jut of her breasts pressed softly against his chest, the toes of her shoes touching the tips of his work boots.

His hands suddenly decided they had minds of their own. Moving forward to clasp her around the waist, they touched silky fabric and heat and a patch of skin where her shirt didn't quite reach her waistband. That alone should have been enough to stop him—what kind of a person wore a tiny, silken shirt to a working ranch?—but of course it didn't. That touch of skin set off something inexplicable inside him.

It always did. That was the problem. Words could be ignored and the sound of her laughter pressed deep down inside him, but one graze of his fingertips on her body and he was lost.

"I've always wanted to have sex on a pile of hay," Dawn said, calling his bluff. She arched into his touch, allowing his hand to slide up her back. He encountered nothing but soft skin and the gentle curve of her spine, both of which promised more of the same, should he give in and *really* cop a feel. Which was tempting for a lot of reasons, including the fact that Dawn was stacked in ways that seemed wholly against nature. "Surely there must be one or two of those in the barn we could try?"

"There are." He brought his lips close to her ear, though he was careful not to press against the gently pounding pulse below it. The moment the kissing started, all other bets were off—including the one that had a Great Dane puppy at their feet and a golden retriever puppy napping under Phoebe's desk. That was the one thing he knew for sure. Dawn had come out here with the sole intention of luring him into lowering his defenses, using her incredible body and the promise of what it could do to get her own way. She wanted Methuselah, and she'd stop at nothing to get her.

Well, two could play that way. In fact, he was becoming something of an expert at this particular game.

"We could slip in there right now, and no one would

know where we are," he murmured. Dawn arched her neck to give him better access, but he didn't kiss, didn't touch. Only teased. "I could throw you into the biggest stack of hay and rip this tiny scrap of a shirt from your body."

A slight, guttural sound indicated how much she liked the direction this conversation was going. *Typical*. With Dawn, the anticipation, the clandestine nature of their meetings, was half the fun.

Who was he kidding? Where that woman was concerned, it was probably *all* the fun.

"No one will think to look for us for hours," he added, still in that low, crooning voice. "It'll just be me and you, our bodies slick with sweat."

Dawn's hips pressed against his, her arms coiling around his neck so that her entire body could melt against him. This was how she always struck, coiled and soft and yielding.

So he struck back.

"Well, that and the snakes."

Instead of pulling back, Dawn only laughed and clasped her hands tighter around his neck. "Good thing I happen to like snakes," she said. Her mouth brushed lightly against his, fluttering like a pair of butterfly wings. "Like the alligators, they make such nice shoes. Purses too."

Even though Adam's body thrummed with anticipation, burning hot in all the places it touched hers, he kept his tone level. "We also get the occasional badger, even though they're pretty rare in these parts. Rats are almost a certainty."

"Why, Adam Dearborn, are you trying to sweet-talk me?"

No, dammit. He was trying to do the exact opposite. Why did this woman refuse to act like a normal human being? She should run at the mention of rats, not press her hips against his until he ached.

"I'm just making sure you know what you're getting into, that's all," he said. His voice sounded strained to his own ears. "Things can get pretty nasty out here in the wilderness."

"That's funny," she purred. "So can I."

It was almost more than he could take. Getting the better of this woman in a verbal battle was almost impossible, and making her see reason was laughable. At least in a pile of hay, he'd have a chance of coming out on top.

Well, he'd have a chance of *coming* on top, anyway.

"Of course, the real thing you want to watch out for is the straw itch mites," he managed before he was lost to all sense of propriety.

"Those aren't a real thing," she protested, laughing. She also slackened her hold, which was the most important thing.

"Oh, they're nasty little buggers—literally." Finally, finally, he was able to slip his hand out from under her shirt. Finally, finally, the pressure of her hips against his gave way. "Zeke was covered from head to toe in the rash last year. You'd have thought he fell into a well of poison oak from the way his body broke out in those welts."

"You're just making this up to scare me. If you didn't want to sleep with me, you could have said so."

Ha. Right. That showed how much she knew. He *always* wanted to sleep with her. He always wanted to be near her—inside her, on top of her, even sitting in the same goddamned room. How pathetic was that?

While she was out living the vibrant, fast-paced life of a woman in her prime, he sat at home and pined.

And his only saving grace—the only way he could continue to hold his head high—was to never let her know.

"I don't want to sleep with you," he lied. "I don't want to kiss or hug or even touch you any more than is strictly necessary. In fact, now that we're on the subject, I don't want your Great Dane peace offering, either."

She laughed. *Laughed.* "I don't believe you," she said, her voice low and crooning. "I think you want me as much as I want you. And I think you're going to throw me into a pile of hay—*clean* hay—to prove it."

"You're wrong," he replied—and she was. Not about him wanting her, but about how much. What he felt wasn't a flash of temporary desire. It wasn't a tepid impulse. It was *need*, pure and simple.

He'd have done exactly as she demanded, given up his dignity and his dog for a chance at having her in his arms again, except for the pounding of light footsteps in the distance. He jumped away from Dawn, ears cocked as Phoebe's panting breath immediately followed.

"Thank the good goddess in heaven. There you are." Phoebe's words were hitched, her breathing labored. "It's that stupid animal, Adam. I tried to catch her before she got away, but I opened the gate so I could start cleaning the yard, and it must not have latched. She took off like a horde of wolves were after her."

"Dawn," he groaned. And since it seemed important to make the distinction, he added, "The cow, that is."

"I gathered as much, thank you," Dawn the human said. "Let me guess—she's going where she's not wanted and creating all kinds of problems?"

Adam was about to nod when Phoebe interrupted. "Worse. She's on Mrs. Benson's property."

He swore under his breath. "Like hell she is."

"I came as fast as I could, but there's no telling what kind of damage she's done by now. I would have gone straight there, only you said—"

Adam nodded his understanding. They needed to tread warily where their erratic neighbor was concerned. There was far too much at stake to send Phoebe in there alone.

"Good call," he said. "You'd better bring the truck around. Grab ropes, the bottle of molasses, and, Lord help us, a tranquilizer. Where's Zeke?"

Although he hadn't directed the question at anyone in particular, Dawn was the one who answered. "Heading out to do laps at the community center, I think. At least that's where he said he was going when I woke him up. Where can I put Uncle?"

It took Adam a moment to work out her meaning. "Out of the question. You're not coming with us."

As usual, Dawn ignored him. "The ropes and tranquilizer I can understand, but what's the molasses for?"

"Dawn has a sweet tooth," Phoebe explained. "She'll do just about anything once she gets a whiff of it. Sometimes, she'll even come when she's called, if you'd believe it."

"Wait—so the cow is *really* named Dawn? Adam didn't make that up to annoy me?"

"Oh, we've been calling her Dawn forever." Phoebe giggled. Like Zeke, she had a joie de vivre that made her seem younger than her twenty-eight years. "But it's not an insult, I promise. She's always been Adam's favorite cow."

"I don't have favorite cows, and Dawn can only be described as a plague." He didn't enlighten the two as to which Dawn he referred to this time. They needed to get moving if he was going to salvage this disaster. Rolling a shoulder in the direction of the house, he said, "You'd better take Uncle inside. He can keep Methuselah company so she doesn't think she's been abandoned. She howls if she's left alone for longer than two minutes. It's heartbreaking."

"Good thinking," Dawn replied.

He wasn't prepared for so much conciliation from a woman who lived to thwart him, so his voice was a little gruff as he added, "I hope you're dressed for getting dirty. This isn't going to be pretty."

Since he knew damn well that she didn't have enough clothes on to protect herself from a mosquito bite, he didn't wait for an answer. Nor was it necessary to. Dawn suggested that Phoebe go for the supplies while she pulled the truck around—an idea to which his sister readily agreed. Adam accepted the leash Dawn put in his hand and did his best to remain unmoved when she said, "I'll be right back. Will you be a dear and introduce the two puppies? This'll be a great chance for you and Uncle to get to know each other."

She didn't wait for an answer. The crunch of her footsteps as she jogged toward the garage was all that was left to him. Well, that and the Great Dane.

He waited until he was sure Dawn was out of earshot before lowering himself into a squat. "I'm sorry about that," he said as he ran a hand over the dog's neck. The animal's hair was short but soft, the thick, healthy texture of it at direct odds with the undernourished puppy he'd left convalescing inside the house. "You seem like a good boy, and I have no doubt that you'll make some other blind schmuck very happy someday. Just not this one."

The puppy licked his face in reply.

"I know. It's juvenile of me, and I should know better than to let her get under my skin, but it's harder than it looks. She slides in there and then latches on like some kind of parasite."

He planted a kiss on top of the animal's head and rose to his feet. If nothing else, this puppy was an exceptional listener. But... "You understand, don't you?" he asked. "I've got nothing against you—I really don't—but she gave me Methuselah, so Methuselah is who I'm keeping. She doesn't get to flit around doing whatever she wants, whenever she wants it. I have some pride left."

He gave the leash a light tug, thinking to lead the Great Dane along the well-worn and familiar path to the house, but the puppy took up a position at Adam's side and waited for him to start walking first. Half an hour in, and Uncle already knew his job better than Adam did.

And so, it seemed, did Dawn.

"I didn't say I had *a lot* of pride left, mind you," he added. "But goddammit, there's enough."

chapter
4

There was no doubt about it—Dawn was a *serious* bitch.

"I swear on everything you love and hold dear, you'll listen to what I'm saying or pay the consequences." Dawn held out her hand, which was smeared in a mixture of mud, molasses, and what she was pretty sure was cow poop. It had neither an attractive color nor an attractive scent. "Get out of the pen right now, or I'll come over and make you get out."

"That's the ticket," Adam yelled from the other side of the fence. The *clean* side of the fence, where the only thing that ruffled his exquisite exterior was a sole lock of hair out of place. The brown swoop fell across his forehead at a perfectly jaunty angle. "Talk to her like a rational human being. That always works. Cows understand every word you're saying."

Dawn relieved the worst of her temper by flipping him the bird with her outstretched hand. Phoebe informed her brother of it with a laugh.

"You don't want to know what gesture she's making at you right now, Adam."

"Don't worry—I can guess. Is she close enough yet?"

"Just a few more feet... Dawn, you're going to

have to get closer than that. Human Dawn, I mean."
Phoebe laughed again. She'd been doing that a lot ever
since they arrived on the scene to find the wayward
cow frolicking in a pit of mud and weeds like she was
never going to see the sky again. "We should probably
give the cow a new name. This is going to start getting
confusing."

"*Start* getting confusing?" Dawn asked. It was a rhetorical question, since both the Dearborn siblings were
intent on the task at hand. As this apparently involved
having her lure the cow close enough for Adam to get a
rope around its neck, it hardly seemed fair that those two
were the ones concentrating so hard. She was the one in
imminent danger of being trampled to death.

"A little closer," Phoebe said. "One more step. There
you go. And…now!"

Dawn shrieked as a heavy coil hurtled past her face.
She knew from the stories Zeke and Phoebe told that
Adam was something of a savant when it came to roping
cattle. Neither of them were able to explain how he did
it, but assuming an animal was within the length of the
rope, he could land the loop around its neck on the first
try every single time.

From a distance, she had no doubt that Adam roping
cattle must be a sight to behold. She'd never known
anyone to be so comfortable in his own skin, so unconcerned with the way others perceived him. He was confident without being cocky, adept without being arrogant.
The hard planes of his body were hewn by hard work.
His clothes were functional rather than ornamental.

In other words, he knew his value, and he didn't need
anyone else to confirm or deny it.

Up close, she wasn't so charmed by the picture he presented. Projectiles whizzing by her head and a five-hundred-pound cow bucking angrily against her restraints had a way of ruining the mood.

Enough. This was the second time in as many hours that this dratted cow was preventing Dawn from appreciating Adam as he was meant to be appreciated. She was putting her foot down. Literally. Without waiting to consider the wisdom of her actions, she squared her stance and faced down the agitated animal. Pausing just long enough to wipe her hands on the seat of her jeans, she put one finger on either side of her mouth and did what she did best—made a lot of noise.

The piercing whistle cut through the air, stopping everyone short. Humans, cow—even the birds in a nearby tree—all halted at once.

"That's more like it," Dawn said. She stepped toward the huge, bulky animal heaving a few feet away, the rope now slack around her neck. "I don't know who taught you how to behave, but if there's one thing I've learned in this lifetime, it's that a lady is only allowed to cause as much trouble as she's worth. And you, my precious, aren't worth this much. Unless—" She turned toward Adam. "How much will a cow like this go for at market?"

"Right now? Twelve hundred dollars, give or take a few hundred. Although at this point, I'd pay twice that just to get someone to take her off my hands."

Dawn turned back to the cow, one finger outstretched. "Then you are *definitely* not worth the trouble. Now, get moving. I've got two puppies to train and one very long shower to take, and you have some serious thinking to do about your actions." She slapped a hand on the cow's massive, muscled back for good measure, more surprised than pleased when it actually worked. The white-and-brown-spotted cow gave her only a mild stare before beginning a slow and careful trudge out of the mud pit.

A round of applause from somewhere behind her had Dawn turning in her tracks. She expected to find Phoebe standing there celebrating their success and was understandably surprised to see a strange woman doing the clapping. The woman was well into her seventies and wore her years defiantly, her wrinkles pronounced and her expression grim.

Like most of the people around these parts, she was also dressed for hard labor. While Adam looked like a flannel god chiseled from stone and Phoebe wore her jeans like they were a second skin, this woman looked as though she'd spent most of the morning rolling around in the mud pit with the cow. Baggy brown pants, an oversized button-down shirt that looked to be disintegrating at the seams, and a pair of boots that had to be six sizes too big for her were hardly what Dawn would consider *cowboy chic*.

"About damn time someone took that animal to task," the woman said. She stopped clapping as suddenly as she'd begun, her eyes drinking in Dawn from the tips of her muddied toes to the spaghetti straps of her chiffon tank top. It was hardly the ideal outfit for working out in the middle of nowhere, but Adam was a tactile man. Dawn loved wearing fabrics that he wouldn't be able to keep his hands away from. "Though it beats me what the hell you're supposed to be."

Dawn laughed. "A puppy trainer, if you'd believe it." She made her way to the edge of the fence, her progress slowed by the clinging pull of mud against her feet. She extended a hand. "Hi. I'm Dawn—Dawn Vasquez."

The woman stared at her hand for a few seconds. Too late, Dawn remembered that it was still covered in mud, but the woman accepted the handshake with a low grumble. Her own palm was rough and warm and none too clean itself. "Bea Benson."

Ah, yes. The neighbor onto whose property the cow had strayed. Although Dawn hadn't had much time to appreciate the scenery before, she took a moment now. Most of the land in this part of the county was flat and uninteresting, similar to the landscape she and Zeke had passed when fleeing with Gigi. The occasional stack of hay, small clusters of trees, and political signs of the conservative variety were all that provided much in the way of visual interest.

This area was similar, though a cute white farmhouse stood not too far in the distance. It was built on a slight rise so that it sat like a beacon against the bright-blue sky, with several fruit-bearing trees growing around it. Dawn had never been much of a one for nature, but she could see how a place like this might appeal.

Not with all this mud, though. For the life of her, Dawn couldn't figure out why this particular area was fenced off. Images of late-night mud battles between buxom, scantily clad women flitted through her mind only to be immediately banished. That was way more fun than most of these people were used to having.

"Why do you have this section fenced off?" Dawn asked. "Does it have some kind of sentimental importance? Oh God…this isn't your family cemetery or something, is it?"

She cast a quick glance around, fearful of finding evidence of mortal remains having once been laid to rest, but Bea just barked out a laugh. It sounded rusty from underuse, but Dawn liked the sound of it all the same.

"Of course it's not a cemetery, you ninny. It's my garden." The laugh stopped short as evidence of the carnage seeped in. "Leastaways, it *was* my garden. Six months of sowing and weeding, my blood in every goddamn leaf."

"I'm really sorry about this, Mrs. Benson." Phoebe stepped forward, wringing her hands. "We had her all penned up this morning, but then the gate got unlatched, and…"

"And she ate my entire life and livelihood," Bea finished for her. "That's fine. No one around here cares if I die of starvation, so why would you be any different? Just don't be surprised if I sneak over in the dead of night and eat your damn cow to make up for it."

Dawn was unable to subdue a shout of laughter. Sneaking around at night and exacting personal vengeance was the same thing she'd have done in this situation. Bea turned a furious eye on her.

"And what do you find so funny, young lady?" Bea demanded. "They weren't your butter beans she ate."

"No. But I hope that when you do come for the cow, you'll let me know ahead of time." Dawn stared down at her outfit in disgust. She'd never be able to wear this tank top again. "I have one or two retributions of my own."

Adam's voice, quiet but firm, came from behind them. "Of course we'll pay you for the damage, Mrs.

Benson," he said. "I know we can't replace the effort you put into the garden, but feel free to name any figure you want."

That seemed inordinately generous to Dawn, who would have unhesitatingly stated a million dollars just to see what Adam would do, but Bea snorted. "A bribe, you mean."

He lifted his shoulder in a half shrug. "I don't care what you call it as long as it leads to what we both want. The checkbook is in the glove box. You know what I'm prepared to pay."

"It's like a Dearborn to think money fixes everything." Bea lifted her chin at a mulish angle and stared hard at Dawn, which seemed a little unfair. *She* wasn't the one trying to buy the poor woman off. "Now, if one of the Smithwood cattle had come over here and turned my vegetables into a playground…"

Both Phoebe and Adam stiffened in a way that was almost comical. It was as though they'd both been jolted by the same electric shock.

Adam was the first to recover, which he did by putting on a smile that would have charmed Dawn right out of her dirty clothes, had it been directed at her. He hitched a thumb in his belt loop, too, which only added to his appeal. "You know we'll match anything the Smithwoods say or do. I've made that clear from the start."

None of Adam's charm worked on the older woman. "They'd have offered to come over and replant this garden from the ground up, keeping a lonely old woman company all the while. Is that what you're prepared to do, Mr. Dearborn?"

His voice remained level as he said politely, "If that's what you want, absolutely. It'd be my pleasure."

"They might even make me a cake, seeing what a sweet tooth I have. In fact, they've made me three this week already. What would you say to that?"

"That you must be getting tired of them by now. What if I were to offer you a pie instead?"

Dawn watched this exchange with interest. Never, not even in the deepest throes of passion, had she ever heard Adam be this conciliatory. He fought and argued and dug his stubborn feet into every challenge that came his way. Likening him to a cow was a bit much, but she was sure there was an ass or two around these parts that fit the bill. She had no idea what power this cantankerous old woman had over Adam, but it must be something good.

"Too bad," Bea said. "I don't want you. Or your milky little sister or that swoopy-haired musclehead you call a brother, so don't go offering me them in your stead."

Adam's smile began to falter. "Excuse me?"

"That boy doesn't have the sense God gave this cow, and if I had to spend as much as five minutes in the girl's company, what with her constant bitching and moaning, I'd shoot myself in the foot."

"Now, see here. My sister does not—"

"Don't, Adam," Phoebe hissed. Her own smile had long since vanished, replaced by a tight line. "She's only trying to rile you up. I'm not worth the fight."

Actually, Dawn disagreed. Phoebe *was* worth the fight. She might not be physically imposing, but looks were often deceiving. Dawn's own younger sister was of the same slight build and mien, and Dawn couldn't think of any person, living or dead, who had as much resolve as her. She'd take one look at this mean old woman and tell her exactly what she could do with herself—all done with such a deceptively sweet air that no one would see it coming.

Since Dawn was much less adorable than her sister, she had to resort to her own tactics, which better resembled a battering ram than a petite Trojan horse.

"Okay, here's the deal." She stared at Bea, holding the woman's gaze until she was forced to blink. "*I'll* be the one to come help you with your garden, and I'll be nice and keep you company while I do it. I might even bring you that pie Adam promised. But I won't hear a word against any of the Dearborns while I'm here, got it?"

"How dare you speak to me like—"

"I'll admit that they have terrible taste in cows," she continued, rising up under the challenge in the woman's stare. Her sisters would recognize the danger of pushing her like this. After the incident with the puppy, Zeke might recognize it, too. But none of the people present knew her well enough to realize that once she took a stand against something, it was almost impossible to get her to sit back down again. When Dawn did a thing, she did it all the way.

Stealing dogs. Confronting mean old ladies. *Falling in love*.

"They should obviously invest in a better gate, too, but they're accepting responsibility and have shown themselves willing to make amends," she added. "Insulting them isn't going to change anything."

Phoebe turned her hiss to Dawn. "Uh, Dawn? Maybe now's not—"

"Oh, now's the best time—believe me. It's no use

letting something like this fester. It's better to get it out while we're all here." She put her hands on her hips. "Well, Mrs. Benson? What do you say? It's me and my hoes coming to do your dirty work, or it's a big fat check from the Dearborn Ranch. Which do you prefer?"

A chuff of something that was either laughter or outrage sounded from Adam's direction, but Dawn didn't turn around to see which. She didn't need him derailing her right now. She was on a roll. Not even her confrontation with No-Pants Shotgun could touch this one.

"Well?" she prodded. "Do you want my help or not?"

A heavy sigh escaped the older woman as she looked away. "You're better than nothing, I suppose," she said.

"I'm a lot better, actually."

Bea pointed a finger at her. "But you'll need to find some work clothes before you come over, because I refuse to look at your tits all day."

Okay, that was a *definite* laugh coming from Adam.

"And you'll have to keep coming for as long as it takes, mind. It's not going to be easy, getting all this back in order. It'll take hard labor and long hours and fingernails that look as though they clawed their way up from the gates of hell. You seem an awful lot like the kind of girl who quits as soon as the nail polish chips away."

"Believe me, Mrs. Benson," Adam said before Dawn could open her mouth to defend herself. "There's a lot I could say about this woman, but if there's one thing she doesn't do, it's quit."

Despite the insult lurking in his words, Dawn's spine straightened. Damn straight she didn't quit. She'd tamed this cow. She could tame this woman, too, if given enough time. She was sure of it.

As for Adam Dearborn?

She gave in and peeked over her shoulder. Adam stood exactly where he'd been at the start of this conversation, stalwart and unmoving and so devastatingly handsome that she found it difficult to breathe. Every angle of him was sharp and strong, every line an architectural masterpiece. Long after the rest of the world crumbled away, he would be standing exactly like that.

No one can tame me, his stance seemed to say. *No one can make me do anything I don't want to. And woe to the woman who tries.*

"That's right," Dawn said, unable to look away. "When I want something, there's nothing in this world or the next that will stop me. And that, Mrs. Benson, is a promise."

🐾 🐾 🐾

"I call dibs on the shower," Phoebe announced.

"I guess that ruins my plans," Dawn said. She leaped out of the driver's side of the truck and watched as Phoebe trotted toward the ranch house without waiting to see if anyone planned on countering her claim. "I was going to try and lure you into something wet and steamy."

"You can lure all you want," Adam replied. He also stepped out of the truck, though with slightly more caution. "But it would be useless to get in the habit of cleanliness on your first day. You have no idea what you've signed on for. By the time you're done helping Bea Benson, you won't know where your skin begins and the dirt ends."

Dawn laughed. Threatening words held no power

over her when they were being uttered by a man who
looked as cool and pristine as Adam. The only signs of
exertion he showed were a pair of mud-splattered boots
and a slightly rakish ruffle to his hair.

She hadn't fared nearly as well, obviously, but that
hadn't stopped him from putting his hands around her
waist and hoisting her into the truck when they left, his
hold much higher—and lingering for much longer—
than necessary. Clearly, a layer of dirt wasn't too much
of a deterrent for this man.

"I already know every inch of my own skin, thanks,"
she replied. "And so do you, if we want to get literal
about it."

"I don't."

"Suit yourself." She shrugged. "But I'm not the
one who was trying to cop a feel while helping a poor,
defenseless damsel into a truck. And while your sister
was just a few feet away, too. Shame on you."

Adam slammed the truck door. "Well, one of us has
to have some shame, and it's sure as hell not going to
be you. What are you even wearing? Is that supposed to
be a shirt?"

Dawn bit her lower lip to keep her laughter from
escaping. The expression on Adam's face was trying so
hard to be outraged, but he mostly looked aroused. "It
used to be one, at any rate. I'll tack the dry cleaning bill
onto my official Puppy Promise invoice."

"This sounds an awful lot like extortion. Can't you
wear normal, machine-washable clothes instead?"

"I could, but what would be the fun in that?" She
waited until Adam had walked around the truck and
joined her before making her way up to the house. He

knew these grounds well enough to walk without assistance or the cane he used in more public places, but she liked to be on hand anyway. "Where'd you leave the puppies, by the way? I'm a little worried about Gigi. Uncle is an absolute sweetheart when it comes to other dogs, but I'm not sure how socialized Gigi's going to be yet."

"*Methuselah* is in the kitchen" came his quick reply. "And if that Great Dane of yours did anything to hurt her…"

That made her laugh, too. One of the first things they did whenever they got a puppy in for training was make sure they got plenty of playtime with the other animals. For the past few weeks, Uncle had been the first face that all of the newcomers met. He was a giant, all right, but as gentle as they came. She'd walked into the kennel the other day to find him sitting patiently in the middle of the room with a Chihuahua dangling from each ear.

She didn't know if it was her laughter that spurred Adam on to the kitchen or if it was genuine concern for the puppies, but he picked up his pace to a near-trot. As he pulled open the kitchen door, he also opened his mouth to call out to them, but Dawn forestalled him with a hand on his forearm.

"Don't," she warned. His muscle twitched under the press of her fingers, but he didn't pull away. "I can see them from here. You'll wake them up."

"They're asleep?"

"*Sound* asleep. Like a couple of babies. Gigi is all curled up next to Uncle's belly, with her head tucked under his chin. It might be the cutest thing I've ever seen."

He hesitated. "You're not making that up?"

"I wouldn't do that, Adam," she said softly. She'd do

a lot of things to rile this man up, but lying about what she could see wasn't one of them. "I told you Uncle is a keeper. He's got really great instincts. He must have known what Gigi needed to feel okay."

As if on cue, Gigi gave a sleepy yawn and began to stretch her limbs, whimpering softly when she strained too hard against one of the sores on her stomach. Adam showed every sign of wanting to leap to her aid, but Dawn held him back.

"I was afraid something like this might happen," she murmured, watching as Uncle licked liberally at Gigi's face until she settled back down. The Great Dane must have heard them, because he cast Dawn a huge, gray-eyed look that seemed to say exactly what she was thinking: *I guess I'm stuck now, aren't I?*

"Something like what?" Adam asked.

"They're attached."

"Attached?"

"Best buds. Inseparable. Soul mates." Dawn heaved a sigh. "Gigi took one look at him and decided no one else would do for her. She'll *definitely* be useless as a guide dog now. A female in love is the worst kind for getting anything done."

Adam squared his shoulders in a gesture of pure defiance. "Okay, now you really are making things up. Either that, or you brought Uncle here on purpose to thwart me."

That made her laugh. "Of course I brought him here to thwart you. Everything I'm doing is to thwart you. Didn't I make that clear? I don't chase down cows and tackle cranky old ladies for fun, you know. I'm only helping Bea with her garden so you give Uncle a *real* try—none of this two-day-trial nonsense."

"You have serious problems."

"What I have is a strong determination to get my puppy back," she countered. "And I'll stop at nothing to succeed."

"That's funny, because I was thinking the same thing."

It was strange that the challenge he offered could make her heart pound like that—the same as his smile, the same as his kiss—but she'd long since stopped questioning the impulses that drove her.

"Well, we'll just have to see what happens, won't we?" she said. "A lot can happen in six weeks."

🐾🐾🐾

"No way." Zeke clomped heavily into the kitchen at the end of the day, still in his work boots and most likely leaving a trail of dirt everywhere he went. The squeak of Adam's bare feet on the linoleum floor indicated that their cleaning woman had come and gone while they were chasing down the cow, but that wouldn't trouble his brother any. "You're really going over to Bea's house to help with her garden? On purpose? The walls aren't really made of gingerbread, Dawn. Don't follow the crumbs, or you'll turn into a pillar of salt."

"That's not how any of those stories go," Adam said, but he wasn't sure if anyone heard him over the clatter of the pots and pans. In addition to the pasta he was making for dinner, he apparently needed to add a pie into the mix. The Smithwoods must be in the homestretch of negotiations if the only temptation they were offering anymore was a cake or two. In addition to today's attempt at a bribe, he'd already doubled his own offer for the Benson lands. There was only so much he could do.

"What made you agree to it?" Zeke continued. The clomping had stopped, so Adam could only assume his brother had thrown himself onto one of the dining room chairs in the attached room. Dawn and Phoebe already sat in there shucking corn. "Are you being blackmailed or something?"

"Nope. I just like being able to hold your brother over a barrel," Dawn said. Her voice was cheerful and triumphant—the same way it had been since her victory over the cow. *And over me.* "Now he *has* to give poor Uncle a try. Isn't that right, Gigi? Soon, you'll be able to come home with me where you belong."

"She's not going anywhere," Adam said. "I promised to give Uncle a chance in exchange for your sacrifice, not part ways with Methuselah forever."

Aware that he was the subject of conversation, the Great Dane puppy approached him from the right. He sidled close enough for Adam to feel his presence, but not so close he got in the way of Adam's movements. *Damn.* The animal was really good at this—of knowing where he needed to be and when he needed to be there, of being present without being obtrusive. Dawn had obviously known what she was doing when she'd chosen him.

"What a good boy you are, Uncle," Dawn said as if to prove it. Her voice was much closer than the dining room table this time, causing Adam to fumble with the can of crushed tomatoes in his hand. "So docile and biddable and eager to please. Remind me—that's how you like them, isn't it?"

He almost *dropped* the can of tomatoes this time, and right onto poor Uncle's head, too. "Stay out from behind the kitchen counter, please," he said by way of answer. "I need a clear workspace to keep track of what I'm doing."

It wasn't much, but it was all he *could* say. Dawn was the least docile and biddable woman in existence, and she knew it. As for being eager to please, well…the less said on that subject, the better. He'd never known anyone to be so specific and demanding with her needs—or so well versed in all the various terms for human anatomy. Every interaction with her was an education.

"Oh, I know you do." Her voice bubbled over with laughter. "This isn't my first rodeo. Gigi and I are just sitting on the island stools and watching you work, aren't we, girl? The corn is behind you next to the fruit bowl, by the way. About eight o'clock."

He nodded a quick thanks and continued tossing contents into the saucepan. He was no gourmet chef, but he liked cooking. There was something soothing about the task of chopping and cutting and combining ingredients, an act of creation that, with the right practice, drew from every sense except sight. Most other artistic pursuits were beyond his reach—he was no Bach, alas—but this was one area where he could put a little of himself into his work. Probably the *only* area. There wasn't a whole lot of room for creativity in the breeding and butchering of cows.

Even naming them was dangerous work. Look what had happened with Dawn the cow. Naming her had given her power. Now she was just as much of a menace as the real thing.

"What's the deal with that Bea lady, anyway?" Dawn asked. "She doesn't seem to think much of you guys."

"Oh, she doesn't like us. She doesn't like anyone."

Phoebe's voice appeared next to Dawn's. It was equally cheerful, though for less ominous reasons. "Is it okay if I put Gigi in my lap? I don't want to hurt her."

"Her name is Methuselah, and yes, you can hold her. Marcia said positive human contact is a must."

"Oh, is that why you let her sleep at the foot of your bed last night?" Phoebe asked, laughing. "And here I thought it was because you were afraid to leave her alone."

Adam ignored her. It would have taken a much stronger man than him to force that whimpering bundle to sleep on the floor. She'd somehow decided that Adam was the only one who could protect her at night, and he was determined not to let her down. Contrary to the opinion of everyone in this room, he *did* occasionally yield to his softer side.

"It was the least I could do," he said loftily. "Puppies who lack affection can have all kinds of problems later on."

"Humans, too," Dawn added mischievously. "We all need a little love sometimes, wouldn't you say, Adam? Just look how miserable that poor lady today was. Does she live in that huge farmhouse all by herself?"

The provocation was strong, but he managed to subdue the urge to retaliate in kind. The only way to beat Dawn at anything was simply not to play.

"She's lived there alone for as long as I can remember," he replied. "She had a husband once upon a time, but he left the picture long before I took over the ranch."

As was almost always the case whenever he mentioned his rise in status at Dearborn Ranch, a somewhat subdued hush fell over the room. Adam had only been nineteen when their father died and put him in charge of this place. *And* of Zeke and Phoebe, who'd only been fifteen. It had been a lot to heap on any teenager's shoulders, let alone one who faced a few extra hurdles in life. Within the space of a few months, he'd had to learn how to cook and make sure the twins got to school, helped with trigonometry homework and prom-date woes—and all of that on top of his regular workload.

It had been hard on them emotionally, too. Their father had been old when they were born; older still as they moved through their teens, but that hadn't made him any less of a presence in their lives. He'd never been a *warm* man—not really, not after their mom died having the twins—but when your whole life and livelihood was tied up in a place like this, it was impossible not to become dependent on those around you.

The fact that they were all still working here was clear proof of that. For good or for bad, he and Phoebe and Zeke were bound. Roped together like a herd of cattle heaving and thronging as one.

Adam cleared his throat—and, in the process, cleared the air. "All that land is a lot for anyone to maintain by themselves, let alone a woman of her age," he said. "I assume that's why she's selling out."

"Selling out?" Dawn echoed.

"Oh, yeah. It's the hottest thing to happen around these parts since that two-headed deer was seen stalking the north woods." Phoebe began fidgeting with the condiments on the counter, the clatter of the ketchup bottle and saltshaker ringing together. "Her acreage is some of the best in these parts. Water access, highly arable land… I won't tell you how much Adam has offered her for it. It makes him turn red to think about it."

Predictably, Adam felt his color rise. There was no denying that he'd already gone much higher than he'd ever planned, but what other choice did he have? Bea Benson drove a hard bargain.

"It would allow us to add an extra hundred head of cattle to our operation," he said in a level tone. "Which, by the way, is a thing all three of us agreed to. This is as much your ranch as it is mine."

"You guys are expanding?" Dawn asked. "Weird. Zeke never said anything."

"That's because Zeke doesn't think it'll actually go through," his brother said. Like the other two, he'd pulled close to the kitchen counter to join the conversation. "If you ask me, Bea's just toying with Adam. Adam and the Smithwoods both. She'll never actually sell. She only wants to see how far he'll bend over."

"And how far will he bend?" Dawn asked. "For purely scientific reasons."

The heat that had risen to the surface of his skin didn't abate any, but Adam busied himself with straining the pasta. The steam was as good an excuse for the flush as any. "I offered a little above market value, that's all. Not that it mattered. She didn't bite. It would have been worth the extra money to see the Smithwoods squirm."

"Why do we want the Smithwoods to squirm?"

Zeke laughed. The sound was followed by the pop of a cork and the gurgle of wine being poured out. Apparently, they were turning this into a whole thing—food and drink and family camaraderie. Adam's heart gave an odd sort of thunk at how good it felt, how ordinary. He couldn't remember the last time they'd done this on a day that wasn't a holiday or a funeral.

"We've been at war with their family for years," Zeke said. "Didn't you know? They're our mortal enemies."

Dawn paused long enough to swallow. "We have a mortal enemy? And no one told me?"

No one bothered to correct Dawn's pronoun usage. It didn't seem to matter that she was just a friend of Zeke's, a dog trainer they'd hired to work on-site for the next six weeks. Now that Adam thought about it, he didn't recall any of them inviting her to stay for dinner, either. Yet for her to leave now would have ruined the evening for all three of them.

"Okay. Spill." Dawn rapped her knuckles on the island top. "What's the matter with them?"

"Oh, not much," Zeke replied. "It's only that they're stuck up and greedy and would love nothing more than to see our entire family in ruins. We've been at war with them for generations. It's a modern-day medieval feud."

"People don't have feuds in our day and age," Phoebe protested. "They just get annoyed with each other on the internet."

"Tell that to the Smithwoods," Zeke countered.

Since Dawn wasn't likely to get any sense out of either Phoebe or Zeke, Adam cleared his throat and did his best to summarize over fifty years of antagonism. "Their ranch is located on the other side of the Benson property," he explained. "It's the only direction either of us can expand, and whoever buys her land will control the best natural water resource in this area. Naturally, we're both very eager to get our hands on it. And even more naturally, Bea Benson knows it. She's been toying around with us both for years."

"Oh." Dawn sounded disappointed. "It's a land dispute."

"It's a lot more than that," Zeke retorted. "Tell her the best part, Adam."

"I don't see what difference it makes."

"The Smithwoods used to own the land our ranch is located on," Zeke said. From the dramatic way he spoke, you'd think he was sharing a deep, dark family secret. Which, Adam supposed, wasn't too far from the truth. "But our grandfather won the deed from Peter Smithwood in a poker game."

"Okay, I like where this is headed."

Zeke lowered his voice to a conspiratorial whisper. "A poker game in which it's reputed that Grandpa Dearborn cheated."

"Okay, now I *really* like where this is headed. I always knew there was something a little dirty about you guys."

Adam coughed heavily. The less time Dawn spent discussing the *dirty* ways of the Dearborn generations — past and present — the better. "We spend way too much time thinking about that stupid family as it is," he said. "I'm sure we can come up with something else to talk about for one evening, can't we?"

"Nope," Zeke replied with a cheerful whistle. "Raising cattle and cheating at poker is all we know. You should try to get Bea to sell the land to us instead of them, Dawn. I bet she'd listen to you. People like you. Even Adam is in a good mood now that you're here. That never happens."

It seemed suddenly imperative that Adam change the direction of the conversation. With more force than finesse, he slid the platter of spaghetti Bolognese onto the kitchen island and said, "Food's ready."

If he'd hoped the promise of home cooking would

divert their attention, he was sorely mistaken. They merely began dishing up and continued the conversation.

"Maybe we can give you a commission if you succeed," Zeke said. "Oh! I know. You can have my share of the ranch—and my share of the ranch work. How's that for temptation?"

"Thanks, but the only thing I want is Gigi. And I'll get her in the end. See if I don't." A light hand touched Adam's arm. "One piece of garlic bread or two?"

"Two, thanks." He replied without thinking, thereby losing any and all opportunity to defend his stake in the puppy. Since quibbling over an animal while balancing a plate of pasta was hardly ideal, he made his way over to the dining room table. Several voices trailed after him.

"You're really going over there, then?" Phoebe asked. "To Bea's, I mean?"

"I don't have much of a choice, do I? I promised to help fix her garden. She's counting on me."

"Yeah, but it doesn't have anything to do with you. Not really. The cow is our problem, not yours. Shouldn't you be focusing on your own stuff?"

Adam hesitated before sitting down, fearful of missing Dawn's answer. In truth, he had no right to ask her to do any of this—to track down rogue cows, to give him a puppy she clearly wanted to keep for herself, to toil in the garden of an irascible old woman for no particular reason whatsoever. Even this meal was way outside her jurisdiction. The check he'd written Puppy Promise covered one service animal and six weeks of in-home training, and that was all.

But her answer, when it came, had nothing to do with either puppies or cows. "Holy crap," she said around a mouthful of food. "This is really good. I had no idea you could cook like this."

Adam grunted a noncommittal reply and took his seat. There were a lot of things Dawn didn't know about him. That was how he preferred it.

"If you promise to feed me like this every day, I'll be only too glad to become Bea's drudge. Do you think she still has some of that cake she was talking about?"

"What cake?" Zeke asked.

"Oh, she said something about the Smithwoods bringing her cake to try and steal a march on the property. I admit I have a lively curiosity to meet these enemies of yours. They're smart. They know that the way to any woman's heart is through her stomach." She paused and brushed her fingers lightly over the top of Adam's hand. "Yes, Adam. That includes you. If you promise to feed me like this every day, I might just marry you."

His hand froze under hers. "I don't recall asking."

"Well, it's the only way you're getting your hands on Gigi, so you'd better start planning the blessed event," she replied cheerfully. "I've always wanted to elope in Vegas, if that helps."

If anything more had been needed to convince him what a terrible idea it would be to have Dawn in his life on a more permanent basis, it was that. She probably *did* love Las Vegas—the noise and the heat, the crowds and the clubs, all those people squeezed together under one roof. He almost shuddered just thinking about it. He could imagine few worse fates than to be plunged into such a morass of overwhelming sensations.

He wasn't one for big-city living. His existence was one of simple means and even simpler pleasures.

In other words, he was the last man on earth who could make Dawn happy.

"Duly noted," he replied. "But not even a tempting offer like a runaway marriage with you is enough for me to give up Methuselah. Nothing you have to offer is worth that much."

Her chuckle was deep and rich. "We'll see about that. You have no idea how persuasive I can be when I put my mind to it."

On the contrary, Adam *did* have a good idea of what she was capable of, and he doubted there was much he could do if she decided to pull out all the stops. She'd take his puppy and his heart, leaving him to sort through whatever pieces remained once she was gone. As much as it pained him to admit it, it was part of the reason he was fighting so hard to keep Methuselah.

He wanted the puppy. He also wanted the trainer attached to her.

Fortunately, Zeke recalled a story about one of the guys he trained with, which served to change the topic of conversation and entertain the two women at the table. Adam was more than happy to sit back and let their light chatter flow over him.

As he did, however, he became aware of a comforting presence on both sides of his chair. He dropped his hands and let his palms graze the soft fur of both puppies. To his right sat Uncle, obediently awaiting his next command. To his left, Gigi stood nervously awaiting events, no longer shaking, but unwilling to go too far from human hands for fear she might be left alone again.

Me too, girl, he thought. *Me too.*

That was the problem with being rescued—with being

loved. Once you got used to things like soft touches and family gathered around the dinner table, it was hard to let go of them again.

Which was why, he knew, it was so important not to get used them in the first place.

chapter
5

Dawn made it through a whole week of puppy training before she noticed the truck following her home.

The summer days were long this time of year, so the sun was still dangling above the horizon when she set out. That was part of the reason it took so long to notice the truck. The light of the setting sun shone directly in her rearview mirror, making it impossible to see much of anything in the background.

The other part wasn't so easily defined. If she had to choose, she'd say it had to do with her reluctance to leave Dearborn Ranch behind for the weekend. There had been no opportunity for she and Adam to do anything more than work with the puppies, and the amount of sexual tension between them was becoming downright painful, but it had been a strangely good week all the same.

A *great* one, actually—the best she'd had in a long time. She'd been busy and active and, well, appreciated.

Her sisters would say that it was the last of those things—the appreciation—she liked the most, but that was only because they'd never understood her need to always be going and doing, to throw herself wholeheartedly into whatever project came her way. She had the sinking suspicion that Adam didn't understand it, either, but that was okay. No one ever had.

Impulsive was the term her parents used. *Tempestuous* was the one coined by a high school English teacher.

Too much was the one preferred by everyone else.

In the mood of abstraction that followed such a profound revelation, it was no wonder she missed sight of the truck at first. Her car zipped down the highway toward Spokane without a care, taking the most direct route home without regard for the consequences.

"Oh shit." She touched the brakes as soon as she realized she was being followed, both her heart and her body giving a lurch. The truck slowed at the exact same rate before giving a warning flash of its lights.

It was impossible for her to make out the shape of the body in the driver's seat or the exact model of the truck, but she had no doubt it was No-Pants Shotgun. He'd probably been lying in wait for a sight of the getaway car that had stolen his puppy.

Instinct warned her to flip a U-turn and hightail it back to the Dearborn Ranch, where Zeke and Adam were on hand to provide protection of the strong, male variety. Common sense, however, told her to do the exact opposite. Heading to Dearborn Ranch would only give Gigi's location away. No-Pants obviously had no idea where they were holding his animal, or he'd have done something about it already.

Dawn wasn't about to enlighten him. Not when Gigi had been curled up so happily in Uncle's embrace. Not when the sores on her stomach were finally starting to heal.

"You won't have a chance to hurt that animal again," she said.

With her heart in her throat, she stepped on the gas, her speed rising accordingly. If Sheriff Jenkins happened by, he would probably take *her* license away this time, but that was a risk she was willing to take. Especially since the truck's lights flashed again in an ominous warning.

Oh, yeah. An officer of the law would come in handy right about now.

At such high speeds, Dawn had to pay close attention to the road in front of her. It was impossible to follow the truck's every movement in her rearview mirror. She knew he was there, though, weaving in and out of traffic, passing other cars like they were toys.

Please don't crash, she told herself.

Please don't shoot, she told the truck.

For the longest time, she wasn't sure which catastrophe would be worse, so she focused on avoiding both. She barely acknowledged the scenery around her, her gaze fixed on the road ahead. It was so fixed, in fact, that she wasn't sure when she lost the truck. All she knew was that when she drew closer to a gas station crowded with evening commuters, she allowed herself a moment to pause, breathe, and look around.

The truck was nowhere to be seen.

With a pounding heart, she pulled in to the nearest pump, her hands firmly clutching the steering wheel. She didn't seem able to let go. The adrenaline that had carried her through the chase began to wane, leaving her feeling shaky and empty.

It spiked again when an older gentleman knocked on her window, his face peering anxiously in.

"Hey, lady…you okay?" he asked, his voice muted by the glass. "You tore in here pretty fast."

Dawn noticed his blue-collared shirt with the gas station logo and relaxed. Rolling down the window, she took a deep breath and said, "Sorry about that. I was in a bit of a hurry."

"Then why are you just sitting in your car?"

There was no good answer for that, so she did what she usually did—told him the truth. "I was being chased by a crazed man in a rusty, dilapidated truck. He's seeking vengeance for the puppy I stole."

"Uh, have you been drinking?"

"Not yet," she admitted with a shaky laugh. "But I may have to before the night is through. What do you sell in there that'll take the edge off?"

She'd meant it as a joke, a way to wipe the anxious look from the gas-station attendant's face, but he only frowned deeper.

Which was why she had to resort to the other—darker—truth. "I promise not to linger too long. I'm just not ready to go home yet, you know?"

The frown on the man's face shifted into a sympathetic smile. "Yeah, honey. I know." He tapped his hand two times on the window frame. "You stay as long as you want. The name's Mel, if you need anything."

He left before she could thank him, which was just as well, because she had no idea how to explain why home held so little appeal.

She knew, down to the exact detail, what would be waiting there for her. Lila had been on puppy duty that afternoon, which meant the kennel would be in perfect order and all the puppies content. There would probably even be a dish of food waiting in the oven for her. None of the Vasquez sisters could cook—and none of them had ever seen the point of learning—so they'd long grown accustomed to takeout and eating at their favorite diner down the street.

Ever since Lila's marriage, though, those restaurant nights had dwindled from three times a week to one. Lila made up for it by regularly bringing by supplies and leftovers cooked by her husband.

So you won't starve, she'd say and then give Dawn a breezy kiss on the cheek. The sentiment was nice, but the underlying message wasn't: *Because you're the last one left. Because you're all alone*.

That was the bare bones of it—of everything, really. Lila would have left the front light on so Dawn wouldn't have to return to a dark house. There might be a loving note or a quick message about tomorrow's schedule. There might even be fresh flowers on the counter to cheer the place up a bit.

But there wasn't anyone who depended on Dawn for their life's happiness. There wasn't someone counting down the minutes until her return. It was a horrible thing to admit, but No-Pants Shotgun chasing her down the highway was going to end up being the high point of her night.

At least *he* wanted to see her again…even if only to commit murder.

These days, she had to take what she could get.

Since the idea of going home was depressing in the highest degree, Dawn turned back the way she'd come.

After a ten-minute drive, she pulled in to the gravel path leading to a beautiful, old farmhouse currently undergoing repairs. Even though it still needed a lot of work, Dawn loved it, if only because it belonged to one of her favorite people in the entire world.

"Dawn!" Sophie came trotting down the steps, a red bandanna tied around her head and splatters of white paint covering her oversized overalls. She was the smallest of the Vasquez sisters in terms of size, but her personality was more than big enough to make up for it. "Am I expecting you? I don't think I'm expecting you. I'd have remembered if I was expecting you."

Dawn laughed and extended her arms for a hug.

"Oh, I'm all painty," Sophie protested, her nose wrinkled.

"What you mean is, I'm all dirty." Dawn laughed again. "Life on a ranch is a lot messier than anyone warned me. Would you mind if I showered here before heading back to town? I really need to start bringing a change of clothes."

It was only partially a lie. Life on a ranch *was* pretty messy, and a shower wouldn't go amiss, but she mostly wanted the company.

"Of course," Sophie replied, seeing right through her. "In fact, you should stay the night. Harrison left for Chelan yesterday, so I'm all alone for the next two weeks."

This bit of news wasn't the least bit surprising. Sophie's boyfriend, Harrison, was a wildland firefighter. Most of his summers were spent in the wilderness, where he and his valiant service dog—a Pomeranian named Bubbles—did their part to save both human and animal lives. Sophie took it in stride, busying herself restoring the farmhouse while they were away.

"Thanks, but I have to get back to the puppies before too long," Dawn replied. "They grow antsy if there isn't someone in the house when it gets dark."

A flicker of a frown crossed Sophie's face, though she tried to hide it by weaving her arm through Dawn's and leading her to the house. The porch appeared to be the current focus of all that white paint, with only a narrow path leading from the steps to the screen door left unpainted.

"I can only paint things on the ground when Bubbles and Harrison are out of town," Sophie explained. "Otherwise, we get tiny paw prints all over everything."

Dawn paused on the threshold for a moment, allowing her eyes to adjust to the change in light. Sophie must have misunderstood the silence that accompanied this because the frown came back.

"It's not fair to you, having to be home every night before dark for the sake of the puppies."

Dawn laughed, though it felt a little forced around the edges. "You mean, it's not *like* me, having to be home every night before dark for the sake of the puppies."

"Well, yes. That too."

"You've been gossiping with Lila." Dawn stated it as a fact rather than a question, and one with no emotions attached whatsoever. "Did she order you to talk me out of adding a pet on top of everything else?"

Sophie shifted from one foot to the other. "Well, it wasn't an *order*, exactly…"

Dawn's laugh was much more natural this time. Nothing Lila said was an order, exactly. It was usually a reasonably couched argument that was impossible to deny. "Don't worry—Gigi isn't mine yet. I have to earn her first."

"Earn her?" Sophie echoed.

"Yeah. I'm starting to get the feeling that Dearborn Ranch is the sort of place where you have to prove yourself the hard way before anyone takes you seriously." She toyed with the long feather of one of her dangling earrings. "Unfortunately for them, I plan on doing just that. They obviously have no idea what kind of beast they awakened when they issued me a challenge. I've done a lot of regrettable things in my life, but giving up easily isn't one of them."

Sophie smiled and dropped to the couch. Despite the fact that she was covered in paint and Dawn had mud clinging to her shoes, she patted for her sister to take the seat next to her. Doing that at Lila's house was unthinkable, but this farmhouse had such a warm, lived-in air that a few extra specks of dirt wouldn't bother anyone.

"Is this about that friend of yours who lives at the ranch?" Sophie asked. "Zeke, right?"

Dawn nodded, allowing the fall of her hair to cover her face so Sophie wouldn't be able to tell she was hiding something. She wasn't sure yet what had driven her to keep Adam a secret from her sisters, since they knew about almost all her sexual exploits and had never once judged her for them, but she'd never mentioned him—not even in passing. Which was weird, because if anyone would get a kick out of Dawn knocking cowboy boots with a tall, handsome rancher, it would be her sisters. The only other time she'd gone anywhere near cowboy boots was when she went through a line-dancing phase a few years ago.

"Partly, yeah. His brother's the one I'm training the Great Dane for." Whether because she liked living dangerously or because she simply wanted to say his name out loud, she added, "Adam Dearborn. He runs the ranch for the family."

Dawn couldn't decide whether she was relieved or disappointed when Sophie didn't react. "The name is familiar, but I'm not sure why. Zeke's the younger of the two?"

Dawn nodded.

"And he's the one with the abs?"

Dawn nodded again, this time with a soft laugh. "Yeah, he's a competitive triathlete—and it shows. But it's not like that between us, unfortunately. No attraction."

That got Sophie's attention. The sidelong look she cast Dawn was one of pure disbelief. "You spend an awful lot of time with him for a man with no attraction."

Dawn dipped her head again and pretended to pick at a clump of dirt on the knee of her jeans. "He has plenty of attraction, don't get me wrong," she said. "He just doesn't have any for *me*."

"Oh, Dawn." Sophie's hand shot out and gripped hers, giving it a meaningful squeeze. "I thought something like that must be in the air. You've been weirdly subdued lately. Do you want to talk about it?"

Dawn didn't contradict her. Sophie might have grabbed the wrong end of the Dearborn stick, but at least she had her hands on it.

"There's not much to talk about. I was never meant to settle down for life on a ranch." She shrugged. "It's for the best, really. Could you see me living it up with all those cows and chickens? I mean, I *do* like to start my day at the sound of a cock rising, but…"

Sophie chuckled obligingly, but Dawn could tell that her heart wasn't in it.

So she put a little more cheer in her voice and tried again. "Don't worry, Soph. I won't break because I found the one man in the world I can't win over with a laugh and a smile. It'll be good for me in the end. My self-confidence was starting to get out of control, anyway."

It didn't work. "Will it be okay, training out there all day every day with him?" Sophie asked.

"So far, so good," Dawn promised. "In fact, if I can convince them to let me keep Gigi, then I'll be more than okay. I'll be like Aunt Nessa, traveling the world and keeping cats in my old age. Except I'll keep dogs instead. Speaking of…do you mind if I hop in the shower now? It's getting kind of late, and I wasn't kidding about those poor dears back at the kennel. By eight o'clock, they start howling."

"Of course. I did a load of laundry about an hour ago, so there should be plenty of hot water by now." Sophie unfolded herself from the couch and readjusted her bandanna. "And stay as long as you want—today, tomorrow, or anytime. We can even trade, and I'll do a few sleepovers at the kennel. I don't mind."

"You're a love." Dawn also rose, pausing to press a kiss on her sister's paint-speckled cheek. "But don't worry about it. You're busy enough around this place as it is. It's starting to shape up really nicely, by the way."

Sophie perked up, her pride in her restoration efforts clear. "You think? I've been trying to keep it as historically accurate as possible, but..." She glanced around as her voice trailed off, glancing at the newly finished fireplace with the same adoration she lavished on their puppies.

"It's perfect," Dawn said, though her knowledge of interior design was slight. "And instead of you offering to come help me around the kennel, I should be offering to help you paint. I can, you know. I'm no good with a spatula, but a paintbrush I can do."

"You're going to add home renovations on top of everything else?" Sophie asked. "Between the kennel, your puppy training, and the demands of your social life, I wouldn't know where you'd find the time."

Dawn laughed, grateful to find herself on familiar ground. "You know what they say—there's no rest for the wicked." She offered Sophie a liberal wink. "And I have yet to meet anyone quite as wicked as me."

chapter
6

"Good morning, Zeke. Hello, Phoebe. What a good boy you are, Uncle." Dawn walked through the front door of Dearborn Ranch the following Monday without knocking. With a sweeping glance, she took in the bustle of early morning in a place like this one—Zeke and Phoebe in various states of readiness, Uncle eating his breakfast, and the scent of coffee percolating in the distance. "Where's Gigi?"

"You mean, where's Adam?" Phoebe laughed and finished whipping her waist-length brown hair into a ponytail. "Don't worry. He hasn't run off with her just yet. They're working together out in the barn. I think he's hoping you'll see what amazing leaps and bounds she's made and have no choice but to give her up."

Dawn snorted. "He obviously doesn't know me very well."

Phoebe glanced at her sideways. The girl's eyes looked heavier than usual, but Dawn assumed that was because it was only eight o'clock. She was looking none too dapper herself. All these early ranch mornings were going to be the death of her.

"You really like that puppy, don't you?" Phoebe asked.

"Of course I do. I'm the one who rescued her."

"Then why don't you just pick her up and leave? She's looking a lot better already. In fact, she ate, like, three of Adam's shoes this morning."

Dawn was startled by the question until she noticed that Zeke, too, was watching her with interest.

"Adam won't really go tattling to Sheriff Jenkins," he said. "Not now that he's already been caught in the lie. You could, um, steal the dog and run. He'd never actually chase you down."

Mentioning the chase reminded her of the altercation with No-Pants. Had she and Zeke been alone, she might have mentioned it to him with a warning to tread lightly. But Phoebe was listening intently, and the last thing Dawn wanted to do was rope another poor Dearborn into her scrapes.

"It's the principle of the thing," she said. "I'm not about to slink away like some criminal in the dead of night. I couldn't, anyway. Adam has already put a down payment on my training fees. It would be a breach of contract to leave now."

To be fair, the agreement stated that she'd train *a* guide dog, not the dog she stole and forced on him, but that was mere quibbling. Besides, she really did have principles.

With a glance down at her hippie-style sundress, which flapped playfully around the upper reaches of her thighs and was wholly inappropriate for a day of hard labor, she had to laugh. She had *some* principles, anyway.

Phoebe seemed to notice her attire at the same time. "When are you supposed to go to Bea's?" she asked.

"Oh, sometime next week," Dawn replied. "I warned her that I needed to make sure the puppies were settling in first. We have such a small amount of time as it is. He's out back, you said?"

Zeke nodded. "And he was up with the sun, so you'd better be careful. Word of warning—he's never at his best before he's had breakfast."

Dawn was never all that sprightly herself until she'd been caffeinated and fed, so she didn't find anything strange about that. With a whistle to Uncle, who obediently rose to his feet and followed her, she headed out the back door.

If she hadn't already succumbed to Adam's sexual allure, the sight that greeted her as she entered the barn would have sealed the deal right then and there. He wasn't, as Phoebe had said, putting Gigi through her paces. On the contrary, he was lying on his back with his hands behind his head, allowing the puppy to crawl all over him. Gigi explored and licked and tugged at the buttons of his shirt, as sure of her reception as any adorable ball of fur had a right to be. And on the hay, too, straw itch mites be damned.

Dawn paused to watch, unwilling to draw too close for fear Adam would hear her and ruin the moment.

I want that, she thought. Not just to crawl all over Adam as her mood and desires demanded—which, admittedly, she wanted a lot—but to elicit that relaxed look on his face, the expression of easy enjoyment. They enjoyed each other's bodies, obviously, but they were never relaxed together. Never easy. Now that she thought about it, few men were with her.

What is it about me that makes it so impossible?

"I know you're there," he said, not bothering to raise his voice. "So you can stop plotting all the ways you plan to make my life miserable."

Dawn chuckled and took a step into the barn. Early-morning sunlight filtered through the weathered boards, highlighting dancing beams of dust and straw. The scent was musty but not unpleasant; this barn was used to store hay rather than animals, so it had a quiet, simple vibe that appealed to her.

"How could you tell?" she asked. "I didn't make a sound."

She fell into a crouch and extended a hand toward Gigi. Much to her dismay, the puppy showed a sudden hesitation, positioning herself behind Adam's safe and solid body. "Gigi, love, it's me. Remember? Your savior? The only person in the world who cared enough to rescue you in your hour of need?"

At the sound of her voice, Gigi's ears relaxed but she still didn't move from her position. Matters weren't helped any when Adam sat up and scooped the puppy into his arms, holding her against his chest.

"I didn't hear you," he said. "I smelled you."

"You smelled me?" She gave herself a tentative sniff. She'd been careful not to wear any scent this morning— not even in her deodorant. It was one of the drawbacks of being a puppy trainer. The little guys were already bombarded with so many stimuli and instructions. To confuse them with perfume at this stage in their lives was just cruel. "Is that supposed to be a hint? I'm not the one rolling around in the hay with a puppy."

For the first time, Gigi noticed Uncle standing in the doorway to the barn and wriggled out of Adam's arms.

With a sprightliness that was heartening to see, she pounced over to the much larger dog and began coyly nipping at his legs.

"Uh-oh," Dawn said. "It seems you've got a trouble-maker on your hands."

"Is she flirting with Uncle again?" Adam asked and hoisted himself to his feet. Straw clung to every part of him, dangling like rustic jewels from his rolled-up flannel. "Typical. The women in my life are fickle creatures."

"If this is where you declare your intention to name her Dawn again? Don't worry—I got the message the first time around. I'm not worth the twelve hundred dollars you'll get for me at market."

A shadow passed over his face, a frown that seemed more serious than the conversation warranted. "You don't smell like anything."

She blinked. "What?"

"That's how I knew it was you. You have a very particular nonscent."

She wasn't done with the other conversation—the one that implied she was fickle—but she allowed herself to be distracted. "How can someone have a nonscent? The absence of smell is just air. That doesn't make sense."

"No," he agreed and rolled his shoulders. "It doesn't. But it's true nonetheless. Well? What's on the puppy-training agenda for today? I got Phoebe to clear me two hours this morning, but Zeke and I need to do a full herd check later. We've got a few late breeders who'll be calving any day now."

"Aw. Baby cows?"

His mouth firmed into a hard line. "Yes. They're adorable and small and all things delightful. Well?"

She sighed, feeling more dejected by his reaction to her arrival than she cared to admit. As usual, she was more of a burden than a benefit, a not-altogether-welcome break in the day. Adam needed her—*for now*—but there would soon come a time when that would no longer be the case.

She blamed that feeling, that pang of inevitability, for what came out of her mouth next.

"I thought we'd begin with a quick blow job in the back of the barn to get things loosened up," she said without a trace of inflection. "Then we should probably do some basic skills training with both puppies before introducing Uncle to one or two of the cows. Just to start. We can bring in the whole herd later."

Adam coughed until his face began to suffuse with red. "That's not what I had in mind."

"I know, but it's best to get him used to the animals a few at a time. He's never seen a cow before, so it's impossible to tell how he'll react. For all we know, he might take one look at them and think he's at an all-you-can-eat hamburger buffet."

Since Uncle stood like a patient giant while Gigi pranced and nipped around him, there was little chance of him doing anything even remotely like that. Still, Dawn had a schedule and she meant to stick to it. Lila might not consider her the most professional dog trainer in the world, but she wasn't completely unreliable. See? She could totally make plans.

"With the exception of that first bit, it all sounds fine to me."

Dawn took a step toward him—close enough for him to *not* smell her, but not so close they were touching. "What if I told you that the first bit isn't negotiable?"

He cleared his throat. The slight tinge of red that had taken over his complexion hadn't abated any, but he held his head at a dignified angle in an effort to counteract it. "I don't remember my sexual services being a part of this bargain."

"Technically you aren't serving anything. All you have to do is stand there. I'll take care of the rest."

He didn't answer, his silence making her feel as though she were six inches tall. Since it seemed she had little to lose at this point, she risked laying a hand flat on his chest. To all outward appearances, it was a sexual gesture, a symbol of intent. Her fingers curved into the plane of his pecs, reveling in the solid strength of him... not to mention everything that solid strength had to offer.

Dawn wasn't able to fool herself that easily. She liked placing her hand over his chest because she wanted to feel the steady thump of his heart. He was so warm and alive, so generous when he allowed himself to be.

"You're tense, Adam. Wound up. The puppies will be able to tell that the only thing you want to do is pin me up against the nearest barn wall, and it'll negatively impact their training. Consider this part of the whole Dawn Vasquez training package." Even though he couldn't see her, she allowed her lips to curve in a smile. "Satisfaction is guaranteed."

He stopped breathing. The rhythmic beat under her palm gave an erratic leap, but he allowed no other outward signs of discomposure to appear. At least, not until his hand gripped her around the wrist. He didn't pull or push her away—just stood there like a statue, holding her.

She let him do it, her own breath caught until his tongue began a slow and tortured journey across his

bottom lip. "Do all your clients get this kind of personalized treatment?" he asked, his voice hoarse.

"Contrary to popular opinion, no. Most of my sexual
partners have been accumulated the normal way."

"Define 'normal.'"

"Oh, you know. Tinder. Bars. Incredibly unsubtle
dinner parties thrown by my sisters. Sometimes, I like
to seduce the brothers of my friends, but that doesn't
always result in a sure thing." She paused before adding,
"It doesn't have to be a life-or-death decision, Adam.
Either you want me before we get started, or you don't.
It's that simple."

He took a wide step back, severing the physical ties
between them. Dawn tried not to let the rejection sting,
but there was no denying the pinpricks attacking her
heart. She also prepared to lead the puppies out of the
barn so they could get to work. She knew from experience that when Adam said he had two hours cleared out
of his schedule, two hours was exactly what he meant.

But he didn't follow. He was still standing there, his
head tilted toward her. "Why are you doing this?" he
asked.

"Training puppies? Or trying to seduce you?"

"Both. Neither. All of it." The words were tumbled,
rushed—both of which were wholly unlike him. He took
a deep breath and began a more careful recitation of her
sins. "Rescuing Methuselah, training Uncle, offering
to help Bea on our behalf, all these promises of sexual
escapades in inappropriate places… Why are you doing
it? What's in it for you?"

She shrugged. It wasn't a very helpful gesture considering that Adam wasn't close enough to feel her move,

but she didn't know what else to do, what else to say. To admit that most of her life decisions were born of impulse would only reinforce the low opinion he already had of her. He thought she was irresponsible and irreverent, that she was only interested in him because she had an itch and he was on hand to scratch it. The thing he didn't understand though, the thing that *no one* understood, was that she didn't regret her impulses.

Yes, she got into trouble sometimes. And, yes, it wasn't always fun to be chased by men with guns or find that she'd committed herself to rebuilding a grouchy woman's garden from the ground up.

But those same impulses had brought her here, hadn't they? Standing in front of the most glorious man in the world, offering the best parts of herself to him? How could anyone who'd had Adam Dearborn inside her feel any other way?

"You mean other than the thousands of dollars I've coerced you into paying my company?" she quipped.

"Don't." He gripped her wrist again, this time in a quick dash that seemed awfully similar to the rope he'd hurled to capture Dawn the cow. His reflexes were incredibly quick, his aim perfect. Like her poor bovine namesake, she didn't even have a chance to struggle. "I'm just trying to understand, that's all. There's a whole world outside this ranch. Places to go, people to see—"

"People to do, you mean."

The circle of his fingers tightened, but he otherwise let the comment pass. "This thing between us is only fun because it's temporary—because it doesn't mean anything. You're not a permanent fixture around here, so it works."

She was having a difficult time determining whether he was making a statement or asking a question. She didn't like the underlying message either way, so she decided to address the few questions she had answers for.

"I rescued Gigi because she needed to be rescued. I'm training Uncle because I believe he'll be a real advantage to you around the ranch. I offered to help Bea because you were in a tight spot and someone had to step up." She took a deep breath, since this last one was the most important. "And I'm offering sexual escapades in inappropriate places because I like it. I thought you did, too, but if I'm wrong, I'll respect your wishes and back off."

"Of course I like it," he said, the words so violent they were almost a curse. "That's not the point."

It was on the tip of her tongue to ask him what the point was, but he answered her before she had a chance to utter so much as a syllable. The answer came not in words and not in gestures, but in a kiss so sudden that even Uncle let out a yelp of surprise.

Adam hadn't let go of her wrist, opting instead to give it a tug and pull her body flush with his. His mouth found hers with unerring accuracy, the crash of lips and shock of intimacy sending her head reeling. Although this had been her goal—to drive him out of his mind with desire, to force him to admit that he wanted her just as much as she wanted him—she wasn't quite ready for so explosive a kiss. In the ordinary way of things, Adam was a highly thorough lover. He rarely left any part of her untasted, took his time making sure that she was panting with desire and dripping with need before he thought of his own pleasures. Dawn had never been much of one for long, leisurely make-out sessions, but Adam refused to be hurried.

This kiss wasn't like that. It was almost as though he'd forgotten everything the two of them had ever shared, had wiped the slate clean and decided to approach this whole arrangement of theirs with renewed vigor.

This kiss was *hungry*.

He didn't wait for her to part her lips and let him in, didn't nibble gently at the edges of her mouth. The press of his mouth was hot and greedy, and there was no chance to hesitate as his tongue swept a victory path over hers.

His free hand came up to grip her around the back of her neck, his fingers spreading wide as if making a claim. He wasn't tugging her hair, but there was a threat of it in the curl of his fingertips, as if he was prepared to go to any lengths to ensure that this kiss didn't end before he was damn well good and ready.

There was at least a full minute of this assault, of his hands and his tongue, of his determination to set every nerve Dawn possessed on fire. On fire was exactly how she felt, too, and in ways that sparked feelings she'd long since thought she didn't possess.

In fact, if she didn't know any better, she'd say Adam was kissing her—that she was *being kissed*—for the first time in her entire life.

"Oh my," she said as soon as his mouth lifted from hers. Her head whirled and her body throbbed, but she still managed to blink up at him until the world stopped spinning. "You *do* like it, too, don't you?"

His laugh was short and gruff, but it was a laugh nonetheless. "You know I do. I always have. But I'll be damned if we're going to go sneak to the back of the barn like a couple of animals in heat."

An animal in heat was exactly what she felt like, so that didn't sound like such a terrible plan. When his arms were around her like this, his body rock hard in all the places it touched hers, she'd do just about anything to keep going—straw itch mites and rats be damned.

"Zeke and Phoebe are in the house, so we can't go there," she mused. "My car's windows are tinted, but it's not very roomy inside. And I suppose we could always sneak to the root cellar, but Zeke once told me that the latch catches and traps people down there sometimes. So that's probably out."

"Yes, Dawn. The root cellar is out."

She scanned her memory for likely trysting places, but it was difficult to come up with a good option while the two puppies sat at their feet. They could hardly take them into a hayfield with them.

Adam heaved a sigh and pulled away, the air between them like a bucket of cold water. "You can stop trying to come up with alternate options, because I'm not having sex with you this morning. There's too much work to do."

"Fine." She gave up fighting. She had to. Adam was right when he said that this thing between them worked because it was temporary, fun. Meaningless.

Just like me.

"But I still think it'd do you a world of good to release some of that pent-up…energy." She bit her lower lip and considered the man standing opposite her. He was like a statue made of lightning. One touch, and he'd break off into a thousand bolts. "In fact, if you'd like to take care of it right now, I'll keep an eye on the puppies. No

one would care if you popped into the shower for a few
minutes."

He gave a short laugh and ran a hand through his hair.
"You think I haven't done that already this morning?"

Every part of her body gave a sudden, lust-filled
pulse. Even the parts of her that shouldn't tingle at such
a thought—her nose and her toes and, from what she
could tell, her appendix—seemed suddenly alive with
possibility.

"You didn't," she said, her mouth dry.

He laughed again, the sound coming much more naturally now. "Oh, I did. Twice."

"Well, shit." It was all too easy to picture Adam in
the shower, all the hard, lean lines of him swirled with
steam as he did his valiant best to work her out of his
system. He was so strong, his hands so rough, that she
imagined he could manage it in a few seconds flat. *Or*,
she thought, barely biting back an unladylike moan,
maybe he took his time with it. "I guess I'm the one
who's going to need a few minutes alone."

"Too bad," he said and grinned. It was his lopsided
grin, the natural one that only seemed to appear when he
managed to get the better of her—in bed, in puppy ownership, in anything, really. "You're on the clock now.
We've got two hours to whip these puppies into shape,
and I don't intend to waste a moment. Don't you agree?"

"The only thing I think is that you shouldn't say
words like 'whip' around me right now," Dawn warned.

The grin deepened. "Whatever you say, Ms. Vasquez.
If it helps, we can stroke them into shape instead."

chapter 7

"Lila, I know it's a huge imposition, but would you mind doing the evening feeding and exercise run for the puppies tonight?"

Adam halted midstep, careful not to make a sound as he rounded the cow barn. He'd been on his way to tell Dawn that she could come meet the newborn calf now, but she was obviously on the phone. It was equally obvious that she hadn't expected the birth to go that quickly. First timers rarely did. The movies liked to make it seem like every calf had to be pulled out by force, with heifer Lamaze and an anxious bull waiting in the wings, but nature usually handled everything just fine. Ninety percent of the time, all he did was catch.

"If I said I'm still at the ranch because I'm helping to birth calves, would you believe me?" Dawn asked. The steady rustle of her footsteps over straw made him think she might be pacing the length of the holding room. "Fine. How about if I said I have a hot date with a ranch hand and it's half-price whiskey night at the local saloon?"

Adam had to fight to keep a laugh from escaping and giving his position away. Their local saloon had recently been updated as a martini bar, and they wouldn't offer fifty-percent discounts even if it was the last day of life on earth. He'd once had something called a Sazerac there that had cost him twenty-five bucks.

"Um, he's tall and wiry and walks with a limp, but his Clint Eastwood impression is spot on. The *old*, decrepit Clint Eastwood, in case you were wondering. Not the young, hot one. Life is rough on men out here."

Adam had to muffle his laugh again, but this time he did it with a twinge of conscience. The right thing to do in this situation was either to make enough noise to announce his presence or to slip quietly back the way he'd come. Eavesdropping on other people's phone conversations wasn't something he did in the general way of things.

But Dawn spoke again, this time with a touch of impatience. "Of course I'm not dating an aged cowboy. I really am helping with the calving. Well, not helping so much as witnessing, but it amounts to the same thing." She paused. "Yes, Zeke is here. Where else would he be? This is his ranch."

The mention of his brother gave Adam a start, but not enough to force him out of his hiding place.

"I'm fine, Lil. I promise. Don't listen to anything Sophie tells you. Ever since she met Harrison, she's got romance where her common sense should be." An exasperated grunt escaped her. "Oh, for Pete's sake. I am not in love with Zeke. He would be the worst boyfriend in the world. The only things he cares about are triathlons and his own mirror image. And not even in that order."

Adam held back a snort. Whatever else could be said

about this woman, Dawn wasn't afraid to call things as she saw them. Her next words proved it.

"If you must know, I'm sleeping with his older brother, Adam—the one I'm training Uncle for. I have been for months." Any idea of retreat was now banished forever, especially when Dawn ended the call with "And before you ask, Adam really *is* like Clint Eastwood. The young, hot one."

He didn't have a chance to do anything but register that remark before Dawn stalked around the corner. She was obviously roiling with emotion—no woman walked with that kind of tread unless there was *something* going on beneath the surface—but he had no idea how much of it he was supposed to ask about. He *wanted* to know more, but that wasn't the kind of relationship they had. She'd made that clear from the start.

As she usually did, Dawn took the guesswork out of it. She came to a halt a few steps in front of him, her presence registering on a purely visceral level. "You sneak," she said, half-laughing, half-outraged. "How much of my call did you overhear?"

"Uh. Most of it?" Adam drove a hand deep in one pocket. It felt good to give one of his hands a purpose, but he wasn't sure what to do with the other one. He ran it over the back of his neck. "I came to tell you that the calf has been born. You can see her now, if you want."

"I missed it?" she asked. Her disappointment sounded genuine. "Damn. I always love watching mama dogs give birth."

"You do?"

"Of course. I mean, it's a little gross the first time, but that goes away pretty quickly. It's amazing how animals are born knowing what to do, isn't it? When to push, when to relax, how to take care of that baby the moment it's here. Humans too, really."

Adam wasn't sure how to respond to that. He and Dawn had spent plenty of time in the act of propagation, but the biological outcome wasn't something they discussed very often.

Dawn sighed. "No one trusts their instincts anymore. We spend so much time thinking and overthinking that we forget how simple some things are. Birth and death. How to do the right thing. The fact that baby animals are the best." She nudged his toe with her own. "Well, Eavesdrop McEavesdropson, are you going to take me to this calf or what?"

"You don't have to stick around," he said by way of answer. "If you have to go take care of the puppies back at your house, I mean. I don't think I realized how much of a burden it was for you to be spending this much time out here."

"That's the part of the phone call you want to discuss?"

A wave of heat moved over him. "It's the part I'm *going* to discuss."

She laughed and took his hand in hers. It was more of a friendly hand squeeze than an overtly sexual maneuver, but there was no denying the way his body flared to life at her touch. "Clint Eastwood was one hell of a dish in his day," she said. "I meant to be nothing but complimentary."

He tried somewhat feebly to take his hand back, but the lacing of her fingers through his felt too good for him to put in much of an effort.

"I'm sorry," he said. "I shouldn't have been listening."

The tug of her arm indicated that she'd shrugged. "I don't mind. I never say anything I don't mean, so it's not like it matters if anyone overhears. I'm not in love with Zeke. I *am* sleeping with you. And to be perfectly honest, whiskey with a Clint Eastwood type sounds like heaven right about now."

Adam could have easily filled in the gap with a comment of his own, but he had the feeling there was more she wanted to say.

Dawn hesitated. He wasn't wrong.

"Whiskey with a Clint Eastwood type would also make my sister feel a lot better. She honestly doesn't mind taking care of the puppies for the night if she thinks I'm getting mindless sex out of the bargain."

"But she does mind doing it if you're helping me with the cows?"

The shrug-tug was gentler this time but still evident. Dawn also began using her free finger to trace the veins along the back of his hand. The light whisper of her fingertips awakened something sharp inside him.

"She doesn't mind so much as worry. A Dawn who shirks her duty in pursuit of the flesh is what she's used to. A Dawn who's spending time at a bovine maternity wing because she genuinely wants to is grounds for a family intervention. We are not a rustic people."

"Okay," he said.

She dropped his hand but the sharp feeling lingered. "Okay, what?"

"Okay, let's have drinks and mindless sex." The offer was out before he could stop it. If he'd been thinking rationally, he could have phrased it a little better, but between her touch and that bit about her genuinely wanting to be with the cows, he was barely holding on over here. People so rarely wanted to stick around. Zeke had been grumbling about being late for swim practice for the past twenty minutes, and Phoebe had slipped out as soon as the afterbirth had been cleared away. And *they* owned this place.

"Really?" Dawn asked. "You want to go out?"

"Well, no," he was forced to admit. "I don't want to leave the puppies home alone, and I doubt Methuselah is ready for a night on the town just yet, so it'll have to be a bottle of butterscotch schnapps and the local country radio station."

"Gross. That's your drink of choice?"

"I can't help if it's delicious." He hesitated. "I know it's hardly the height of entertainment, but I can at least promise to pour with a heavy hand. You in?"

He held his breath, trying not to wince as he waited for Dawn's response. The date, if it could be called as much, was no more and no less than anything else he'd given her before. It was also no more and no less than what their banter had been leading up to.

Still. It felt different somehow. Probably because *he* felt different somehow. He'd never spent this much time with Dawn before while their clothes were on, and he wasn't sure whether or not that was a good thing. For the first time, she was seeing him in his real element—how tied he was to this ranch, how routine were his days. For the first time, he wasn't just a convenient and fun way to spend a few hours.

"To be honest, I'm a little wary," she said.

Adam's heart gave an odd thump. This was it. The

end of the road, the day of reckoning. Dawn had taken a good, hard look at the real Adam Dearborn and realized she had better things to do with her life.

"I can't help thinking about all that time you spent in the shower this morning." Her voice dropped, her hand coming to rest lightly against his chest. "All that rubbing and cleaning. All that intense self-care. Are you sure you're…up for an evening with me?"

Adam's heart stopped altogether. It was accompanied by a stop to all his other bodily functions— breathing and blinking and moving his lips to form human words. As Dawn's fingers trailed down his chest to the waistband of his jeans, the only thing he seemed to be capable of was excessive and healthy blood flow.

"Never mind. I see that everything seems to be working just fine. But I still want to meet that baby cow first, so don't think you can get off that easy." She lifted her hand away and laughed. It was a delicious, tormenting sound. "Well, you're going to get off incredibly easy, if I have anything to say about it. But you know what I mean."

He did. He also knew that as much as he'd have loved to forget everything but this woman and the promise of a few hours alone with her, there was work to do first.

In a life like his, there was *always* work to do first. And whether he liked it or not, Dawn was finally starting to see that for herself.

🐾🐾🐾

"Oh, don't worry about me." Dawn waved Zeke away at the front door. His swim bag was slung over one shoulder, a bright-blue towel peeking out over the side. In his haste to get out the door after the calf had been born, it was a wonder he'd remembered to grab the bag at all. "I'm going to get Uncle and Gigi settled for the night and then I'm heading home. It's been quite a day."

"It always is around here," Zeke replied as he began heading toward his car. "Welcome to life on the wild side."

Although there was no way No-Pants Shotgun would associate Zeke's beat-up Volvo covered in bumper stickers with her Jetta, Dawn felt a twinge of conscience at letting him head off into the great unknown without a warning.

"Uh, just so you know, I had bit of a run-in with our pants-less friend last week."

Zeke stopped to turn and stare, the car door hanging open to reveal piles of sporting equipment inside. "Are you kidding me?"

"It's fine. I handled it. But there's an eensy-weensy chance he's lying in wait somewhere along that stretch of highway looking for us, so tread warily."

Zeke slammed the car door shut and stalked back up to the house. Dawn cast a nervous glance behind her, fearful that Adam would overhear, but neither he nor the puppies had come in from the barn yet. "Dawn, you idiot. What happened?"

"Nothing, I swear!" She held up her hands as if proving her innocence. "He flashed his lights at me and gunned his engine a few times, but he was easy enough to outrun. I doubt he'll recognize you in your own car."

"You've been outrunning criminals on your own?"

"Just the *one* criminal, and he's hardly a mastermind of villainy."

"That's it. We're going to the sheriff's office and telling him what's going on." Zeke planted his feet in a stance that made the most of his physique. He wasn't as tall as Adam and didn't have the same cowboy leanness, but his shoulders were wide and powerful. With his arms crossed like that, he looked as though nothing and no one could ever argue with him.

Dawn did anyway.

"No way. Sheriff Jenkins will drag us in on theft charges. Or, worse, make us give Gigi back."

Zeke released a snort. "Of those two possibilities, you think losing a dog is worse?"

Dawn thought of that sweet little puppy, her round little belly finally starting to swell with good meals and better care, and nodded. "Yes. And if you go to the authorities behind my back, I'll deny everything. I'm a very good liar. I can even pass lie-detector tests. I dated an FBI agent once."

"Of course you did."

"He *might* have been making that up to impress me, but he was definitely affiliated with law enforcement in some way. Lila thinks he might have been the guy they hire to serve papers to deadbeat dads trying to avoid paying child support."

Zeke tossed up his hands. "I don't know why anyone even tries talking to you." He cast a quick look around, though whether he was checking to see if his brother was around or if No-Pants Shotgun was hiding behind one of the bushes framing their front porch, Dawn couldn't say. "If you won't let me go to the police, what's the point of telling me? Am I supposed to start carrying a shotgun, too?"

Dawn shook her head. "Of course not. He doesn't actually know where you live. I was careful to lead him off the scent so he won't know where to find us."

"Is that a trick you learned from your FBI agent boyfriend, too?"

"He wasn't my boyfriend," Dawn clarified, "and no. It's a trick I learned from being a woman living in the twenty-first century. The first rule is never to lead the murderers directly to your house. If they want to turn you into a skin suit, they're going to have to do it in the street where the witnesses are."

Zeke looked as though he had plenty to argue with in that statement, but he didn't give voice to any of his feelings. He glanced at his phone and sighed instead. "I'd stay and try to talk some common sense into you, but I'm already late for open swim."

"That's good, because I don't need you to treat me like I'm a child. I'm sorry that I dragged you into this, but I'm not sorry I did it." She crossed her own arms and did her best to glare Zeke into submission. "Some things are worth the risk."

"I have half a mind to tell Adam and let him deal with you," Zeke muttered, but he didn't make good on the threat. "Please be careful when you leave here tonight," he said instead. "And for the love of everything, try not to steal any other highly valuable animals. One of these days, you're going to end up getting us both killed."

Dawn wasn't sorry to see him go, and not just because his departure meant that she and Adam were alone in the house. She liked Zeke, she really did, but she didn't always like that he saw her as a person to be humored—a person to be *handled*. There was nothing she hated more than that.

Doing things her own way didn't make her wrong. It just made her Dawn.

The house was eerily silent when she stepped back inside. Adam should have returned by now, not to mention the two puppies who'd become his shadow. There was no sound of any of them scuffling around, but as she moved into the kitchen, she noticed that a bottle of Adam's weird butterscotch-flavored liquor had been set out along with two glass tumblers.

With that, Zeke and No-Pants were all but forgotten. That bottle was a declaration of Adam's intent, a promise that he planned on delivering. He really was like the silver-screen Clint Eastwood that way. A man of few words, yes, but one who could be trusted to keep them once they were uttered.

"Gigi?" she called, since the fastest way to find the man was to find the puppy who adored him. She probably should have called out Methuselah, since Adam was doing his best to confuse the poor animal, but she refused to give him the satisfaction. "Uncle? Where are you two hiding?"

The answer came as the thump of Uncle's long, gray tail on the hardwood floor. Dawn turned down the hallway where the bedrooms were located to find both animals lying in a tangle of limbs in front of Adam's closed door. Gigi blinked up from her comfortable position curled next to Uncle's stomach before emitting a tiny, pink yawn.

"Oh, Gigi. You're killing me." Dawn squatted down

and offered the smaller dog her hand, but she'd already fallen back asleep. "You can't go falling in love with Uncle. That's not how this is supposed to work. He's a hardworking service animal and you're... Well. *Not*."

Uncle yawned, too, an almost apologetic look in his sleepy gray eyes as he tucked his head possessively over Gigi's resting form. Dawn should have been delighted to see him taking such a deep and unprompted interest in his malnourished protégé, but she mostly wished she'd never brought Gigi here in the first place. It would be almost impossible to separate these two now that they'd become a bonded pair. Impossible *and* cruel, and that was the one thing she was determined not to be. The poor animal had suffered enough already.

It was with conflicted emotions that she rose to her feet and dropped a light knock on Adam's door. The sound elicited no response, so she clicked the handle and pushed the door open a crack.

"Hello?" she called. "I know you're in here. Your watchdogs are keeping a vigilant lookout."

The only answer was the distant patter of water over tile. It took Dawn all of two seconds to place that sound, and only one more to suck in a sharp breath at Adam's audacity.

"Oh, hell no." She marched across his bedroom, taking quick note of the familiar sparsity of it—everything in neutral tones, nothing scattered over the tabletops, the only clutter a set of headphones on the side table that Adam used to listen to audiobooks. It had felt strange at first, this room with no pictures or knick-knacks, every single item of clothing and sock tucked exactly where it was supposed to be, but she liked it now. There was something profoundly comforting in so much constancy.

There was also something profoundly appealing in it, but that wasn't what Dawn intended to focus on right now. Without knocking this time, she pulled open the adjoining bathroom door.

"You'd better not be doing what I think you're doing in there." Without waiting for a reply, she reached for the hem of her dress and pulled it over her head. "If you're wasting even an ounce of your stamina, you're going to pay dearly for it."

The blur of Adam's naked body behind the semi-transparent glass wasn't clear enough for her to make out *all* the details, but the scent of his alpine shampoo and the fact that his hands were up near his head seemed to indicate that he was only washing his hair.

Still. She wasn't taking any chances. Not when she could practically feel the slide of his wet skin under her fingertips.

She wriggled out of her panties and unclipped her bra, making short work of the disrobing process. In fact, she was so quick that Adam barely had time to utter a protest before she pulled open the door and joined him inside the compact shower.

"What are you doing?" he demanded. "Zeke is—"

"Already well on his way to swim practice," she finished for him. "We're alone in the house. I think the real question is, what are *you* doing?"

She glanced down at his glorious nudity, marveling, as she always did, that a man could be so perfectly molded without hours of careful and strategic weight lifting at the gym. She'd dated enough gym rats to know that most men had to work very specific muscles to get that buff, sculpted physique so prized by Hollywood and Instagram influencers. Adam, on the other hand, never did anything that wasn't related to this ranch. He didn't have time for gym memberships, and even if he did, he'd probably scoff at the notion of spending energy working on something as silly as physical appearance.

Not that it seemed to matter to his body in the slightest. His thighs were a perfect picture of masculine power, his abdomen flat without being overly defined. Most of his musculature was in his arms and across his chest, a testament to all the heavy lifting required in a place like this.

And his ass, well… Dawn bit her lip. She could only be glad that he was face-to-face with her right now. There was a lot to be said for full frontal, but his ass made her feel unnatural things. It made her want to *do* unnatural things.

"I was afraid you'd gotten started without me," she said when all he did was continue to stand there, his head soapy and his body on display. "I had all sorts of punishments planned."

His laugh was slightly mocking. "Just having you here is punishment enough, wouldn't you say?"

Considering how *robustly* he was adapting to her presence in his shower—and she hadn't even touched him yet—she wouldn't have said that at all. "It doesn't look like you mind. In fact, I'd have to say you're about to enjoy every second of my presence." She paused and held her hand out to catch the drops cascading from up above. "This water is freezing, by the way. How can you stand it?"

"I can't." He reached out and turned the knob to a much warmer temperature. "But it was the only way I could keep myself from, ah, getting started without you."

That was all Dawn needed to hear to have every nerve ending in her body thrumming. Call her crazy, but self-imposed preventive torture had to be one of the hottest aphrodisiacs on the planet.

She stepped under the spray and allowed the water to surge over her. The shower was so small that there was no way to do this without their bodies coming into contact. It wasn't much to start out with—the brush of her nipple against his chest, her hip pressing against his— but it was enough. Especially since Adam was so soapy that everywhere they touched was smooth and slippery.

Smooth and *slippery* were two of Dawn's favorite adjectives when crammed naked into a compact space with a man, so she made the most of it. Turning this way and that, letting a small moan escape as the water crashed over her head and washed away the grime of the day, she became a body in constant motion.

Adam noticed—and in a *big* way. With a groan, he reached down and gripped her just below her waist, his fingers pressing into the roundest parts of her hip. "Stop wriggling around like that, dammit. I can't concentrate on what I'm doing."

She laughed at how irritated he sounded—a strange thing when he was so obviously *not* irritated with her right now. "Then duck your head, stupid. I'll wash your hair for you. I'll wash anything you want me to. Just tell me where you'd like me to start."

"I thought we were going to have a drink first," he

grumbled, but he lowered his head enough so she could reach it. "I had a whole plan."

"I hate plans," she replied and threaded her fingers through the wet, soapy strands of his hair. Her nails weren't very long, but she used what she had to massage his scalp, tilting his head this way and that as she rinsed. "They take all the fun out of everything. Why don't you tell me about what you had in mind instead?"

He hadn't yet let go of her hip, and at this request, his fingers dug even deeper into her flesh. "You don't deserve to hear it."

She laughed and renewed the wriggling undulations that had unsettled him so much before. The movements were intended to entice Adam to the point where he had no choice but to pin her up against the shower wall, but she'd underestimated his ability to hold himself in check. *Her* arms were starting to turn to gelatin, and *her* legs were throbbing with the desire to have him between them, but he seemed able to control his limbs just fine.

"Fine," he said and ran his free hand along his jawline. "The first thing I was going to do is shave. Otherwise, it's going to feel like sandpaper against your lips later. Or between your thighs. I hadn't yet decided where I was going to focus my attention."

She stopped all movement at once. Despite the fact that they were surrounded by water, her mouth went dry. "Why not both?" she managed.

"Unfortunately, we don't have as much time as I'd like. I figured I was either going to have to start at the top and work my way down, or start at the bottom and see where my tongue ended up. It was turning into a kind of dilemma, to be honest."

"It just so happens I love sandpaper," Dawn said. She reached for the shower knob. Enough of this wet, steamy foreplay. She was going to kiss this man soon or die trying. "It's my favorite thing. On my lips, between my thighs, pretty much anywhere you'd like to rub it…"

His hand dropped over hers before she managed to get the water turned off. "I've never understood why you're always in such a hurry. Some things aren't meant to be rushed." He gave a gentle *tsk* before grabbing a razor from a clip on the shower wall and pointing it at her. "Here. You do it."

She looked at the razor but didn't reach for it. "You want me to shave you?"

"I want you to be naked with me for five minutes *without* forcing me to move faster than light," he replied, his voice low. He gave the razor a wiggle. "I want you to have to focus on something that isn't my cock."

She took the razor. "Well, I don't see why you're always determined to take things slow. There's something to be said for a hard, fast shower quickie."

Partly out of a desire to punish him for eking this process out, and partly because she was thrilled that he was so determined to make this worth the wait, she nudged him into a more comfortable shaving position. As this entailed her legs spreading open and straddling his in a semistanding position, *comfortable* was a matter of debate. Their bodies were touching in all the places that throbbed and yearned for more, and it would have been incredibly easy for her to shift a little bit to the right and feel the full glory of him inside her.

But that wasn't the game. For whatever stoic moral

code Adam lived by, they were going to make this as
painfully prolonged as possible.

"I can't hold this position for very long, or I'm going
to slip and accidentally slice your jugular," she warned.
"You'd better hold me in place."

Actually, she did enough spin class at the gym to be
able to brace her thighs like this for hours on end, but
she wanted to feel his arms around her. This seemed as
good an excuse as any, especially when he grumblingly
did as she asked. Those oh-so-powerful forearms, made
for catching cows and hefting bales of hay, wrapped
around her. His hands spanned the smallest curve of her
waist, the glide of his skin over hers like falling down
a long, wet chute.

"This seems like a trap," Adam said, every muscle of
his body tensing around hers.

"You're the one who wanted a precoital grooming
session," she pointed out. "Do you normally use any
kind of product? I don't see any shaving cream."

"Third bottle on the right. Between the conditioner
and the shower cleaner."

Like most parts of Adam's house, the shower was
neatly and simply organized, every item in its place.
Dawn had no idea how long it took to get a house like
this—with every end table in a perfect location, every
spice in the kitchen arranged to be quickly and easily
pulled out—but she liked it. So few things in her life
were like this. Her own bedroom was a haphazard
whirl of discarded outfits and lost earrings, her shower
a smorgasbord of broken razors and empty shampoo
bottles that needed to be thrown out.

"Seems like dangerous work, putting a blade against

your skin without being able to see what you're doing," Dawn said as she filled her palm with a handful of white, lightly scented foam. "But you never seem to have any nicks or cuts."

Since she was busy lathering him up, all he could offer in reply was a soft grunt.

"I know, I know. It's because you're not in a hurry to get it done." She moved her fingers in a circular pattern along the sharp, finely chiseled lines of his jaw. "Adam Dearborn is a careful man, a meticulous man. When he sets about doing a thing, he does it all the way."

"You say that like it's a bad thing."

"It's not," she replied, tilting her head to view her handiwork. She'd missed a small spot near his ear, so she reached up and finished the job, her hand lingering to touch the side of his face a moment too long. "It's the opposite of how I do things, that's all. No one has ever accused me of being careful. To be perfectly honest, I'm not sure I know how."

She'd meant the words playfully, a light banter to keep this whole shower situation moving along to its natural and inevitable conclusion, but Adam's hold on her tightened. One of his hands was pretty much cupping her ass by this point, but he hadn't strayed *too* far from neutral territory.

"I trust you," he said simply.

"You shouldn't. I could easily hurt you."

"Yes," he agreed. "You *could* cause me pain. But I think you'll find that I'm not so easy to crack."

She didn't argue with him. Adam Dearborn definitely wasn't an easy man to crack. She'd spent the last six months trying to find a hole somewhere in this ironclad exterior of his, but nothing seemed to work. Nothing she knew how to do, anyway.

If there was one thing she *did* know, however, it was the landscape of this man's body. If she could paint, she'd have been able to perfectly re-create his likeness on canvas. If she were a poet, she might be able to describe every scar that told the tale of his youth. Unfortunately, she was neither of those things and never would be.

She was Dawn Vasquez, decent at training puppies and great at sex. It wasn't much of a curriculum vitae, but it was all she had.

Although she'd done a lot of things with men in her lifetime, this was her first time shaving one. As soon as she started, she realized why. Nothing could have prepared her for the sheer intimacy of running the safety blade over Adam's jaw. She couldn't hear the scrape of his stubble giving way under the pounding of the shower, but she felt the low rumble of it. Over his strong, wide cheekbones. Down his square jaw. Skipping lightly over the scar that ran from the bottom of his chin to the side of one ear—an accident he laughingly referred to as the time Phoebe had thought it would be a good idea to rearrange the living room furniture. She even took a moment to press her thumb in the small divot in the middle of his chin before moving the razor over it. Each part of him took on new meaning as she explored his skin at such close proximity.

"Tilt your head up a little?" she asked when she reached the bottom of his jawline. Her voice was oddly quiet, but her face was so near to his that he didn't have to strain to hear her. "I need to get your neck."

"Uh-oh. That's where the danger is. I'll try not to breathe."

"You laugh, but I can see your pulse." She stopped her index and middle fingers on top of the gently throbbing beat of his carotid. "One wrong move, and I could end you right here and now."

"You could end me at any point, Dawn, and you know it. You've known it from the start of this."

She opened her mouth to protest but wasn't sure how to set about doing it. Mostly because he was wrong on every level. Not only was she physically incapable of getting the better of this man, but she doubted she had much emotional sway, either. That kind of power required him to feel something for her. Something *real*. Not this temporary, meaningless fling.

Even though she hadn't yet finished with the scruff on his neck, she clipped the razor back into its place on the shower wall. She also straightened her legs so that she was no longer halfway propped up by Adam's arms. She was on her own two feet again—on familiar ground, so to speak.

"I don't want to end you, Adam," she said, watching him. She'd missed a patch on his left cheek as well as his neck, but she wasn't about to let that bother her. Especially since she had every intention of turning her attention—and her hands—elsewhere. "What I want, and what you're making very difficult, is to *enjoy* you."

She punctuated this statement by running her hands down the smooth, hard lines of his abdomen, stopping just shy of making contact with his cock. Every part of her yearned to grab him, to show him how easily she *could* end him. Or that part of him, at least.

"Believe me," Adam said, groaning softly. "The feeling is mutual."

She didn't have time to ask which part of that sentiment he shared—the desire or the frustration—because
he grabbed her around the back of her neck and pulled
her in for a long, demanding kiss. Dawn imagined that
must be what the cows felt like when they felt the heavy
rope land squarely around their heads. It was a shock,
yes, but it was also compelling.

Come to me, it said. *Don't fight. You're mine now.*

She gave in to all three. As the water sluiced down
over their heads, Dawn allowed herself to be pulled into
Adam's hard embrace. She didn't fight the insistent
press of his mouth, and she didn't question where she
belonged. Like poor Dawn the cow trying to enjoy her
few blissful stolen moments of freedom, she knew when
the battle was over.

Well, mostly.

She dropped her hands the last tantalizing inch before
she had Adam firmly in hand. Without waiting to see
how he intended to react, she slid her hand up the length
and back down again, her movements aided by the water
and soap and steam. Adam wasn't slow to return the
favor, dropping his hand between her thighs. There was
no need for water or soap to ease that friction, since
she'd been in a state of high desire for days now.

"I was going to make you do this yourself so I could
watch," Dawn said as Adam slid a finger inside her.
He crooked that same finger and pulled her forward,
so close their bodies were now touching almost everywhere. Her legs slithered up and down his, her breasts
pressed against his chest. Even seemingly innocent parts
like shoulders and elbows took on new meaning as they
slipped and slid together.

A gasp escaped her as Adam slid his finger out and back in again, his thumb expertly grazing her clit.

"If you don't start behaving, I still might make you take over," she added, but they both knew it was a lie. His erection was a hard, insistent pressure between their bodies—a hard, insistent pressure she was powerless to ignore. She drew her hand up and down between them, pausing only when his own careful movements took her breath away.

As it turned out, that was most of the time. Adam's hands were one of his best features, which was saying a lot considering how well crafted the rest of him was. But his hands were large and rough with work, and dexterous in ways that defied human nature. They were also intimately familiar with Dawn's body. Adam knew when to push and when to pull away, exactly where to hitch her leg so he could plunge his fingers deep.

He didn't hesitate to do any of those things now, forcing her to brace herself on the shower wall or risk having her legs give way underneath her. Her eyes were closed, her back pressed against the cold tile, one palm flat against the side wall to keep herself from toppling over. She was, in a sense, pinned against the wall and unable to escape, but she didn't mind in the slightest. Especially not when he stopped with all the teasing and began to focus his attention on sending her over the edge.

"I thought you were yelling at me for always being in a hurry," she said between gasps.

"Do you want me to stop?" came his strained reply. She flicked her thumb over the head of his cock, delighted when his entire body gave a convulsive twitch. "Because I can stop. All you have to do is say the word."

"You know, I don't think that's true." She flicked her thumb again, this time without pausing before pumping her hand steadily up and down his length. His breathing was growing labored, his entire body a thrumming chord waiting to be plucked. One or two more thrusts, and he was done for. "I think there's nothing you can do right now but finish the job I started. Go ahead. You can come first. I don't mind."

"Like hell I will."

Just as Dawn was ready to enjoy the sensation of Adam losing his control, he slid his hand out from between her thighs and grabbed her around the ass. Without giving her time to consider what could possibly come next, he whirled her around so she was pressed face-first against the wall instead. The tile was a surprise of cold against her nipples and belly, bringing to the surface of her skin a tingling, almost electric shock. A gasp—partly of outrage but mostly of delight—escaped her lips as Adam brought his hand between her legs again, this time from behind. His other hand gripped her around the wrist and brought her arm straight up above her head.

If she'd been trapped by Adam before, she was imprisoned by him now. His body was holding hers at every pressure point, his hold like a shackle that allowed her no room to escape. In fact, the only movements she seemed capable of making were the repeated undulations of her hips.

He dropped his lips to the back of her neck and kissed her—long and hard and deep, not to mention likely to leave a hickey of the kind she hadn't enjoyed since high school.

"There's nothing you can do now but finish the job *I* started," Adam murmured into her ear. He ground his hips harder against her, restricting her movements even more. "Go ahead. You can come first. I don't mind."

It would have brought Dawn immense satisfaction to thwart him. The press of Adam against her backside was likely to be causing him just as much agonizing delight as it was giving her, and she was sure that if she could hold out a few seconds longer, he wouldn't have any say in the matter of who was the first to give in. But everything about this position—being pinned against the wall, Adam's hand between her legs, nowhere for her to go—had her spiraling closer and closer to release.

And then he bit her.

Dawn had read plenty of vampire erotica in her lifetime, so she knew, in theory, how powerfully sexual a well-timed bite could be. She wasn't saying she wanted to *bleed* or anything, but there was something deliciously possessive, something ruthlessly primal about the whole thing.

Adam seemed to know it. Whether because he'd also spent his fair share of time in the erotic vampire library or because he simply couldn't help himself, he sank his teeth into the sensitive skin on the side of her neck. She cried out as that final sensation was added onto all the rest, the strength of her orgasm outstripping any other considerations. There were too many parts of her body being stimulated at once—too many parts of her being told what to do and how hard to do it. She was so overpowered with sensory overload that her orgasm throbbed longer and harder than any she'd experienced before.

Her only saving grace was the fact that as soon as the cry left her lips, Adam proved himself just as far gone as she was. He changed the bite to another one of those long, hard kisses, pressing his mouth against her neck as he gave in to the pull of his own release.

Her legs were weak and her breathing labored, but neither of those things seemed to matter as he continued cradling her from behind. He was holding her up without even trying, supporting her simply by being near.

Shower sex had always been one of Dawn's favorite kinds in terms of cleanup, since the mood remained unbroken. Cuddling in the heady afterglow had never been one of her strong points, but the act of soaping one another off under the continued spray of the water was a pure delight.

"What was that bite all about?" she said as she ran her hands up and down Adam's abdomen, rubbing soap far more thoroughly than was necessary. "I'm going to be walking around like the victim of an animal attack for weeks."

A guilty flush arrested his expression. "Is it bad?"

"I can tell what great orthodontic work you had done as a teenager, if that's what you're asking."

The guilty flush didn't abate, and his hand shot out to trace the line of her neck where he'd planted his teeth. He missed, grazing her shoulder instead, but he managed to find the location by running his fingertips over her skin. It remained unbroken, but there were clear indentations. "Oh shit. I didn't mean to—"

She laughed and turned off the shower spray. "Don't worry. I liked it."

"You did?"

With the water turned off, an immediate chill overtook the bathroom. Dawn used this as an excuse to wrap her arms around Adam's naked torso, basking in the warm, wet lull of him for a moment before dropping a kiss on his lips. It was meant to be a quick kiss, but there were still so many naked parts touching, she got a little carried away. Her mouth softened as she gave in to the kind of slow, leisurely tangle she normally found a waste of time.

"It's been a long time since a man has felt the need to visibly mark me as his territory," she teased as she drew her lips from his. "Aren't you afraid of what Zeke and Phoebe will say if they see it?"

"Not really, no. I think they know you well enough by now to accept signs of depravity as part of the complete Dawn Vasquez package."

She couldn't help but laugh. "Gee, thanks. You paint such a lovely picture of me."

She stepped out of the shower and was reaching for one of the oversized towels on the opposite wall when Adam reached out and grabbed her around the wrist. "I didn't mean it like that."

Leaning down, she dropped a quick kiss on his hand before disentangling herself from his grip. "I know you didn't. I just think it's cute, that's all, how obsessed you are with making sure you brand your herd."

"I wasn't—"

"First Dawn the cow, then Dawn the human... I'll warn you right now, there'd better not be any marks on those puppies, or I'm hauling you in for animal abuse."

"Dammit, Dawn, I didn't—"

"Hey, Adam. I know." She cupped the side of his face, aware as she did that she'd done a deplorable job of shaving him. "I told you already that it's fine. It felt good, I don't mind the marks, and I like that you're uninhibited enough with me to go where the moment takes you."

"But—"

"Don't worry. If you ever overstep a boundary, I'll make sure you know it."

He didn't appear to be comforted by this, worry puckering his brow.

"What is it?" she asked as she reached for the towel again. She took only a moment to wrap herself up before handing a second one to him. "Why do you look so upset?"

Instead of wrapping himself up, as most people would, he used the towel to dry his hair. He was supremely indifferent to the picture he made as he did it, all naked and chiseled and gleaming.

"You're not like anyone I've ever known, that's all," he said. He finished toweling off his hair and started drying his body. Dawn could have easily pointed out that *he* wasn't like anyone she'd ever known, either, but she was too busy enjoying the show. "I don't think you realize how rare it is—or how useful—to find a woman who says exactly what's on her mind."

The words he was saying were a compliment, she knew. Forthrightness and honesty were things Adam valued, and they also just happened to be values that she possessed. But something about the way he said them made her feel like she was being pushed away.

"Well, what's on my mind right now is food. Between the ranch work, the puppy training, and the shower sex, I'm ravenous."

Adam laughed obligingly, but that worried pucker

was still evident. "Right. I can promise to feed you, but I don't know how much more time we'll have before... Well, until..."

"Until one of your siblings comes home and sees me all bitten and sated." She nodded. The action made her feel better somehow, more in control. "Noted. We'd better get me spirited away before our devious deeds are uncovered."

"That's not what I meant."

"Yes it is, but that's okay. It's all part of the charm, right?"

She reached for her pile of clothes, which were still incredibly dirty and not at all what she wanted to put on after such a thorough and satisfying shower, but there wasn't much she could do about it unless she started packing spare underwear in the trunk of her car.

Which, to be fair, had been something she'd done for the bulk of her early twenties.

"Out of curiosity, what would you want to do?" he asked. "Besides eat."

It took her a moment to work out his meaning. "If I didn't have to slink off into the night, you mean?"

He nodded, looking boyishly shy. It might have been because of the single damp lock of hair that curled down his forehead like he was a wet Superman, but Dawn thought it had more to do with the hesitant way he reached for her before dropping his hand again.

"Do you want the fun, sexy answer I'd give to the man I'm sleeping with, or would you prefer the real one?"

"The real one, please."

She didn't have to think about it. "I'd put on one of your oversized work shirts and nothing else. I'd pour us each a huge glass of that disgusting butterscotch schnapps out there and lounge with you on your couch watching Netflix until we fell asleep together."

"Netflix?"

"It's not as selfish as it sounds. They have really good audio description tracks on some of their shows."

"I know that," he said carefully. "But I didn't know that *you* knew that."

She turned away, even though he couldn't see the blush that had crept into her cheeks. "I got curious and googled it one night." Since she was still feeling oddly exposed, she added, "And strange as it seems, having someone to watch Netflix with is every woman's dream."

"You lie."

"Okay, *some* women might prefer to binge-watch their favorite shows alone, but I'm not one of them. I watched all of the *American Horror Story* seasons a few weeks ago, and I still have to sleep with the lights on. I'm pretty sure there's a ghost trapped in my basement."

Adam clearly assumed she was making another joke, so she let the subject go. How could she explain to him that she wasn't kidding, that the sum of all her hopes and dreams was to find a place where she could comfortably loll about, half-dressed and half-drunk, with a man who accepted her for who she was?

It was a truth as bleak as it was simple—she'd never be as professionally driven as Lila, and she'd never be as sweetly determined as Sophie. She'd never reach any great personal heights or distinguish herself in any way. The only thing she was good at was enjoying herself, and even that was a struggle these days.

"He's a friendly ghost, though," she said, careful to

insert a smile into her voice. "Like an erotic Casper. His moans are a little *too* enthusiastic, if you know what I'm saying."

"Considering what you just did to me in that shower, I know what you're saying."

It was as good a segue as any. The flirtation was back on, the lighthearted note returned to the air. There would be no lounging and no Netflix, but that was okay. She hadn't really expected him to take her up on the offer.

After all, that was the sort of thing *real* couples did. If there was one thing Dawn had learned in this lifetime, it was that real couple stuff—*real love*—wasn't designed with women like her in mind.

chapter
8

Adam wasn't sure whether to be relieved or disappointed when he woke up the next morning to find that Dawn had already come and gone for the day.

"I was up and about at an obscene hour, so I've taken the puppies to Bea's to help me garden," Phoebe read aloud from the note that had been left on the kitchen counter along with an oversized box of pastries. "If I'm not back after lunch, assume I've been murdered and used as fertilizer. One of you can have my vintage movie-poster collection."

The sound of whooshing paper filled Adam's ears as Zeke swept in and plucked the note from Phoebe's hand. "I call dibs on the posters," Zeke said.

"Shame on you!" Phoebe laughed. "I thought she was your friend."

"She is, but you wouldn't believe how good that collection is. Valuable, too. She likes the really porny ones."

Phoebe choked on another laugh, but all Adam could manage was a sigh. Only Dawn could turn her last will and testament into a sexual escapade. "Of course she does," he said, resigned. "What time is it now?"

"A little after eight."

He reached for one of the pastries. They were sticky and sweet and not at all the kind of food necessary to fuel a morning of hard labor.

And, he hardly needed to add, delicious.

"Then we're fine," he said around a mouthful of apple-flavored goo. "She can't possibly be dead yet."

"How do you know that?"

He licked one of his fingers. "Because these are still warm. She must not have left here too long ago, and it'll take Bea at least an hour to do her in. Possibly two. Dawn seems like the type who won't go down without a fight."

"See, Phoebe?" Zeke said, triumphant. "Adam doesn't seem too worried about her untimely demise, either."

"That's because I'm not. Dawn's death would solve a lot of our problems."

There was a short, shuffling sound before Zeke spoke up. His voice was more subdued than before, a hesitation in the way he chose his words. "You don't like her, do you?" he asked.

Adam noted his error at once. Where Dawn was concerned, his best route—no, his *only* route—was to have no emotional response. Too little enthusiasm was as dangerous as too much enthusiasm, too little interest worse than no interest at all.

"Oh, she's fine," he said as neutrally as possible. "A little high maintenance for my tastes, but she seems to know what she's talking about when it comes to dogs. I was just thinking that if Bea murdered someone and we could prove it, she might finally be willing to sell us her land. *And* at a discount."

Zeke chuckled obligingly, but he wasn't finished with the topic. "Dawn's not a bad person, Adam, when all is said and done. I mean, I'd never date the woman, but you have to admit that she's generous with her time."

Adam's only response was a grunt. She was generous with her time, all right. Her time, her laughter, *and* her body. The only problem was, he had no idea what he was supposed to give her in return.

"Why *don't* you date her?" Phoebe asked. "I've always wondered that. She's super fun and drop-dead gorgeous—and she seems to like you, which is pretty rare in someone with a functioning nervous system."

Phoebe cried out as Zeke either punched her playfully in the arm or flicked her ear—his go-to ways of antagonizing his twin. "Because I value my sanity too much, that's why," he replied. "The man who ends up with that woman will be called upon to lie, cheat, and steal every day for the rest of his life—when he's not already busy trying to keep up with all her other demands. Between the ranch and my training, I'm exhausted enough as it is."

Adam felt a twinge of guilt. Zeke *did* do a lot around here, especially considering how many other things he had going on his life. Maybe he should look into giving his brother a few extra days off in the near future—Phoebe, too. Grandpa Dearborn had worked hard. His father had worked hard. Adam would spend the rest of his life working hard.

But that didn't mean they had to suffer the same fate.

"Dawn doesn't lie!" Phoebe protested. "She's one of the most honest people I know."

Zeke snorted. "If you mean, does she tell the truth,

then yeah—I guess you could call her honest. But if you want to avoid someday finding yourself stranded in a third-world prison or explaining why you had to go ninety miles an hour down Highway 395 in the full light of day, then lying becomes a necessity."

There was something about that second example that caught Adam's attention. "You were doing *ninety* down the highway?"

Zeke quickly changed the subject. "One of us should probably head over to Bea's house to make sure she's all right. I'd volunteer, but I was just about to check on the new calf and then move that huge pile of fertilizer. Unless you'd rather switch, Adam? Personally, I find piles of shit much less daunting than trying to tackle Bea and Dawn at the same time."

It was on the tip of Adam's tongue to point out that there was a good chance Dawn had already tackled Bea, hog-tied her, and turned her house into a bed-and-breakfast, but he refrained. He wasn't supposed to know about how much energy and enthusiasm that woman had, how easily she transformed people and made their lives better simply by being near. Even this—standing in the kitchen eating breakfast pastries with his siblings before their shared day's work—was almost unheard of.

Yet here they were. Laughing. Talking. Enjoying one another's company. Dawn wasn't even in the house, but she'd somehow managed to make that happen.

"Don't worry—I'll go after I make my morning rounds," Adam said. He did an admirable job of making it sound like a chore, too. "I'd like to stop by, if only to make sure that Dawn hasn't run off with my dog."

"Which one is your dog, again?" Phoebe asked. There

was enough irony in her voice that Adam didn't miss her real meaning. "The one that's actually fit for work out here, or the cute one you want for no real reason?"

It's not "no real reason," Adam wanted to tell her. Okay, so an undernourished puppy who was rapidly developing a taste for footwear wasn't the ideal guide dog. And, yes, he'd been doing some research into early canine trauma, and there was a chance the golden retriever would never fully overcome whatever had led to her abandonment.

But he liked her, dammit. He liked how affectionate she was, how playful. He liked how she made him feel—not like a hard taskmaster, the way Phoebe and Zeke saw him, and not like some staid and boring ranch owner, the way the rest of the world saw him.

To Methuselah, he was just someone to love.

"As of right now, I consider them both mine."

"If you want to *keep* both dogs, she'll make you *pay* for both dogs," Zeke warned.

Adam shrugged and popped another bite of pastry into his mouth. "I'm not worried about the money."

"Money isn't what I meant," Zeke said with a knowing chuckle. "When it comes to Dawn, you can expect to pay in blood."

🐾🐾🐾

"Oh God. She *is* dead." Phoebe pulled her Jeep to a sudden stop, propelling Adam against the seat belt. "Bea probably forgot all about their agreement and shot her on arrival. She has about fifty guns in her bedroom, you know. She told me she likes to keep them in case of invasion."

Adam didn't find that hard to believe. Bea also regularly stopped by the town hall meetings to warn the community about chemtrails and unidentified lights in the night sky. She had some strange theories.

"Unless you're looking at an actual body lying in the driveway, I'll thank you not to exaggerate," he said. Then, more sharply, "Please tell me there isn't an actual body lying in the driveway."

Phoebe giggled. "No, but there's no sign of anyone doing any yardwork out back. In fact, it looks as though the garden is an even *bigger* mess now than it was last week."

Adam held back a sigh and pushed the car door open, reaching for the telescoping cane he kept under the seat before swinging his legs out. He didn't spend enough time at his neighbor's house that he was willing to tackle it without aid. "Define 'bigger mess.' How can anything be worse than the disaster Dawn leaves wherever she goes?"

"Don't forget to mention that you mean Dawn the cow," a voice called from the front porch. "Otherwise, Phoebe's going to think you're being rude."

Adam felt a disproportionate amount of relief to hear the musical laugh in Dawn's voice. It wasn't that he *actually* feared Bea would do away with another human being, but there was no denying she had a tendency to rub people the wrong way. And by *rub the wrong way*, he meant she usually grated them down until they were nothing but a blubbering mess of their former selves.

Call him sentimental, but he didn't care to see that happen to the woman he was sleeping with.

"You're just in time," Dawn added as a screen door creaked in the distance. "Bea and I were about to have some lemonade and pie out on the back porch. Fair warning—her lemonade is like ninety percent vodka. Sip slowly."

Phoebe laughed and said that nothing sounded better, but Adam wasn't so easily fooled. He came up the steps carefully. "You and Bea are having alfresco cocktails?"

"And pie," Dawn pointed out. "I bought it from the diner near my house. But don't worry—I told her that you made it, since you did promise her and all. It seems that in addition to vodka, Bea likes a man who delivers."

"I was going to make one. I haven't had a chance yet, that's all."

"Yes, well." Dawn's hand touched his arm to indicate that the door was open and he had a clear path inside. "Maybe if you didn't spend so much time in the shower, you'd have more time for things like baking."

"What's that you're saying?" Bea demanded as Adam walked through the door. He'd only been inside Bea's house a few times before—usually to beg her to consider his continually rising offer for her land—but it always had a damp, musty smell, like a sock forgotten in the bottom of the washing machine for too long.

The sock scent was still there today, but in much less concentrated amounts. A cross breeze hinted at several open windows, at least one of which was near the back garden, if the loamy tang of upturned soil was any indication.

"It's about damn time you got here," Bea added without waiting to hear their answer. Which was just as well, since there was no telling if Dawn might follow up on that shower comment. In the right mood, she had every likelihood of making life uncomfortable for him.

Hell, who was he kidding? She *always* made life uncomfortable for him. Morally, emotionally, physically…

"Do you still own that backhoe?" Bea asked.

Adam halted. "Uh, backhoe?"

"The patio door's about four feet to your right and ten feet back." Dawn brushed past him lightly, allowing her hip to touch his. Her voice lowered to a near-whisper as she added, "You don't have a backhoe. You don't know where to rent one, either. In fact, you read an article about how backhoes have been contributing to higher rates of certain kinds of cancer."

Phoebe must have overheard that last part, because she giggled and answered for him. "Sorry, Mrs. Benson, but we got rid of that old thing years ago."

"What'd you do that for?" Bea demanded. "I need one."

Phoebe and her ever-fertile imagination had a response for that, too. "Unfortunately, it went rogue and ran over Zeke's foot. He's lucky to still have it. You should have seen how many stitches he got."

Adam was almost certain Bea wouldn't buy such a ridiculous story as that, but she gave a harrumph and moved in the direction of the back porch. "It's just like a Dearborn to go wasting a valuable piece of machinery because it's got a minor hitch. You people think nothing of money, do you? There's always more where that came from."

There was no response that would allow Adam to maintain both his dignity and the respect necessary to keep him on Bea's good side, so he didn't say anything. He also regretted the impulse that had allowed him to send Dawn here to help Bea with the garden repairs. No one deserved to be subjected to this woman's company for hours on end. She took bad manners to a whole new level.

"Well, you know your way around a cherry pie, at any rate," Bea said as Adam found a seat at the table and settled into it. He was almost immediately greeted by twin canine noses, one in each palm. Uncle's felt as warm and friendly as it always did, but Methuselah's appeared to be covered in mud.

"What the—" he asked, running his fingers up Methuselah's muzzle to find that the mud continued well into her upper body. "What have you done to my poor dogs?"

"You mean, other than feed them and train them and otherwise do the job I'm being paid for?" The question must have been a rhetorical one. Dawn paused only long enough to draw a breath before adding, "Uncle spent the morning learning useful farm words, so he'll know how to recognize things like fences and roads and where to find people out here in the middle of nowhere. Gigi, however, preferred to chase butterflies."

Phoebe muffled her laugh. "I can't say I blame her. I'd rather be chasing butterflies, too. But, uh, I thought you were coming over here to help Bea fix the garden. No offense, but it looks a little…discombobulated."

Bea released a laugh that could only be described as a cackle. "Yes, well, I decided not to bother with that whole mess. I'm going to take a backhoe to the whole thing instead." Her pause held all the power of a menacing glare. "Or rather, I *was* until you decided to throw yours away."

"You're not going to bother?" Adam echoed. "But what about your butter beans?"

"Fuck the butter beans. Dawn helped me see reason."

The words *Dawn* and *reason* had no place in the same conversation, let alone the same sentence. "I'm almost afraid to ask," Adam said.

"Well, you shouldn't be. This girl has more sense than the entire lot of your family put together. Why should I put this garden to rights if all I'm going to do is sell this place by the summer's end? It's not as if any of you will appreciate my hard work and keep it up."

"*Your* hard work?" Phoebe murmured.

If Bea heard Phoebe's remark, she let it pass. Adam, however, wasn't about to allow any of this to slip past him. He sat up straighter, wiping his muddied hand on his jeans. "You've finally decided to sell? To us?"

Finally, it was here. Finally, he was going to get the land needed for the expansion. If Dawn had somehow managed to convince Bea to do this in a single afternoon, he was going to kiss her. With tongue. And in front of everyone here, too.

"I didn't say that now, did I?" Bea smacked her lips. "Next time, you'll want to add a little more cinnamon to this pie, Adam. It could use a kick of something."

His excitement began its slow and inevitable deflation. Of course it wasn't going to be that easy. Dawn might be capable of making him act contrary to everything he knew and believed in this world, but her magic obviously didn't extend to a woman like Bea Benson.

"Cinnamon," he agreed flatly. "Sure thing."

"Bea hasn't yet decided who she wants to sell to," Dawn supplied. "It's a delicate situation because of the promise she made to Peter Smithwood."

Adam didn't care for the sound of that. "Promise? What promise?"

Bea gave that cackling laugh again. She also paused to take a long sip of her vodka lemonade, which would explain why she was in such a conciliatory mood. "You obviously never got the full story from your grandfather."

That got Adam's attention. Phoebe's too. Neither of them had known their grandfather very well—he'd passed away not long after Phoebe and Zeke had been born—but he was something of a legend around these parts. He'd started their ranch with nothing more than a hundred dollars and the deed to the land in his pocket. And, as Adam knew from his own experiences, a hell of a lot of hard work. All those rumors of his infamy, of having cheated the Smithwoods at cards, were just that—rumors. In a community the size of theirs, that sort of thing was inevitable when something as large as a three hundred acres was involved.

And when the Smithwoods were involved, but that part went without saying.

"What story?" Phoebe asked. "No one ever said a word about a promise to me."

"Well, of course they didn't," Bea said. "It's none of your damn business. It all happened long before you and that swoopy-haired twin of yours were a twinkle in your parents' eyes."

Methuselah gave a whimper at Adam's feet, so he reached down and wordlessly plucked the puppy from the ground. He could hear Dawn's cluck of disapproval at how quickly he'd given in to her demands, but it wasn't as though he had a choice. Methuselah *needed* him. In fact, as soon as he started running his fingers over the silken threads of her ears, she settled down, her head resting contentedly on one knee.

Since he knew he was in the wrong—and because offense was always the best defense—he pointed an accusing finger in the direction of Dawn's chair. "I thought you came over here to be helpful."

"Training your guide dog to recognize fences *is* helpful," she replied, laughing. It perfectly matched the tinkle of ice against her glass. "Besides, Bea had more interesting things to tell me than where to put the tomatoes. You never told me she knew so many things about your family."

"She doesn't."

"Like about how your grandfather was a con man and a philanderer."

"He was *not* a con man and philanderer."

"And about how he used to make his living fleecing people at cards until he settled down on the ranch."

"There's nothing illegal about a friendly game of poker."

"Or about how after Peter Smithwood lost half his ranch to your grandfather, he sold Bea this piece of land for the sole reason that he didn't want any part of his property touching yours."

Adam paused. "I didn't know that one."

There was something self-satisfied about the way Dawn settled back into her chair, a puff of air rising from the seat cushions. "Then I'm guessing you also don't know that he made Bea and her husband promise never to let you guys get your hands on it. Apparently, it was part of the original purchase contract. She literally can't sell it to you."

Adam let out a long breath. All of his hopes and dreams for the future seemed to vanish with the air in his chest. It caused him a pang of regret, but not nearly as much as the realization that Zeke's and Phoebe's futures were vanishing along with it. Oh, the ranch was fine right *now*, with the three of them sharing the responsibilities and the income, but he didn't know how long it could stay that way. If one of them got married, one of them had kids... A ranch the size of theirs could support a single family, but it couldn't support three separate ones. Expansion was the only way to keep the holdings intact.

"Is that true?" he demanded.

"Of course it's true!" Bea said. "I don't know where the paperwork is, but Dawn says she's happy to sort through all that crap in the basement to find it. Seeing as how I'm letting her off the hook with the garden and all."

"I didn't say I was *happy* about it..."

"She also thinks I should hire a professional cleaner to come through here and lend a helping hand, but that's where I draw the line. I've never met anyone with so many opinions on things that aren't any of her god-damned business."

It would have been easy for Dawn to take offense at this, but she just laughed. "I could say the same of you, but you'll notice I refrained."

Adam cleared his throat before they got too far off course. This conversation was more productive than any of the ones he'd tried to start with Bea for the entire past year combined.

"Are you serious about this, Mrs. Benson?" he asked. "All this time, all these negotiations, and there's literally no way you can sell us the property?"

"Goddamn lawyers," she said by way of answer. "They're part of the Illuminati—did you know that?"

Dawn coughed gently. "What Bea means is that she's not overly fond of legal entities imposing their will on her."

"No, what I mean is that they'll take the skin off your back and prance through town wearing it like Lady Godiva."

Dawn's hand stole under the table to touch Adam's knee. It was a quick gesture and could have easily been interpreted by anyone at the table as a way for Dawn to pet the puppy rather than the man, but he found it comforting all the same. *Trust me*, that touch said. *Believe in me. Give me all your problems, and I promise to make them okay*.

She obviously had no idea how tempting that was.

"I won't know until I find the papers she's talking about, but it sounds as though it's pretty straightforward." A gurgle of laughter escaped her throat. "And easy to get around. *Bea* can't sell to you, but there are no limitations once the property has been moved out of her hands."

Adam's heart rate picked up. "You mean..."

"I mean that what the next owner does with this godforsaken mud pit is no concern of mine," Bea said. "*Or* the damn lawyers."

"Yes, Adam," Dawn said in a much gentler tone. "That's what she means."

"Wait...I'm confused." Phoebe scraped her fork across her plate. The high-pitched sound caused Methuselah to twitch, but Adam stilled her by running his hand over the back of her neck. "What are we talking about? I thought we just decided that the sale is off."

"It is," Adam said. "At least, the sale to Dearborn

Ranch is off. But if *Dawn* were to make an offer, what's to stop her from signing it over to us as soon as the dust settles?"

This neat—if somewhat immoral—summary of the situation shocked Phoebe into momentary silence, but Bea's cackle rose anew. It was accompanied with a hearty slap of her hand on her leg. "Damn if I don't almost like you, Adam Dearborn. You've got grit. Your grandfather had grit."

Coming from Bea Benson, that wasn't much of a compliment, but Adam took it as one anyway. There were worse things in the world than to be compared to the man who'd built the Dearborn name into what it was.

"I'm not saying my mind is made up," Bea warned. "Until Dawn finds those papers, there's no saying what will happen. But I'm willing to let her poke around a little. She has grit, too."

Dawn had a lot more than that going for her, but Adam wasn't about to start listing her virtues. Once he got started, he wasn't sure he'd be able to stop. Once again, she was doing so much for him—for his whole family. And for no reason he could easily discern unless it was the novelty of it all.

"I wonder if I should do it under cover of night," Dawn said in a laughing, teasing voice that made Adam feel like *novelty* might not be too far from the truth. "Sneak in when no one is looking, sort through the boxes away from the prying eyes of the Illuminati."

"I'm not so sure that much secrecy is required," Adam said. "I doubt either the Illuminati or the Smithwoods pay that much attention to what goes on around here."

"Don't be so sure about that," a slow, somewhat

dry male voice said from the doorway to the house. "Contrary to what the Dearborns believe, some of us are able to see what's going on right under our noses. Uh, no offense."

Adam's hand stopped on top of Methuselah's neck. The puppy took instant exception to this, squirming her body so that her stomach was exposed and he could continue his ministrations. There was no denying such a demand, though it made Adam feel like a villain, sitting in his chair and stroking his pet while his nemesis approached.

"Hello, Charlie," he said, trying to keep as much of the villain out of his voice as possible. There was no need to add to the theatrics around here.

"Adam." Charlie Smithwood's voice was equally level. "I hope I'm not interrupting anything."

He was, and they both knew it, but the unspoken arrangement between the two families was one of unperturbable—if resentful—civility. Even when they'd been kids meeting across the schoolyard, Charlie had been unfailingly polite in the way he'd put them all down. *Oh, look. There are the Dearborns. Did you want to play on the monkey bars, or would you rather sneak in the classroom and steal everyone's pencils while their backs are turned?*

"Of course not," Adam lied. "We were just having some lemonade with our favorite neighbor."

Bea snorted her appreciation for this remark but didn't add anything to the conversation. No one did, which was something Adam never enjoyed. He didn't like feeling as though he was missing something.

Dawn must have realized it, because she quickly and

easily stepped into the breach. "I'd offer to pour you some of it, but it's highly alcoholic and you don't look like much of a day drinker. Now *I*, on the other hand..." The ice in Dawn's glass clinked as she presumably took a sip.

From the conversation that followed, that wasn't the only distraction she intended to provide. "Oh no!" Phoebe cried. "Dawn, what happened to your neck? It looks like someone bit you."

Adam did his best to appear natural, but it was difficult when most of his body functions had all but stopped. He wished he knew what Dawn was wearing, whether she'd made an attempt to cover up the proof of his loss of control or if she'd brazenly bared it all just to provoke him. He wasn't a betting man—and neither was his grandfather, goddammit—but he'd have put everything he owned on the latter.

"Someone *did* bite me," Dawn said, and with such a saucy air that no one could mistake her meaning. "I like to live dangerously."

Bea made a sound that could only be classified as a *harrumph*. "We had a name for girls like you back in my day," she said. "It starts with the letter—"

As much as Adam hated to admit it, Charlie proved himself a gentleman when he interrupted Bea before she could get one more syllable out. "I'm sorry, I didn't catch your name. I'm Charlie Smithwood, but considering the conversation I walked into, you must already know that."

"I managed to put two and two together," Dawn said, her arm brushing past Adam as she extended it for a handshake. "I'm Dawn Vasquez. I came with these two gorgeous creatures—the canine ones, not the humans. The big, gray one with the eyelashes is Uncle. The pampered one on Adam's lap is Gigi."

"Methuselah," he said mechanically, but his heart was no longer in it.

"I'm training Uncle to be Adam's service dog. Gigi is my personal pet, but she's recently discovered that Adam's lap is the best place to be."

"I imagine that's a matter of taste," Charlie said. His voice was filled with the heavy sarcasm that almost always accompanied any conversation in which both he and Adam played a part, but Adam found himself almost warming to the man. Whatever else his faults, he was taking this whole situation in stride. If Adam had overheard someone talking about plans to steal land out from under his nose, he'd have reacted a little more forcefully.

"I didn't mean to interrupt your party, Mrs. Benson, but my mom sent over a box of her famous lemon bars and a gallon of that cider you like," Charlie said. "The *good* cider, if you know what I mean."

Bea knew. "Your mom knows the way to my heart, that's for damn sure. Pie and cake are all well and fine on an afternoon like this one, but that cider gets me through many a long, lonely night."

Considering that the Smithwood cider also had enough alcohol content to set the entire county ablaze, Adam could see why it appealed to her.

"Why don't you come help me carry them in, Phoebe?" Charlie asked with an air of innocence that Adam didn't trust for a second. He doubted Phoebe did, either. His sister was no fool. "I left them out in the truck."

"Oh, let me," Dawn said before Phoebe could answer. "I'm glad to be of use. And if it just so happens that a few of those lemon bars don't make it to the kitchen on the way, I refuse to be blamed."

"Didn't you just eat half a pie?" Adam asked.

"Manual labor always makes me ravenous. All physical activity does, actually. When I work up a sweat, it's like I become insatiable."

It was to the benefit of everyone sitting around the table that Dawn and Charlie headed off to grab the bribes. Nothing Adam could think of to say to that was appropriate for company—especially *this* company. When Dawn worked up a sweat, he had a tendency to become insatiable, too.

"In case you're wondering how to win me over next time, I could use a new transmission for my truck," Bea said with a whoosh of her hands rubbing together. "If your two families are going to be battling for my favors from here on out, I might as well get something more than food out of it."

"You're already getting free labor," Adam pointed out.

"Free?" Bea snorted. "That damned dog trainer of yours wasn't here five minutes before she talked me out of working in the garden. She's not much of a one for sitting back and letting life happen to her, is she?"

Adam had a lot to say on that subject, but Phoebe interrupted before he could get started. "If I'm not needed here, I'm going to head out," she said. "Adam, you can get a ride back to the house with Dawn, yeah?"

Adam tilted his head in assent.

"And please don't remind me that we have that call with the bank later this afternoon," she added as a parting shot. "I know already. I'm the one who scheduled it. I promise to be home in plenty of time."

That seemed a little unfair, since the bank was the last thing on his mind, but he just raised a hand in farewell.

"Well, well. A call with the bank? You're taking an awful lot for granted, aren't you?" Bea didn't wait for him to defend himself. "Provided we find that paperwork, I don't see why we can't come to some sort of arrangement. I wasn't kidding when I said there's nothing keeping me here. I'm an old woman and a tired one. Dawn thinks I should go somewhere with sun and sand and young men in those tiny swim trunks."

"That does sound like Dawn's idea of paradise." Adam was forced to agree.

"I'm not so sure about that," Bea replied, but she didn't expand on the topic. "Tell Dawn I'll see her later, yeah?"

She didn't make any further attempts at conversation, so Adam took it as their cue to leave. Setting Methuselah carefully on the ground, he gave his low whistle to bring Uncle to attention. Once again, the Great Dane outdid himself in terms of obedience. He came immediately to Adam's side, his gentle press directing him where to go to safely leave the porch.

Bea must have noticed it, too. "That big one seems like he could come in handy," she said. Adam was about to agree when she added, "But for my money, I like that soft, brown-eyed one better. Useless for ranch work, of course, but she knows her value. The beautiful ones always do."

Adam could no longer tell if they were talking about the golden retriever or the woman who'd foisted herself into his life, but it didn't matter. He knew damn well that

Methuselah—*Gigi*—would never fit in his life. At least, not in any way that counted. Marcia had warned him that she'd probably always be a little on the small size and more inclined to take naps than perform work duties.

She'll be more work than she's ever worth, I'm afraid, Marcia had said. *But she's got a certain something about her, doesn't she?*

There hadn't been anything to say to that, either. Everyone was trying to talk him out of a puppy that wasn't technically his to begin with, yet here he was, holding on to her leash like it was his only lifeline.

Uncle did an admirable job of leading him back through the house and down the front steps. Adam was half-afraid that Charlie would still be there, chatting with Dawn and spilling more family secrets, but Dawn greeted him with a brief explanation.

"Charlie took off as soon as he put the food in my hands. He didn't even help me take it into Bea's kitchen, the louse. I can see why you dislike him so much."

"His manners have always left a little something to be desired."

"The lemon bars are good, though. I shoved a few in my bag, if you want one. Bea will never notice they're missing."

He chuckled and opened the passenger door to Dawn's car, waiting patiently while the dogs tumbled into the back seat. "You're stealing an old woman's food now?"

"Um, have you ever been in her basement? It's wall-to-wall junk down there. It'll take me weeks to clear it. She's lucky I didn't pinch the cider, too." She paused while Adam settled himself in and allowed the golden retriever to wriggle her way over the middle console and into his lap.

"Don't say it," he warned.

"I wasn't going to!"

"I can hear you thinking."

"In addition to being able to smell my nonscent, you can hear my not-sounds now, too?"

Yes, he could. He could also feel her not-touch and taste her not-kiss. It was starting to seriously unbalance him.

Dawn reached over and gave the puppy a gentle pat. "She's destined to become a great lapdog someday, that's for sure."

"You mean *ranch* dog."

"Not if I get you what you want, I'll wager." She started the Jetta and pulled out of the drive, but so slowly he could not-see her looking at him. "That's how your family works, isn't it? Place a bet and watch to see how everything unfolds? Stake half of your lands and hope the dice fall in your favor?"

"First of all, it was poker, not dice," he retorted. "And how was it my grandfather's fault that Peter Smithwood was a degenerate gambler who put half his family's fortune up for grabs?"

Dawn gave a crow of laughter. "I *knew* you couldn't be nearly as upright as you want us all to believe. What other scandalous deeds litter your family's past? Are there bodies buried in the woods? Illegitimate Dearborns in every cradle across the county?"

"I'm not dignifying either of those with a response."

"Well, what about my wager, then? Does that warrant a response?"

"Not really, no," he said, but of course Dawn couldn't let it rest there.

"You heard Bea for yourself. The property is all yours." She paused a beat. "Provided I act as mediator, that is."

There were so many things he wanted to say to her—to thank her for—but the words lodged in his throat. He and Dawn didn't have that kind of relationship. They could tease and taunt and take steamy showers together, but heartfelt honesty was off the table.

"You're only offering to act as mediator because you think I'll give you Gigi if you do," he said.

"I'm sorry—*who*?"

He realized his error at once. In his distracted state, Dawn's name for the puppy had just slipped out.

"Am I wrong?" he asked, ignoring the implication of having given in. *Methuselah* was a ridiculous thing to call the puppy—and had been from day one—but saying so out loud would only be the start. Once he opened those floodgates, he'd also have to admit that there was no way he could keep Gigi forever. A few weeks of Uncle's company had more than proven to him that what he *wanted* and what he *needed* were two very different things.

A few weeks of Dawn's company had done the same. Already, he was falling way behind schedule, letting his ranch duties slide so he could have vodka and pie on Bea's back porch. Already, he found himself wishing Dawn would stay for more than just the day, her laughter and whirlwind existence sweeping him up and away from the realities of his life.

He sighed and rubbed his hand along the back of

his neck. All he had to do was say no. All he had to do was decide to go on the way he always had, without a puppy of any kind in his life. All he had to do was shut the door against Dawn and pretend that he didn't live for those stolen moments they shared both in and out of bed.

"You're not wrong," Dawn agreed. "I'm just surprised to hear the words from your own lips. So it's a trade? If I get you the Benson lands, you'll give me Gigi? Just like that?"

Adam shrugged uncomfortably. It sounded so sordid when put into words like that. So *final*.

But "Why not?" was what he said. "Even if you don't succeed, it'll piss Charlie off something fierce to know you're at Bea's every day, bringing us closer to the final purchase. It'll be worth it just for that."

Dawn pulled the car up the crunching gravel drive to the ranch and slowed to a stop. "Well, I guess that's as close to a deal as we're going to get, isn't it?" she said. "I'm on basement and Uncle training duty. You can keep shamelessly spoiling Gigi, because that is literally what you're doing by letting her sneak onto your lap like that. Between the pair of us, we'll wrest that land out of Bea's hands and keep the Smithwoods from regaining their familial stronghold. If that's not the plot for one of my Aunt Nessa's favorite telenovelas, I don't know what is."

"My life was perfectly ordinary last month." Adam felt compelled to protest. It was a feeble protest, though, since the golden retriever had rolled onto her back again in a shameless bid for tummy tickles. "Then you introduced this girl into my life and, well…"

He didn't dare finish that statement. Dawn had introduced Gigi into his life and, well, he'd fallen in love. He had the feeling that when it came to this particular woman, love was the worst possible thing to admit.

chapter
9

"Uh, Dawn? Is there any chance you've been seeing another cult leader?"

Dawn glanced over at Sophie, who sat in the passenger seat of her car with a takeout pizza balanced on her lap. She'd managed to convince her sister to spend the evening at the kennel with her…though, honestly, that was never a difficult task where promises of hot food and melted cheese were concerned.

"Not to my knowledge, no," Dawn said. "But you can't always tell if someone is a cult leader right away. They're very charismatic, you know. That's how they lure people in."

The response had been meant as a joke—the only way *to* respond when someone who shared your blood knew all of your darkest dating secrets—but Sophie's expression grew thoughtful. "Huh. I guess I never thought of it that way."

Most people didn't. That was the one benefit of experience as vast and scattered as hers. You learned that charisma wasn't a trustworthy trait and sisters rarely said what they were really thinking.

Dawn decided to save Sophie the trouble. "Besides,

you know very well that I've been sleeping with Adam Dearborn. There's no way Lila didn't call you the second she got off the phone with me the other day." She poked her sister in the arm. "Admit it. You guys gossiped about it for hours."

"Not *hours*," Sophie admitted, her brow lightening a little. "It was twenty minutes at the most. Unless you count the ten minutes after that spent trying to finding a picture of him online."

That made Dawn laugh. It was no less than what she would have done in similar circumstances—*had* done countless times before, in fact. She was quite good at Google stalking her sisters' former beaux.

"And did you?" she asked.

"Yes. His brother and sister both have public Facebook profiles. Adam appeared in a few of the pictures they'd posted. He's very, um, nice-looking."

Nice-looking was one way to put it. Dawn would have said something more along the lines of *stern, striking*, or *sexy as all hell*…but some things didn't need to be explained.

"Okay, but if you aren't dating a cult leader, have you broken any federal laws lately?" Sophie cast an anxious look into the rearview mirror. "This is going to sound silly, but I could almost swear we're being followed."

"Oh balls," Dawn said, choosing a milder oath than she normally would have. She didn't want to send Sophie—or that hot pizza—into a flutter. "Is it a big truck that was once blue but is now mostly rust? Looks like it probably has Confederate flag stickers in the back window and a pair of fake testicles dangling from the hitch?"

Sophie peered closer at the mirror. "Yeah, that sounds about right. Friend of yours?"

"I wouldn't exactly call him a friend. He's the guy I stole Gigi from."

"Dawn!" Sophie's eyes widened.

"I know. But he can't go very fast in that thing. I've already outrun him twice. Well, Zeke did it the first time, but you know what I mean." She made a quick survey of the highway before stepping down on the gas. "Sorry, Soph. This might not be very fun for you."

"But it *is* fun for you?"

Dawn laughed, though the sound was shaky around the edges. This wasn't the same part of the highway where No-Pants had followed her before, which was a worrisome development. Either he was covering more extensive ground in his search, or he was learning which routes she was most likely to be on. She couldn't decide which option was worse.

"I'll head in the direction of the sheriff's office. He won't follow me there." She paused, thinking of the audacity of a man who'd chase a woman in the broad light of day, and amended her statement. "Well, he might *follow* me there, but he won't kill me there. At least, I hope not. Cult leaders I'm familiar with, but rural psychopaths are a new one for me."

Sophie offered the shaky laugh this time. "I don't know why I find that comforting, but I do."

"It's because it shows how resourceful I am," Dawn said with confidence she was far from feeling. "This isn't my first time running away from an angry man, and I'm sure it won't be my last."

Concentrating on the road took up most of her

energy, so she didn't spend too much time chatting with Sophie after that. Fortunately, it was a sunny and clear Saturday afternoon, which meant there were lots of families heading out to enjoy the weather. No-Pants might be scary, what with the way he was gunning his engine at her and weaving on and off the graveled edge of the road, but she wasn't the only one who objected to his style of driving. Several cars honked warnings at him, and one oversized SUV even moved to the middle of the highway to prevent him from passing.

"God bless giant cars and the people who drive them," Dawn said as No-Pants got caught behind a truck with wheels so big they belonged on a semi. She caught sight of an opening in the passing lane and zipped neatly toward it. She had to push her car up past eighty, but she managed to put several car lengths behind them. Either No-Pants gave up after that, or his truck decided it could no longer maintain such high speeds, because he dropped from sight.

Dawn waited only until she was sure he was gone before she let up on the gas. "One of these days, No-Pants is going to learn that I don't give in that easily."

"No-Pants? His name is No-Pants?"

"Technically, I've been calling him No-Pants Shotgun, but I didn't want to scare you with that last bit."

Dawn glanced over to make sure Sophie wasn't going to fall into a maidenly swoon. Far from showing signs of collapse, her younger sister was sitting bolt upright in her seat, her hands clutching the pizza as though she were prepared to hit someone over the head with it.

"And he's really done this more than once? Chased you down? Tried to run you off the road?"

"I mean, he's never gotten close enough to do more than alarm me, but yes. I'm not sure what his endgame is. Does he think I have Gigi in the car with me at all times? Or that I'd let him come within five feet of her after what he did?"

"That miserable rat bastard."

Dawn blinked at her sister's vehemence. "Thanks, Soph. I'm glad you're on my side."

"How dare he try to scare you?"

"I know, right?"

"Who does he think he is, coming after *my* big sister like that?"

Dawn chuckled and laid a restraining hand on Sophie's leg. She doubted No-Pants would look at the five-foot-two woman and feel a qualm of fear, but he should. No one was more terrifying once she put her mind to something—Sophie was the fiercest, most tenacious person Dawn knew.

"Easy there, tiger. He's not worth the energy. There are much worse bad guys out there."

As before, the adrenaline of the chase had given way to a shakier, less exciting sensation that left Dawn feeling drained. Drained *and* guilty. It was one thing to embroil Zeke in the theft of Gigi, since he'd known what he was getting into ahead of time and had the kind of physique that would cause a man like No-Pants to think twice before confronting him. Sophie, however, hadn't asked for any of this.

"Look, Soph," Dawn began, choosing her words carefully. "I never would have invited you to come with me if I'd have known No-Pants might show up. I mean, I *should* have considered the possibility, obviously, but, well…"

There was no good way to put it. She hadn't been thinking. In true Dawn Vasquez style, she'd barreled into action without considering all the repercussions first.

"Don't worry. I won't tell Lila." Sophie made the motion of a zipper over her lips. "It'll be our little secret. Just you and me and this stuffed crust with double pepperoni. And *this* guy will soon be in our bellies, so he barely counts."

"That's not what I was going to say! I don't care if Lila knows about that part." She considered her older sister's displeasure and winced. "To be fair, it's probably better if we downplay the danger factor an eensy-weensy bit, but that's not what I'm worried about."

"Oh?"

Dawn struggled to find a way to put her feelings into words. She'd never been the sort of woman to regret her mistakes or even to worry too much about making them in the first place. Part of being alive was just that— *being alive*. Puppies needed to be saved sometimes. So did lonely old women who lived alone in ramshackle farmhouses. *Not to mention tall, gorgeous cowboy types with the most magical hands known to mankind.*

It was just that for once, it would have been nice to not have to defend herself—not to Lila or to Sophie, not to Bea or to Adam. For once, she wanted someone to take in all the parts of her—the good and the bad, the recklessness and the honorable intentions behind it— and say, "You know what? This is exactly what I want."

She must have taken too long to answer because a sympathetic smile crossed Sophie's face. "Poor Dawn."

"Poor Dawn?" she echoed. "What are you talking about? I'm the one leading *you* on a dangerous car chase, not the other way around."

"It's making you crazy, isn't it, being cooped up in that house all day?"

It was on the tip of Dawn's tongue to tell her sister that she wasn't cooped up in the Dearborn house all day—that life on a working ranch was turning out to be exactly the constant whirl of activity and adventure she craved—but Sophie's voice softened. "It wasn't very nice of us to abandon you to the sole care of the kennel, was it? Of all of us, you're the last one anyone expected to stick around holding the mop bucket."

Dawn turned off on the road that would lead them back to Spokane, her attention on the asphalt leading off in the distance. It had to be. Otherwise, she'd be forced to give Sophie her full focus, and there was nothing she wanted less right now.

"You know I don't mind being in charge of the kennel," Dawn said. "I *like* the puppies. I *like* that they need me."

"Yes, but you also like being able to come and go at your leisure—and don't sit all stiff like that. It's not a judgment. Anyone would." Sophie paused in a considering way. "Mom was saying something along those lines just the other day. Do you know, this is the longest you've ever lived in one place?"

"Oh, great. Mom is keeping track of me now?"

Sophie laughed. "I'm pretty sure she has records of everything you've ever said or done. She has one for each of us. It makes her happy. It's the longest you've gone without one of your emergency dating texts, too, in case you're wondering."

Dawn glanced over at her sister so quickly that the car gave a lurch.

That just made Sophie laugh more. "Oh, don't worry. Mom doesn't keep track of those."

"But you do?"

"Not officially, no," Sophie said. "But I used to get one of those texts at least once a month, if not once a *week*. You haven't been going out."

They'd reached a red light by then, so Dawn had nothing to distract her except the tap of her fingers on the steering wheel. "I go out," she protested.

"I'm sure you do. What I mean is, you're not going out with the kind of men who require your sister to come up with a last-minute emergency so you can make a safe escape." Sophie sighed playfully. "I miss them. I was getting really good at coming up with new ones. The next one was going to be an outbreak of listeria. Harrison and I watched an exposé a few months ago. It's scary, how often people get poisoned from restaurants that way. Most of the time, you don't even know that's what caused it."

"Soph, it's not like that. I—"

Sophie reached over and put a hand on Dawn's leg. Her palm was warm from where it had been holding the pizza. It was weirdly comforting, that residual heat, a mixture of pepperoni and sisterly love. "It's that Adam guy, isn't it?"

Dawn stared at the red light, trying her best not to cause her sister unnecessary worry. Part of it was a lingering habit from childhood, when it had been their family's sole mission to save Sophie from any and all pain. The leukemia Sophie had battled for most of her youth had been more than enough for her to bear already.

But it was more than that, too. The truth was, there was nothing to worry *about*. Dawn was doing the same thing she'd always done—seeing a man she liked, sleeping with him when the mood struck, enjoying the fun and flirtation that came with it. This was no different than dating the cult leader or the quasi-FBI agent or any of the other men who'd caught her fancy over the years.

Except it *was* different. She didn't know how or why, but this thing she had with Adam was unlike anything she'd experienced before—and had been from the start. There'd been no expensive dates or hours of clubbing. No drunken public sexcapades or late nights of partying. Not even a fake FBI job or a circus ring hiding in the background.

There'd been only him: Adam Dearborn, solid and stalwart, honest and real. He was the first man to offer her that—not some flashy lifestyle designed to charm her out of her panties, but just himself.

"*He*'s the one you can't win over with a laugh and a smile, isn't he?" Sophie prodded softly.

Dawn took Sophie's hand and didn't let go, clutching those fingers with a grip that felt strangely unlike her.

"You *really* can't tell Lila about this," she said. "Promise me. I don't care if you divulge every detail of the No-Pants road chase, but I need you to keep this one between you and me. Please."

Sophie returned the press of her fingers. "Of course."

And that was it. She didn't ask any prying questions,

the way Lila would have, and she didn't crack any hot cowboy jokes, the way Dawn herself would have. The one thing Sophie had always been great at was her quiet, unassuming strength.

"Just remember that I'm here to talk if you ever need to, okay?"

"There's nothing to talk about," Dawn said with stark truthfulness. "It's exactly the way you guessed. We're sleeping together. It's fun. That's all there is to it—and it's probably all there will ever be."

Sophie must have sensed that Dawn had reached her limit of openhearted girl chat, because she released her hand and placed it reverentially on top of the pizza box. "If that's the case, then we need to get somewhere where this pizza and I can get better acquainted. When Harrison's out of the house, there's no one to cook for me. I'm starving."

That was all Dawn needed to hear to set her foot heavily on the gas pedal. She might not be any closer to deciding what she planned to do regarding No-Pants Shotgun or Adam Dearborn, but she was close to dinner.

For now, that had to be enough.

chapter
10

"Today is harness training day," Dawn announced as she entered the kitchen. She spoke with the air of one carrying an executioner's ax over her shoulder and a golden retriever puppy in her arms. "You know what that means... It's also Adam-has-to-go-with-me-into-town day."

"I can't. The irrigation system on the south field is having problems." Adam held out the coffee mug he'd just finished filling, keeping it there until Dawn took it with a murmur of thanks. Like him, she took her coffee black. No muss, no fuss—all she asked was that it was hot. He reached for a second cup and began pouring himself one.

"No, it's not." Zeke took the coffee from his hand before Adam had a chance to finish pouring. "I took a look at it this morning. The pressure tank was off, but I added some air. It's working just fine now. Ugh. Didn't you use the flavored kind?"

"Of course not. I'm not a heathen." Adam paused before filling a third cup of coffee. "And what do you mean, you took a look at it this morning? It *is* morning."

He knew before Phoebe plucked the last cup from his

hand that there was no way he was going to be able to
enjoy this pot of coffee in peace. His siblings were mer-
ciless. Didn't they realize how little sleep he'd gotten
last night, staying up well past his bedtime listening to
American Horror Story?

Dawn hadn't been kidding about that show. It was
terrifying. He was pretty sure there was a ghost in *his*
basement now.

"He means that we were up before the sun, doing
every possible chore that might be on your list today,"
Phoebe said. "So there's no excuse."

"No excuse for what?" The pot in his hand sloshed
with the tiny bit of coffee left. He'd have to make do
with the dregs. "Harness training can't possibly take all
day."

"It can and does take weeks, actually," Dawn said.
"But I think they're referring to Zeke's race."

Oh. *Oh.* "Shit, Zeke. I forgot. The Trailblazer Tri,
right?"

His brother shifted slightly, the rustle of his athletic
pants carrying new meaning now that Adam remembered what day it was. His brother had been competing
in the triathlon around nearby Medical Lake for years—
and he usually won. It wasn't a very big race, and it
didn't come with any prize money, but Zeke entering it
had become something of a tradition.

"What time are you supposed to check in?"

"Eleven, which means I need to get moving if I want
to make it on time." His brother gulped his coffee. With
an anxious inflection, he added, "It's okay, yeah? Since
I got the irrigation system up and running again, you
don't mind if Phoebe and I lope off for the rest of the

day? Michael's out of town, so she has to be my whole support crew."

"I've got water bottles, salt packs, and the first aid kit ready to go," Phoebe said. "He's going to need them. It's supposed to reach a hundred degrees today."

Adam felt a pang of mingled remorse and regret. Zeke and Phoebe didn't ask for a lot in terms of time away from the ranch—not compared to the number of days off included in a more traditional job—and he did his best to accommodate them when he could. But there was no denying that it was a strain. Days off required coordination and planning and a lot of extra work picked up late into the night.

That was something most people would never understand. Ranching wasn't a job; it was a way of life. It was an existence, and one that included a lot of hard work and sacrifices. In fact, now that he was thinking about it, it was kind of like being a service dog. Since the moment he'd woken up this morning, Uncle had been at his feet—never in the way, of course, but on the job. He was ready to come the moment Adam called, to sniff out his boots or accompany him across the yard or even to entertain Gigi, who was both at Adam's feet *and* in the way. Uncle didn't complain, of course, and Adam liked to think that the animal was starting to feel happy and settled in his new home, but there was no denying that Uncle's life was one of restriction and duty—would, from here on out, be one of continued restriction and duty.

"Of course you guys can go," he said, waving them off and almost spilling coffee all over himself in the process. "I'm only sorry I didn't remember before. I would have been up early to fix the irrigation system with you."

Now that his blessing had been bestowed, both of his siblings showed themselves eager to get out the door.

"Nah, I thought it'd be nice you to sleep in for a change," Zeke said. "Besides— you know I can never sleep before a race."

Actually, Adam hadn't known that. Between all the training and the manual labor he did around here, Zeke almost always slept like the dead.

"Make sure he behaves himself, okay?" Phoebe asked before dropping a quick kiss on Adam's cheek. He thought for a moment that she was telling him to make sure *Uncle* was being good, but Dawn laughed and promised to do her best. "You laugh now," Phoebe added, "but just wait until Adam starts talking to the grocery clerk about crossbreeding and the latest in artificial insemination methods. It's mortifying. He sometimes forgets how to act around normal, noncattle people."

"Ooh, that sounds right up my alley." Uncle shifted at Adam's feet as Dawn drew closer. He hadn't realized *how* close she was until Gigi's wet nose pressed against his forearm. "What do I need to know about the latest in artificial insemination? Please tell me it involves giant turkey basters and bulls masturbating in dark corners, or I'm going to be disappointed."

"You're bound for disappointment, I'm afraid," Phoebe replied with a giggle. "It's all very straightforward and clinical."

"Just like me," Adam said. It was mostly an attempt to move the conversation along, but he was afraid it came off sounding much more pathetic than he'd anticipated.

"Well, good luck to you both," Dawn said brightly. "I promise not to sully your family name by letting Adam discuss anything but *human* insemination in public. You have my word on that."

That remark, as well as a few others about wishing Zeke well on the upcoming race, had Adam's family leaving the ranch in one of the best moods they'd been in for a long time.

"How do you do that?" he asked as Dawn shut the front door behind his siblings and returned to the kitchen. He'd already started a new pot of coffee, which was bubbling to life in the background.

"Do what? Get rid of your brother and sister as fast as possible?" Her voice dropped to a lower, coy note. "It's not that tough when there's such strong motivation standing here making me coffee."

As easy—and as fun—as it would have been to let her divert the subject, Adam shook his head. "No, not that. I mean that no matter who you're talking to or who you're with, you always leave them in a better mood than before you arrived. Zeke. Phoebe. Marcia. Bea Benson." He hesitated. "Me."

The silence that greeted this filled Adam with a worrying amount of foreboding. One of the unspoken rules of their relationship was that they never veered into any kind of territory where real human emotions lived. Flirtation was fine, and insults were basically foreplay, but actual compliments weren't something they dealt in very often.

He busied himself by brushing a hand over Uncle's head, taking comfort in the strong, silent bulk of him.

"I think that might be the nicest compliment anyone has ever given me," Dawn eventually said. Her voice was distant, but he knew she was standing close because he could feel the air moving around her. "Thank you."

The sincerity in her voice unsettled him. "Does that mean you're not going to tell me how you do it?"

"You've seen me in action. You probably know better than I do."

"Not really. From what I've been able to glean, most of it is sex jokes."

That made her laugh. "Never overlook the power of a well-timed and well-hung pun." She paused. "You're not wrong, though. People like jokes, and they like sex. If they like me, too, it's mostly because I give them an excuse to enjoy both themselves."

Considering how much he laughed with Dawn, Adam wasn't in much of a position to argue this fact. Her open and honest approach to sex was, in fact, one of his favorite things about her, but that wasn't confined to the bedroom. She was open and honest regarding just about *everything*.

"You do more than that," he said, trying—and failing—to share some of what he was feeling.

"Yeah, I also remind them of a time when they were as fun-loving and carefree as I am—back in their wayward and regrettable youth." She changed directions before he could contradict her. "Well, where do you want to go today?"

"Uh…to the south field?"

She dropped a hand to his forearm and gave it a gentle squeeze. "Sorry. I should have been clearer. Where do you want to go that will give the puppies an opportunity to work in a public setting? Uncle has had some basic harness training, but he'll need to learn your specific needs. Things like where the elevators are in a store or how to find a person to help when you're somewhere new. Gigi, well…it might be too late for her either way. We'll have to see."

Until that bit about Gigi, Dawn's plans had been sounding pretty good. Adam did quite a bit of his shopping online, and he was able to get around most places with his cane, but it would be nice to diversify his options. However, he didn't much care for the implication that Gigi wasn't fit for duty. It might be impossible to teach an old dog like himself new tricks, but Gigi was young. She had her whole life ahead of her.

"It's not too late," he protested. "Gigi's been doing really well with your basic training instructions. We did sitting and staying for thirty minutes last night without a single hitch."

He could hear the smirk in Dawn's voice. "Okay, okay. Don't shoot the dog trainer. I only meant that it might take her a few weeks to catch up. Sheesh. You really love that little puppy, don't you?"

His chest clenched. Love was only the start of it. "I care about her well-being, that's all. If you bring me a broken animal, I'm going to fix it."

"What about broken women?" she asked. "Do you fix them, too?"

The coffeepot dinged its cheerful completion, making it impossible for him to get an accurate read on Dawn's tone. She seemed lighthearted enough, and she'd never given him reason to doubt her word before, but he had no way of knowing for sure.

He took the easy out.

"I have a destination in mind, but I don't know how realistic it is," he said as he poured himself a fresh cup of coffee.

"The sky's the limit," she replied. "Literally. Short of parachuting out of an airplane, I can't think of anywhere you might want to go where these two can't follow. What's on your mind? The feed store? The Deer Park bowling alley? Oh, I know—it's Bea's house. You had such a good time last week, you're dying to go back, aren't you?"

Adam took a long, careful sip of his coffee. "No, it's not Bea's house," he said. "But if you want company the next time you head over there, say the word. No one should have to face that woman alone."

"My white knight. So gallant."

"It's not gallantry. It's basic human decency—especially since you're only going over there for me." He ran his free hand along the back of his neck, finding it strangely difficult to get this next part out. "The thing is, I'd really like to go to Medical Lake."

"Medical Lake?" she echoed. "You mean, to watch Zeke's race?"

"I know, it's dumb. Phoebe told me once that the spectators sit there for hours just to cheer for five seconds when their racer flashes by, but I've always wondered what it was like. It's supposed to be ridiculously hot today, and I don't know if all the crowds will be good for the puppies, but—"

Dawn's hand stole to his cheek, stopping him short. "I think it's a great idea."

"You do?"

"Absolutely. I mean, I don't know how Gigi is going to react to all those people, but Uncle loves crowds. He's like a circus strongman walking through the center of town. Everyone oohs and aahs over him, and he eats it up. Don't you, Uncle? Your secret ambition is to be adored."

Actually, his secret ambition was to sleep lengthwise next to Adam and Gigi in the bed rather than on the special cushion next to the door, but he wasn't going to rat the poor animal out.

"Besides, I've always wanted to watch Zeke in action," Dawn added. "He loves that stuff."

"I know."

"Do you? I sometimes wonder how much either of you knows about the other." She lifted the coffee cup from his hand. He thought that was rather rude considering he'd had to brew a whole second pot for himself, but she replaced it with the warm, squirming bundle of golden retriever. "I've got a couple of training vests for them in the car, but we can wait to put the harnesses on when we get there. I think you'll be surprised at how much Uncle loves it."

No, he wouldn't. If there was duty and obligation involved, then Adam knew full well that Uncle would rise nobly to the task like, well, the white knight Dawn had accused him of being.

"One of these days, we're going to have to give Uncle a day off just to have fun," he said. "You're working that poor animal to death."

That poor animal gave a long, happy whine and began thumping his leg—both clear signs that Dawn was scratching the back of his ears. *And* that he was loving it.

"You're right," she replied, laughing. "Uncle is definitely starting to show signs of strain."

🐾 🐾 🐾

"So, all you have to do is hold the harness at his level like this." Dawn put a slim handle into Adam's hand and showed him where to hold it. "Say 'harness,' and he'll walk right into it."

"This feels an awful lot like a metal cage," he said as he ran his free hand over the harness. It was simple in design, the handle a U-shaped piece that connected directly to the apparatus so that the animal wearing it could quickly and easily lead him in any direction. "You're sure he won't mind?"

"I'm one hundred percent sure. Uncle has been using one of these since he was just a few weeks old. He likes it."

"Okay," Adam said doubtfully, but he did as Dawn instructed. Both of the puppies had been well behaved on the long drive out here, but while Uncle was now standing at attention and ready for duty, Gigi was prancing around and nipping playfully at Adam's feet. He suspected it was his shoes she was really after, but he didn't dare say so in front of Dawn. That woman had enough ammunition against him—and against Gigi—already.

"Uncle, it's time to get in your harness," he said. If he'd had any doubts about Uncle's feelings toward it, they disappeared as a powerful surge pulled at his hand. The Great Dane had practically leaped into the thing.

"Now just slide that buckle there, and he's good to go. Feel how he pushes and pulls on it? It's like having a harness on a horse—you have to work together to get where you need to go."

He gave both himself and Uncle a moment to adjust. Dawn had parked her car near the back of the parking lot, which was apparently a large dirt field in the middle of nowhere. They had plenty of room to test the puppies without danger of being run over.

"Now, Gigi—it's your turn. Please get in your harness."

Adam was busy holding Uncle, so he couldn't tell for sure what kind of struggle was going on as Dawn attempted to introduce Gigi to the harness, but it didn't sound good. There was a whimper, a cry, and the clang of metal—none of which filled him with much in the way of confidence.

"I know, girl. It's a little strange at first. But see how nice Uncle looks, leading Adam around? So big and strong and noble." She laughed. "The puppy's not bad, either."

"Flattery will get you nowhere," he said, though it was a lie. He could feel himself swelling already. He wasn't sure anyone had called him noble before. "What's wrong with her?"

"Nothing is wrong with her. She's just sniffing it, checking out the mechanics. Will you let me put this little part on you right here?"

An even louder cry sounded this time. Adam dropped the handle to Uncle's harness. "Is it rubbing against her sores? Dammit, Dawn. You can't force her into it. She's not used to being told what to do."

"I'm aware of that, thank you," she said, her tone clipped. "It's not touching her wounds. It's not anywhere near them."

"Then why is she making that sound?"

There was a slight pause. In the background, Adam could hear cars pulling into the better parking spots in the distance, the twitter of birds not too far behind them.

It was a good reminder that they were standing in the middle of an open field, the sun blaring high above them. The puppies would need shade before long. Uncle didn't seem to mind the heat, but Gigi had a strange dislike of direct sunlight.

"It could be lots of reasons," Dawn admitted. "If I had to guess, I'd say it's because she doesn't like being restrained. I was afraid of something like this happening."

Something about her tone—so matter-of-fact, so unalarmed—snagged at him. "Afraid of what?" he asked.

"It's not a big deal."

Uncle drew underneath Adam's hand so he could pick up the harness handle again. "What's not a big deal? What aren't you telling me?"

"I warned you that she wasn't cut out for this kind of work."

"What aren't you telling me?" he repeated.

"I told you time and time again that she's more of a pet than a service animal."

"Out with it already."

"It's just…" She sighed. "When I first found her, she had a chain wrapped around her neck. Like, a big one. *Scary* big. It weighed almost as much as she does."

"What?" Adam was already feeling anxious, the prospect of Zeke's upcoming race and worry about Gigi working together on his nerves. This bit of news—which would have been nice to know earlier—only served to ratchet up his tension. "Some bastard had her chained up?"

"I know. It was awful. The poor thing could barely

move with it on. She was just lying there in the heat, all pitiful and resigned to her fate."

"Why didn't you tell me?" he demanded. "Why didn't you tell Marcia?"

"I didn't think the specifics were relevant. I told you she'd been neglected."

He knew he was misplacing his anger—that his feelings weren't directed at Dawn but at whoever had thought it was acceptable to put a huge chain on a puppy as small and loving as this one—but he couldn't seem to stop it.

"Of course she doesn't want to wear a harness," he said, putting a hand out in Gigi's direction. She put a wet, pitiful nose in his palm before heaving a whimper designed to break a man's heart. "It was cruel of you to even try."

He thought it sounded like Dawn threw up her hands before dropping them to her thighs again. But when she spoke, it was with nothing but sweet submission. "You're absolutely right, Adam. I'm a horrible monster."

"Yes, you are."

"I saved this puppy from her chains and agony only to force her into servitude."

He felt a growing sense of discomfort. "Wait. I never said—"

"I wrested her from death's door only to put her in the care of a man who's determined to make her earn her keep. I mean, *I* wanted to take her home to be loved and coddled, but—"

"Dawn, that's not what I meant!"

She laughed and pressed a kiss on his cheek. It was just like her to do that—to repay his outburst with affection, to playfully defuse the situation—but that only served to make him feel worse.

"I know what you meant, Adam, and it just so happens to be what I like best about you. You take good care of your animals. Your people, too."

His sense of discomfort only mounted. He *didn't* take very good care of his animals, obviously. Dawn had known at the outset that Gigi would struggle with things like harnesses and restraints, but he hadn't listened.

And his people, well, just look at what a bungle he'd made of that. He'd forgotten about Zeke's race—hadn't even gotten up early to help with the ranch chores so Zeke could enjoy his big day. If his brother lacked the energy to win, it would be Adam's fault for failing to see to the irrigation system himself.

"I'll just put Gigi on a loose leash," Dawn said. "That'll get her used to being tied up without feeling like she's under some kind of punishment. Why don't you tell Uncle where you want to go?"

"He knows how to find the spectator stands?"

"Well, no. But he should know how to find someone who can tell you how to find the spectator stands." Dawn paused. "Ask him to find 'help.' He knows what that means."

Adam felt a little foolish speaking to his dog in plain English, but only because he wasn't used to having an audience. He talked to the cows all the time—even sang them songs when they were feeling nervous—but it wasn't the same. "Okay, Uncle. Find us some help. We have a race to watch."

It worked. With the competence he was coming to expect from the Great Dane, Uncle started moving away from the car. Adam had ridden enough horses in his lifetime to feel comfortable being attached to an animal—and in trusting one. If Gigi had been doing the leading, he might have been wary of cars backing into their parking spots or divots in the dirt under his feet, but Uncle knew what he was doing. He walked along, keeping pace with Adam, refusing to be sidetracked by the sounds and smells of hundreds of people gathering for an event.

"Wait—why's he stopping?" Adam asked as Uncle's movements started to slow.

"We're coming up on a nice family lifting a cooler out of the back of their car," Dawn said. "He wants you to stop and ask them for directions."

"Oh. That's smart. Can he tell the difference between nice families and serial killers?"

Dawn gave a gurgle of laughter. "You know, I didn't think to include that in his training. Would you like me to work it in tomorrow?"

"Nah. I'd rather you train him to recognize attractive young women. Preferably single ones."

A playful pinch sent a jolt down his arm. "If that's what you want, then you're much better off with me. I could give you the names and numbers of six potential candidates right now. I'm an excellent wingman."

He didn't doubt it. Dawn probably knew hordes of young, attractive, single women—and would, if he so desired, set him up with any number of them. And she'd do it all without a single glimmer of jealousy.

In order to be jealous, she'd have to care about him—about *them*—first.

"Excuse me," he said as Uncle came to a complete

stop. "Could you tell me how to get to the spectator stands?"

"Puppies!" A loud squeal drowned out any response the nice family might have made to his request. "Mama, look—two puppies!"

"Oh, um." Adam cleared his throat. He knew, from what Dawn had told him during the first week of their training, that it was important to be firm with people when he was out with his service animals. No matter how much he might want to let squealing children pet Uncle and Gigi, they had to learn to ignore anything but the task at hand. "I'm sorry, but—"

"How clever you are," Dawn said, her voice somewhere near the region of his feet. He assumed she was either squatting at the child's level or at the animals'. Probably both, considering how much squirming Gigi seemed to be doing. "They *are* puppies. Most people take one look at this big guy and assume he's like a hundred years old. But he's only seven months."

The girl giggled. "He's hugemongous."

"That's true—and he'll get even bigger as he grows up. When he stands on his hind legs, he'll be as tall as your dad."

"Gracie, honey, you can't pet those dogs." A woman's voice, brisk but friendly, was followed by the slam of the car's trunk. "They're service animals. That's right, isn't it?"

"I'm afraid so," Adam apologized. "And we're training them to recognize when I need directions. Are the stands near here?"

"Sure thing, hon. What you're going to want to do is head about ten feet to your right..." The woman continued with her directions. Adam knew he was supposed to be listening, and that the woman's clipped recital of the easiest route to the stands was better than most people were able to provide, but Dawn and the little girl were distracting him with their continued discussion of the puppies.

"That small one doesn't look very good at his job."

"It's a girl puppy, and between you and me, she's not."

"Oh. That's too bad. What's wrong with her?"

"You mean other than her love of chasing bugs and eating shoes?" Dawn waited for the girl's giggle to subside before continuing. "Nothing. It's just that some puppies are good helpers, and some aren't. That's all there is to it."

"Did you get all that?" A man laughed as the woman finished her recitation of the directions, obviously aware that Adam had only been paying half attention. "It might be hard to find the path, but we can walk with you to where it starts, if you want."

"Thanks, but my friend should be able to get us the rest of the way."

"No problem. Come on, Gracie. Say goodbye to the nice lady and her puppies."

"Bye, lady! Bye, puppies! See you later!"

The family moved off, but Adam and Dawn didn't start walking right away. As if aware that something was holding him back, Uncle hadn't made the least push to start moving again.

"What is it?" Dawn asked. Her hand touched his arm. "Why do you look as though someone just told you that you're going to have to put one of the puppies down?"

Because that was essentially what *had* happened. Adam had known for some time now that Gigi wasn't likely to win any guide dog awards, but he'd been holding out hope that she might be able to step in and give Uncle the occasional day off. Unfortunately, not only was the harness an issue now, but that girl—a child—had noticed within five seconds that Gigi wasn't suited for the life he had planned for her.

Some puppies are good helpers, and some aren't. That's all there is to it.

"She's never going to be any good at this, is she?" he asked. He put his hand out only to have Gigi leap full tilt into it, almost oversetting his balance. Only Uncle's solid bulk kept him from sprawling in the dirt. "No matter how much work we do, no matter how much time she spends on the ranch. She's always going to be like this."

Lots of women—men too—would have used this opportunity to remind him that this was precisely what she'd said from the start. It had never been Dawn's intention to give him Gigi, even less to spend six weeks of her life training Uncle as an alternate. She had every right to be frustrated with him, with the job that had been foisted on her, with the fact that he'd practically forced her into helping Bea Benson with her nonsensical chores in an effort to get Gigi back.

But not Dawn. With her familiar laugh, she said, "Oh, hell no. Don't you dare."

"Don't I dare what?"

"Reverse psychology me."

"Is that what I'm doing?"

Her fingertip hit the middle of his chest and stayed there. "I can tell you right now that your evil machinations won't work, so you can wipe that smirk off your face."

"I wasn't aware that I was smirking. Or, for that matter, reverse psychology-ing you."

She drew closer, her finger still wedged between them. Something about that connection—her hand the only thing separating their hearts—made him suddenly feel relaxed. Well, either that or the fact that her laugh was the one thing in the world that had the capability of lighting his whole world. "You think that if you suddenly start telling me that Gigi is no good, I'll fight harder to make her work out."

"Um…"

"You think the challenge will only make me want to prove you wrong."

"Does it?"

She laughed, her mouth so close to his by now that he could feel, smell, *taste* the ruffle of her breath. "A little bit, yes. I never could resist a dare."

Adam believed it. He also believed that nothing would make him happier than having Dawn prove him wrong about Gigi—about *everything*. "So…if I told you that you're no good, either, would you fight to prove that wrong?"

Her answer came immediately. "Yes."

His heart leaped in his chest, the steady beat so off-kilter that he was afraid Dawn must have somehow been able to feel it. "Oh, yeah?" he asked, striving to keep his voice level. "What would you do? How would you fight?"

"You already know the answer to that, Adam." Her voice was low and sultry and *dangerous*. He didn't realize just how dangerous until she placed her palm flat on his chest and began a slow, tortuous journey down his abdomen. Every movement of her fingertips over his body was both a promise and a threat. "Dirty. I fight dirty."

"Adam! What are you doing?" Phoebe's voice broke in just as Dawn grazed the top of his jeans. He jumped back, startled into immediate action, but Dawn only laughed.

"Hey, Phoebe," she said easily. "I guess you caught us."

"I didn't know you guys... You never said..." The sound of Phoebe running a hand over Gigi's head was followed by "Yes, Gigi. That's enough. You're beautiful and perfect and everything I want in the world, but you have to get *down*."

The puppy's misbehavior didn't bother Adam nearly as much as it might have a few minutes ago—and not just because Dawn had promised to fight dirty for him. He was too busy trying to discover what kind of damage control was needed now that he and Dawn had been caught in the act.

They'd have to admit their relationship. They'd have to come out in the open. They'd have to move forward as two people who were unquestionably sleeping together.

And the only thing Adam felt about any of it was profound, enthusiastic relief.

"I wish I'd have known you two were coming. I would have reserved front-row seats." Phoebe wound her arm through Adam's. "They designate a few for family members, but they fill up fast. You'll have to make do with some dusty outpost. You don't mind, do you?"

Adam's relief disappeared in a flash.

"I mean, Zeke's going to be crazy excited that you're here no matter what. And surprised. You didn't say a word this morning, you sneak."

"He's been planning it for weeks," Dawn said in a calm, easy lie. "Now that he has Uncle to lend him a hand, it seemed as good a time as any."

Phoebe paused long enough to plant an affectionate kiss on Adam's cheek. "That was really sweet of you, Adam. It's going to mean so much to him to have you here. Lately, he's been feeling...well...you know."

On the contrary, Adam *didn't* know, but he was starting to get a sense of the general lay of the land. And to be perfectly honest, he didn't feel as though he stood on stable ground. It shouldn't have been that much of a shock for him to be here today. If the bubbling voices in every direction were any indication, this was a well-attended race. Family members, friends, people who just liked being supportive—they were all here in abundance.

Because this was a normal thing to do. Run triathlons. Be supported by those you love. Live a life that didn't include twenty-four hours a day of chasing down rogue cows and fixing irrigation systems and trying to buy up the neighboring lands.

"He's feeling cooped up?" Adam suggested. When that elicited no response, he tried again. "Hog-tied? Fenced in? Imprisoned?"

"Not *imprisoned*," Phoebe protested. "Let's just say he's been feeling his lack of a social life lately."

Dawn laughed. "I tell him all the time that I'm the only real friend he has, but he thinks I'm being full of myself. I'm obviously much more important to his well-being than he realizes. Yours too, Adam."

"Oh, don't worry. I realize it just fine," he admitted. These days, it was pretty much the only thing on his mind. "I never would have come out here if it wasn't for you. Thank you."

"You're welcome," she said and left it there. She also turned her attention to Phoebe with a sharp reprimand. "Now let go of your brother's arm so Uncle can lead him to the stands. Unlike you, I don't have a day off today—and neither does Uncle." In an exact imitation of Bea's voice, she cackled and added, "Just like a Dearborn, slacking off when there's work to be done."

Phoebe burst into laughter at that, but Adam couldn't help feeling hollow. As happy as he was to be here—and as thrilled as he was to find that Uncle was exceeding expectations—he could no longer pretend there was any hope of keeping Gigi for himself. The only problem was that he couldn't admit it out loud. To acknowledge defeat, to relinquish his negligible hold on Gigi, would also mean letting Dawn go.

And that, unfortunately, was something he was finding it more and more difficult to do.

chapter

11

Dawn might not have been adept at making dinner, but she was excellent at making reservations.

"Yes, there will be four of us, and we want the best seat you have in the house. We're celebrating tonight." She pressed the phone against her shoulder and glanced over at Zeke. He was leaning against the now-empty spectator stands, but the fact that he was still on his feet was a testament to how good an athlete he was. Dawn was exhausted just thinking about how many miles he'd covered today. "Can I tell them it's your birthday? I don't think they give out congratulations-you-won-a-triathlon cake, but they do this amazing flourless chocolate thing for birthdays."

She didn't wait for an answer. The chocolate was that good. "Yes, it's a birthday. *Four* birthdays, actually. We're quadruplets."

"Make it triplets," Adam called from where he was sitting and lavishing praise on Gigi for *not* making a meal out of Zeke's sweaty running shoe. "You'll have to celebrate without me. I'd like to get back to the ranch before it gets dark."

A chorus of protests went up around them. Phoebe's

was the loudest, though how that woman had any of her voice left after all the cheering she'd done today, Dawn had no idea. Zeke had easily won the competition, but they'd been caught up in the spirit of the chase quite a few times. Her own throat felt awfully scratchy.

"It won't be the same with just the three of us," Phoebe said with a pout of her lower lip. "Come on, Adam. It's only another hour or two. What difference will it make?"

"Do you want the actual answer to that? Because I can recite a whole list—and most of it involves cattle in various states of neglect. There's no telling what's happened at the ranch in our absence. For all we know, Dawn has escaped and made it to the Canadian border by now."

"I'm sure they're fine," Phoebe protested. "They're cows. And someone would have called us by now if Dawn was making a nuisance of herself or the place was burning down."

"Are you sure about that?" Adam countered. "The Smithwoods would love to watch us go up in smoke, and if there's a fire, I'm guessing Bea Benson isn't too far away holding the match."

Dawn would have laughed out loud at this pessimistic—if accurate—summary of the situation back at Dearborn Ranch, but no one else seemed to see the irony. *She* was the one everyone assumed lived a life of chaos and intrigue, but she obviously didn't have a monopoly on it. She'd never met a family so determined to make everything more difficult than it needed to be.

As if to prove that, Phoebe's pout deepened. "I knew this would happen," she said. "I knew we couldn't just enjoy an entire day off together."

"There's no such thing as a day off when you live on a working ranch."

"The Smithwoods take days off all the time. That's what hired hands are for."

Dawn felt it was timely to intervene before things descended into a squabble. In a voice that was audible to both the hostess on the phone and all three of the Dearborn siblings, she said, "You know what? Let me place an order for pickup." Without waiting to take requests, she ordered all of her own favorites—lasagna and pasta primavera and parmesan-encrusted tilapia and an entire flourless chocolate cake to wash it all down. If any of the Dearborns didn't like it, that was too bad. She was planning a goddamned party.

"An hour?" she asked as the hostess completed the order and rattled off the total. "Yes, I can make that work. Thanks."

When she hung up, it was to find their entire party looking sheepish and ashamed of themselves. Well, Phoebe and Adam looked ashamed of themselves. Zeke mostly looked sweaty.

"It's just as easy to have the celebration back at the ranch," Dawn said in a matter-of-fact voice that was meant to rob the situation of any more drama. "Plus, this way I can pick up a whole case of cheap wine for us to share. I don't know about you guys, but there's no way I'm pairing the world's best parmesan tilapia with butterscotch schnapps."

Phoebe glanced over at her, a glint in her eye. "Wait. How do you know about the—"

For the second time, Dawn felt a need for intervention. "Phoebe, you can take Adam back to the ranch and perform all the necessary bovine labors. I'll run Zeke to my house so he can help me settle the puppies. By the time we're done, the food will be, too, and we can bring it out. Voilà! Problem solved. Chocolate decadence acquired. It's a shame she didn't believe me about the birthday thing, though. Cake is always better when it's free."

Only Adam seemed to be aware of how hard she was trying to make this work. "Dawn—" he began.

She quelled him with a bright, cheery voice. "I know. I'm being overbearing and presumptuous and foisting myself on you without invitation. But you guys have to let me come over now. Otherwise, I'm just going to be a sad, lonely, single woman eating an entire chocolate cake by herself. And I will too. I'll eat every last bite just to make you feel bad for abandoning me."

Phoebe assented to the plan. Her smile was strained and flat around the edges, but at least it was a smile.

"I don't know how much help I'm going to be at the kennel" was Zeke's contribution. "My arms won't lift all the way."

"They're puppies, Zeke, not half-ton cows," she said in a tone that brooked no argument. "Are there any wine requests, or should I just grab my favorites?"

"Dawn, we really don't need you to " Adam began again, but she cut him short. It wasn't necessary to hear the end of that sentence. They really didn't need her to patch things up. They really didn't need her to feed them. They really didn't need her to direct their lives and overstay her welcome.

Well, it was too late for that. As was usually the case, she'd already invested both her time and her emotions into this family before any of them had asked her to. They might assume she was doing this because it was in her nature to throw a party at the least provocation, but not even she could spend every minute of every day in celebration mode.

"If I agree to this, can we at least stop and grab some Gatorade on the way?" Zeke asked. He hoisted his athletic bag over his shoulder. "Wine might kill me if I don't build up a base layer of electrolytes first."

From the looks the three of them were wearing, a quick, painless wine death was preferable to continuing this conversation a minute longer.

"You know, you guys could at least pretend I haven't just ordered you to attend your own funeral," she said. "None of my parties have ever ended in death before."

Zeke was opening his mouth to argue this point, so Dawn forestalled him before he could make her feel any worse about herself. "And no, Zeke. There's no need to remind me that it's come close a few times. How was it my fault that the stripper cake we ordered for Raul's birthday two months ago wasn't gluten-free? I didn't actually expect anyone to eat it."

"What else are you supposed to do with a stripper cake?" he asked, laughing. It was a real laugh, and it was accompanied by real smiles from Phoebe and Adam.

There. Balance was restored, the universe set right again.

"If you can't think of a few seedy alternatives, then I have no use for you," she said, pressing both her hands on Zeke's sweaty back and giving him a shove in the direction of the parking lot.

❧ ❧ ❧

"Their food amounts are listed on the clipboard. Don't overfeed them, and make sure you initial after each one. Lila likes us to keep records of each feeding."

"I still don't know how I got roped into doing your job for you," Zeke grumbled as he scanned Lila's clipboard. "It's my first real day off in months, and I'm ankle deep in kibble."

"That is a very fine blend of roasted chicken, rice, and high-nutrient puppy chow, thank you very much," Dawn said primly. "Nothing but the best for the residents of Puppy Promise. You can try a bite if you want. It's not bad, especially after a hangover."

Zeke relaxed enough to laugh. "I'm not going to ask."

"That's probably for the best. And I wouldn't recommend trying the same technique at home. I doubt hay and grass would have the same effect."

Mentioning cows and their dietary habits was a mistake. Zeke's easy air dissipated in a flash. *Damn*. And after she'd been making such painstaking efforts to elicit and maintain it, too.

"Thank you for today," he said, his pencil poised above the clipboard. He made no move to either mark the page or to feed the black Lab at his feet, who was rapidly working herself up into a frenzy of anticipation. "Adam has never come to one of my races before."

"He really enjoyed it."

"Adam has *never* come to one of my races before."

"Yes, I heard you the first time. It was fun for all of us, although I'm still trying to figure out how you got in and out of that wet suit so quickly. Is it Vaseline? Or just regular lube? Adam seemed to think it was Vaseline, but I'm holding out for Astroglide. The kind you buy in bulk."

"I don't think you understand. *Adam has never come to one of my races before.*"

Dawn bit back a sigh. This wasn't a conversation she was either prepared to have or looking forward to right now. It was an important conversation, obviously, but all she really wanted was to get the puppies settled and get her hands on that chocolate cake.

"Speaking of, we'd better get moving if we plan to pick up that food while it's still hot." Dawn settled the Chihuahua she'd been cuddling back in his pen, making sure to slip him a chew toy before she moved on to the next puppy. Gunner was in a fierce chewing phase and already making headway on his dog bed. By morning, there'd be nothing but fluff and fabric as far as the eye could see. "I wonder if I should just bring this guy with us. How many puppies are too many puppies as far as Adam is concerned? Six? Seven?"

When Zeke didn't answer, his brow furrowed in a way that made him look as though he was working out a particularly difficult calculus equation, she added, "No, you're right. Chances are he'd fall in love with Gunner and decide to keep him, too. It's better not to risk it."

"It's weird," Zeke said as though she hadn't spoken. He did start feeding the Lab, though, so that was good. "He's been doing a lot of unusual things lately—making dinner and visiting with Bea and showing an interest in my well-being. Phoebe's too. He's been talking about giving her a week off to take a trip to the Yucatán with her friends. All he has to do is announce his plans to run off with his secret girlfriend, and I'll know he's been taken over by body snatchers."

It took every ounce of willpower Dawn had not to balk at that last bit, but she managed it by moving on to the next puppy, an adorable beagle with eyes like liquid amber.

"Adam has a secret girlfriend?" she asked in a tone of what she hoped was only mild interest.

Zeke snorted. "Of course not. A regular girlfriend would require him to take a few evenings off. I can't imagine how much more work a secret one would be. But not only did he offer to do my chores last night, but he sang show tunes while he did it. *Show tunes*. I can't think of anything else to account for that kind of behavior. Can you?"

Dawn saw a chance of salvation and reached for it. "Um, hello?"

"Hi?"

She waved a hand over herself. She was looking particularly good today, with a pair of stretch jean overalls layered over a white crop top. It was the kind of outfit one wore to *pretend* to work on a farm, as it was more suited for low-key clubbing at a country-western bar than actual hard labor, but that had been the whole point. Nothing drove Adam crazier than her showing up to work in the least ranch-appropriate attire possible.

"He's obviously in a good mood because he has me in his life now," she said.

Her ruse worked. Zeke took the bait. She might even have felt relieved at such an easy success if he hadn't laughed *quite* so hard and long over it.

"Dawn, you know I love you, but no man who has

to put up with you for eight hours a day is going to be happy about it," he said.

"Why not?" she asked. Even though she'd spoken in jest, the mockery in Zeke's voice caused annoyance to pluck at her nerves. "People love me. I'm nice. I'm fun."

"The word you're looking for is 'exhausting.'"

"Excuse you. I'm not the one who just ran and biked like a zillion miles today. You're much more exhausting than I am."

"I don't mean physically exhausting," he said, and with so much condescension that it took all her resolve not to step on his foot. *Hard*. "I mean emotionally exhausting."

She didn't respond, just crossed her arms and stared at Zeke until he sighed and added, "You know what I mean, so don't look at me like that. Adam obviously didn't want to celebrate with us tonight, but you kept pushing until he had no choice but to give in. That's what you do. You push and you intrude and you make a man so fed up that he'll get behind the wheel of a getaway car and help you steal a puppy just to get you to leave him alone. Couldn't you, like, scale it back a little? Just for once?"

It was the final straw, the tipping point, the place where common sense departed and her impulses took over.

Okay, yes. Dawn knew she was exhausting. She knew people got tired of her after a few months, always telling her to step back, step down, *be less*. She'd heard it so many times before—from teachers, from employers, from relatives, from friends—that she could practically recite a list of her sins in her sleep.

What she didn't understand, however, was why these particular sins were so off-putting. There were people out there who lied, who cheated, who wrote long, painstaking checks in the express lane at the grocery store. When was it universally decided that the one unforgivable offense was for a woman to be herself? Why did her desire to be accepted for who she was turn her into some kind of unlovable monster?

"Well, I think you're a chickenshit, so there." She tightened her arms across her chest. "We're even."

Zeke almost dropped the clipboard on the black Lab's head. "I'm *what*?"

"A chickenshit," she repeated. If they were going to throw out painful truths, he needed to see his as well as hers. At least she'd always been able to own who she was, even if it made other people view her as a nuisance. "I've been at your ranch for almost a month now, and I have yet to hear you mention to your brother even once how much it chafes you—how badly you want to leave. Adam is so deep in his expansion plans that he's sending me to Bea's house to uncover some kind of long-lost legal document, but I have yet to hear you raise one word of protest."

"Dawn."

"Ezekiel."

"You know it's not like that."

"I know you *think* it's not like that."

Zeke tucked the clipboard under one arm and glared down at her, but Dawn wasn't put off. He'd already done the worst he could—said the words that always made her feel like someone was trying to cut out the best pieces of her and replace them with something else. Something, well, *less*.

"I've been spending quite a bit of time with him lately, and I think he'll understand better than you realize,"

Dawn added, softer this time. "Look, my older sister is the same way. Supersmart and always on top of things. Keeps everything running without a word of complaint. Kind of makes you feel like she has more value in the tip of her pinkie finger than you have in your whole body."

Zeke continued holding himself tense, but Dawn could tell that he was listening. *For a change*.

"Tell him what you want," she urged. "Feel him out. Who knows? Maybe he'll be relieved not to have to worry about all that stuff with Bea. He can just go back to focusing on his cows."

Zeke's laugh carried no mirth. "Your sister might understand you, but I promise Adam doesn't understand anything but the ranch."

It was on the tip of her tongue to point out that Zeke was totally wrong. Adam was dedicated to his work, yes, but he was also warm. Funny. Caring. He drank like a sorority girl at a bar for the first time, couldn't resist a dare once it had been laid before him, and had fallen so much in love with a golden retriever puppy that he literally carried her around like a baby. He was goal-driven to the point of being obsessed, but she hadn't been lying about how much he'd enjoyed Zeke's race. The look of pride on his face as the announcer gave a play-by-play of the final moments had been nothing short of breathtaking.

He'd been so happy for Zeke. So glad to be there sharing it with him.

"I can't take it away from him, Dawn," Zeke said. His voice was softer—pleading. "The ranch is literally all he has. It's all he is. How could he manage it without me there to help?"

An anger unlike any Dawn had ever felt took over. The idea that a person could be boiled down to one thing—a job, a passion, a *condition*—wasn't just stupid; it was cruel.

"I don't know," she retorted. "What does everyone else out there do when someone leaves? Buy them out? Hire a few ranch hands? Work a little bit harder until a more practical solution presents itself? Jesus, Zeke—it's not prison. It's a family business."

"That shows how little you know," Zeke muttered.

Dawn opened her mouth to say more, but Zeke lifted a hand and shook his head. "Don't. I know you mean well. You *always* mean well. But you have no idea what you do, whirling in and taking over like this without thinking things through. In the past month, you've committed larceny, been chased by a man with a gun—not just once, but multiple times—and turned the entire fucking neighborhood upside down. You convinced Adam to come to my race, yes, but to what end? He'll feel guilty about the time away from the ranch for at least a week, which means I'll have to suffer through twelve-hour days to make up for it."

"You don't know that."

"Oh, I know it. I've lived with the man for twenty-eight years, and you've known him—what—all of five minutes? Yet here you stand, dressed like Old MacDonald, pretending like you know what's best for us. Well, surprise. You don't." Zeke tightened his jaw. "And don't you dare mention anything to him about this, or I'll tell him where Gigi really came from."

She held herself perfectly still, not trusting herself to move or speak or even breathe. Nothing Zeke had just said wasn't true—or wasn't something she'd heard dozens of times before—but he was supposed to be her ally, her friend.

"Don't look at me like that, Dawn. I'm only telling the truth." He crooked a smile. "And you're a *cute* Old MacDonald, if that helps."

She managed to start breathing again, but only because it was obvious that was what Zeke expected.

He slung an arm over her shoulder and gave it a light squeeze. "You don't mind, do you?" he asked. "Me being honest? I wouldn't say it to anyone else, but you're not like other girls. You don't mind hearing the truth with no sugar added."

Everything Zeke just said rankled, but Dawn knew what was expected of her. "I mean, I could use a *little* sugar."

He laughed, taking this remark as the joke she'd intended. It was obvious what he wanted—for everything to be nice and clean and easy again—but she wasn't sure it was possible after this. Zeke obviously enjoyed her company because she introduced no deep, troubling thoughts into his life. She was always happy, always fun, and never expected anything of him that he wasn't willing to give.

In other words, she was like one of the puppies currently scampering about in anticipation of dinner. Simple and adorable—and, yes, exasperating sometimes, but that was all part of the package.

"I think we'd better get these puppies fed and hit the road soon," Zeke said. As far as he was concerned, the conversation was over, the waters settled flat again. "I can feel the Gatorade starting to wear off. I need carbohydrates—and fast—or I'm going to start getting mean."

"Start?" Dawn echoed.

Zeke took this as a joke, too. With a hearty laugh, he pulled the clipboard out from under his arm and resumed his feeding duties. "Either that or I'm going to eat your miracle canine hangover cure. I'm not going to lie—the longer we stand here talking, the better it's starting to smell. You might be onto something with this after all."

chapter
12

"Three hours." Dawn walked through the front door to the ranch without knocking or ringing the doorbell or announcing her presence in any way. Despite the lack of ceremony, not one of the Dearborn siblings expressed the mildest surprise to find her there.

Since it was late in the afternoon and there was no puppy training on the schedule for the day, Adam should have been surprised. He had no right to expect her to stop by on her day off.

But she had, and he was glad.

Too glad, if the sudden spike of his heartbeat was any indication. His fingers fumbled over the fluted edge of the piecrust he was attempting.

"Three hours," she repeated when no one offered an immediate response. "That's how long it took to clear the door to Bea's basement today. Not—I tell you—to clear the basement. To literally move all the boxes and broken furniture piles that were in front of it. Did you know that wicker will disintegrate on touch if it's been sitting and rotting for twenty years?"

"Interesting," Adam murmured.

"Gross," Phoebe said from somewhere in the living room.

"I warned you not to do it" came Zeke's contribution.

Dawn released a long sigh. "Gee, thanks. I'm so glad I came here for moral support." A brief pause and an onslaught of happy puppy noises ensued. "At least a few of you are glad to see me. Hello, Uncle. Gigi, love— *down*. When you greet a person, you do it on all four legs."

Adam released a low whistle. It worked in getting Uncle to come to him, but Gigi had no intention of following orders. Ever since the day of Zeke's race, she'd been getting worse and worse at behaving herself the way a well-trained service animal should. He'd brought it up to Marcia that morning only to have the veterinarian laugh at him.

"It's a good sign, all things considered," she'd said. "It means she feels safe with you. She knows she can misbehave and not get beaten for it. Don't you, beautiful girl? You know just how to wind this man around your paw."

The conversation had driven home the truth that Adam was finally willing to admit—Gigi would never be a service dog. To force the kind of discipline necessary to get her to become one would be to crush her spirit, to change who she was at a fundamental level.

He loved her far too much to want to change her.

"There's a box of chew toys by the back door," he said as he returned his attention to the pie in front of him. He'd opted for peach, since Marcia had brought a huge box from her orchard, with extra cinnamon and a dash of bourbon to win Bea over. "See if you can redirect her to one of those."

"Ooh, look at you, using fancy dog-training words

like 'redirection.'" Dawn laughed, but he could hear her rummaging around in the wooden box he'd hammered together to house Gigi's rapidly growing collection of behavioral bribes. "You've been doing some research."

"Yes, well." He put the final touch on the pie and stepped back. "You're not the only one who spends all her free time being productive."

"Me? Productive?" All of Dawn's rummaging came to a stop.

"You just said you spent three hours at Bea's house."

"Oh, that. That doesn't count. I like Bea. Apparently, I have a thing for bitter, reluctant curmudgeons who don't want me around. Who knew?"

"Don't be silly. No one actually *likes* Bea. We tolerate her because we have to." Phoebe approached Adam from behind and placed her chin on his shoulder. "Nice work, brother dearest. That looks amazing. Are you sure we're going to waste it on an ungrateful neighbor?"

"It's not wasteful if it gets us what we want in the end." He slipped the finished product in the fridge, where it needed to sit for a few hours before he could pop it in the oven. "I'd bake her a thousand pies if I thought it would get us closer to the final sale. Wouldn't you?"

"Seeing as how I can't bake, probably not," Phoebe admitted with a laugh. "But I appreciate your commitment on my behalf."

There was a brief pause before Dawn spoke. "What about you, Zeke? Don't you think your expansion plans are worth a thousand pies?"

Adam knew something about the question was off the moment it left Dawn's lips. Like her nonscent, it carried a feeling, a sensation, a *weightiness*. So did Zeke's answer, which took a little too long in coming.

"I'll reserve judgment until I actually taste the damn thing," he said. "I've never cared for peaches."

This was the first time Adam had heard anything to that effect, but he wasn't about to start an argument over pie. Nor was he going to protest when Zeke changed the subject by asking Phoebe to help him finish checking the inventory lists.

"And then I'm heading into town to watch a movie and think about literally anything but cows," he announced in a tone that dared someone to contradict him.

"Ooh, you should go see that new one with Channing Tatum," Dawn said. "My sisters and I saw it last week. It was amazing. He's shirtless for like nine-tenths of the movie."

"Channing Tatum?" Phoebe's voice took on an audible perk. "I didn't know he had a new one out. Take me with you, Zeke, I'm begging you. I'll even spring for the large popcorn."

"But I wanted to see that one with all the explosions," Zeke complained.

Dawn laughed. "You should offer him the large popcorn *and* pretzel bites. And take your big purse so you can smuggle in a few beers. That's the only way I've ever gotten him to see a rom-com with me."

"Goddammit, Dawn. I'm trying to spend less time with my family, not more." Even Adam could tell that Zeke's sigh was offered only as a token protest. Neither of them was very good at denying Phoebe what she wanted. "I'm a grown-ass man who can't even go to the movies without dragging my little sister along."

"Oh my God. Two minutes, Zeke. You're literally two minutes older than me." Phoebe's voice began trailing off in the other direction, Zeke's footsteps not too far behind. Adam took it as a sign of his brother's capitulation. "And maybe if we hurry, we can make it a doubleheader. That way we both lose. You'll be all right without us, Adam, yeah?"

"Have fun," he said with a wave of his hand. "I'm going to finish cleaning up in here and then spend some training time with the puppies. I'd like to do some more harness work with Uncle."

He spoke lightly so his siblings wouldn't feel it incumbent upon themselves to invite him along. They did that sometimes, but it was almost always because they felt guilty leaving him alone at the house rather than an actual desire for his company. No matter how many times he told them that he preferred it here, that spending a beautiful afternoon outside with two puppies was pretty much everything a man could want, they always assumed he stayed home to wallow and brood.

Phoebe proved it by offering him an alternative. "Oh, I know!" she said. "You should have Dawn take you into town to pick up that new cattle bander we ordered. They called a few minutes ago to let us know it came in. After three hours of Bea's company, she deserves a treat."

Dawn's laugh filled the kitchen before he could offer a protest. "You think cow-related errands are a treat? Gee thanks, Phoebe. You sure know how to make a girl feel special."

"Cow-related errands and reluctant movie dates with my brother—welcome to my world," Phoebe said and popped out of the kitchen.

Adam waited only until he was sure Phoebe and Zeke were out of earshot before saying, "I'm sorry about them. You don't really have to take me to—"

Dawn cut him short with a hand on his lower back. The sudden contact caused him to jolt. He'd had no idea she was standing so close to him, but he liked the proprietary way her hand stayed in place—holding him until his heartbeat resumed a seminormal state.

"Are you kidding?" she asked, her lips so near his ear he could feel her breath move over his neck. It was both a whisper and a caress, the soft pout of her lips practically touching his skin. "After I worked so hard to get rid of those two? *Three hours*, Adam. I don't even spend that much time with my own grandparents. If I don't have at least that many orgasms this afternoon in return, I'm giving up this whole project."

There was no chance of his heartbeat doing anything normal after that. Only her hand on his back—that light, easy touch—kept him grounded in place.

"Why is it that everything you do seems to come with strings attached?" he managed. "I've never known a woman so determined to wheel and deal her way through life. You could have just helped Bea out of the goodness of your heart."

"No one has ever accused me of having a good heart before" came her prompt reply. Her hand slid lower. She wasn't *quite* groping his ass, but the case could be made. "Nice legs, sure. A great rack, of course. Unfortunately, the curves of my cardiac system have never made the list."

Bullshit. Adam had never known anyone with a better—or a bigger—heart than Dawn. She was the sort of person who had something nice to find in everyone, who gave her time and herself freely for no reason except that the spirit of generosity was ingrained into her soul. He wasn't going to argue about her legs and her boobs because, well, they were amazing, but she was mistaken if she thought that was all she had to offer.

"Does this mean you're in?" she asked, her voice low.

As if he had any choice in the matter. "Of course I'm in."

Her lips moved the fraction more needed to make contact with his neck. The kiss she planted there was soft and slow, full of tongue and promising many more delights in store. Anyone who hadn't been kissed by this woman might think that was an awful lot to promise in the ten seconds it lasted, but Adam knew better. Once her lips started moving over his body, they wouldn't stop until he could no longer remember his own name.

"Excellent. Get your shoes—if you have any left— and we'll run into town to pick up your stupid cattle bander. I'm sure the puppies will be fine without us for an hour."

"Wait. What?"

"I know how you are," she said, but with such warmth in her voice that he couldn't feel insulted. "You're the opposite of me. Work first, play later. A dog at his bone. You won't be able to give me your full attention unless you've got all the tools where they belong in your toolbox."

"I could make an exception this once," he suggested. He was a man who liked to have his to-do list wiped clean, it was true, but he was still a man. And Dawn— her breath soft on his neck, her hair tickling his cheek, her hand still trailing toward his ass—was very much a woman.

"Oh no you don't." She pulled away. "I'm not about to let you get away with anything but the full Adam Dearborn treatment. Come on. If we hurry, we'll be back in time to finish cooking this pie of yours before Zeke and Phoebe have even started their second movie."

"Why do I get the feeling it's never going to make it to Bea's house?"

Her chuckle was warm and rich. "Because I wasn't kidding when I said that food is the way to my heart. Well, one of two ways, anyway. The other takes a more direct course right up my—"

He coughed heavily. There was no way he was letting her finish that sentence while his brother and sister were somewhere inside the house. He knew most of the words for what she had in mind, and all of them would cause a hot blush to rise to his cheeks.

They'd cause other parts of his body to heat, too, but there was no help for that now. There hadn't been help for that from the moment Dawn Vasquez had entered his life.

🐾🐾🐾

"What I don't understand is why you guys don't order this stuff from Amazon like normal humans." Dawn's car zipped along the highway, the familiar twists and turns leading into Deer Park so much a part of Adam's memory that he could tell exactly where they were. "Two-day home delivery is what separates us from the apes."

Adam allowed himself to relax into his seat. He

should have known that an afternoon with Dawn would be a playful thing—an easy thing. *He* might be pining for her every second they were apart, but she was clearly here to enjoy herself.

"I love Prime shipping as much as the next guy, but I draw the line at buying specialty castration tools from Amazon." He heaved a mock sigh. "Damn my principles."

Dawn touched the brakes. "Wait—we're picking up a *castration* tool?"

"Of course." Adam felt his lips twitch into a smile. "What do you think a cattle bander is? They're very humane, I promise. All you have to do is reduce the blood flow to the testicles and they just sort of—"

She touched the brakes again, this time enough to send him lurching against the seat belt. "You monster. Those poor little cows. You're robbing them of their manhood—their prowess."

There was enough genuine horror in her voice to set him laughing. If nothing else, at least Dawn was consistent in her appreciation for masculinity in all its forms.

"Not that I spend a lot of time feeling up my puppies, but I'm pretty sure you've had Uncle neutered," he pointed out. "What about *his* prowess?"

She released a harrumph and regained her previous speed. "That's different. There are already too many unwanted dogs in this world. Besides, his job is to take care of you, not get down and dirty with any bitch who saunters by."

"Poor Uncle. He'll never know what he's missing. Getting down and dirty is my favorite thing to do."

"You're such a liar," she said, laughing. "I just can't

believe you're going to pick up something literally designed to remove a cow's testicles and then take me back to your house and fuck me senseless. It seems cruel. Like eating cake in front of a dieting person or—*Oh shit*."

This time, her touch on the brakes was more like a slam. Even though he was buckled in, Adam's hand shot out to catch himself on the dashboard. He fully expected to hear the screech of metal or to feel the car come sliding to a halt on the side of the highway, but no sooner had Dawn slowed down than the engine revved and they lurched forward once again.

"What is it?" he asked, his voice sharp with anxiety. It wasn't often that he felt encumbered by his blindness, but moments of danger were one of the exceptions. Until he knew what was going on, he was powerless to come to Dawn's aid. "What happened? Did we hit an animal?"

"No, but an animal is trying to hit us. Hold on tight, Adam. I can outrun him, but I have to speed a little to do it."

"A little?" he asked as they started racing even faster. Despite the obviously high rate of speed they were undertaking, he risked laying a hand on Dawn's thigh. It was rigid with tension, her attention so focused on the task of driving that she didn't seem to notice his touch. "Dawn, relax. Tell me what's going on. Who is *him*? And why is he trying to hit us?"

She didn't answer. He thought for a moment that she was too intent on the task at hand, that she had to concentrate on the road or risk their imminent death, but there was something deliberate about her silence.

"Dawn?" he prodded. "It's not fair to keep me in the dark. You know I can't assess this situation for myself."

She released a soft curse. "I know, Adam. I'm sorry. It's just—" She heaved a sigh. Some of the tension lifted from her body, though their speed stayed exactly where it was. "It's this guy. He sort of…lies in wait for me."

He bolted upright in his seat, his hand falling away. "He lies in wait for you? As in, this has happened before?"

"A few times, yes." She swerved to the right and beeped her horn in a quick, friendly staccato. "Thank you, semi-truck driver. You're a doll for letting me by. See? I'm already four SUVs and one hauler ahead of him. A few more minutes, and he'll be nothing but a blur in the distance. I don't think he does a very good job maintaining his engine."

"His engine?" Adam echoed. He was still trying to process what Dawn was telling him—and how coolly she was doing it. The last time he checked, a man lying in wait to chase a woman down the highway was something to be alarmed about.

"Yeah. I don't pretend to be a wizard when it comes to cars, but even I know to top up the oil and spring for the new air filter every year or so. My dad's really insistent about stuff like that. He wouldn't let me or my sisters take our driver's tests until we learned how to change a tire on our own." Her laugh, at least, was shaky. It was oddly comforting to know she could show *some* fear. "He didn't want us to be at the mercy of any crackpot with a truck on the side of the road. Sorry, Dad."

"How many times has this happened?" Adam asked, his voice grim.

"This is technically the fourth."

"And you know him?"

Dawn didn't answer.

It was all he needed to hear—or not-hear, as the case turned out. "You know him."

"I don't *know him* know him," she protested. "He's not a crazed ex-lover or anything like that. He's, well…"

Adam froze. He knew that tone. He recognized that tone. It was the same tone Phoebe had used whenever she'd gotten in trouble at school and didn't want him to know about it. He'd never gotten angry with her for skipping classes or talking back to her teachers—and he definitely skimped in the punishment department—but that hadn't seemed to make a difference. He was older and ostensibly wiser, which meant that the lines were drawn and there was nothing he could do about it.

He hadn't cared for it then, and he didn't care for it now either. He wasn't that old and he didn't feel particularly wise, but the barriers were there all the same.

It was bad enough coming from Phoebe, but from *Dawn*…

As she usually did, Dawn both surprised and delighted him with her frankness.

"I lied to you, Adam, and I'm sorry." This time, it was *her* hand that found its way to *his* thigh. She probably found him just as tense as she'd been, though for entirely different reasons. "I didn't find Gigi abandoned on the side of the road. She was chained up in that rotter's backyard—though how anyone could call it a backyard is beyond me. It was more like a dirt pit, without any shade or any water or even a place where she could comfortably lie down. He had her chained so tightly that she could barely move."

Every muscle in Adam's body hardened. "He *what*?"

"Her little body was heaving—with the heat and the

dehydration and the fact that the chains were literally pinning her down." Dawn drew a deep breath. "I tried calling animal control, but they weren't any help. They said I could lodge a formal complaint, and that they'd process it through the normal channels, but it would have taken *weeks* for them to get around to checking on her. She didn't have weeks to spare, so I made Zeke help me steal her."

The car had slowed considerably by this time, so Adam could only assume the moment of danger had passed.

"I don't regret it," she said, her voice heavy with meaning. "I'd do it again in a heartbeat. That man had no business owning a dog if he meant to mistreat her like that. If he hadn't had a gun, I might have given him a strong piece of my mind."

"A *gun*?"

She ignored him. "And the truck chases aren't that bad—really, they aren't. The first one took me by surprise, I'll admit, but I think he's only trying to intimidate me. He never does anything but flash his lights and gun his engine."

"Stop the car."

"Adam, I know it sounds crazy and totally irresponsible, but it wasn't. Something had to be done for her."

"Stop the car," he repeated.

"I'm not going to apologize for it. I *am* sorry about lying to you, and we probably should have told Sheriff Jenkins right away rather than make up that story about her being your support dog, but I only wanted to get her somewhere safe. The rest was just details."

"Dawn, for the love of everything, will you please pull the car over to the side of the road?"

She eased up on the gas but didn't stop. "Why?"

"Because I'm asking you to."

It was the sort of comment that drove Phoebe and Zeke crazy—this autocratic demand for compliance. It was also the sort of comment that drove a wedge between them, since Adam was always the one who had to make them. But Dawn didn't take offense. Nor did she hesitate. The click of the blinker was on for only a few seconds before the car crunched to halt on the side of the highway.

"Does Zeke know about this?" Adam asked.

"About the man? Yes. I wanted to warn him in case he started getting followed, too."

"And he didn't do anything to stop him?"

"Well, no." A note of genuine curiosity crept into Dawn's voice. "Why? Is that what you're going to do?"

"Damn straight it is." He unclipped his seat belt and stepped out of the car. "With any luck, he'll see us and stop."

The whir of traffic zooming by whipped up the air into a mix of hot asphalt and dirt, but Adam didn't mind as much as he probably should have. He was far too busy trailing one hand on the car, following the line of it until he reached the trunk.

And then he leaned against it to wait.

It took Dawn only a few seconds to join him, the press of her body next to his giving the car a little push. "This is my fight as much as it is yours," she said. "I hope you aren't going to tell me to get back in the car."

"I'm not. I could use the backup."

"Oh. Okay. Good." She paused a moment before giving him a traffic update. "There's no sign of his truck yet, but there's a good chance he's broken down somewhere a few miles back. I wasn't kidding about how easy it is to outrun him. Honestly, if you were planning on chasing a woman down, wouldn't you get a tune-up first?"

Adam was forced into a laugh. "I'd like to think that any woman-chasing I did would be entirely consensual and occur either in a bar or a bed, but I guess I'm unusual in that regard."

The shift of the car seemed to indicate that she'd turned to face him. It was a theory that held when it took her a good twenty seconds to respond. He could almost feel her nonstare.

When she finally spoke, her question took him aback. "*Have* you ever chased a woman, I wonder?"

Although it technically only required a simple yes or no, there were an awful lot of layers to unpack beneath a question like that one—far too many to discuss while standing on the side of a highway waiting to confront a gun-toting madman, at any rate. The truthful answer— no—wasn't the whole picture. If he was being perfectly honest, he'd chase Dawn right now, pursuing her with every ounce of strength and determination he had, if he didn't think it would be criminal to catch her.

Dawn Vasquez wasn't a woman to be tied down. His favorite thing about her was how free she was, how unapologetic about everything she did. She was some- one who wouldn't blink at the thought of being chased by a man with a gun, who'd steal an abused puppy when it needed to be done, who'd tackle runaway cows and cranky old ladies and go home smiling each time. She'd been to extraordinary places, met extraordinary people, made extraordinary love.

In other words, she was worth chasing.

"I've always left the running to Zeke," he said by way of answer. It wasn't even close to what he wanted to say, but it had to be enough. There was nothing he could offer, no future the two of them shared, where her way of life wouldn't have to be sacrificed for his.

That was one thing he could give her—the one thing he could never ask. The only way he'd be able to live with himself was if he refused to throw the rope that would catch her forever.

"Well, that's probably for the best because there's no running now," Dawn said as tires screeched in the distance. They were followed by a waft of burned rubber and the rattle of an engine that *definitely* wasn't running at its peak. "He's here."

Adam pushed himself off the trunk and did his best to look like a man who was accustomed to confronting bullies. Since he wasn't, the best he could do was cross his arms and wait.

Dawn touched his shoulder. "It's him all right, and he doesn't look pleased to see me. I can't see a gun, but that doesn't mean he's not packing."

He nodded his thanks. "Noted."

He waited only until he could smell the man drawing close. Unlike Dawn, this man's scent was a *definite* presence, pungent and festering in damp bodily crevasses. "Hello, there," he said in as pleasant a voice as he could muster. "Do I have the pleasure of addressing the previous owner of a certain golden retriever puppy?"

The polite address must have taken the man off guard because he offered a bewildered grunt before directing his attention toward Dawn. "I knew it was you. I been waiting for you. You're that bitch who stole my—"

"Bitch?" Dawn suggested.

Adam had to choke back a laugh. This wasn't supposed to be a comical confrontation, but Dawn never did anything according to script.

"Yes, this is Dawn," Adam said before she could manage to derail him further. "She stole the animal at my request."

A spit bubble of a whistle sounded from between the man's lips. "Your what?"

"My request." Adam untucked one of his hands and held it out. He wasn't excited about making contact with a man who obviously hadn't seen the soapy side of a shower in some time, but he was hoping to make this as painless as possible. "When she told me about the puppy's condition, I had her bring the animal directly to me."

The man didn't take his hand, which Adam could only attribute to his bad manners. This theory bore out when the man said in a tone dripping with belligerence, "What the hell are you talking about? All I know is this bit...I mean, *chick* broke into my property and stole what's mine."

"Stole?" Adam echoed blankly.

"Yes. Stole. It's trespassing, that's what it is. Trespassing and robbery. I know my rights. I want my goddamned animal back."

"Of course, of course. I was wondering why we hadn't heard from you yet." He turned in Dawn's general direction. "Dawn, please tell me you informed this gentleman where he could collect the puppy."

"Oh. Um." Dawn paused only slightly before picking up on his intention—or at least the important parts of it. "I forgot?"

"Forgot!" Adam threw up his hands and sighed. "*Forgot*. I am so sorry, sir. She always seems to be forgetting something. She's new. In fact, we only hired her on a trial basis. I'm afraid things aren't looking good for her now."

"Oh, please don't fire me," Dawn protested. The waver in her voice could have been taken as a piece of supreme acting, but Adam knew for a certainty that she was only quelling her laughter. "Not when I was finally starting to get the hang of things. I'll do better next time. Honestly, I will. Right, Mr...? Um, well... You see, I think I forgot..."

Adam sighed and shook his head. "You don't even remember his name, do you?"

"No." Her voice took on a hangdog innocence. "But I'm sure it's something nice."

"My name is Murphy Jones, dammit, but I don't see what that has to do with—"

"Oh, that *is* nice."

There was such feminine sweetness to the way she spoke that Murphy cleared his throat and waited to see what else she might have to throw his way. Unfortunately for him, it wasn't Dawn pitching this bullshit. That privilege belonged to Adam.

"Well then, Mr. Jones. You have my sincerest apologies for the lack of communication, and you can trust that Dawn will be severely reprimanded for her error."

"All I want is my goddamned—"

"Puppy back. Yes, I know. You're more than welcome to come collect her at Dearborn Ranch, where she's been receiving her rehabilitation."

Dawn drew in a breath at Adam's use of his actual home and business, but she didn't say anything to ruin the game. If he ever took to a life of crime, she was the exact person he wanted at his side. Bold, brilliant, beautiful...

With a start, he forced himself to focus on the task at hand. This wasn't the time to extol Dawn's less-than-moral virtues.

"Of course, given the misunderstanding, we'll reduce our usual fees by ten percent," he said smoothly. "That should represent a savings of... Ah, Dawn? I don't suppose you have the total figure handy, do you?"

"Four thousand five hundred and sixty-four dollars," she said with admirable promptness. "And fifty-six cents, but we can just drop that."

Adam nodded. "There you go. Ten percent off will save you four hundred and fifty-six bucks. Not bad, considering the puppy's state when she was brought in. The antibiotics alone set you back several thousand. Will that be cash or check?"

"Now, see here—"

"We also offer payment plans, but you'll need to provide us with your social security number so we can do a credit check first."

Adam felt Murphy draw close. It was a move designed to intimidate, he was sure, a puffed-up chest pressing near to his own, but Adam pretended not to notice.

"We also provide high-nutrient puppy food that you can purchase directly from us, or you can make your own arrangements with the feed store in town. Either way, we'll need you to sign the contract stating your intentions to continue her care plan."

"Antibiotics? Payment plan? Contract?" The man's breath was warm and sour and filled with flecks of his spittle, but Adam didn't back down. "I didn't ask nobody for any of that."

"*You* may not have, but my good friend Harold Jenkins at the County Sheriff's Department did." The game was up, Adam now determined to end this. As much fun as it was to taunt a man who clearly didn't know a bluff when it stood up to him, making sure Dawn and Gigi were safe was the real focus here. "If you want your puppy back, you can either cover the full cost of her treatment, or you can take it up with him. Those are your options."

"But I didn't… You can't do this—"

"I can and I have," Adam said, his jaw tight. "I don't have any cards on me, and we both know how useless my associate here is, but if you have a pen, you can take down my name and address for the payment. It's Adam Dearborn of Dearborn Ranch. We're located at—"

"I'm not giving you five thousand dollars for my own fucking dog!"

"You're right. You aren't. You're going to turn around, get back in your truck, and drive back to whatever miserable hole it is you crawled out of." He could feel Dawn straighten next to him, her stance echoing his own. "You won't stalk this woman, and you won't make any attempts to see or touch that puppy ever again. Men like you don't deserve to be anywhere near animals. Or women, for that matter."

"You fucking bastard. You have no idea who you're dealing with, do you?" The spittle flew with renewed vigor, but Adam didn't back down. He withdrew a handkerchief from his back pocket and carefully wiped his mouth instead.

"Yes, I do. I took your measure the second that puppy was placed in my arms. Anyone who treats a vulnerable animal like that is both a fool and a coward." He allowed a slow smile to spread across his face. "The real question is, do you have any idea who *you're* dealing with?"

The answer to that was an obvious *no*. Murphy had clearly stepped out of his truck expecting to intimidate the pair of them, to leverage their fear into getting his own way. But that was his first mistake. Adam Dearborn wasn't someone who intimidated easily.

Neither was Dawn Vasquez.

"I'm not really as dumb as I let on," she said as if to prove it. "I know where you live, Murphy Jones. I know you carry illegal firearms. I know you haven't paid your taxes in years, and we both know that Sheriff Jenkins would love any excuse he can find to haul you in."

Murphy's only response to that was a glib "fuck you."

"No, my friend. Fuck you." She touched Adam's arm. "Come on, Adam. Let's go. I don't want to waste another minute of my life on this scumbag."

He gave a curt nod and made a move to return to the passenger seat. He had no idea how much of what she'd just said was true, but she sounded convincing enough to him. It would take a much stronger man than he—and, he was guessing, Murphy Jones—to stand up to the fire in that woman's voice.

But she wasn't done. Before she made it very far, she halted and added, "Oh. And if I ever drive by your house to find another animal being abused, you'd better pray that I decide to call in the authorities rather than take matters into my own hands again."

Murphy heaved an inarticulate grunt. "I ain't scared of you."

"You should be," Dawn said simply. There was no sign of emotion in her voice, no tremor of nerves as she confronted a man who had to be at least twice her size. "I make a mean Molotov cocktail, and my aim is impeccable. Good day, Mr. Jones. I hope I never have cause to meet you again."

There was nothing Adam could say or do to top that, so he didn't even try. All he did was raise his hand in a cheerful farewell and slide back into the car. The sound of the truck roaring to life behind them was followed by a screech of tires and a honk of several horns as Murphy presumably pulled back onto the road.

Dawn wasn't long in joining him. However, she didn't, as he expected, get behind the wheel. No sooner did he register the passenger door being opened than he felt the warm press of her body pouncing onto his lap.

"What the—?" he began.

The door slammed shut, shaking the small car and trapping them both in place. With a finesse that had to be practiced, Dawn reached down and pulled the lever that moved the seat back as far as it could go. The extra legroom was nice, but it hardly mattered when she began ruthlessly kissing him.

Dawn was always a passionate woman, but the way her lips moved over his went beyond anything they'd shared before. She didn't swoop in with her tongue, the way she did when it had been a long time since their last meeting. Nor did she nibble playfully at his lips, the way she preferred when trying to rouse him to action only minutes after he'd already climaxed. This was a soft, warm, heavy planting. Her lips pressed down on his as though she were breathing life into him—or possibly breathing life out of him. He couldn't tell which, and to be perfectly honest, he didn't care. If she was a succubus sent to destroy him, to pull the very air out of his lungs and the life out of his chest, then so be it.

Adam couldn't think of a better way to go.

But she pulled back just as his senses were starting to grow dizzy, her hands pressed against his cheeks to hold him in place. He was pinned and trapped at every turn. She straddled him with thighs bare and hot from the summer sun, the full weight of her body on top of his. She was looking at him too, he knew. There was no other reason for her to hold him like that, so quiet and yet so alive. Her pulse thrummed against his leg, her breath coming hard and fast, her heat intoxicating.

But still she didn't move.

"That was the single most erotic experience of my life," she said. "I swear to God, if you so much as flicked my nipple right now, I'd come screaming on the spot."

A devilish urge to test that theory took him by force, but Dawn had planned her ambush too well. He could barely even twitch his arm, let alone pull it out from under her.

"I had no idea you had a thing for stale tobacco and men who sweat whiskey," he said, since words were the only tool she'd left him. "I'll start my transformation immediately."

The punishment for his insouciance was another one of those long, crushing, soul-searing kisses. She managed to slip a little tongue in this time, too—a slow, careful opening of her mouth against his. She was

inviting him in, tantalizing him. Every part of her was
hot and wet and somehow linked with the coiling, curl-
ing urgency that thrummed in his veins. He had no idea
where she ended and he began.

Nor did he care. By the time the kiss was over, he
knew down to his toes that if she so much as flicked his
nipple, *he'd* come screaming on the spot.

"No man has ever done anything like that for me
before," she said. Her breath came short and panting, but
she had yet to relinquish her hold on him in the slightest.
"Stepping up. Stepping *down*."

Maybe it was because all the blood was leaving his
brain, but that bit didn't quite make sense. "Wait. Did I
step up or down?"

"You did both, you idiot."

"I did?"

"Yes, Adam. You did. You stepped up to protect
me—and then stepped down to let me finish the job."

Although there wasn't much he could do to facilitate
whatever sort of interlude was about to happen inside
a hot, stuffy car on the side of a very public highway,
Dawn was more than happy to pick up the slack. She
thrust a hand between them, not stopping until she
reached the fly of Adam's jeans.

In her distraction, he got his own hands free. They
gravitated naturally toward her hips, which were pressing against his with an urgency that neither one of them
could deny. As usual, she was wearing a skirt that was
far too short to make ranch work or puppy training reasonable. Her underwear was even less so. There was a
bit of lace, a strap or two holding it on, and that was it.
The rest was all glorious curves and smooth, hot skin.

He slid his fingers around until he was cupping her ass in two hands. It would have only taken a few small adjustments for Adam to remove his jeans and be inside her, but he held back. For one, he didn't have any protection on him. For another, the car seemed an awfully public place for this. Sheriff Jenkins would have a field day.

"You did say these windows are tinted, right?" he asked as Dawn's hand slid up and down the front of his fly. She had a knack for knowing just how to press her fingers to reduce him to nothing more than a pile of nerve endings. "Very dark?"

"Dark enough for me, anyway," she said with a laugh. "I meant what I said, by the way. Thank you for rescuing me."

A growl escaped Adam's lips, but he wasn't sure if it was the memory of Murphy Jones that elicited it, or if it was just that Dawn did that thing with her fingers again. Considering how good she felt in his hands, he assumed it had more to do with the latter.

"Thank *you* for rescuing Gigi," he said. "You're a good person, Dawn Vasquez. Probably the best one I know."

"I'm not," she said. "But thank you all the same."

Her thanks was more than enough to set the seal on their exchange, but she followed it up by adjusting her body so that there was nothing but delicious friction between them. Every part of him yearned to free himself and do this the right way—hard and fast, careful and slow, over and over—but he hadn't been kidding about that protection thing.

"Wait," he said with a low groan. It took all his willpower to resist the sweet, intoxicating pull of her, but he managed it. He feared her skin would tell the tale of his restraint, the press of his fingers probably leaving a mark, but she didn't murmur a word of complaint. "Unless you've got condoms in your glove box, we're going to need to put this on hold."

She didn't, as common sense demanded, pull her body back from his. If anything, she tilted her hips even more, her breasts pressing up into his face and burying him with their pillowy softness.

"I'm good if you are," she said. "I recently started the pill."

Although nothing would have delighted him more than to take this woman right here and now, his own common sense refused to budge. It was the Adam Dearborn way—duty and safety first, pleasure second. Not very glamorous, sure, but much less likely to result in the spread of HPV.

"We still can't," he said. "What about—?"

"I'm good if you are," she repeated. "I got tested about six months ago and received the A-OK."

The A-OK sounded wonderful. The A-OK sounded like everything he wanted in this world.

"There's nothing standing in the way of us doing whatever we want, whenever we want to," she said. "Personally, I think we should do it soon. I don't know how much more suspense I can take."

He didn't either, but he still managed to croak out, "But what about your other partners since then?"

Her movements stopped, her thighs straddling his. For what had to be the first time in the entirety of their relationship, she seemed unsure of herself—hesitant. He might have regretted his practicality in asking such a question except that it was the exact sort of thing that made Dawn such a delight. She didn't hold back from being who she was, didn't shy away from the fact that her generous sexuality was as much a part of her as her generous heart.

Which was why her next words came as such a blow.

"There haven't been any other partners, Adam," she said and ran a hand through his hair, tucking a loose strand behind his ear. From where he sat, it felt like a loving gesture—a possessive one. The kind a woman might give a boyfriend or husband of long standing. "Since the moment we met, there's only been you."

The seat fell back with a sudden start. Adam went from being mostly vertical to knocked flat in less time than it took to blink—and in more ways than one. His hands fell away from Dawn's body, his head whirling as he took stock of his bearings.

He was in her car, he knew. He'd just reduced a man to an angry, sputtering mess. He was harder than he'd ever been in his entire life.

And he also felt as though the world had suddenly started spiraling out of control.

"Oops. Sorry." Dawn laughed and positioned herself more comfortably astride him. "I meant that to be a lot smoother. I forgot how fast these seats move. You okay?"

It took him a moment to find his tongue, a moment longer to muster the word he knew he needed to say.

"No."

"Did you hit your head?" She leaned down and planted a kiss on the center of his forehead. Like the hair ruffle, it was an incredibly romantic gesture—and one so much unlike her that he felt the world starting to tilt again. "Don't worry. I can fix that. I know just where to kiss you to make you all better."

As if to prove it, she slithered down his body, her movements neat and agile and designed to make him forget his own name. And he wanted to do that—he really did. He wanted to abandon himself to Dawn's laughter and light, let her kiss away all his troubles, enjoy a quickie in her car on the side of a busy highway.

"No," he said again.

This time, she took note, halting the tug of her hands on his fly. Adam struggled to a sitting position. Instead of feeling intoxicated, the stuffy heat of the car was starting to feel overwhelming.

"I'm sorry, but do you think we could open a window?" he asked.

"Of course." Her reply was swift and free of embarrassment, and she made quick work of getting a semi-cool breeze moving into the car. "Is that better?"

"No," he said for the third time. It wasn't exactly a lie—the temperature was much more bearable, yes, but he was still finding it difficult to gain his bearings.

"Adam, are you okay?" Dawn scooted off his lap and climbed into the driver's-side seat, moving over the console and emergency brake with easy agility. "You look really pale. Let me get the air-conditioning going, and then we can—"

He stopped her with a hand on her arm. "I'm fine. The temperature is fine. It's just..." He shook his head in an effort to collect his thoughts. They felt scattered, abandoned, *lost*. "Is that true? What you said?"

"What I said?" she echoed.

"About you and me. About your partners." He

swallowed. "That you haven't been with anyone but me in the past six months."

"Oh. Um. Yes." Her voice carried a note of light anxiety. "Why? That's not a problem, is it? You don't... mind?"

He could have laughed out loud at such a ridiculous question. Did he mind that the woman he was sleeping with—a woman he admired and adored—wasn't sharing her bed with other people? Did he mind that he was the only man to feel her squirm underneath him, to capture her screams of ecstasy with his kiss? Did he mind that the best thing that had ever happened to him was his and his alone?

He wasn't so unique that the thought of having Dawn to himself didn't thrill and delight him. Under any other circumstances, he'd have pulled her back into his lap and shown her exactly how thrilled and delighted he was.

But that wasn't the deal between them. That wasn't the game.

"Adam, don't look so worried," Dawn said. Even though they no longer needed the air conditioner, she started the car and shot a blast of cold air out the vents. The hum of the engine and the coolant masked any detectable emotion in her voice, making it difficult for him to get an accurate read on her. "I don't mind if you've been seeing other women. Exclusivity isn't a conversation we had."

It was on the tip of his tongue to tell her that of course he hadn't been seeing any other women, that like her, he'd been faithful from the moment they first met. Not only was serial monogamy an intrinsic part of his nature, but what man could even consider kissing another woman once he'd felt Dawn Vasquez's lips give way under his? The idea of seeing anyone else—of *being* with anyone else—was ludicrous to the point of being laughable.

In fact, he doubted whether he'd ever be able to fully recover once Dawn left his life for good. And he didn't just mean the sex. Yes, it would be difficult to find anyone so uninhibited and explosive and, well, fulfilling, but those weren't everything.

He'd never find anyone who made him laugh like she did. Who filled his days with a light he'd never known was missing. Who gave his life meaning and purpose beyond the gates of Dearborn Ranch.

Dearborn Ranch—his first life, his first love, and the worst thing in the world he could tie Dawn down to.

Fuck. The realization hit him harder than the blast of cold air, chilling him to the bone. What he'd never find again was a woman he loved even half as much as he loved this one.

"Why?" he found himself asking. His lips felt dry, and it took almost everything he had to get the word out. He already knew that he'd fallen too hard and too fast for Gigi, and that letting her go would mean ripping the heart out of his chest. It would hurt, but it had to be done.

But to add Dawn to that pain, to listen as she faded in the distance, would end him.

"Why didn't we have the conversation? Well, I presume it's because there was no need. I mean, it's obviously not something you're ready for. Not," she added quickly, "that I'm judging you for it. You're an attractive, virile man. I'd be more surprised to find that you *don't* have hordes of women lining up to take advantage of you."

It was just like her to say something so easy and generous, but Adam forced himself to brush that part aside. What he wanted to know—what he *had* to know—was why she'd put all other men aside for him.

"No, why haven't you slept with anyone else?" he asked. His voice didn't sound like his own, but at least it didn't sound how he felt. Wild. *Desperate.*

He felt her shrug next to him before she began tapping a random beat on the steering wheel. "I didn't want to."

"Why?" he persisted. He had to know. He had to understand.

The tapping stopped. "Because you're enough."

All of the air left his lungs at once. It was such a simple thing for her to say—such a normal collection of words—that emptiness shouldn't have been his first reaction at hearing them. If anything, he should have been filled, buoyed, delighted.

He wasn't.

The woman he loved thought he was enough. The woman he loved wanted only him.

The woman he loved was categorically, devastatingly *wrong*.

"Oh," he said flatly, fearful of what would happen if he loosened the rein on his emotions even a little. "That's nice. Thank you."

"So…are we good?" Dawn's voice was equally flat, equally controlled. "We'll keep using condoms, keep this conversation in the wings where it belongs?"

"Yeah. That's probably for the best."

He almost crossed his fingers in an attempt to draw as much luck around him as he could. He needed Dawn to put the car in drive. He needed her to take them to town, where the shiny new cattle bander would force any and all thoughts of intimacy out of their minds. Otherwise, there was a good chance he'd tell her what he was really thinking.

You're enough for me, too.

It was an easy enough sentence to say—full of meaning yet promising nothing—but he knew he wouldn't be able to stop there.

Dawn was enough for him. She was everything to him. She was the first thing he thought about in the morning and the last thing he dreamed of at night.

And he couldn't, shouldn't, *wouldn't* ask her to share in a life as small and demanding as his. Not because he was afraid she'd say no, but because there was a chance, however remote, that she'd say yes.

"Well, that felt good, didn't it?" Dawn asked, her voice bright. She also did all those things he'd been hoping for—buckled her seat belt and got the car moving again. "Not as good as a quick fuck on the side of the road, obviously, but I wish you could have seen the look on Murphy's face when you threatened to tattle to Sheriff Jenkins."

Adam relaxed into his seat and gave himself over to the familiar comfort of Dawn's playfulness. He should have known that she wouldn't fall into maudlin tears or berate him for not saying what was in his heart. This feeling of complete and utter heartbreak might be new for him, but she'd seen enough of this world and its inhabitants to be able to move on with her life.

And moving on with her life was exactly what Adam needed her to do. Not for his sake, but for hers. She was a woman who deserved to reach incredible heights, to experience everything this world had to offer with joy and enthusiasm.

He couldn't be the reason she settled for anything less than extraordinary.

"I didn't tattle," he protested, his tone matching hers. "I threatened in a highly masculine and intimidating way."

She laughed before pressing her foot heavily on the gas and shooting them into traffic. "Well, whatever you call it, it was a glorious thing to behold. I'll always consider you my white knight, Adam Dearborn."

He made a face. "Please don't. If there's one thing I can promise you, it's that I'm not the hero you've been looking for."

She paused. The exigencies of traffic might have been demanding her attention, but Adam had the feeling there was more to her silence than that.

"Don't worry," she eventually said. "If there's one thing I know, it's that fairy-tale endings are never everything they're cracked up to be."

chapter
13

It was just like Dawn's sisters to know exactly when to show up with fun surprises and serious distractions.

"It's about time you got home!" Sophie yanked open the front door to the home they'd once shared just as Dawn was about to slip her key in. Her sister had a bottle of champagne in one hand, her whole body vibrating with some unknown excitement. "We were about to give up and start drinking without you."

Dawn blinked, taking in the sight of her sister with a slightly bemused air. It was always nice to see her, yes, and she'd never say no to hand-delivered Veuve Clicquot, but she was still reeling from her day with Adam.

"Hello to you, too, Soph," she managed. "What's the party for?"

Lila appeared next to Sophie and dropped an airy kiss on Dawn's cheek. "Have you ever needed a reason for a party?"

Actually, yes. Contrary to popular opinion, Dawn didn't regularly crack fifty-dollar bottles of champagne and invite everyone she knew to drink it with her. She liked parties, it was true. Most people did. They also liked champagne and having a good time and the occasional bout of casual sex. None of these things made her an anomaly.

To hear the people in her life tell the tale, however, everything Dawn did was completely and utterly frivolous. With her sisters, it wasn't so bad, since they assumed her frivolity took the form of fun-filled sprees of drink and dance. With Adam, though…

She took a deep breath and forced a smile, since to do anything else would only open the floodgates to questions she had no intention of answering.

Adam sees me exactly the way everyone else does, and that's all there is to it. It didn't mean anything. He was allowed to sleep with all the women he wanted, share any parts of himself he felt inclined to, hide any parts he wanted to keep tucked away. In fact, that probably explained what he was doing with her in the first place. With Dawn Vasquez, what you saw was what you got. She promised a good time, a quick fuck, easy intimacy with no strings attached—and that was exactly what he asked of her. Nothing more, nothing less.

She wasn't going to punish him just because somewhere along the way, she'd made the mistake of falling for him.

"You're right," she said brightly. Her smile felt like it was about to split her face, but she wasn't going to look this gift champagne in the mouth. Not today, at any rate. "I don't need a reason to party. Crack that sucker open and blast some Lily Allen. We haven't had a feminist sing-off in ages."

Sophie pulled the bottle out of her reach, taunting her with the radiant happiness shining out of her eyes.

Harrison had gotten back to town a few days ago, so Dawn could only imagine that they'd been reunioning harder than two people had ever reunioned before. Sophie *always* glowed like that when he returned from his fire crew.

"It just so happens that we're here on a mission," Sophie said. "We've got a surprise for you."

"A surprise?" Dawn echoed. In the normal way of things, she also loved surprises, but she wasn't sure how many more of those she could take today. The look on Adam's face when she'd admitted her fidelity had been enough to last a lifetime. "What kind of surprise?"

"One that's hopefully going to take care of a few of those bags under your eyes." Lila swung her key ring around her finger and grabbed the oversized beige purse she carried everywhere. "No offense, Dawn, but you're looking a little peaked."

Peaked was polite Lila-speak for looking like hell—a thing Dawn had been fully able to ascertain for herself in the rearview mirror on the way home. Her skin was pale, and her mascara showed an alarming tendency to run.

"Thanks, Sis. I feel a little peaked."

"This doesn't have anything to do with that guy, does it?" Sophie asked with an insight Dawn would have gladly dispensed with.

"Which guy?" she asked. As if just remembering his existence, she added, "You mean Adam?"

Sophie nodded and watched her. Lila's gaze became downright dangerous. If Dawn wanted to get out of this day intact, she was going to have to tread carefully.

"After the things we did in my car today, I definitely hope not," she said with a toss of her hair. It had grown sweaty and shiny with the heat, its usual bounce flattened to match her spirits, but she pretended not to notice. "In fact, it's better if one of you drives to wherever we're going until I can get that thing detailed."

Lila's eyes widened, but Sophie just laughed and linked her arms through Dawn's. "Let's take Lila's car," she said. "That way she can drive…and you can tell me all the sordid details."

🐾 🐾 🐾

"Uh, guys?" Dawn blinked as Lila lifted her hands away from Dawn's eyes, taking a moment to adjust to the suddenly bright lights. "I hate to break it to you, but an empty living room in an empty house isn't a surprise. It's depressing."

A cork popped as Sophie opened the bottle of champagne and began liberally pouring it out into three plastic flutes. "There. I filled yours to the top. *Now* it's a celebration."

Dawn accepted the glass but didn't sip, looking around the house with interest. Her sisters had pulled out all the stops to make this an affair worth noting, even going so far as to tie a blindfold around her eyes and make her swear not to count the stoplights to guess where they were going.

For a brief moment, Dawn's heart had swelled with the thought that Adam had somehow gotten to her sisters, asked them to intervene on his behalf so he could pull out a grand, romantic gesture fit for the movies. But that moment hadn't only been brief; it had also been foolhardy. Things like that didn't happen to her. Men liked her just fine. A few of them had even loved her.

But the ease with which she slipped into their lives was matched only by the ease with which she eventually slipped back out.

So as soon as *that* moment of madness had passed, Dawn had settled back and allowed her sisters to lead her to the supersecret surprise. Which, as it turned out, was this house.

It was a nice enough place, if a little on the suburban side. She watched enough HGTV to know that features like vaulted ceilings and quartz countertops were a thing to be valued, but it all looked a little tame for her tastes.

"Okay, I give," she said. "What am I looking at?"

"Welcome to the future home of the Ford family," Sophie announced in her best television anchor voice. "It provides over two thousand square feet of modern living, complete with walk-in closets on both floors and a pantry big enough to feed a family of twelve. There's radiant heating throughout the main floor, and I have it on good authority that there's a jetted tub in the master suite."

Dawn broke into a genuine smile. The house, which had looked so barren before, suddenly took on new meaning.

"No way, Lil!" she cried. "This place is fantastic."

Lila blushingly thanked her. Her sister would never be the sort to fall into rhapsodic ecstasies, but her pink flush betrayed her pleasure.

"I can't believe you bought a house without me knowing about it," Dawn said. "I mean, I *can* believe it, but you know what I mean. You guys seem so happy where you are."

"In the place where we literally live on top of one

another and can't have more than five people over at a time?" Lila asked. She laughed to strip the words of any malice. "It's silly to be this excited about a house, but what can you do? It took us forever to find one that fits. This one's still in Emily's school district, and it's within walking distance of our old neighborhood, so we won't lose contact with any of our friends. *And* it's big enough for us to stretch our arms and not hit both walls."

"It's not silly." Dawn handed Sophie her champagne so she could wrap her arms around Lila and give her a hug. She held her long and firmly, making sure her sister knew how happy she was for her. Her own life might be a hot mess of romantic disappointments, but she was genuinely invested in Lila's happiness. Hers and Sophie's both. "It's great. You guys deserve to have everything you want. But I should probably warn you ahead of time that I'm busy the weekend you're moving in, so don't count on my muscle or my great trunk space."

"I didn't tell you when we're moving in."

"I know. I'm busy all the weekends until every last box is unpacked and put away."

Both Lila and Sophie took this as it was intended, as a complete and utter lie. One of the rules of the Vasquez sisterhood was that all of life's unpleasant tasks had to be shared. Cleaning toilets, moving to new houses, singing at karaoke bars—none of it was optional and, in the case of that last one, none of it was very good, either.

"There's more," Lila said. She clasped Dawn's hand and started leading her through the white-and-beige glory of the kitchen to a pair of french doors at the back. "And I think you're going to really like this part."

"Is it a hot tub?" she asked. "A tiki bar? Oh! How

about a giant trampoline? I always wanted one of those when we were kids, but you know how Mom gets about things like severed spinal cords. She's never been any fun."

She had every intention of continuing in this vein, running a dialogue of jokes that no one was really listening to, but Lila gave her hand a warm squeeze. That warm squeeze told Dawn everything she needed to know, and none of it was good.

"Ta-da!" Sophie pushed open the doors and waited while Dawn stepped through to the backyard beyond. "It looks small from here, but wait until you get inside. I've never seen anything like it."

The smile felt plastered to Dawn's face as she followed her sisters down a stone path to the two-story detached garage at the end of a huge, rolling lawn. There were plenty of reasons why Lila and Ford might have chosen a house with all this acreage, including the fact that Lila's seven-year-old stepdaughter would love being able to run around at liberty with her hearing service dog, a cockapoo named Jeeves von Hinklebottom.

But that, Dawn knew, was a secondary consideration. It wasn't just Jeeves who would be playing fetch and practicing obedience back here.

"The people who lived here before used to keep goats," Lila explained. She pulled out a key and opened the door to the garage. A slightly musty scent mingled with the recent use of organic cleansers. "They also turned the upper story into a mother-in-law suite, so we can set it up as an actual office. No more answering the phone in our underwear or having clients tromp through the living room and kitchen to get to the kennel."

"And no more Dawn having to spend every night home alone with the puppies," Sophie added as the lights flicked on. "Can you believe this place?"

No, she couldn't. It was almost too good to be true. After one quick sweep of the main floor of the garage, she could see water hookups, heating and cooling appliances, and plenty of space to set up the individual puppy pens. It was light and bright and airy, and a staircase at the back led up to what she was sure would make an admirable headquarters for this new phase of Puppy Promise.

"Ford and I have talked about it, and we don't see any reason why we can't handle most of the off-hours puppy care between the two of us," Lila said. Her voice had more vibrato than usual, her excitement difficult to subdue. "Since he works from home and I'm around most of the time anyway, we should be able to set it up so you and Soph only have to come when you're doing actual training for the clients. Or when we want the occasional weekend or evening off, but Sophie promises that won't be a problem."

"Are you sure?" Dawn asked. "It's a lot of work, being the only one around at night, and—"

"And you've already done your fair share of it," Lila finished for her. "I know, Dawn. Sophie and I both do. That's why this is going to work so well. Ford is weirdly excited about learning the training routines, and Emily has been bouncing off the walls since our offer on the house was accepted. She promises to name any and all of the puppies who haven't yet been christened. I'm afraid there are a lot of Sir Reginalds and Princess Brandywines in our future."

"Princess Brandywine is a beautiful name," Dawn said, hoping to keep things light. "We could do a whole line of alcohol-themed royalty. I call dibs on King Kahlua."

"Taking care of that many puppies is too much for one person," Lila said, once again ignoring her. "That was the whole point of the three of us living under one roof, the entire reason we started this company in the first place. To share the workload."

Dawn opened her mouth and closed it again, searching in vain for the right words. This thing Lila was doing for her—for all of them—was kind and generous and everything that Dawn had asked for.

"If it's okay with you, we'll put the old house and kennel up for sale next week," Lila said. "It's going to take a little money to get this place in perfect puppy condition, but there should be plenty left over in your share to put a down payment on another house or get a condo or even…"

Lila held her hands out to Dawn as if offering her the world. Which, in a way, was exactly what she was doing. That house was the only thing tying her down. As long as those puppies needed a home and a caretaker, Dawn was bound to it. She had rules and responsibilities, had to spend every night with her head on her own pillow.

"Well?" Lila prodded. "What do you think? Does that timeline work for you?"

There was a look of anxiety in her large brown eyes, a question that Dawn would have been a monster to answer any other way.

"It's perfect," she said and meant it. With her usual acumen and efficiency, Lila had found a way to solve all their problems, and in such a way that no one would be asked to put forth any more effort than they were willing—and able—to give. "This place is ideal, the puppies will love it, and I couldn't ask for anything else. But I'm still busy on moving weekend, so don't even ask."

Both Lila and Sophie laughed at that, allowing themselves to be diverted by lighthearted chatter about paint colors and canine running tracks and what licensing paperwork would have to be filed before they could start moving the puppies over. More than anything else, that laughter kept Dawn's smile pinned in place. Her sisters obviously needed her to be fun, easygoing Dawn Vasquez right now—the fun, easygoing Dawn Vasquez who balked at duty and enjoyed nothing as much as her freedom. In fact, she had the strong suspicion that if she raised one word in protest—one syllable, even— they'd put all their plans on hold until she was ready. Lila would probably even let this house slip through her fingers, asking her whole family to let go of their dream home for the sake of Dawn's feelings.

She knew exactly how Lila would sell it, too. *Dawn doesn't have anything else. Dawn doesn't have* anyone *else. No matter what life throws at us, we'll always have each other, but she's all alone.*

And the worst part was, she'd be right. Dawn had dozens of friends, more family than she knew what to do with, and plenty of hobbies to fill her time.

But that wasn't the same as having a husband and daughter, like Lila. It wasn't the same as having a boyfriend who was desperately in love with her, like Sophie. Even her parents had one of those mushy-eyed romances that spanned the decades. The amount of PDA those two indulged in had been a constant source of mortification in Dawn's adolescence, though she found it awfully sweet now. They'd been married for thirty-five years and still considered every day they had together a gift.

"I guess it might not be so far-fetched for you to bring that stolen puppy home as a pet after all." Lila hooked her arm through Dawn's as they headed up the stairs to check out the future offices of Puppy Promise, LLC. "Heck, if you get a big enough place, you can start stealing all the dogs you want, and I promise not to say a word."

Even though she still felt more like crying than laughing, Dawn forced herself to do the latter. It was what was expected of her, and what was more, it was all she really knew how to do.

"You'd better be careful with offers like that," she said and prepared herself to find nothing but delight in the mother-in-law suite on display. "You know me. Now that I've had a taste of crime, it's going to be awfully hard to rein me back in again."

chapter
14

"Well?" Adam stood hovering in the doorway to the kitchen, anxiously awaiting the results of Marcia's exam like a father anticipating news of his new baby. "How's she doing? Does she get the all clear? Is she safe to travel?"

Marcia's laugh told him everything he needed to know.

"Relax, Adam. She's great. More than great, actually. You've got one very healthy and surprisingly happy golden retriever on your hands." She laughed again as Gigi's low, playful growl indicated that she was trying to tempt the veterinarian into a game of tug-of-war. "And not the least bit afraid of me, it seems."

"Sorry. She's a bit spoiled."

"A bit?" Marcia groaned as she presumably rose to her feet. "I've never seen a dog go from malnourished to pure menace in such a short time."

He was about to apologize again when Marcia placed a hand on his shoulder.

"Good for you. It takes someone special to be able to manufacture that kind of transformation. I'm not saying you won't see signs of her early trauma crop up from time to time   that's inevitable—but there's no question that she made it over the worst hump with flying colors. She's good to go wherever you want to take her."

It should have been a moment of triumph. After only five weeks, the healing effects of Uncle and Dawn and the good Dearborn Ranch air had done their work. Uncle supported her, Dawn trained her, and Dearborn Ranch gave her room to explore. That magical trifecta meant that Gigi wasn't just physically healed; she also displayed a mental resilience they could all be proud of.

"Where are you taking her, if you don't mind my asking?"

And that, right there, was the only dark spot.

"I'm not," Adam replied. Gigi bounded over to him and pawed at his leg in a plea for affection. Dawn had instructed him not to give in, to ask her to sit patiently until her good behavior warranted attention, but he gave in anyway. As he crouched down and began lavishing Gigi with love and a scratch on her favorite spot right underneath her left ear, he could practically hear Uncle sighing his disapproval.

Too bad. Wise, sober Uncle could judge him all he wanted. It wouldn't change his mind. If this was going to be his last day with Gigi, he was going to indulge in a little ear scratching.

"I'm going to send her home with Dawn today," he said. The words felt stiff on his tongue, but he hoped that the more he said them, the easier they'd come out. "As much as I'd like to keep her with me, it's not practical. It's time she went to her forever home."

"Oh, how sad!" Marcia quickly added, "Not that she's going to live with Dawn, of course. Just that you'll have to say goodbye. This puppy obviously means something to you. Hear how fast her leg is thumping?"

Adam stood up so abruptly that his head swam, and Gigi whimpered her displeasure at being abandoned when he was getting to the good part. He relished the dizzy feeling, welcoming how off-balance and uncomfortable it made him. It was a feeling he was going to have to get used to—disappointing the females in his life, learning to live in a world without them.

"This isn't the place for her," he said, his words necessarily curt. "Not for the long term, anyway. I've known it from the start. To keep her here any longer than necessary would only be cruel."

"Yes," Marcia agreed. "It would."

"So I'm saying goodbye," he added. There was no need to keep going. Marcia knew and understood animals better than anyone. She also knew and understood *him* better than anyone. "It's going to be hard enough for her to move on as it is. Better to rip the bandage off now."

Marcia's hand came down on his shoulder again, this time lingering long enough for her to squeeze and hold the pressure. "Are you sure it's *her* attachment you're worried about?"

There was no use pretending—not now, not with Marcia. He had no idea if she knew that Gigi was only part of the equation, but he needed to say this to *someone*, if only to keep himself from breaking down when Dawn arrived.

He allowed the detached facade he'd been wearing all morning to fade. "You're right. It's me who's really going to suffer. I don't know what I'm going to do without her."

There was no opportunity to hear what words of wisdom Marcia had to offer him. He had the feeling she'd do what she always did, which was gently question him—never pushing harder than he was comfortable with, never forcing him to say or do anything he didn't want to. It was one of the things he appreciated most about her...and also one of the things that made him appreciate Dawn that much more.

Dawn pushed him. Dawn opened him up to experiences he'd never known existed. Dawn didn't shy away from difficult conversations.

Dawn put herself out there, wholly and wholeheartedly, and damn the consequences.

She'd done it yesterday, offering him the sole use and glory of her body for no reason other than that she wanted to. She was doing it again today, bursting in the front door with the ringing, musical tones of her laugh.

"Is that Marcia's van I see out in the drive?" she called.

Her answer was the full-force skitter of Gigi's nails on the hardwood as the puppy shot out to greet her preceptress. Witnessing how happy the golden retriever was to see Dawn was a consolation, but Adam's heart still hung like a wrecking ball in his chest.

"It sure is," Marcia replied. She squeezed Adam's shoulder one more time, making him think that she *did* know more about this situation than she let on. That, too, was only half a consolation. "I've just been telling Adam the good news. Methuselah—Gigi—whatever it is you're calling her these days—has the all clear from me. You guys have done wonders in terms of her recovery."

"The all clear?" Dawn asked. "All clear for what?"

Adam had hoped to make his capitulation in private, but that didn't seem to be in the cards. Making the most of the situation, he shrugged and said the words he'd been practicing for days. "You win."

"I win? Like…a prize? A million dollars? An all-expenses-paid trip to Cabo?" She heaved a playful sigh. "I hope it's that last one. I could use a vacation."

"You and me both," Marcia said. "I can't remember the last time I saw the bottom of a margarita glass."

"Then don't be surprised to find me standing on your front porch one of these days with a pitcher of Don Julio's finest. You've laid the challenge on me. I won't rest until you've seen the bottom of at least a dozen."

A lot of people would have made an offer like that purely for form's sake, but Dawn meant it. Even on such a short acquaintance, Marcia could tell. All Dawn had to do was bring a bottle of tequila, and her presence became a party.

"You're an absolute darling. Anytime this week would be great—just make it after six. My husband's been dying to meet you."

Adam was tempted to ask her to make it right now instead, whisking Dawn and Gigi out of here before he lost his resolution, but Marcia made her excuses and bid farewell to the puppy.

"Make sure you bring Gigi when you come, yeah?" she added before she stepped out the front door. "Our home is open to both people and dogs."

"That's nice, but how do you feel about rogue cows?"

"Rogue cows?" Marcia laughed. "If you mean that beast that's been running all over this county since the day Adam birthed her, the answer is no. My kids would take one look at her and beg her to stay forever."

The women's voices trailed off out the door and onto the front porch, then down the front porch and to the driveway. There the conversation continued for quite a few minutes, the two of them chatting as though they'd been friends for years instead of weeks. Adam used the time to get a grip on himself, marshaling the two puppies into a semblance of order and stationing himself behind the sink in the kitchen. He'd already done the breakfast dishes, but that stainless-steel barrier was better than nothing.

At least that was what he thought until Dawn walked in.

"You bastard."

Adam picked up the sponge he kept stored at the back of the sink and began randomly scrubbing the counter. "Zeke is still in his room, and Phoebe has been coming and going all morning, so you might want to watch what you say."

"Oh, I'm sorry. You *rat-faced* bastard."

He scrubbed harder. "I think maybe you misunderstood me earlier. I said you win, Dawn. As in, you're the victor. You get the spoils—or in this case, Gigi."

"Yes, I gathered as much, thank you." She paused. "Would you please stop trying to wear a hole in your kitchen counter? I'm trying to insult you and your underhanded tactics, and it would be a lot more satisfying if you were paying attention to me while I did it."

He couldn't help but chuckle. Only Dawn would continue to do and say exactly what was in her heart at a moment like this one. Tossing the sponge negligently aside—a thing he almost never did—he braced both hands on the edge of the sink, hunched and facing straight ahead.

"I thought you'd be pleased," he said, striving for nonchalance. It was difficult when every muscle in his body was tense enough to snap, when he was so close to falling to his knees and begging Dawn and Gigi to stay with him forever, but he managed it. Somehow. "I'm giving you Gigi. No more jumping through hoops, no more searching for mislaid legal documents, no more selling yourself out as a drudge to Bea Benson. She's yours, free and clear."

"Too bad. I don't want her."

Adam felt an absurd urge to take this conversation somewhere else—somewhere the puppy wouldn't overhear—but the sound of Gigi's happy chewing indicated that she wasn't paying them the least bit of attention.

"Well, I don't want her either," he retorted. "I've decided to keep Uncle instead."

When Dawn didn't reply right away, he felt a nervous qualm. There was no saying what she was doing right now—what she was thinking. For all he knew, she was getting ready to throw something at him.

Which, to be fair, he fully deserved.

"I'm telling you that you're right, Dawn. You've been right since the start of this thing." He released his death grip on the sink and pushed himself to a standing position. "She's not suited for life on a ranch. She'll never be much of a guide dog—not compared to Uncle—and it's selfish of me to keep her just because it seemed like fun to see how far you'd take it. I'm only sorry it took me this long to admit it."

The only sounds in the kitchen were Gigi's erratic chewing and Uncle's steady breathing. Well, that and the thump of Adam's pulse beating in his ears. Every word he was saying was a lie—and also one hundred percent true. He *was* sorry and he *was* selfish, but not enough to change his mind.

He also wanted to reach out and touch Dawn. Not in an intimate or erotic way, but in a reassuring one—to know she was there, to remind himself that they were still very much a part of each other.

He didn't though. He wasn't selfish enough for that.

"Is that why you wanted her in the first place?" Dawn eventually asked. Her voice sounded small and tight, almost as though she was controlling it through sheer force of will. "Just for fun?"

No. Never. "Yes."

"You never thought you might want to keep her forever?"

Yes. *Always.* "No."

"You never felt her curl up next to you and wondered what it might be like to have her there every day of your life?"

Adam had to put a stop to this. He couldn't keep lying, couldn't keep standing here pretending like they were talking about a dog and not the woman standing on the opposite side of his kitchen sink—the same kitchen sink that had stood here for generations, the same kitchen sink that would remain exactly like this for as long as Adam lived.

"Of course I thought about it," he admitted. "How could I not?"

Running a hand through his hair, he allowed his

natural expression to emerge for the first time. He was sad and tired. He wished there were a way to go back and shut his heart against both Gigi and Dawn. He was also resolute.

Dawn knew it. And she wasn't afraid to make him admit it out loud. "But?"

"But you and I both know that's not realistic. I like Gigi, yes. She's fun and playful and turns every day into an adventure."

"But?" she prodded again.

"But fun and playful and adventurous aren't enough. Not for me, anyway. I'm sure there are some people out there, some men who…" He let his voice trail off, unable to finish the sentence. Not that he needed to. They both knew what he meant. There were some men—thousands of them, probably—who would be able to give Dawn the life she deserved, matching her step for step, accompanying her on every adventure, supporting her through every dream.

"Some men who'd be willing to overlook her faults? Some men who could look beyond the surface to see what else she has to offer?"

She was wrong, of course—laughably so. Dawn's faults weren't what kept him from jumping in with both feet. His own were.

But he nodded anyway. There was no other way to end this conversation and remain standing. "She's not cut out for life on a ranch. It's better to end things now, while she has a chance at being happy somewhere else. *With* someone else."

The pause that settled over them was heavy and uncomfortable, broken only by the jangle of something that sounded like either a harness or a leash. It was enough to draw the attention of both puppies, who clamored over to Dawn's side to see what delights were in store for them.

She murmured something low and soothing as she presumably attached the devices, but Adam didn't move. He didn't move, didn't blink, barely even breathed as he awaited Dawn's response.

It was everything he expected…and offered no satisfaction whatsoever.

"Okay." She drew a deep breath. "They're all set. Uncle is in his harness and ready to go on a perimeter walk with you. Ideally, you two should make it all the way around the ranch, but I know this place is like eleven million miles, so only go as far as you're comfortable today. But you'll need to finish tomorrow—I'd like him to learn the full extent of his boundaries while I'm on hand to make any necessary corrections."

"You aren't coming?" he asked, surprised.

"Nope. You've made your decision." There was no rancor in her voice, no accusation. "If you and Uncle are going to make a real go of this, then you need to learn to depend on each other."

From a logical standpoint, Adam had known this moment was coming. Six weeks sounded like a long time to spend in the company of just one person, but not when that person was Dawn. He'd have gladly extended the training for another six weeks, six months, six *years*, but that wasn't the point. Uncle was here to make him more independent, to reassure his friends and family so they could enjoy their time away from the ranch.

In other words, Uncle was all he had left.

"What are you going to do?" he asked gruffly.

"Head over to Bea's, probably."

"But—" Adam had to shake himself as a reminder that his interest from here on out needed to be cool and casual. "I'm not sure I follow. Gigi is yours. The bet is canceled. It doesn't matter whether or not you find those papers of Bea's anymore. In fact, you can forget that whole arrangement with you buying her house as our intermediary. I'm sure there's another, less morally questionable way around it."

"Oh, I know." This time there *was* rancor in her voice. And accusation. "But I promised her I'd help, so that's what I'm going to do. Contrary to what many people believe, I *am* capable of sticking around and seeing a project through to its finish, even when it isn't covered in glitter and lined up with vodka shots."

He had to suppress the argument that sprang naturally to his throat. That *wasn't* what he believed—it was just what he needed Dawn to believe he believed. "I'm not sure I even want the land anymore," he lied. "I'm sure I can find other ways to expand the ranch's holdings. We'll invent micro-cows or something."

"Oh, it's not *you* I'm getting it for," she retorted. "It just so happens that I'm homeless—or, rather, I'm going to be homeless here in the next few weeks. I'm thinking about buying it for myself."

Adam's hand stopped on top of Uncle's head. It had been his intention to pet the puppy, to reassure him that they'd start their walk soon, but he suddenly needed the large, stately Great Dane to hold him up. "Wait—what? You're moving? *Here?* What about the puppies?"

"We're moving them to a kennel in the garage of

Lila's new house. I'm free of them forever." She gave a bitter little laugh. "That's me, Free Forever Dawn. I have no ties, no responsibilities. I can go wherever I want, and no one will have any reason to miss me. Well, except for Gigi, I guess. Although from the way she's looking at you right now, it's obvious I'm not her first choice."

That was bullshit. Gigi owed her life to Dawn. Adam couldn't think of any other person on the planet who would have so unhesitatingly tackled a man like Murphy Jones and lived to tell the tale. If Gigi preferred him now, it was because he'd behaved like an ass. There was no other name for a man who refused to give up a dog he had no right to, who'd gone against all advice and reason because he was too weak to say no.

He opened his mouth and closed it again, searching in vain for the right thing to say.

He didn't make it in time.

"I'm not *your* first choice either, but that's what makes this so deliciously ironic, don't you think? Who'd have thought that I'd develop a taste for country living at the same time Bea lets go of such a prime piece of real estate? By this time next week, you and I could be neighbors."

🐾 🐾 🐾

"I understand why a person might want to keep one broken rice cooker, but are you absolutely sure you need all three of these?"

"Yes."

Dawn looked down at the box in her arms and then back at Bea. The older woman sat on the top of the basement steps reading a mystery novel, not even bothering to glance at the rice cookers in question. If she had, she'd have noticed that they were all at least twenty years old and so covered with mouse droppings that it had to be breaking some kind of food safety law to use them.

"Maybe we can just pick the best one, and then you'll be able to—"

"I need them for parts," Bea explained. She flipped a page of her book and kept reading. "Each one has a different broken component. Put them together, and you get one perfectly working rice cooker. Fresh and fluffy every time."

Dawn wrinkled her nose. The idea of mishmashing three broken appliances together to make a single functional one was ridiculous. That wasn't how things got fixed. It wasn't how people got fixed either. *Or puppies.* You could push and shove and show up on a man's doorstep every day, but there was no way to combine Adam Dearborn, Dawn Vasquez, Uncle, and Gigi to make a cohesive unit.

She'd tried. She'd given him the option. But that hadn't stopped him from giving up on Gigi.

From giving up on *her.*

"Do you eat a lot of rice?" Dawn asked.

"I eat enough."

"How many times per year?" she persisted. She needed to start making progress down here, and fast. At this rate, clearing out the basement was going to take the bulk of her youth—the good, fun-filled years that were already starting to feel miles away. "If you had to make an estimate?"

"What are you, the CIA?"

Dawn sighed. Clearly, Bea had no intention of making

this task easy on her. "Yes, Bea. I'm with the Central Intelligence Agency, and my sole mission is to discover the exact amount of rice you eat per year. The fate of our nation hangs in the balance."

That got Bea to look up from her book. She pointed a finger at Dawn. "You're the one who wanted to do this."

Want seemed like an awfully generous term for what she was doing. This basement looked as though Bea had done nothing to it for the past twenty years but stand at the door and toss things down as the mood struck. Even Gigi had taken one long sniff and decided that she'd rather wait with Bea at the top of the steps.

Although that might have been because she'd been slinking around with her tail between her legs ever since Adam and Uncle had taken themselves off on a grand adventure without her. Dawn had tried to console her with treats and belly rubs and promises of half a dozen puppy friends at home, but to no avail. The golden retriever obviously held Dawn responsible for her broken heart.

"You can hardly take three rice cookers to Bali," Dawn pointed out.

"Bali?"

"Bora Bora. Cancún. Thailand." Dawn paused. "You know—the tropical paradise that awaits you? When you move?"

Bea's brow lifted a little. "Oh. That. Sure, sure. My tropical paradise. I guess you can put those in the donate pile. There should be three or four bread machines you can toss in there, too."

Dawn made a mental note to give everything in the donate pile a thorough disinfecting before she dropped it off. She also was careful to count out a full minute inside her head before speaking again.

"Have you given any more thought to where you want to go?" she asked in what she hoped was a casual voice. It was helped by the fact that she spied a box of paper-like objects in the far corner. Maybe Bea's organizational system wasn't so defunct after all. "If you don't end up somewhere warm and exotic, I mean?"

When Bea didn't respond right away, Dawn added, "Is there a family member you've been meaning to visit? Friends nearby?"

"You know what?" Bea said by way of answer. "I think I *will* keep those rice cookers."

Dawn's heart sank. It would have been very easy to assume that Bea was just being contradictory, but Dawn had always been a realist. Bea had no more intention of leaving this place than Adam did of changing his mind about Gigi.

So much for moving into the neighborhood. There was going to be no farmhouse in Dawn's future, no opportunity to buy this place for the sole purpose of holding it over Adam's head and gloating about her victory.

Yet another door was closing right in front of her.

"You know, I've been doing some thinking about this Smithwood-Dearborn feud," Dawn said as she busied herself clearing a path toward that box in the corner. Her own future might look bleak, but she still had an opportunity to make something good come out of all this.

"Oh?"

"Yeah. It's strange how something like that can go on for so many years. About sixty? If I did the math correctly?"

Bea grunted. She was still holding her book open, but she didn't appear to be reading it anymore. Her free hand rested on Gigi's neck, her fingers brushing absent-mindedly over the puppy's fur. Gigi accepted this as her due; even *Bea* had more of a hold over that animal than Dawn did. "That sounds about right."

"And you've lived here all that time?"

Bea's eyes narrowed in a look of shrewd suspicion. "If you want to say something, girl, just come out and say it. Don't use any of your animal-training tricks on me."

Candor suited Dawn down to her last freckle. She gave up on the pursuit of the box.

"Sixty years is a long time to live in a place," she said, frankly but—hopefully—with kindness. "And from everything I can tell, you don't have a lot in the way of family. There are no framed photographs, no grandkids' drawings on the fridge, no personal mementos shoved into any of these boxes. I've never even seen a picture of your husband."

"Good riddance to bad rubbish." Bea spat over her left shoulder.

"I'm hoping that means he left you, not that I'm going to stumble across his dead and decaying body somewhere in this heap."

Bea fell into one of her signature cackles. "I wish I *had* thought to murder him, the lying bastard." On a more sober note, she added, "He left not long after we moved in. Didn't care for the nightlife out here. Or the fact that I was the only one in it."

Dawn nodded. She could see how the long, wintry nights out here might wear on a person, how an unhappy marriage could fracture under the strain of so much isolation. She could also see why a woman like Bea Benson—or a man like Adam Dearborn—refused to leave. There was something about the pace of it, like stepping back in time, that soothed the soul. People talked out here. They worked together. They relied on each other.

Once upon a time, Puppy Promise had been like that. Dawn had never been happier than when she and her sisters had sat chatting about the day over cups of hot chocolate, laughingly breaking down both their training cases and their latest loves, occasionally stepping out to make sure the puppies had everything they needed. Everything *she'd* needed was under one roof, and it had brought her a measure of peace that she hadn't known existed.

She missed that—missed it so much that she suspected that was the true reason she was so upset at losing the last thing tying her down. It wasn't the puppies or the job or even her sisters that had changed. It was *her*.

Her mind was so preoccupied with this that her next question slipped out unaware. "Bea, if you end up selling this place, do you have anywhere to go?"

As much as Bea claimed an appreciation for coming right out and saying a thing, this seemed to take her aback. Her face grew pale, and the book dropped from her fingers. It narrowly missed landing on Gigi's head. "And what is that supposed to mean?"

Now that the question was out, Dawn did what she always did—leaned into it.

"It means, do you really have any intention of selling to Adam and his family, or is this a ploy to get me to come over here and keep you company? The garden, the basement, the constant influx of baked goods… It seems to me that you don't actually care about any of it. You just like having people around."

Bea shot to her feet with an agility that belied her age. "Now, see here, young lady—"

"It's okay if you do," Dawn said. "I'm the same way. I don't like spending a lot of time alone. I never have."

That bald confession—the first time Dawn had ever allowed herself to say it out loud—had a calming effect on Bea. The older woman sat back down again, her knees a little wobbly, her hand braced on the banister to give her leverage.

Bea's gaze caught hers. "I wasn't lying about that contract," she finally said, her tone somewhat mulish. "I really did have to sign something promising not to sell to the Dearborns."

Dawn moved toward the stairs and took a seat on the bottom step—but not before brushing away what appeared to be more mouse droppings. "I believe you."

"And that damned cow really did trample the yard, living it up like a trollop at her first disco. There just... wasn't much of a garden back there. It was mostly dirt to begin with."

Dawn believed that too. She'd thought it was odd that there weren't more remnants of demolished vegetables scattered about. Not even Dawn—*the cow*—at her most destructive could pull up potatoes and carrots from the roots.

"You're not going to tell them, are you?" Bea asked with an anxious inflection. "The Dearborns, I mean? The last thing I need is the whole lot of them trampling through here, full of sympathy and whispers for the sad, lonely lady next door. I'm not some dying old crone."

"No, not a *dying* one," Dawn agreed.

That got a laugh out of Bea—not to mention the glint back in her eye. Dawn was both glad and wary to see it.

Bea's next words justified the wariness. "It might just so happen that a copy of the paperwork you're after is filed in my estate lawyer's office." She held up a hand before Dawn could shout her protest. "Now, I'm not saying it *is*, only that it seems a likely possibility. I don't have a mental record of everything they've got squirreled away, but that seems like the sort of thing that would go with the deed, don't you think?"

Yes, Dawn did think it. She also suspected that Bea knew down to the last tax receipt what was being kept on her behalf. Bea might be a sad, lonely woman, but she was as sharp as they came.

"I'll give him a call one of these days and have him pull my files out. Not," she added as a warning, "because I've decided for sure what I want to do about this property, but because I like you. You remind me a lot of myself at your age."

Dawn's whole body jerked, though she did her best not to show it. Although she *liked* Bea—in the same way one liked a cute pair of shoes that started causing arch damage after just one hour of wear—she didn't see a lot of common ground between them. Dawn enjoyed puppies and men, love and laughter. She did her best to fill her days from sunup to sundown, enjoying a whirl of activities and plans that kept her constantly on the go. She did everything she could to avoid going home, where the four solid walls stood as a stark testament that no one was waiting there for her...

Oh dear.

Bea must not have picked up on the sudden chill that moved down Dawn's spine because she laughed and said, "I was a bit of a tart myself back in the day."

Under any other circumstances, that admission would have done much to bolster's Dawn spirit. Today, however, she could only stare at the woman. Bea was so lonely that she'd grown old in this house without anyone to care about what happened to her. She had no friends or family to brighten her golden years. Her neighbors were conspiring to get rid of her through any means necessary.

She's me in about forty years.

Dawn swallowed and tried to think of something to say—something irreverent and light, something that would prove she was nothing like this woman who had to manipulate and lie just to spend time with another human being.

She came up short. Manipulation and lies were exactly what had gotten her into this position in the first place. She'd lied about Gigi's origins and manipulated Adam into letting her train Uncle as a way to stay close to him. She'd lied about her true feelings and manipulated everyone into thinking that her only ambition in all this was to be the proud owner of a golden retriever.

With the end result, of course, that she'd gotten exactly what she asked for. She had the golden retriever and not a whole lot else.

"You know what?" Dawn sprang to her feet and wiped her hands on the seat of her shorts. "I *am* a tart."

Bea blinked down at her. "Well, shit. Anyone with eyes in her head can see that."

Dawn didn't let that remark faze her. With the same

emboldened belligerence, she lifted her chin and said, "I like men in general and Adam Dearborn specifically."

"Anyone with eyes in her head can see that, too."

That remark *did* faze her, but Bea only laughed and added, "What the hell else would you be doing here day in and day out? Anyone who thinks you're digging through some old lady's basement for shits and giggles has to be *blind* as well as blind. If you know what I mean."

Dawn did know what she meant. She also knew that there was only one way she could prove to the world—and to herself—that she wasn't some milquetoast of a woman who was willing to sit back and let a man dictate the terms of her life.

She liked Adam Dearborn, yes. She probably even loved him. But she wasn't going to grow old and lonely in a slowly decaying farmhouse waiting for him to come around.

"Bea, how soon do you think you can get your hands on that paperwork?" she asked.

"Well now. That depends on the reason."

Dawn had the feeling that *true love* wasn't the sort of answer that would move a woman like Bea to action, so she said the next best thing.

"A poker game."

Every sparkle in Bea's eyes lit up at once. "You saucy minx—are you saying what I think you're saying?"

She was. Once upon a time, Adam Dearborn's grandfather had wanted something so much that he'd staked everything he owned to get it: a chance at a better future, an opportunity to build something worthwhile. More to the point, he'd done it even though it had cost him his reputation and probably his dignity.

"If I were to set up a friendly poker game among neighbors, you'd host it, right?" Dawn asked. Considering how much effort would have to go into a party like this one, she hastened to add, "You wouldn't have to do any of the work, I promise. You can leave it up to me. All I'd need from you is one tiny little stake to get things rolling."

Bea didn't pretend not to understand. "And by tiny, you mean every acre of land I own, don't you?"

"I'll make sure you get whatever price you want for it," Dawn promised. "And this way, no one can argue that it wasn't fair or that you played favorites in deciding who the property goes to. Adam, Charlie, and I can play for it. Winner takes all—with or without the cheating this time."

That was all Bea needed to hear to set her cackle roaring. "Say no more. I don't want to be an accessory before the fact. You tell me when and where, and I'll make sure the deed and agreement are in hand."

Dawn trotted up the stairs and threw her arms around the older woman. Bea was much smaller and thinner than she'd expected, her frame hidden underneath the oversized clothes and dingy layers she always seemed to wear. This hidden frailty, unnoticed for too long, made Dawn hold the hug longer than she might have otherwise. She also dropped a kiss on Bea's cheek. Her skin felt soft and papery under her lips, and would probably bear the bright crimson mark of her affection for the rest of the day.

Neither woman cared.

"Bea Benson, you are a treasure," Dawn announced.

"Dawn Vasquez, you are a pain in my ass," Bea replied. "But damn if that isn't exactly what this entire sorry neighborhood needs."

chapter
15

"I hereby call this family meeting to order," Dawn announced.

Lila's brows rose, but she pursed her lips and folded her hands primly on top of the table, ready and willing to listen. Sophie was also ready and willing, but since she held a squirming Gigi in her lap, her attention wasn't quite as focused.

"This is the worst-behaved service puppy I've ever seen," Sophie said as Gigi started snuffling her way inevitably to the floor. That was where the shoes were, which meant that was precisely where she intended to go. "What exactly are you training her to do?"

"To sit still for five minutes and not get us kicked out of our favorite restaurant," Dawn replied. Even though Gigi bore the vest proclaiming her service training status, they'd already received the side-eye from several of the waitresses. Fortunately, they were such regular patrons—and often with a puppy-in-training or two on hand—that no one had asked them to leave.

Yet.

Gigi finally latched on to Sophie's shoelace and pounced to the floor, eager to celebrate her victory by chewing it to pieces.

"These laces should give us about ten minutes," Sophie announced with a chuckle. Like everyone else who'd ever held Gigi for longer than two seconds, her gaze was one of adoration and indulgence. "So you'd better talk fast. Either that, or we need to get one of Lila's pumps ready."

Lila promptly tucked her feet under the red vinyl booth. "Are you kidding? I love these shoes. I don't see why you can't just train her to behave. You're more than capable of it. You once transformed an entire litter of hyperactive Jack Russell terriers into docile little lambs."

"Because I don't want to," Dawn replied. She could have left it at that, but she needed to tell them this. She needed to tell them everything. "She bounced back from her trauma like a trouper and acts as though all she has to do is bat her eyes to have the whole world eating out of her hand, but it's not like that."

Last night had been a clear example. Adam had warned her that Gigi didn't much care for the dark, but not to what extent. As soon as the lights had gone out for the night, that little puppy had jumped into Dawn's lap and refused to move. Not even the promise of a leather-thonged flip-flop had been enough.

"Her spirit isn't unbreakable," Dawn said, stealing a glance under the table at her protégé. In addition to Sophie's shoelaces, she seemed to have found a stray crust worth snuffling out. "She puts on a good show, I know, but that's only because it's what's expected of her. Happy, playful, energetic puppies are what people prefer, so that's the facade she's learned to wear. She chases anything that moves and refuses to listen to commands and then makes up for it by licking your face until you can't breathe. In other words, she's charming as all hell. But deep inside, she's a neurotic, chaotic mess."

She glanced back up again and held her sisters' stares—first Sophie's, and then Lila's.

"A lot like me."

To her sisters' credit, neither one of them burst out with protests or exclamations that she was no such thing. They knew her well enough to recognize the truth.

"I'm struggling, you guys," Dawn said with a quick dash at her suddenly moist eyes. Her winged eyeliner was perfectly on point today. There was no way she was ruining it. "I should have said something earlier, but I didn't want to infringe on your happiness. The truth is, I don't like living in the house without you, but I don't like losing all responsibility for the kennel and puppies, either."

"Oh, Dawn." Lila reached across the table, holding her hand in place until Dawn took it. "Of course you're not infringing on our happiness."

"I am, and you know it. How many times have you had to abandon Ford and Emily to bring me food and flowers?"

"It's not like that—"

"It's exactly like that. Emily once offered to come stay with me for a few weeks so she could teach me how to make my own peanut-butter sandwiches. When a seven-year-old is offering you life-skills training— and you actually consider it for a few minutes before declining—something is wrong."

Dawn turned to Sophie before she could interrupt.

"And how many hours have you wasted on the road, driving to and from Deer Park to make sure I'm not moping around and feeling sorry for myself?"

"Excuse you. My time on the road is never wasted. I love those murdery podcasts." Sophie smiled and took Dawn's other hand. It was an awkward position, and made it difficult for Dawn to protect her eyeliner, but her sisters held fast. "In fact, I listened to one the whole way here. They just found three more bodies."

Dawn refused to let herself be distracted. That was supposed to be *her* job, not theirs—cracking jokes, bringing smiles.

But Sophie beat her to the next line. "It's a few minutes on the road, Dawn, not a lifetime of jury duty. I visit you because I want to, not because I feel like I have to."

"And Emily only offered to come live with you because she likes you better than the rest of us," Lila added. "*Everyone* likes you better than the rest of us, but you always find a way to do this."

"Do what?"

In tandem, both Sophie and Lila squeezed her hands. They also released their grips and sat back against the booth cushion. Dawn thought for a moment that their food had arrived, but the waitress bustled by carrying someone else's plates.

"It's true. Do you remember the time she broke up with that quarterback in high school?" Sophie's question was directed at Lila, who nodded in reply. "He was—what?—six foot two and had more muscles than an entire beach-body competition. I remember because I was in for my second round of chemo, so she kept sneaking photos of his abs to help pass the time."

"But then he dumped her, so she had to steal photos from the internet and pretend they were him." Lila laughed. "I'll never know where she found so many pictures of half-naked men."

"His name was Chad," Dawn said carefully. Like Lila and Sophie, she had very clear memories of this incident—few of them good. "And naked pictures are everywhere, Lil. Do you even know how the internet works?"

They ignored her, and this time, it was Lila's turn to traipse down memory lane.

"Or there was the time I was finishing my master's thesis, and she broke her ribs in that skiing accident. Remember, Soph? She didn't want to distract me when I was up against such a tight deadline, so she pretended she'd fallen in love with her ski instructor and hid at her friend Malia's house until she was healed."

Dawn sat up straight in her seat. "Wait—you *knew* about that? Sophie, you told her?"

Sophie blinked innocently at her. "Of course not. You don't have to tell Lila things. She already knows."

"It's true," Lila agreed, her expression softening. That was almost worse, since Dawn could guess what was coming next. "I know everything—including the fact that you'll do or say anything rather than reveal what's really in your heart. Especially if it might cause anyone else the least bit of discomfort. You loved that overly chiseled quarterback... Admit it."

"Please. I could never love a man named Chad."

"Dawn," Lila admonished.

Dawn felt heat flush to her cheeks. "At the time, yes, I thought he was the hottest thing since popped collars. In retrospect, however, I think I would have gotten tired of him within the year. He never stopped talking about his passing yards. You did me a favor, Soph, getting chemo when you did. Searching the internet for PG-13 porn got me through a real tough spot in my life."

Sophie didn't accept the thanks. Like Lila, her expression grew misty around the edges, her soft, lilting voice even softer and more lilting than before. "And you would have much rather convalesced at home instead of your friend's house," she said. "I remember because Malia had that boyfriend who was always trying to get you to sleep with him while she was at work. You must have hated being stuck there."

Dawn pulled a face, remembering. It *had* been hard to stave off an ardent cheater when her ribs were cracked in three places, but she'd managed it. Of course, it had required her not bathing the entire time she was there. There had been things growing on her bandages that no woman should have to face alone.

"It was my own fault for trying that jump in the first place. My skiing skills have never been quite as high as my confidence."

"Dawn," Lila said.

"Dawn," Sophie echoed.

A feeling of profound discomfort settled onto Dawn's shoulders, holding her in place and making it difficult to protest her sisters' gentle treatment of her. All the things they were saying about her were true, but they were wrong about the motivations behind them. From the way they were looking at her, as though she was some kind of saintly being dedicated to their life's happiness, anyone would think she'd acted from motives of pure self-disinterest.

But that wasn't it. That wasn't it at all. It wasn't self-disinterest that caused her to act the way she did—it was self-preservation.

"You guys don't understand," she said. Pled, really, her voice taking on a wheedling tone that caused even Gigi to sit up and take notice. Although Dawn doubted she would ever be the puppy's favorite, the animal was perceptive—and generous—enough to lift her head and place it on Dawn's knee.

She dropped a hand to the puppy's head and ran her fingers over her silken ears.

"Then tell us," Lila said. "Please."

If that one word wasn't persuasive enough, Sophie only added fuel to the fire. "I can't think of a single time in my life when you didn't give up everything to come running to my aid. No matter what you had going on in your life, no matter what you had going on in here." She leaned across the table and tapped her temple. "Won't you tell us what's going on? Just this once?"

There were lots of ways Dawn could have fulfilled Sophie's request. Adam Dearborn was one of the things going on, taking up way more room in her heart than she appeared to be taking in his. Bea Benson was there, too, all her grumbling and cackling intended to hide how lonely she was. Then there was Zeke and his inability to talk to his brother about how much he hated the ranch; Gigi and the fact that it was wrong to take her away from Uncle, even if Adam didn't want her anymore; even the puppies at the kennel, who would soon find much more joy in the company of a little girl than they'd ever found with her.

But of all those things, the person who loomed largest and took up the most space was herself.

"It's easier to deal with other people's problems than it is to deal with my own," she said. *There*. It was out now—the dark truth, the deep secret behind it all. "A smile, a laugh, a party, a mad plan to steal a puppy—I know how to fix things. I'm good at fixing things. Sometimes it's pictures of a quarterback's abs; sometimes it's a flourless chocolate cake and a case of wine. In fact, when Sophie needed help figuring out how to break down Harrison's walls, I knew just what to do. Remember?"

Sophie tilted her head thoughtfully, the sway of one dangling earring touching her shoulder. "Show a little skin, drive him a little crazy. Of course I remember."

Dawn's lips lifted in a slight smile. That had been a fun problem to fix. Sophie had been able to get that man eating out of the palm of her hand within days. "And when Lila was trying to figure out what to do about Ford, it was easy for me to jump in and help with that, too," she added.

"Dressing me up as a princess and spinning plates like a circus clown. Emily still talks about that. She thinks you're the most talented person in the world. Come to think of it, I do too." Despite the laughter in her voice, Lila's brows came down in a tight line over her eyes. "So what's wrong? You don't know how to fix your own problem?"

Oh, she knew how to fix it, all right. Re-creating the poker game that had gotten Dearborn Ranch started was just the kind of far-fetched plot Dawn specialized in. It was unexpected and ridiculous and would most likely end in tears, laughter, or explosive bursts of anger—just as all her plots did.

"I do have an idea," she admitted. Gigi decided that a

head on the knee wasn't enough comfort, so she pawed at Dawn until she gave in and lifted the puppy to her lap. "And it's right up there with partial nudity and princess role-play. But…"

Her sisters watched her without blinking or breathing, the air of expectation heavy enough to touch. There was nothing Dawn could do with it except reach out and grab with both hands.

"But I'm terrified of what will happen if it doesn't work," she said. The words came out so rushed and soft, it was a wonder they heard her. But the looks of wide-eyed sympathy from both told her there would be no turning back now. She'd cracked open the deepest recesses of her heart, and there would be no shoving everything back inside again. "I've come up with a way to make Adam face me, but I'm afraid he might not want me. It might not be enough. *I* might not be enough. What happens if I put myself—the *real* myself—out there, and he says no?"

She pulled her lower lip between her teeth and held on to Gigi as if she'd never held on to a puppy before. Of everyone at this table, Gigi alone knew what it meant to be rejected by Adam Dearborn, to give one hundred percent of herself to that man and have the door slammed in her face because of it.

"Then you figure out a way to live without him," Lila said as though it were the easiest thing in the world. Considering how happy she was with her own soul mate, the response seemed a little callous. "Your heart breaks and your world falls apart, and it sucks more than anything has ever sucked before. Maybe you grow old and bitter and lonely because of it, or maybe you reinvent yourself by scaling mountains or opening a great essential-oil scented-candle shop on the beach."

"I would absolutely invest in your essential-oil scented-candle shop on the beach," Sophie promised.

Dawn knew she was supposed to laugh and accept this gesture in the same vein it was being offered — cheerfully and without tears — but her stupid eyeballs weren't paying attention. A hot stinging behind her eyes made her hug Gigi even tighter.

"But I don't want to open a candle shop," she said, her voice thick.

Lila had the audacity to smile at this. To *smile*. "Then don't. It was only a suggestion. All I meant was that whatever happens, you're still going to be you. Beautiful, talented, generous, fun, resourceful, adventurous—"

"Don't forget softhearted," Sophie interjected. She started to smile, too. Dawn had never felt so betrayed in all her life. How dare they look so ridiculously gleeful at the thought of her heart being crushed in one of Adam's large, work-worn hands?

"*Definitely* softhearted," Lila said. "Dawn, please don't cry. Or do, actually. Open those tear ducts and let it all come pouring out. I don't think I've ever seen you cry before. Not even when we watch *Legends of the Fall*, and that movie makes me sob for days afterward."

"Even thinking about it is making me misty," Sophie agreed.

The waitress stopped by with their food before either of them could say more. Dawn had never been so happy to see a cheeseburger and fries in her life, and there had been times when months of no-carb dieting made for some serious competition.

Unfortunately, the waitress was one they knew well. They'd even thrown her a baby shower a few months back when her sister had been stuck in a layover from hell and couldn't make it in time to get everything set up.

"Uh-oh," she said, whisking the tray of food up out of their reach before Dawn could touch so much as the parsley decorating the plate. "I can see that there's some serious girl talk happening here. Want me to put this under the heater until you're ready?"

"Yes, please," Sophie and Lila said in unison.

"Don't you dare," Dawn warned. "They're ganging up on me. I need sustenance."

"Five minutes should do it," Lila said without regard for either Dawn's feelings or her stomach. Her air of authority was such that the waitress took her word as law. "We're just trying to convince Dawn that she's the most amazing person in the world."

The waitress blinked down at Dawn. "You mean she doesn't know it already? Damn, honey. And here I thought you had all your shit figured out. If *you're* having doubts, then what are the rest of us supposed to do?"

"See?" Sophie demanded as the waitress whisked herself off—and took all their food with her. "Even Wendy knows what you're worth, and she's seen you pick lettuce out of your teeth and eat cookies that have fallen on the floor."

"I only did that one time, and it was the macadamia-nut kind!" Dawn's protest was offered through a haze of half-shed tears and a bubbling laugh that was building up in the back of her throat. It was too much—an emotional confrontation in the middle of Maple Street Grill during a dinner rush, her sisters cracking jokes about floor cookies, a puppy trying to lick her ear, the waitress stealing her food and holding it for ransom. Didn't they know she was supposed to be miserable over here? "And I don't see what that has to do with anything. We're supposed to be talking about my future life's happiness."

Lila extended her arms over the top of the table and held them there until Dawn placed Gigi in them. The puppy had no problem with this high-handed approach to her care. In fact, she made a quick dive for the cracker packets on the side of the table, sending an accusing look at Dawn when Sophie swooped them out of her reach at the last second.

"We *are* talking about your future life's happiness," Lila said. "Look—you're laughing."

"I am not. I'm crying." She yanked a cracker packet out of Sophie's hands. "*And* I'm hungry."

"You're also getting a taste of your own medicine for once," Sophie pointed out. "It's not so easy, is it? Being forced to laugh when you feel like crying? Being surrounded by sisters who know how to make you smile even when you're breaking apart inside?"

"I don't do that."

"You *always* do that," Sophie said. "You always have. No matter how dark things get for us, no matter how fast the world is slipping out of control, you've always been ready to lift us back up again. God, I used to curse you something fierce for it. There's nothing worse than someone who denies you a really good wallow."

It was enough to set Dawn cry-laughing again, but Lila had more to heap on top of Sophie's words. "Does Adam love you? I don't know. I've never met the man. Is he going to break your heart? Maybe. Men do that sometimes. But we'll be here, Dawn, no matter what and for as long as you need us."

"That's why we know you'll be okay," Sophie added, her eyes crinkling around the edges. "We won't let you be anything else."

As if on cue, Wendy swooped back in with the tray and their plates of food. The parsley was a little wilted from the heat, and the cheese on her burger was starting to curdle at the edges, but Dawn didn't care. She'd never seen anything so wonderful—and not just because she was starving. Those three plates—plus the small breast of chicken for Gigi—represented the Vasquez sisters at their best. Eating food they didn't cook themselves, chatting over their woes and pleasures, figuring out what was next in the life they all shared.

Laughing. Crying. Sometimes both at once.

"Now." Lila leaned across the table and stole one of Dawn's fries. "Tell us about this plan. I don't know about Sophie, but I'm ready to meet this cowboy of yours."

Sophie—small and petite and looking more ferocious than Dawn had ever seen her—added, "And if he doesn't know how good he's got it, I'll personally kick his ass."

chapter
16

"Adam, we're not asking you to join us on a trip around the world. It's one night, for crying out loud." Phoebe's voice was filled with impatience, the tap of her foot keeping a steady beat from the hallway. Adam had hoped, with his door shut and a pair of headphones on, that his siblings would take the hint and go away.

They hadn't.

"I can't," he said as he pressed Pause on the audiobook he was listening to. It was a thriller—dark and twisty and perfectly suited to his mood—but he'd already figured out who the bad guy was.

The older brother, naturally. The one who'd spent his whole life taking care of an ungrateful family.

"Why not?"

He racked his brains trying to think of a reasonable excuse. For the first time, he regretted that he didn't have more of a social life. It was impossible to pretend he had a prior engagement. No one knew better than Phoebe and Zeke what a lie that was.

"Uncle is sick" was the best he could come up with. It had the benefit of being a believable lie, considering how heavy and morose the puppy felt on top of his feet.

It was the exact location where Gigi used to sleep. Uncle had been cruising all her favorite spots over the past few days, holding on to her scent for as long as he could.

"Uncle isn't sick; he's sad," Phoebe countered with alarming accuracy. "You gave away the love of his life. He needs an evening out as much as you do."

"No one needs an evening out as much as Adam," Zeke muttered. Adam wasn't sure if he was supposed to have heard that, because his brother raised his voice and added, "Bea promised to make it worth our while, so you might as well suck it up and come. She hinted that there might be some papers to look over."

For the first time in days, Adam's interest perked. He'd been living in daily expectation of hearing the news that Dawn had purchased Bea's property and planned on installing herself next to him for the rest of her life. The prospect both thrilled and terrified him, and not just because of what it would mean for his expansion plans.

A lifetime of Dawn was everything he wanted—and exactly what he'd been trying to avoid in the first place.

"Papers?" he asked. "But I thought we gave up on that plan."

Phoebe laughed and pushed open the door, unwilling to leave him to his privacy any longer. "*You* gave up on it, not me. There's still a chance we can beat the Smithwoods at their own game. We might as well take her that coconut cream pie you made yesterday and see if it doesn't do the final trick."

"How do I know this isn't a plot to lure me out of the house?"

Phoebe's response to this was to yank the phone out

of his hand and toss it aside. She grabbed one of his hands and pulled, helped along by Zeke, who took hold of the other one and did the same. Decades of ranch work made them both far too strong to resist.

"You don't," Phoebe answered as they hoisted him up off the bed. Uncle went too, leaping up and stationing himself at attention. Despite his morose state, he was too much like Adam to let anything stand in the way of what needed to be done. "But you also don't know if we're telling the truth—and the only way you're going to find out is if you come with us."

He wanted to ask if Dawn would be there so he could prepare himself, steeling his heart against the pain that would inevitably accompany such a meeting. But he couldn't. To do so would be to admit out loud just how deeply he'd fallen in love with her.

"Fine," he said, resigned to his fate and the fact that he was going to eventually have to get used to this new relationship with Dawn. Things might have ended between *them*, but she was still Zeke's friend, and there was still technically about a week of puppy training left to do. There would be meetings and chance run-ins, the occasional moment when they were left in a room alone together. The bandage would have to be ripped off and the wound cauterized with burning steel sooner or later. "But I'd better come home with a hundred acres in my pocket, or I'm holding you both accountable."

🐾🐾🐾

Adam realized something was off the moment he walked through Bea Benson's front door.

For starters, the air hung heavily with the scent of

expensive cigars and Dawn's nonsmell. If someone had offered him a million dollars to explain how a room could smell like both smoke and nothing, he'd have walked away without a penny more to his name. But there it was—and so was she. It was almost as though Dawn moved through a bubble of her own making, a force field against the things that normal people dealt with on a daily basis.

There was none of the house's usual mustiness or the stifling feeling of being closed off, either. As Adam walked through the front door, he expected to find the same side table on his right that had been there the last time.

It was gone. As he made further explorations under Uncle's gentle guidance, he discovered that so were the couch, the overstuffed chair by the fireplace, and the stack of old newspapers that had contributed so strongly to the smell.

She's done it.

That was the only thought to leap to Adam's mind, the only explanation that made sense. Dawn had found the papers and convinced Bea to move. This was a house being emptied for its new tenant.

"Uncanny, isn't it?" The sarcastic male voice that sounded at Adam's elbow caused him to jerk. Poor Uncle grunted as Adam gave the harness a hard yank. "I did the same thing when I got here. I have no idea what your girlfriend did to Bea, but the house looks amazing."

"She's not my girlfriend," Adam said. It was a stupid thing to say in light of everything else, but it was the only thing he could think of when hit from the side by Charlie Smithwood. A Charlie Smithwood who, it seemed, had deeper powers of perception than he'd ever given him credit for. In an attempt at recovery, he added, "What are you doing here, anyway?"

"They didn't tell you?" The sarcasm in Charlie's voice was replaced by genuine amusement. "I should have guessed. I thought it was odd that you'd have agreed to this."

It was on the tip of Adam's tongue to demand an explanation, but he held himself stiff. As much as he disliked not knowing what was going on, he disliked even more to be at a disadvantage.

A thing his siblings knew full well. A thing *Dawn* knew full well.

"Cigar?" asked a voice at his other side. It was feminine and familiar in a distant way—almost as though he remembered it from a dream. "I also have every kind of whiskey known to mankind, actual legitimate moonshine, and butterscotch schnapps." There was a slightly breathless pause full of withheld laughter. "Dawn warned me about your deplorable taste, so I promise not to judge you for that last one. I swiped a swig earlier. It's not the worst thing I ever tasted, but I wouldn't want to wake up to a hangover full of that stuff."

Recognition clicked almost at once. "You're Sophie."

"And you're Adam. Well? What'll it be?"

"He's going to pretend to consider it for twenty seconds and then get the schnapps." Phoebe's voice was just as amused as Sophie's—a thing that was seriously starting to get on his nerves. Was everyone in on this weird party except him? "Here, Adam. You'd better give me Uncle. Gigi is out back, and she's getting frantic about being here without him."

He handed over the harness without question. "Gigi's here?"

"Yes," Sophie answered as she placed a glass in his hand. The ice tinkled and sent up a waft of butterscotch. "In addition to Charlie, so are both my sisters, your brother, a nice veterinarian named Marcia, and the grumpy old lady who owns this place. It should be a lot of fun."

As much as he appreciated the quick rundown of the guest list, Adam was finding it more and more difficult to make sense of all this. Was it a send-off? An intervention?

"If you want to come with me, I'll show you to your seat," Sophie said without providing any kind of enlightenment. "Your stack of chips will be waiting for you. Both they and the cards came from your house, so they should be familiar."

If it weren't for Sophie standing next to him, Adam would have reared back at this. Chips? Cards? *Cigar smoke?*

Enlightenment was starting to dawn—and with it, the sinking feeling that he'd been duped. There was no way that Zeke and Phoebe hadn't known about this ahead of time. He'd been lured here under false pretenses, set up to take a terrible fall.

This wasn't a party. This was a motherfucking poker game.

"Is it too much to ask to speak to Dawn right now?" he asked, his teeth clenched. "I'm sure she's very busy, having set all this up and put it into execution, but it's important that we talk."

"She'll explain everything in a minute," said another

familiar-but-not-familiar female voice. *Lila*. These were hardly the circumstances under which he would have chosen to meet Dawn's sisters, but it felt oddly good to be given this opportunity. A woman who had written him off forever wouldn't introduce him to the two most important people in her life.

"She could have explained everything before I left the house and saved us all a lot of trouble," he said.

"True," Lila agreed. "But you wouldn't want to upset everything after all the work she's done on your behalf, would you?"

There was a note in her voice that caused Adam to do nothing more than shake his head. Maybe he'd been a little preemptive in his optimism. That wasn't the voice of a woman who'd been on the receiving end of high praise in his honor.

The two Vasquez sisters led him to a chair around an octagonal felt table. *That* wasn't from his own house, he knew, but he didn't dare question where it came from. He dropped to his seat and did his best to appear unconcerned instead.

He also carefully set his drink aside. As much as he could use something sweet and alcoholic right now, he wanted to keep his wits about him. The scuffle of footsteps and the general murmur of voices grew subdued, and Dawn's nonscent grew more pronounced. Even without those signs, he'd have known Dawn was near because he was ruthlessly attacked by the puppy he'd been separated from for all of five days.

It was a little disconcerting to have Gigi wriggling and whimpering and leaping up into his lap while the entire room watched, but he could hardly berate the

poor thing. From the way she was burrowing her face
into his side, almost as though she was trying to take up
residence inside his skin, it was obvious that she'd felt
the separation as keenly as he had.

"Yes, Gigi," he said, giving her his hand to lick—a
thing she did with exuberance. "I missed you too, girl.
Uncle and I both did. But this is no way to behave in
public. You're embarrassing yourself."

She didn't care. She transferred her affection from his
hand to his face, licking and snuffling until she reached
a comfortable spot with her head crooked against his.
Literally. This was how people swaddled babies.

"What on earth did you do to that poor animal?"
Charlie asked—presumably to Dawn.

This theory was confirmed when Dawn sighed and
said, "Loved her. Took care of her. Offered her the very
best parts of me. As you can tell, they're not up to par."

They are too up to par, Adam wanted to say. Maybe
not for Gigi, who clearly had her priorities wrong, but
for him.

"Well, now that Gigi has chosen her seat, we can
all get started." Dawn clapped her hands once. It
had the effect of bringing any remaining lingerers to
attention. "As most of you know, we're currently on
a plot of land whose ownership is highly sought after.
The Dearborns would like it to expand their ranch.
The Smithwoods would like it to regain some of their
lost holdings from a similar poker game over half a
century ago."

Such was the power of Dawn's presence that no one
interrupted or contradicted her.

"And *I* would like it because now that I've spent a

few weeks out here, I realize that there's nowhere on earth I'd rather live."

At this, Adam's entire body tensed, but Uncle settled himself directly on top of his feet. Between that solid bulk pressing on his toes and Gigi's warm snuffling as she burrowed deeper into his neck, there was no escape for him.

"Which is why Bea has been so kind as to agree to sell to the winner of this poker game. The winner will be expected to pay full market value, of course, but this should put the question of who deserves the land to rest. No more fighting. No more bribes. This whole affair began with a poker game and will end with a poker game. Right, Bea?"

"Hell yes. I'm tired of all this nonsense. You people exhaust me."

"You agree, Charlie?"

"Sure. Why not? Provided there's no funny business involved…"

Adam tensed even more, ready to leap to his family's defense, but Zeke beat him to it. "Oh, pipe down, Smithwood. You know as well as we do that your grandfather was a lazy waste of space. Our granddad did more with this land than he ever could have."

"I thought this was going to be a friendly game," Marcia interjected. Adam had been wondering what brought her to this spectacle, but even that was beginning to make sense. Marcia spent as much time on the Smithwood Ranch as the Dearborn one and was on friendly terms with both. If Dawn wanted to bring in a peacekeeper, she couldn't have chosen a better one. "If you guys can't leave off with the smack talk, I might sit down and join the game, too. Just imagine—a veterinary clinic right between my two biggest cash cows. Pun one hundred percent intended."

Light laughter dispelled the tension.

"That leaves you, Adam," Dawn said. Was it his imagination, or did she sound less friendly now that she was talking to him? "Can you find it in yourself to agree to those terms?"

No, he couldn't. Everything about this situation was ridiculous in the extreme. No matter what had happened in the past, people didn't play poker for land in this day and age. They should have been able to sit down like adults, discuss their options, and come to terms that were agreeable to all of them.

"Hell yes," he said, speaking more forcefully than he intended. He didn't take his words back, though. He was tired of acting like an adult, even more exhausted with being the only person in the room who put a damper on everyone else's dreams.

He wanted things, too. Tangible things like land to expand the family ranch. Intangible things like love and acceptance and the prospect of waking up every morning next to a woman like Dawn.

Shifting Gigi just enough so that his hands were free to play poker, he turned his full attention to the felt in front of him. The intangible things he wanted might not be so accessible, but here, at least, was something he could do. Like most of the things he'd achieved in life, it had taken him more time and more work than most people to master the art of poker. He couldn't read faces the way others did, forced to rely instead on audio clues and card counting. Forced to rely instead on *himself*.

That one lonely constant. The only thing he could hold onto in times like these.

So, yes. He could agree to those terms. Win or lose, the game would end today. "Ante up," he said.

chapter
17

Dawn had been steadily losing since the game began.
It had been her intention to start off with a bang,
frightening her competitors into upping their stakes
and playing recklessly, turning this poker game into
something worth noting. She should have known better.
Where Adam Dearborn was concerned, intentions meant
nothing.

"Full house, aces over fives." He sat back in his seat,
buoyed by his triumph but determined not to show it.
Dawn could tell. She knew all the signs of that man's
excitement—the way he flushed just at the tips of his
ears, the way his movements slowed down to become
careful, methodical, *purposeful*.

This was normally the point where he demanded that
she slow down and enjoy herself, when he told her that
he was going to take his time and nothing she said or did
would deter him from that path.

She was annoyed. Annoyed *and* aroused, which made
the annoyance that much more difficult to bear.

"Goddammit, Dearborn." Charlie threw his cards
down in disgust. "I was sure you were bluffing that time."

"He never bluffs," Dawn retorted, tossing her own

cards into the middle of the table. "He never lies, never says anything he doesn't mean."

Charlie cocked an eyebrow at her from across the table. He was a good-looking man, if a little uninteresting in a bland, all-American sort of way. His height was average, his build stocky, and his eyes so blue it looked as though his parents had plucked them from the wide prairie sky. From the way Phoebe kept shifting her glance his way, it was obvious she admired his style, but Dawn had been with enough guys like that to know all that corn-fed goodness had a tendency to pall after a while.

"Making up for the sins of the father?" Charlie asked. He coughed gently and added, "Or grandfather, as the case may be?"

Adam flushed darkly, though he still held himself careful and stiff in his seat. He was all hard lines and rigid angles, a tower of strength that might fall at the least provocation. "Are you accusing me of cheating, Smithwood?"

He made a big show of rolling up the sleeves of his red-checked flannel shirt, exposing his sinewy forearms one tantalizing inch at a time. Dawn tried her best not to stare and was forced to take her lower lip between her teeth and fix her gaze out Bea's front window to the twilight beyond.

Her sisters saw it, of course. So did Marcia and Bea and, unless she was very much mistaken, Zeke. His eyebrows shot to his hairline, but he didn't move from where he sat on the couch.

"There." Adam flipped his hands from palm-side down to palm-side up and back again. "Anything else I can do to address your concerns? Should we have Bea cover the mirrors? Clear the room? Strip me down to my shorts?"

He made a show of standing and reaching for the buttons of his shirt as if to disrobe right then and there. The forearms Dawn could withstand, but there was no way she'd be able to concentrate if Adam sat there in nothing but his underwear.

And concentrating was something she seriously needed to do.

"Cut it out, you two," she said, sounding so much like Lila that her sisters had to stifle their laughter. "No one is accusing anyone of anything. Well, except for Adam being a cocky bastard with all the luck, but there's not much we can do about that. Shall we keep going, or do we need a break?"

"Keep going," both men said without a moment's hesitation.

"Unless you'd like to take a few minutes?" Charlie asked with a glance down at Dawn's rapidly dwindling pile of chips. "You, ah, aren't looking so flush over there. If you'll pardon the pun."

She pardoned the pun but not the fact that Adam looked so smug about it. His intentions were obvious—he wanted Bea's land, but more than that, he wanted to make sure she *didn't* get it. He couldn't stomach the idea of having her as a neighbor, was so determined to cut her out of his life that he'd sit here and carefully demolish her at poker to ensure she was exorcised forever.

"I'll be fine," she said in as sweet a voice as she could muster. And she would, too. She had her sisters at her back, and she knew now that she didn't need anything else.

But, oh, she wanted more. So much more, and with so much longing that it was all she could do not to upend this poker table and demand that Adam see this game for what it really was.

She was reaching her hand out as far as it could go. All he had to do was reach back, just a little, and she'd hold on with every ounce of strength she had.

"Then ante up, and we'll get this next hand going," Marcia said as she gathered the cards and began shuffling them. As the most neutral party in this whole thing, she'd been designated as the dealer. "I'll keep an eye on the sleeves from here on out."

The next few hands went as well as expected, which was to say that Dawn was quickly and steadily losing her ground. Charlie was also losing, but he still had enough chips to make a recovery—provided the cards fell in his favor.

They didn't. At least, Dawn assumed they didn't because as Marcia tossed the next round of cards their way, Dawn picked them up to find herself facing the knobby braille of a straight flush.

Finally. Here was her chance to regain some of her lost ground, to show Adam that she was a contender worthy of the title. She needed to make a big show of this hand, to shake Adam out of his calm and make him realize that if he wanted this land, he was going to have to fight her directly for it.

"All in," she announced, pushing her pile of chips toward the center. "I've got you beat this time, boys. I'm looking at a straight that's dripping with diamonds."

Marcia's hand stopped over the top of the deck. "Um, aren't you supposed to keep that a secret? The hand's not over yet. In fact, I didn't even call for your bets yet."

"It's also not her turn to start the betting," Charlie said, his head tilted as he considered her. "Are you sure you know how this game works?"

"Playing games is the only thing I'm any good at," she replied. Although she spoke to Charlie, her words were meant for Adam's ears. From the looks of him, he knew it. His mouth was firm and his concentration more focused on her than the cards in his hand. "And I repeat—I'm all in."

"She's bluffing," Adam announced as he matched her bet. It barely made a dent in his own chips. "She doesn't have anything. She's just making a mad last-ditch effort to throw us off since she knows this is her last hand."

Dawn's lips curved in a smile. Now they were getting somewhere. Now she could force Adam to discuss the real matter of importance between them. "Are you sure about that, Adam? I've always been straightforward with you before—told you exactly what I wanted, exactly what I was thinking. What makes this time any different?"

His lips pressed into a firm line. "She's bluffing," he repeated.

"I don't know, Dearborn," Charlie said. "She looks pretty serious to me."

"No. She doesn't actually want Bea's house. In fact, this whole thing is a sham. She only set up this game to thwart me."

"Are you absolutely sure about that?" Dawn asked. Even though she knew they were in a room full of people, that there would be no more pretending to Zeke that she wasn't in love with his brother after this, she went all in on this matter, too. "Because I'm willing to place everything on this hand. In fact, I'll even raise the stakes higher."

"With what?" Adam asked. "You don't have any more chips."

Being down for the count had never stopped Dawn before, and she wasn't about to let it stop her now. A stirring at her feet reminded her that the things she possessed went a lot higher than poker chips, that the things that mattered were a lot more valuable than a stupid house and a hundred acres.

"No, but I do have Gigi. She's worth—what did you say, Marcia?—about a thousand dollars?" She fought a pang of regret as Gigi resettled herself, this time placing her head firmly on the top of Dawn's foot. The poor puppy was exhausted by the day's activities, and instead of sitting by Adam, she'd opted for Dawn. It had been a nice—if unprecedented—move on her part. "I'll add her to the pot. That should help sweeten the deal, don't you think?"

Adam's mouth twitched and his hands faltered on the cards, but Charlie spoke up before he could say anything. "Uh, no offense, but I don't really want a dog."

"Oh, but this isn't any dog," Dawn replied sweetly. "She changes lives. She charms uncharmable men. Isn't that right, Adam?"

"What do you think you're doing?" he demanded. "You can't stake the puppy I gave you literally last week."

"Yes, I can. She's mine, which means I can do anything I want with her. You didn't say I had to keep her forever."

"Dawn." Adam set his cards down, accidentally tipping over the one on the end in the process. It was, she noted, a two of spades—hardly the card necessary to beat her straight flush. "You absolutely cannot stake a living, breathing creature—especially not a living, breathing creature you've spent the past month trying to wrest out of my hands. Are you drunk?"

Her laugh came out a little breathless. "No, not drunk. This butterscotch schnapps only has like fifteen percent alcohol. I'd have to drink two bottles of it to even make a dent in my determination. I stake Gigi against everything you have in your pot. You and Charlie both. Winner takes all."

"You can't!" Adam protested, pushing his chair back from the table. The jostling movement had the effect of waking both puppies from their naps. Uncle lifted a weary head while Gigi gave a long, endearing yawn. "Marcia—will you please put a stop to this nonsense? I thought this was supposed to be a clean, fair game."

Marcia took a long look at Adam before transferring her gaze to Dawn. Dawn was careful not to give anything away, but the veterinarian paused only a moment before speaking. "I don't see why not, provided Charlie agrees."

"Yeah, um, I don't think—" Charlie began before his chair gave a lurch. Dawn glanced over to find that Phoebe had given it a healthy kick. "What the hell? What's the matter with you, Phoebe?"

Phoebe gave him a look of such blandly sweet innocence that Dawn knew it to be a fake. "I must have tripped. I'm so sorry. You were saying?"

Charlie didn't look fully convinced by Phoebe's excuse, but he ran a hand along the back of his neck and tried again. "I was saying that as nice as I'm sure that dog is, I don't think I'm willing to stake my entire chance at—"

This time, it was Zeke who kicked his chair, and he was much more violent about it. The chair tipped sideways on two legs. Charlie had to catch himself by gripping the table with both hands. There was no way Adam didn't feel it—either the table shaking or the reverberations of Charlie's chair—but he gave no sign of noticing.

Charlie did, though. As soon as his chair was righted again, he leapt up from the table and turned to face Zeke. They were of a level height and build, but Zeke bore the same look of determination that had been on his face the entire time he'd been competing in the triathlon.

"Sorry," Zeke said as he crossed his arms. "I tripped too. There must be a loose board right here."

"There is something seriously wrong with your family, you know that?" Charlie replied. He looked around at the three Dearborns—Adam coloring up with anger, Phoebe smiling sweetly, Zeke scowling at him— and threw up his hands. "I don't know why I came over here today. I should have known this was a trap. You guys can't do anything honorably."

"It's no trap," Dawn replied. She cast a pointed look down at the chair until he took the hint and lowered himself into it. "In fact, I'm doing you a favor. You and I can either sit here for a few more hours while Adam eventually demolishes you, or we can end things right here and now. What do you say? You have anything in that hand that's better than my straight flush?"

"She doesn't have a straight flush," Adam said with

a stubborn jut of his chin. "She's only saying that to get to me."

Dawn ignored him. "If you win this hand, you get bragging rights, the opportunity to buy Bea's property, and a beautiful golden retriever puppy," she said to Charlie. "What's there to lose?"

"You are *not* staking my dog," Adam said.

"She's my dog, and I can stake whatever I want." Dawn turned to Charlie with a smile. "Well? What do you say? Just think how much fun you can have if you win. You can take Gigi for long walks along the edge of your new property every day."

The underhanded side of this plan must have made its way through to Charlie, because he stopped long enough to consider what Dawn was offering him—not a plot of land, and not a puppy, but a chance to annoy Adam in ways that would rankle him for the rest of his life.

"What the hell," he said and picked up his cards again. "I'm in. But you'd better not actually have a straight flush, because what I'm holding doesn't even come close."

Dawn turned to Adam. Her smile was still fixed in place, so she allowed it to drip into her voice. "That just leaves you, Adam. What do you say? How sure are you that I'm bluffing? How much do you really know about me?"

There were two people—maybe three, if you counted Zeke—in that room who could tell Adam exactly what to do. Her sisters knew her well enough to realize that Dawn would never stake something or someone she cared about unless she was absolutely sure of her win. No matter how much she wanted to shake Adam out of his apathy and his obstinacy, she loved that little puppy far too much to let her go without a fight.

She loved Adam far too much to let him go without a fight, too. She wouldn't be here—pushing him, poking him, prodding him—otherwise.

"How much do I know about you?" Adam echoed. He tilted his head her direction. "Are you sure you want to ask me that? Right now? In front of all these people?"

She nodded. It was a silly thing to do, but it was all she could manage. Her throat had suddenly gone thick and dry, blocking off everything except the rush of blood through her veins. Since she had to say *something*, she fortified herself with a sip of his disgusting liquor. It was far too sweet and much too cloying, but it had the effect of loosening her tongue enough to say, "Go ahead, Adam. Do your worst."

Dawn had no way of knowing when everyone else in the room disappeared, but she suspected it was only a few seconds after Adam opened his mouth to speak. After months of hiding their relationship, of pretending that their feelings didn't factor into things as long as they maintained a cloak of invisibility, it was the height of irony that they'd do this in front of an audience.

And that the audience didn't matter to them one tiny bit.

"You are, without a doubt, the most difficult woman I've ever had the misfortune to know," Adam said. He spoke without anger but with plenty of heat, as though the words burned on his tongue but he'd say them even if it pained him. "Which is funny, because when I first met you, you made it seem like everything was going to be easy. You laugh easily. You live easily. You *love* easily."

She wanted to point out that there was nothing easy about loving Adam Dearborn, but he wasn't done speaking. In fact, from the way his voice had taken on a rhythmic quality, it seemed as though he planned to keep going for hours.

"You sweep into people's lives and take over without being aware of how much havoc you wreak," he said, still with his head tilted toward her. "And why would you? No one ever stops you. They're either too hesitant to step up or, as is more often the case, have no idea how to do it. They just let you in to do your worst, and you do it every time. To Zeke. To Bea. To poor Charlie here. And Lord knows Murphy Jones would have something to say about all the pain you've caused him."

She held herself stiff, waiting for him to add himself to the list of her victims, but he didn't.

"You think nothing of facing down half-ton cows. You think even less of facing down the men who wrangle them. In fact, I can't think of a single thing that scares you. People chasing you with guns mean as little to you as the laws governing human society. In your twenty-nine years on this planet, you've managed to live the kind of life most people only dream of, and you have decades more of it to look forward to."

At this, his jaw tightened and he paused, almost as though he was wrestling with some unseen ghost. "You *will* have decades more of it to look forward to," he repeated, more forcefully this time. "And you'll have hundreds more lives to change. That's the one thing— the only thing—I can promise."

Even though Dawn knew that Adam couldn't see her—not literally, anyway—she'd never felt more exposed. He had to know about the hot tears building up in her eyes, how fierce her grip on the poker table had become. The things he was saying about her were hard and stark and one hundred percent honest. They were also deeply, painfully kind.

"You turn every room you walk into upside down," he said, his voice as raw as her emotions. "But you also turn them into somewhere everyone wants to be. You make the entire fucking world a better place just by being in it. You've made *my* world something I never thought it could be."

Dawn's breath caught and her heart took flight. *I knew it.* There was no way Adam would let her walk out of his life without a word, no way he'd reduce their time together to a meaningless fling. This thing of theirs meant something, even if he wanted to fight it with every ounce of strength he had.

"Adam—" she began.

He flung his hand up to stop her, that firm set of his jaw even more apparent this time. "Which is why I'm calling your bluff. You and I both know that you don't really want Bea's house. You don't really want to live out here in the middle of nowhere, surrounded by nothing but cattle and hard work." His voice dropped so much that Dawn could practically feel the entire room leaning close to hear the rest. "You don't really want to live out here with me. And even if I'm wrong, even if it costs me everything—Gigi, the extra acreage, *you*—I won't ask you to do it."

Dawn reared back, her entire body suddenly grown cold. Even with all the windows in Bea's house open and a few fans blowing in the background, it was well over eighty degrees in here, the summer night refusing to cool. It could have been over a hundred degrees, and Dawn would still have broken out in goose bumps.

He's calling my real bluff. He's saying no.

She had no idea where she found the strength to keep standing, let alone reach out and flip her cards. This wasn't even close to how poker games were supposed to go, and a stickler for the rules would point out that there was still a round of cards to pass out before the game was over, but she didn't care. Like Adam had pointed out, she never had much use for the rules.

"Well, you're wrong," she said. "It's a straight flush, sparkling diamonds and all. Sorry, Adam. Sorry, Charlie. It looks like you're both out a prime piece of real estate. Bea's property is mine."

Adam grew as white as she felt. "*No.*"

Even though it was the last thing Dawn felt like doing, she smiled. "I guess you don't know me nearly as well as you think," she said and snapped her fingers to bring Gigi to attention. It didn't work, of course. The puppy lifted one lazy ear and decided to pretend she hadn't heard. "Come on, Gigi," she said anyway. "Our work here is done. The winner is taking all."

chapter

18

"Goddammit, not again!" Adam heard the jangle of dog tags in time to stop his ax midswing. He lifted the blade well out of puppy range and wiped the sweat dripping down his brow. "Would it kill that woman to invest in a decent fence?"

His answer came as a twenty-pound puppy running into his legs with full force. It was a good thing he'd anticipated Gigi's exuberance ahead of time, because she knocked him to the ground. Only by turning the ax head down was he able to save them both from a Lizzie Borden incident.

Sensing a reunion, Uncle bounded over to join the fun. He'd have happily and obediently sat there in shade for hours while Adam made dents in the woodpile, but the presence of Gigi was a cause for celebration.

Considering she'd managed to find her way over to this house every day for the past month, Adam felt Uncle's excitement was a little misplaced, but what he could he do? He was covered in dogs.

"I'm not the one who needs a better fence" came a cool, detached voice from somewhere above his head. Dawn gave a low whistle, but Gigi failed to heel or come or do any of those things a puppy was supposed to do when called. "I come bearing gifts. Or gift, rather."

Adam released a soft curse. "Don't tell me."

"I managed to round her up before she ate *all* the flowers I just planted, but you owe me fifty bucks for the rosebushes. I was going to use them to start my essential-oil scented-candle business."

He ignored the first half of this remark, since there was no need for elaboration. Just as Gigi managed to find her way over to his house every day, so too did Dawn the cow visit Dawn the human with regularity.

"You're starting an essential-oil scented-candle business now?" he asked instead.

"I make very nice scented candles, thank you. It's something of a hobby of mine. The only problem is that they have a tendency to rub off on my hands, which means I no longer walk around with a nonsmell." She paused. "That must be why you didn't know I was coming."

Oh, he knew she was coming. She was *always* coming. Bea Benson had lived alone in that house for all thirty-three years of his life, and he'd seen her maybe once a month. Dawn had moved in four weeks ago, and he'd already lost track of how many times they'd run into each other. She'd even volunteered to help organize the annual town-hall fund-raiser this year—a thing he always took part in and now had to pretend he was too busy for.

"It must be tough, finding things to fill your time out here," he said, aiming for the right balance of sympathy and bland disinterest. From the way Gigi licked mournfully at his hand, he must have sounded a lot closer to pathetic. "I guess roses are one way to do it."

"Oh, I'm finding plenty to do. Don't you worry about

me. I could find ways to—how did you put it?—wreak havoc even if I lived all by myself on the moon. It's a gift, really."

Adam bit back a short laugh. He wouldn't call that particular talent a *gift*. It was his curse, plain and simple.

Her first week out here had been a given, since Dawn had been busy with moving trucks and trying to get Bea to throw out enough stuff to carve out her own space in the house they now shared. The second week hadn't been too hard to swallow, either, since she'd been fueled by her perverse determination to prove to Adam wrong.

Then week three had come and gone.

And now there was this. Neighborly greetings and friendly chats in the fields. Chance run-ins at the store and community events into which Dawn gave herself heart and soul. She'd even thrown a barbecue a few days ago for her friends and family. The sounds of loud music and laughter had carried over the fields so well that Adam halfway suspected her of faking the whole thing just to get to him.

But of course that was preposterous. He'd been invited to the damn thing. Zeke and Phoebe had done their best to lure him out, but he'd refused to cross the threshold. A man had his limits. Attending a carefree, see-I-don't-need-you party thrown by the love of his life was that limit.

"Look, Dawn," he said and ran a hand through his hair. He was sweaty and dirty, and he left a trail of wood chips behind, but he couldn't find it in him to care. There had to be an end to this torture, to this plan she had of punishing him for loving her too much to tie her down. He couldn't live the rest of his life knowing she was only a short walk away, aware that she might be curled up in bed and dreaming of a world where the two of them made sense. "We really need to sit down and discuss—"

"I thought I heard barking out here!" The sound of Zeke's voice came as an unwelcome interruption. "And talking, but that's not as uncommon as you might think these days. Adam has taken to having long, rambling conversations with Uncle at all hours of the day. Poor Uncle always casts me the most pleading glances, but what can I do? He's stuck in this life of servitude now."

Dawn laughed and smacked a pair of loud kisses that Adam assumed landed on both of Zeke's cheeks. "I can't judge. You should hear some of the conversations I have with Gigi. She's rapidly becoming the best friend I ever had. She even helped me pick out my outfit this morning. You like?"

"No," Zeke said baldly. "I've told you a hundred times that you need to start wearing jeans and boots out here. A dress that short and flimsy is only going to cause trouble. As soon as you come across your first patch of poison oak, you'll see what I mean."

Adam could easily imagine the sensation of her dress under his fingertips. There were any number of short and flimsy dresses Dawn might wear, but all the ones he'd encountered had been very similar in makeup. They slid over her skin and bunched under his fingertips, rustled like silk and fell to the ground in slinky heaps. He'd risked asking Zeke once, back when he and Dawn had first started sleeping together, to describe how she looked. Zeke's answer had been short and far more descriptive than Adam could have asked for.

"I don't know how it is, but some women wear clothes in a way that makes you aware, from every angle, that they're naked underneath."

Phoebe had been in the room at the time and snorted, saying, "That's the stupidest thing I've ever heard. All women are naked underneath their clothes."

"Yes," Zeke admitted. "But when Dawn walks into a room, you know it."

Adam did know it. He'd never have the privilege—or the pain—of seeing Dawn the way other people did, but when she walked into a room, he was always aware of how naked she was underneath her clothes.

"I'll take my chances on a rash, thanks," she said now. "A lady likes to look her best, even when she's relocated out to the boonies. Speaking of, I put Dawn in the cow barn for you, but you might want to go nail boards across the windows or put an arc of salt around the baseboards. Burning some sage might help, too."

"We tried that," Zeke admitted with a laugh. "Not even a hex will keep that animal where she's supposed to be."

Adam didn't contribute anything to the conversation. There was nothing he could say, so why bother? He didn't know how to make cows do what he wanted them to, he didn't know how to make women do what he wanted them to, and he *definitely* didn't know how to make his heart do what he wanted it to.

"It's weird, isn't it?" Dawn agreed. "It's almost like you can't control either animals or people. Like they have wills and agendas of their own, and nothing you do can change that."

Even though Dawn had basically just said the exact same thing he was thinking, Adam pressed his lips in a flat line and scooped Gigi up. Wordlessly, he held the puppy out. "Sorry about your rosebushes," he said. "I'll send a check."

She didn't respond for a painfully long time, forcing him to stand there holding out a wriggling animal like an idiot. When she did eventually come forward to take Gigi, she acted as though nothing had ever been amiss between them. "Thanks. Although it might be better if we just wait until the end of the month and make a full tally then. I'd hate for you to waste all those stamps."

Adam continued to feel like an idiot as Dawn's footsteps crunched in the distance, accompanied by Gigi's happy barking. He knew Zeke was still there, waiting until she was far enough away before saying what was on his mind.

"Don't worry," Adam said in an attempt to preclude him. "I give it two more weeks, tops. Either she'll get tired of playing Farmer John by then, or Bea will get tired of having a roommate and kick her out. It's only a matter of time before we're back to negotiations for the land."

"Adam, you are one hell of an expert on cows, but you have absolutely no idea what you're talking about when it comes to women."

Adam halted, taken aback by the forcefulness of Zeke's outburst. His brother was the most easygoing person he knew. Nothing ruffled him—not Dawn asking him to steal puppies, not the idea of running twenty miles at a time, and not even the poker game that had led to this disaster in the first place.

"I do too," he protested. "Trust me. This is all part of a game she's playing."

"Yeah. A game called life." Zeke touched Adam's shoulder. His hand lingered there, making Adam fear what came next.

He was right to be scared.

"You love her, don't you?" Zeke asked.

Instinct and months of practice almost had Adam voicing a flat denial. No, he didn't love Dawn. No, he had never loved her. It had all been a fun, frenetic, fleeting relationship based on how nicely their bodies fit together. Period.

"Yes," he said instead.

Zeke hefted a sigh. "I was afraid of that. You've loved her for quite a while, yeah?"

He shrugged, causing Zeke's hand to fall off his shoulder. The absence of it felt heavier than its presence. "Do you really need an answer to that?"

"No, but I'd like to hear it."

There was nothing else he could say. Even if he *had* kept his mouth shut that day at the poker game, the way he'd been moping around the ranch for the past four weeks would have been a serious clue.

Besides—he was tired of pretending. He was tired of holding everything inside.

"Yes. I've loved her since almost the first moment we met."

Zeke's response was automatic and underscored with a laugh. "Then you should know better than anyone that she's not leaving until she's damn good and ready. Dawn Vasquez does exactly what she wants to do when she wants to do it, and there isn't a man, woman, or puppy on the planet who can stop her." Zeke made a clucking sound with his tongue. "Hand me that ax, would you?

We might as well make some headway on that woodpile while we talk."

Adam pulled the ax from the ground and handed it to him. "Are we talking?"

He heard the thunk of a log being dropped to the splitting stump followed by a whoosh and a crack as Zeke's aim landed dead-on. "I think we should. I've put this off long enough."

Adam would have liked to have ahold of the ax so *he* could be the one distracting himself with work, but he had to make do by calling Uncle over and settling onto the ground next to him. Although it seemed almost impossible, the puppy had doubled in size since the day Dawn had first brought him over. It was like sitting next to one of his cows.

"You're leaving the ranch, aren't you?" Adam asked.

The whiz of the ax stopped midblow. "What? How did you—?"

"Call it an educated guess. Your heart hasn't been in it for a long time." He lay back in the grass, enjoying the tickle of the blades against his skin. Speaking of long times…he couldn't remember the last time he'd done this—lounging in the yard, talking to his brother about the things that mattered, the things that were in their hearts. "I wish you'd said something before I went through all the trouble of trying to oust Bea, but better late than never, I guess. Do you want me to buy you out?"

Zeke sucked in a breath so fast it whistled through his teeth. "*Can* you buy me out?"

"Not out of pocket, obviously, but I'm sure the bank will step in to help."

Zeke began talking a mile a minute. "I don't want to put a financial strain on you and Phoebe, and we'll have to find someone to replace me for the daily chores, but if you think it's possible… Adam, do you really think it's possible?"

A few months ago, the answer to that question would have been an unequivocal no. There was too much work and too little predictability, too many things that could go wrong on a ranch of this size.

But a few months ago, he hadn't had the most amazing service dog by his side. He hadn't witnessed one of Zeke's races for himself. He hadn't realized that to force someone you loved to live a life not of their own choosing was the worst thing you could do.

"I mean, I don't *like* it, but if it's what you want, then we'll do whatever it takes to make it happen." He sat up, the fingers of his right hand toying with a weed. "I love this place like it's my own child, but I can't expect everyone to share my feelings. I'm not going to tie you down to it. I'm not going to tie *anyone* down to it."

"Uh-oh. We're talking about Dawn again, aren't we?"

Adam yanked the weed from the dirt. "No. I don't know. Maybe." There was no use pretending about this anymore, either. He heaved a sigh and tossed the weed aside. "Yes."

The jangle of dog tags was just as much of a surprise the second time around. Since there wasn't an ax in his hand, he was able to open his arms and catch Gigi. She was just as exuberant and enthusiastic as before, which meant Adam had to be just as stern at subduing her. Things couldn't keep going on like this. They *couldn't*.

"Gigi, love," he said, giving her a gentle push back to

the ground. "You can't keep running over here. I appreciate your affections, I really do, but you aren't mine. You never were."

"Uh, Adam?" Zeke asked.

"I know. Dawn is probably standing right there. There's no help for it. We've got to train this dog to understand where she belongs, or it's going to keep being painful for all of us."

"But she's not standing right there," Zeke said. The swish of his legs trailed off, which explained why his voice sounded equally far away. "In fact, I don't see her anywhere."

Adam sighed and hoisted himself to his feet. He hadn't been anticipating a long walk between properties today, which meant he hadn't brought Uncle's harness with him, but it seemed he'd have to go retrieve it anyway. Under no circumstances could Gigi stay here.

"Then I guess we're going to take in the scenery," he said, resigned. "How could she have possibly lost control of you in the fifteen minutes since she left? Uncle, where are you?"

He snapped his fingers to bring the Great Dane to his side, but for the first time since that puppy had been introduced into his life, no large, wet nose pressed into his waiting hand.

"Uncle?" he called. "Zeke—what is Uncle doing?"

"Oh shit," Zeke said by way of answer. "He took off. Fuck—he and Gigi both."

Adam whirled in the most obvious direction of their departure, his ears on alert for the sounds of Dawn's footsteps and laughter. Neither came.

"Uncle stopped at the rise to the southwest," Zeke

said. "He's looking back at us like he wants us to follow. Adam, you don't think Dawn and those shoes…?"

Adam bit back a curse. "Yes, actually. I do think it, and it serves her right. I hope she fell into an entire field of poison oak. Come on. We'd better go pull her out."

Zeke took his arm and began walking with him in a generally southwestern direction. His speed was fast and anxious, making Adam wonder if his brother knew something he didn't.

"You know as well as I do that there isn't any poison oak around here," Zeke said, his voice tense. "We only said that to scare her—which, now that I think about it, was our first mistake. She isn't afraid of anything. I accused her once of being afraid of you, and all she did was laugh and say she'd stab you with her EpiPen if she had to."

Adam halted, yanking Zeke to a stop with him. "Her EpiPen?"

"Yeah. She's super allergic to bees. They're the only thing in the world that has a chance of slowing her down."

At those words, every part of Adam stopped—his breathing and his steps, the steady beat of his heart. So many times, he'd cursed the speed and joy with which Dawn moved, stood by in wonder as she did and said exactly what she wanted. From the start, it had been what drew him to her. There was so much life in her—so much love—that just being near her had been an experience worth having.

Knowing there was something that could bring all that to a crashing halt ripped something from his soul.

"Why the hell didn't anyone tell me that?" he demanded, whirling on his brother. "There's a hive the size of a watermelon along the riverbank at the edge of Bea's property. I've told her a dozen times that we'd be happy to take it down for her, but—"

"*Fuck*." Zeke's oath matched the rush of blood that was suddenly pounding through Adam's veins. "There was no way Dawn had her EpiPen on her today. That dress barely had a skirt, let alone a pocket."

"Go to her house and get it."

"I will, but first—"

"Go to her goddamned house and get the goddamn medical device she needs to stay alive." Adam's entire body flushed hot and then cold, his skin breaking out in goose bumps despite the heat of the day. If anything happened to that woman, if they didn't get to her in time…

"I'll find her even if I have to crawl over every inch of that riverbank on my hands and knees," Adam said, though he wasn't sure which of them he was saying it to.

"But—" Zeke began again.

"Please, Zeke." Adam's voice cracked. He didn't bother trying to hide his desperation. Asking for help wasn't something that came easy to him—and he doubted it ever would—but some things were more important than pride. "It'll take me too long to get somewhere I can call for help. Her best chance is for you to bring the EpiPen to her. *Run*, Zeke. I know you know how."

Zeke didn't waste any more time in arguing. With quick assent, he loped off in the direction of Bea's farmhouse.

It would have been a lot easier to search for Dawn if he had either Uncle or Gigi to provide him with some guidance, but Adam hadn't spent thirty-three years on this land for nothing. If he remembered correctly, the hive was located in a grove of trees by the creek's edge. He and the twins had spent hours there as kids, climbing the branches and daring each other to swing from one to the other. Adam had spent quite a few hours there as an adult, too, enjoying the breeze that lifted up off the surface of the water and scented the air.

He hadn't been kidding when he said he loved this place like his own child. He knew every leaf in every tree, every furrow in every field. It was in his soul and in his blood—a gift from Grandpa Dearborn, who had loved it just as much as he did.

None of that mattered now. Leaves and trees grew everywhere. Cows could be relocated. Even the family farmhouse was just a pile of cement and wood and carpet that only mattered because of who lived there. If someone were to offer him the opportunity to give it all up for a promise that Dawn would be okay, he'd take that deal in an instant—signed, sealed, and never once regretted.

Sorry, Grandpa.

"Dawn!" he called, even though he had no idea if she'd be able to respond. His knowledge of anaphylaxis was slight, but he knew that time was the most important factor. "Dawn Vasquez, you pain in my ass and general plague upon the earth, where are you?"

The only answer was a rustle of a breeze and the sound of a rock kicking off the toe of his boot. Drawing a deep breath, he forced himself to slow his steps and follow the map of this land that had been laid out inside his mind for decades.

"If you acted like a normal human being, none of this would have happened," he continued. Yelling at her wasn't at all how he wanted to do this, but his heart was thrumming too hard for anything else. "Of course there are bees around here. Hundreds of them. Thousands of them. You're in the goddamned wilderness, for crying out loud."

This time, he heard a low whimper in the distance. He latched on to that sound like it was a lifeline—a rope he could follow through a blizzard to make it home.

"If you're going to stay out here for the rest of your life, you're investing in steel-toed boots and a backpack full of supplies," he said. "Or one of those buttons you can push when you're old and you fall down. I'll buy it myself if I have to. Tie it around your neck. Wrap it around your finger and hold you close—"

"What on earth is wrong with you?"

Adam almost shouted his surprise at hearing Dawn's voice from a few feet away. He subdued it just in time, which meant the sound came out more like a grunt.

"Is it me you're talking to, or your stupid cow? Because if she got loose again, it is *not* my fault. I secured her."

"Dawn." It was all he could say—an exclamation and a sigh of relief, the weight of the world lifting off his shoulders. Oddly enough, the loss of that weight didn't make him feel more stable on his feet. His knees were suddenly weak, his joints like liquid. It was as though every feeling he had was pouring out of him all at once. "Oh, thank fuck. You're okay."

"Of course I'm okay. I mean, I'd be better if my silly dog would stop running off, but that's your fault."

Adam had been so sure that disaster awaited him at the end of this journey—that he'd swoop in to find

Dawn hurt, damaged, even dead—that he wasn't sure what to do next. Overwhelming relief at finding her intact was there, obviously, but even stronger was the feeling that he was being given another chance. There were hundreds of ways this might have ended differently. Dawn could have been stung by a bee. She could have tripped on one of the rabbit holes that were Adam's personal nemesis. She could have been attacked by coyotes or even decided that she'd had enough of country living and escaped this place as fast and as far as her feet would take her.

But she was okay. She was alive. She was here.

Despite everything, she was *here*.

"My fault?" he echoed, almost laughing. Of course it was his fault. He'd done nothing but push this woman away from the outset. In all that time, it had never occurred to him that Dawn couldn't be pushed. He'd said it so many times—she did what she wanted, when she wanted it. She never let anyone dictate her actions. She was one hundred percent herself, and it was the most beautiful thing about her.

And she's still here.

"Of course it is," Dawn replied. "Gigi only runs over to your house because you had the audacity to make her fall in love with you. What else did you expect?"

Adam's throat felt tight with fear and longing, with the clamping sensation of a love he'd never be able to shake. He wanted to speak, but the words were stuck. "Dawn…" he managed.

"And what is all this nonsense about tying things around my neck? What are you accusing me of doing now? From all I can tell, I'm standing on my own land.

In fact, *you're* the one who's trespassing right now."
There was a pause and a shuffle of feet. "Actually, how
did you get here? I don't see Uncle anywhere."

"Dawn."

"I know. You don't have to say it. I've ruined your
life, and you'd like nothing more than to see the back of
me. Don't worry. I got the hint." She laughed, a sharp
edge rendering it brittle. "I mean, I didn't *take* the hint,
obviously, but I got it."

"Dawn."

"I'm not going anywhere, Adam, so you might as
well reconcile yourself to having me as a neighbor."
There was a challenge in her voice but also kindness.
Warmth. Honesty. All those things that made Adam fall
for her in the first place. She was giving him the truth
with no varnish on it—and leaving it entirely up to him
to decide what to do.

Because that was what you did when you respected
someone. That was what you did when you loved them.

"I won't force myself into your company, and I'll
do my best not to heave *too* many lovelorn sighs when
you're near, but I like it here. I like the scenery. I like the
people. I like knowing my sisters are nearby but not so
close that it gets in the way of their own lives."

"Dawn."

"Would you stop saying my name like it's a bad
word?" She grunted her irritation. "I get it, Adam—you
don't want me. It's fine. It *hurts*, obviously, and I wish
things had ended differently between us, but I've never
been one to howl at fate. I know you don't believe me,
but I can learn to live in a world where we're just neighbors. I can and I will and I *am*."

The vise in his throat unclamped, and he gave in to the powerful urge to reach for her. She was standing much closer than he anticipated, that tiny dress and the hot flush of her skin practically rubbing up against him. Even though he'd aimed for her arms, he hit her waist. The fabric bunched under his touch, sliding up over her body in that oh-so-familiar way.

"Yes, but I can't," he said, his fingers digging desperately into her sides. "I can't and I won't and I'm *not*."

"You can't what?" she asked.

There were so many ways to answer that question. He couldn't live in a world where they were just neighbors. He couldn't stop thinking about her—her laugh and her touch and the simple joy of having her near. He couldn't imagine a lifetime spent without her in his arms.

"Do you know why I came running over here?" he asked. Without waiting for an answer, he continued, "Zeke thought you might have been stung by a bee. A *bee*. I was ready to burn this whole place to the ground, to give up everything I've ever owned, to cast aside every cow and every piece of hay, all to murder one fucking bee."

"That seems a little drastic. You love this ranch."

His grip on her tightened to the point of desperation. He had to be hurting her, but she didn't make a whimper of complaint. He remembered what she'd told him once—that she'd always tell him when he stepped over the line—and dared to drop a kiss to her lips.

For once, she wasn't expecting it. Her lips were slightly parted, as though she'd been on the verge of speech, so he took shameless advantage. Knowing this might be the last time he ever felt her mouth opening under his, he took stock of every breath, every taste, every brush of her tongue against his.

She tasted like honey, which seemed ironic considering the panic that had driven him out here, but he leaned into it—into her—his arms holding her as though he feared to let her go.

"I love *you*, Dawn Vasquez," he murmured against her mouth. "More than this ranch. More than life itself."

"Oh."

That was it. One word, one syllable, one breath. *Oh*. It was hardly the encouragement a man wanted to hear when making a declaration like this one, but he didn't care. Dawn had always been brave enough to say exactly what was on her mind. The least he could do was return the favor.

"I know I should have said this weeks ago—*months* ago—but I'm only just now realizing it," he said. "What it means to love someone this much, how much my happiness depends on yours. I think that's why it scared me so much—why *you* scare me so much. If you asked me to, I'd pack everything up and elope with you in Las Vegas. I'd join a cult in the backwoods of Idaho. I'd follow you on a circus tour through Europe. I thought…"

She didn't pull out of his embrace, but she did draw her head back so that her mouth was no longer within kissing distance. "You thought?" she prodded.

"I thought that tying you to this place was the worst thing I could do." His voice cracked, but he didn't bother to hide it. Mostly because his heart was cracking wide open along with it. "But it isn't, is it? We're already tied. Not to a ranch or a house or even a lifestyle, but to each other."

"You think we're tied to each other?"

No. He *knew* they were—knew it down to his very bones.

But that was the thing about being tied to someone else: there were two of them in it together, both of them bound by the same power. It wasn't up to him to say what happened next. The burden of their relationship didn't rest entirely on his shoulders.

How could he have been so stupid?

Dawn wasn't asking him to change or give anything up. She was only asking that he make room for her at his side.

"The worst thing I did was deciding that I knew what was best for you—and for us," he said, brushing his thumb across her cheek. It was damp with her tears. "You know yourself better than anyone. In fact, it's one of my favorite things about you. Who am I to tell you what you can and can't do? Who you can and can't love?"

"You can't," she said simply.

He knew it for the truth it was. He also knew that everything hinged on what he said next. Unable to help himself, he slid his hands up her back, holding her so close that she could feel how entangled his heartbeat was with hers.

"That day in the car when you told me that there hasn't been anyone else, I realized there was nothing on earth I wouldn't do for you, nowhere I wouldn't go. There hasn't been anyone else for me, either. Not since the moment we met."

"Oh. I didn't know."

He nodded but moved on, determined to get the rest of this out. "It happened again at the poker game when you tried to shake me out of my stupidity. To set all that up, to put yourself so far out there, and for me? I didn't understand. I thought—I *hoped*—that if I cut the ties between us, I'd be the only one who got hurt."

"Well, you weren't," she said.

His heart roared—with joy at hearing how much he mattered to her and with agony at realizing what he'd done to her.

"I'm sorry," he said. It was an inadequate thing to say, barely scratching the surface of the remorse and regret that flooded through him, but it was all he had. "I know it's taken me a stupidly long time to come around, and I don't deserve it, but if you give me another chance, I'll spend the rest of my life trying to make it up to you. Even if it means selling this place and starting over somewhere new with you. Even if it means uprooting an entire field to plant your rosebushes."

He drew a deep breath, since this last one was the most difficult to get out. "Even if it means stepping back and giving you the time and space you need to make this community your own. I'm yours, Dawn Vasquez, any way you'll have me. I'm yours even if you won't have me at all."

"Oh, Adam." Dawn somehow managed to get her hands free and lifted them to his face. The press of her palms against his cheeks was so much more intimate than their kiss had been because she held it there. Long after the moment passed, even as Gigi and Uncle descended upon them and began prancing around their legs as though they'd been separated from them for hours instead of minutes. She just held him. Loved him. *Accepted* him.

He couldn't wait to start offering her the same thing in return.

"You're such an idiot," she murmured. "You've always been such an idiot. Don't you know that I'm already exactly where I want to be?"

"You mean Dearborn Ranch?" he asked.

"No." She got up on her tiptoes and kissed him with a light flutter of her lips and a sweet sigh. He knew, in that moment, that Dearborn Ranch would never be as much a part of him as this woman.

Places were just places. But people were everything.

"I mean right here with you."

Epilogue

"I'm still not sure I understand. Why are we all wearing hats?" Alice Vasquez adjusted the elastic band under her chin so that the paper cone on top of her perfectly coiffed brown hair sat at a jaunty angle. "Everyone else seems to be wearing their normal clothes."

"Because, Mom." Dawn reached forward and tucked a stray lock behind her mom's ear. "This is a celebration. We've been counting down the days until Dawn's auction date for months."

"I'm not sure I understand why you and the cow have the same name," her dad put in. Both of her parents had just returned from a luxurious semester of lecturing in Spain, so they were looking tan, well rested, and not at all pleased to be attending a cow auction in paper hats. "Is it a joke?"

"Yes, Daddy," Sophie answered for her. "It's an inside joke between Dawn and Adam. She was always his favorite cow."

Their dad glanced askance at the animal. This was the first cow auction for the entire Vasquez clan, and all of them could say with complete sincerity that they hoped it would be their last. There was something unsettling about all these pens of cows being sold to the highest bidder for a future as a nice chuck roast. Even Dawn, who had long since inured herself to the ranch-to-table process, was finding it difficult to look the cows in the eye.

"You know I've never questioned your life choices, Sunshine, but this whole rancher thing is just plain weird. And considering your past, that's saying a lot." That seemed to be all her dad had to say on the subject, because he shook his head and offered his wife an arm.

Dawn waited until he was out of earshot before releasing the laughter welling up in her throat. Lila and Sophie chimed in, holding up their paper cups in a mock toast.

They were also the only ones who'd thought to bring celebratory drinks to a cow auction. Sophie and Dawn were sipping from a very cheap bottle of champagne, but Lila was on a strict sparkling cider diet. The gentle swell of her stomach, now halfway into her first pregnancy, had turned her into a teetotaler.

"Poor Dad," Sophie said with a giggle. "We broke him. At this point, I think we could all shave our heads and start a zombie-training boot camp, and all he'd do is say that he supports our dreams."

"Mom, too," Dawn said and gave Lila's stomach a gentle pat. "As long as Lil here promises to pop out grandchildren on a regular basis, she'll let us get away with anything."

"*One*, you guys," Lila warned. "I'm giving her one grandchild. Two, if you count Emily, which she most definitely does. Someone else can take the next round."

Sophie and Dawn shot each other accusing glances, which only made them laugh harder. They probably should have laid off the champagne a *little*, but Dawn needed the fortification. She was going to miss that silly old cow.

As if sensing how emotional she was getting over an animal that had thus far eaten two dozen of the rosebushes she'd planted, Adam appeared at her side. The arm he dropped around her shoulder was playful and casual, but she knew how anxious he was that everything went well today. And not just because his entire year's income depended on the outcome of the auction. He was weirdly worried about making sure her family had a good time. Never mind that Emily was gleefully running around and naming each cow, every title a little more ridiculous than the last. Or that Ford and Harrison were running after her, anxious lest she or her service dog get trampled underfoot. Or that Harrison, equally anxious about *his* service dog, was wearing a Pomeranian strapped to his chest in a baby sling. Add in Uncle trotting faithfully at Adam's side and Gigi, who refused to be left alone in the truck, and it was a veritable zoo.

Needless to say, the old cowboys who filled up the rest of the place were giving their party a *very* wide berth.

"It's going okay, right?" Adam asked. "I left Phoebe in charge of the rest of the herd, but Dawn is going up on the auction block now."

"It's going fine," Dawn promised, giving his waist a squeeze. To be perfectly honest, she had no idea if any of this was going according to plan, but that was half the fun of it. Anyone who said that to live on a ranch was to live a life of monotony had clearly never spent time at one. She had cows to chase and puppies to train, neighbors to visit and town hall meetings to attend, sisters to plan dinners with, and a gorgeous, hardworking, faithful man to come home to every night. It was a wonder they had any time for sex, really.

They always managed to find time, though. In fact, there had been a promising little storage shed she and Adam had passed on their way out of the parking lot…

"I think they just called her number," he said, forcing any and all thoughts of the storage shed out of her mind. Well, *mostly* out of her mind. That arm around her shoulders moved to her waist, Adam's fingers trailing awfully near… "Yep, that's her. It's time."

Dawn held her breath as her fellow Dawn ambled down the chute to where the rest of the cows were being held. The animal's statistics were rattled off by the very loud and efficient auctioneer before the bids were opened. It started much as the other auctions had so far, with low numbers being tossed around as interest heated up.

"I think I changed my mind," Adam said suddenly. "Dawn—quick. Get up there and tell them the sale is off. I don't want to get rid of her. She's a pain, yes, but she's *my* pain."

"Relax." Dawn slipped a hand in Adam's back pocket. "It'll be fine."

"I'm serious," Adam said. "I know it sounds stupid, but I already tried this twice. First with Gigi and then with you. It never works. I started missing both of you before you even left. We'll find room for her. We'll build her a barn of her own. We'll—"

"And that's an unheard of bid for three thousand!" the auctioneer called. "Does anyone dare to step up and offer more?"

Adam groaned. "Quick, Dawn. Place a bid before I change my mind. Offer them four thousand. No—offer them five."

"No way. I am *not* paying five thousand dollars for that cow."

"Going once—"

"Please, Dawn. She's part of the family."

"Going twice—"

"They're going to murder her. You know that, right? None of these cows are making it out alive."

"And sold!" The auctioneer was barely audible among the sudden burst of applause that sounded all around them. "To the gentleman in the oversized gray shirt. Oh. Nope. I'm sorry. To the *woman* in the oversized gray shirt. My apologies, ma'am. My vision isn't what it used to be."

"Oh, shove off," an irascible voice said. "You've known me these thirty years and more."

As soon as Adam heard it, he turned his head toward Dawn. "Dawn. That's not… It can't be…"

"And you'd better take that damn heifer around back. She looks innocent now, but give her ten minutes, and she'll have the entire lot of you running for your lives."

"Bea!" Adam dropped his arm from around Dawn's waist. "That sounds exactly like Bea."

Bea's signature cackle rose through the air, dispelling any and all illusions Adam might have had that he was hearing things. "She's going to be worth every god-damned penny. Just you wait and see. We're kindred spirits, Dawn and I. The next time one of my neighbors tries to kick me off my own land…"

Adam could only chuckle as Bea's voice trailed off. It was followed by an audible groan a few feet away.

"Well, fuck," Charlie Smithwood said. "There goes the neighborhood. *Again*."

About the Author

Lucy Gilmore is a contemporary romance author with a love of puppies, rainbows, and happily ever afters. She began her reading (and writing) career as an English literature major and ended as a die-hard fan of romance in all forms. When she's not rolling around with her two Akitas, she can be found hiking, biking, or with her nose buried in a book. Visit her online at lucygilmore.com.

BIG CHANCE COWBOY

At Big Chance Dog Rescue, even
humans get a second chance

After a disastrous mistake disbanded his army unit, Adam
Collins has returned home to Big Chance, Texas. He doesn't
plan to stay, but when an old flame asks him to help her train
her scruffy dog, he can't say no. As his reluctant heart opens
up, the impossible seems possible: a place where he, his friends,
and the other strays who show up can heal—and a second
chance with the woman he's always loved...

"A real page-turner with a sexy cowboy, a sassy
heroine, and a dog that brings them together."

—Carolyn Brown, *New York Times* bestseller

RESCUE ME

WILD ON MY MIND

Love runs wild and big-hearted animals help unlikely
couples find love—from debut author Laurel Kerr

When Katie Underwood discovers a litter of newborn cougar
cubs, the last person she expects to come to the rescue is her
former crush—and high school nemesis—Bowie Wilson. But
he doesn't seem to remember the trouble he caused her years
ago…

Single father Bowie is all ears when it comes to getting
his beloved but cash-strapped zoo on the map. He considers
himself lucky when Katie agrees to lend her publicity skills to
the zoo's rehabilitation programs…until their rivalry resurfaces.
He can't figure out why the beautiful redhead hates his guts—
and she's determined to protect her heart from the infuriatingly
attractive zookeeper. But there's not much they can do once a
lovelorn camel, a matchmaking honey badger, and a nursemaid
capybara are convinced these two are meant to be…

For more info about Sourcebooks's
books and authors, visit:

sourcebooks.com

COLD NOSE, WARM HEART

First in a fun, funny contemporary romance
series about the passions and perils of a
local dog park in trendy Miami Beach

All Caleb Donovan has to do to redeem his family name is take a
rundown Miami Beach apartment building and turn it into luxury
condos. Easy, right? Unfortunately, that would also turn the
local dog park into a parking lot and the neighbors aren't having
it. Caleb is faced with outright revolt, led by smart, beautiful
building manager Riley Carson and her poodle, LouLou.

For Caleb, this project should have been a slam dunk. But even
more challenging than the neighborhood resistance is the mutual
attraction between him and Riley. It would be so much easier
just to stay enemies. Can Riley and her canine sidekick convince
Caleb that what's best for business isn't always best for the heart?

"Full of humor and heart..."
—Publishers Weekly

For more info about Sourcebooks's
books and authors, visit:

sourcebooks.com

PUPPY LOVE

Wildland firefighter Harrison agrees to a service dog, but he wants the biggest, baddest dog he can find. Instead, he gets a 4-pound bundle of fluff named Bubbles...and his trainer, Sophie, whose poise hides a heart just as fierce as his own.

When Sophie Vasquez and her sisters dreamed up Puppy Promise—their service puppy training school—it was supposed to be her chance to bring some good into the world. But how can she expect to do anything when no one will take her seriously?

Enter Harrison Parks, a rough, gruff, take-no-bull wildlife firefighter in need of a diabetic alert service dog. He couldn't be a more unlikely fit for Sophie or Bubbles—the sweet Pomeranian she knows will be his perfect partner—but when Sophie insists he give them both a shot, something unexpected happens: he listens.

As it turns out, they all have more than enough room in their hearts for a little puppy love.

For more info about Sourcebooks's books and authors, visit:

sourcebooks.com